My Life as a Troll

Susan Bohnet

FIVE RIVERS PUBLISHING

WWW.FIVERIVERSPUBLISHING.COM

Published by Five Rivers Publishing, 704 Queen Street, P.O. Box 293, Neustadt, ON N0G 2M0, Canada

www.fiveriverspublishing.com

Published in Canada

Library and Archives Canada Cataloguing in Publication

Bohnet, Susan, 1966-, author

My life as a troll / Susan Bohnet.

Issued in print and electronic formats.

ISBN 978-1-927400-63-0 (pbk.).--ISBN 978-1-927400-64-7 (epub)

I. Title.

PS8603.O35M9 2014 C813'.6 C2014-902940-3

C2014-902941-1

Contents

Chapter One

After all the questions—all the deep, personal, weird questions—Jared was finally finished. "What? I don't have to pee in a cup?" asked Jared aloud. He felt a little freaked out by the questions the game had thrown at him just so he could set up his account. Look at his troll, though! A thrill as intense as electricity moved through him as he examined his troll in glorious 3-D. That was *exactly* what he would look like as a troll. It was him, only better and more mature than his thirteen years. The troll's arms were lean but the muscles were defined. His torso was solid, and his legs looked strong. He had dark brown hair and a red fohawk—a Mohawk-like strip—down the center of his head. Trolls were the only creatures that could have fohawks, so he wanted it, big time. Satisfied with his appearance—blue eyes, thin nose, and small build which translated into quarterback size in Lavascape—he pressed his right index finger against his thigh to click the correct button on the game glove to accept. The gloves were white and seemed to be made of soft leather, but were stretchy and fit perfectly. They were so thin he hardly noticed he had them on. A metal chain at the wrists cinched the cuff just right. Jared had chuckled when he saw that: the metal reminded him of handcuffs.

He sat in his computer chair facing away from the monitor; this placed him in the center of his bedroom where there was space to move his arms and legs or even get up and move around. The sensors in the gloves and another set strapped to his ankles would send all the information to the game. There was one more question on the screen of his funky Lavascape mask: 'Ready to begin Quest?' The mask went on like a pair of glasses but it had advanced 3-D graphics and covered not just his eyes but his whole face, curving under his chin. Microphone and earphones were built in, but it weighed next to nothing, didn't fog up, and was surprisingly comfortable.

He clicked the glove over 'yes' and switched to first-person vision to see the view from his troll's perspective. The view in the mask became black; streaks of light flew past him as if he were soaring through space. A red orb was visible to the left and grew as he sped toward it. It was a sun, a brilliant, beautiful red sun. The second planet in this system became his focus when he swerved toward it. The screen became misty and Jared could see only blurred images through the thick, peach-colored fog. Then he landed with a plop on a blood-red bush. "Welcome to Lavascape," Jared said to himself.

He manoeuvred his troll to standing position with glove controls; he'd try standing up later. As Jared turned his head, however, the troll did the same thing. There was a bubbling stream flowing to the right. A spray of mist rose from the water…no, it wasn't mist, it was steam; this must be lava. "Lavascape is a landscape of lava," Jared reminded himself.

Straight ahead was a lava sea. The molten stream emptied into it with a gloppy rhythm. The lava mist thickened, making it difficult to see. Blue bushes that looked like the tops of palm trees grew on the ground. The leaves were so large they were almost up to his shoulder.

The sudden clang of metal on metal startled him. Someone was nearby. He heard grunts of exertion and a wail of pain. Through the mist, Jared could see the shapes of two approaching fighters. They were both several inches taller than he was, and though their features were blurred, their outlines reminded him of professional wrestlers.

Suddenly, a streak of brown fur hit him from the side. He rolled with the creature several times before coming to a stop. Then, lying flat on his back, he found himself looking up into the beady, black eyes of an animal with wolf-like ears and a rodent face. It was almost as large as he was. "Are you trying to get yourself killed?" the creature asked under its breath.

"No," Jared replied.

"Then where's your sword? You were standing right out in the open!"

"The sword's digging into my hip. Get off me."

Back in his bedroom, Jared's hip seemed to ache. It was the weirdest feeling.

The rat-like thing in Lavascape pulled Jared under the fronds of one of the large blue ground palms. "Whisper!" he hissed. Heavy footfalls stomped past them, then stopped.

"I heard someone," said a whiny voice from just beyond their hiding place. "I'm sure I saw another troll over here."

"Is that who was talking?" said another voice, deep and scratchy.

"Must have been."

The huge palm leaves above swayed and Jared saw the creature who had just spoken. He had a large pale, muscular body and fuzzy blond hair standing out from his head like little springs. As comical as the hair was, his face was more than serious enough to make up for it with thick ropes of muscle over his cheekbones. He held an axe over his right shoulder, the blade jagged and menacing, tinted red at the tip.

The axe swung through the air now. The being that wielded it looked Jared's way and sliced off one of the fronds over Jared's feet.

Jared moved his troll back into the brush using the movement pad on the game gloves. It was a square area on the palm and worked like a touch screen mouse. The rat creature beside him inched further under the palm leaves, too.

"I see one. On the cliff. Way over there. Do you see it?" said the dark-haired one with the deep voice. He was looking off in the distance.

"Yes! I love having super sight. Don't you?" said Blond Springs.

"Let's get him before he finds the rest of his army."

"But what about that other troll?" His axe continued to swing in a big arc just inches from Jared's hiding place.

"Maybe that's the one we saw."

"Naw."

"Well, if we wait around, we might not get either one. Come on."

When they moved away Jared whispered, "What's happening? Whose side are you on?"

"I just saved your neck, buddy. You better not be questioning my loyalty."

"What are you and what were they?"

"What am I? Seriously? You're that new?" He seemed to be laughing at him.

"Yes. I'm new," Jared admitted. "Now, what's going on?"

Susan Bohnet

7

"It dumped you in the middle of a battle! Wow, that's just cruel. You almost died as soon as you got to Lavascape."

The rat was definitely laughing and he hadn't answered any of Jared's questions. Jared switched back to 'third person view.' If he was in a fight, he wanted to see what was coming from every angle, including behind him.

In the distance, the unsuspecting troll stood at the edge of the cliff overlooking the lava stream. He didn't see the enemy stalking him. "We've gotta help him," Jared said.

"Don't be such an eager newbie; you don't know anything about fighting."

This overgrown rat was getting on his nerves. Jared had played all sorts of video games before and wielding a sword would surely be a simple matter of stabbing the right enemy. There was no complicated gun to learn how to use, no tricky mode of reloading or finding more ammunition. Now that he wasn't lying on his sword, he pulled it from the sheath at his left hip. It was a little clumsy and primitive looking, but it appeared sharp.

Back in the bedroom, Jared felt a shiver run down his spine. He could actually feel the sword through the gloves. He considered removing his mask to be sure he wasn't actually holding a sword, but the rat was talking to him.

"Do what you want. I'm outta here."

"You're scared."

"I'm not scared; I'm smart. Each one of those guys is twice my size. They know I'm not on their side and would love to take me down."

"So, run away," said Jared. "That's really showing 'em."

The rat's face turned down a notch, his eyes lowered. His features changed, he seemed to clench his teeth. The image of Jared's troll also altered. There was a fleeting wide-eyed expression, then, shifty eyes, turning head, raised hands.... mask off.

Jared gasped. Looking at his troll had been like looking in a mirror. The face shield did more than give a surround view of Lavascape; it also transmitted his movements and facial expression back to Lavascape. No doubt, it was part of the 'ultimate interactive experience' the game boasted.

"You still there?" asked the rat. Jared heard it faintly through the mask on his lap. He steadied his breathing and slipped it back on.

"I'm here."

"You just noticed how the mask puts your attitude on the troll."

"Yeah."

"Who's scared now?"

"It threw me a bit," Jared admitted.

"Cool Beans," he said.

"Huh?"

"I just mean, it's cool, isn't it?"

"Sure. It would also be cool to help the troll over there."

"And dangerous."

"You claimed to be loyal..." said Jared. He let it hang in the air. Then he crouched his troll low and followed the two wire-headed creatures.

Jared couldn't see him, but he heard the stealthy movements of the rat-dude following him. "Help me put these guys in their place," whispered Jared.

"First day here and you think you're going to save the world?"

"If it looks like you're going to get defeated, just leave."

"You're not allowed to do that," hissed the rat. "You can't leave just to get out of trouble; so once you start this you have to finish."

Jared didn't answer.

The rat continued, "I just escaped from those two and you're going to jump into a battle with them! You're new here. Learn a few things before you start challenging elves."

"Those were elves?" They were a far cry from the tiny leprechaun, Santa's-helpers kind of creatures he'd always thought of as elf-like. Once again, he was happy he chose to be a troll. Even if elves did have great vision, trolls ruled. Besides, these two were probably new to the game, too. They were still in awe of their vision powers. He could take them. "I want a battle. That's why I'm here."

He must have spoken louder than he thought because the two elves turned, searching with their special vision. Jared crouched a little lower. Their heads snapped in his direction. He was too late. They'd seen him.

Chapter Two

The elves were coming his way. Jared called to the other troll, "Hey! Troll! Elves at six o'clock! Help me!"

The other troll turned, pulled his sword, and thundered through the brush toward him. He looked taller and stronger than Jared's troll and had big bushy eyebrows. Jared had a moment's regret. Why hadn't he chosen the larger body type? Just because he was small in real life didn't mean he couldn't be bigger in Lavascape.

Blond Springs came around the side of an evergreen and grinned right in his face. Jared gasped. He turned and took a few steps away only to realize that the other elf was waiting for him there, chuckling in his scratchy voice. He lunged at Jared; his tightly wound black hair straightening briefly as he jerked forward. Jared jumped out of his reach. Then Jared jabbed with his sword but missed the elf and caught the tip of his sword in the lava rock hidden under a dense layer of pine needles, dead leaves, and loose dirt. He stumbled.

"Have you ever done this before?" said Blond Springs standing a few paces off. "What a N00b! You take this one, M; I'll go after our other 'friend'." He ran off, and judging from the sound of their confrontation, Blondie was having some trouble with the bushy-eyebrow troll. The sound of their weapons was sometimes the sharp clang of sword on axe and sometimes a sickening thud that Jared assumed was the sound of blows hitting body parts.

Jared took a couple of practice swings. The game allowed a combination of actual arm movements and glove commands for manoeuvring. He could toss the sword from one hand to the other and the gloves automatically adjusted. The non-weapon hand could control body movement. Some of the sensors in the gloves could be activated by pressing his fingertips against his thighs. It was turning out to be a heck of a lot harder than simply stabbing in the right direction. He still found it remarkable that he could feel the weight of the weapon.

Plus the 3-D vision was fantastic. He could see the Lavascape world out of his peripheral vision to the sides and even on the ground. He faced M. The elf looked strong. Jared blocked M's axe with stiff sword movements but he wasn't steady and stumbled backwards each time. The jolt of the contact jerked through his hand and up his arm. He didn't even have a chance to attack; he was too busy defending himself. Where was that stupid rat? Was he off gloating somewhere because Jared was going to lose a life his first hour in Lavascape?

Blond Springs called to his friend for help but Jared's attacker didn't pause in his relentless strokes, leaving Jared breathless as he retreated away from the barrage of axe falls. The next blow was so strong that Jared fell backwards, and his sword flew from his hand.

"Help me, M! Get over here! Now!" called Blond Springs.

This time, Jared's opponent seemed to hear his friend's cry and left at a run.

Jared scrambled around, looking for his sword. It was lost in the debris of leaves and rotting logs on the forest floor. He looked toward the fight. The blond elf was up against a poplar tree, his axe locked under the troll's sword. The elf's arms shook and gave way. He turned but the troll's sword caught his forearm before he rolled. The elf, M, arrived and plowed into the troll while his sword was down. Then he stepped back to ready his axe.

"Thanks," said the wounded elf as he got to his feet, panting. The elves moved as if performing a choreographed dance, except there was fear in the air instead of music. The other troll looked like he was fighting off a pack of wolves. The elves swung their axes like wheels in a machine. The troll, strong as he was, couldn't rebuff all the blows. M's axe caught his thigh and he pulled his lips back. His teeth were clenched and his eyes wild. The mimic feature was somewhat disturbing. It mesmerized Jared for a moment. He needed to help him. This instant. Where was his sword? Surely, it hadn't fallen into the lava stream! Jared searched through the ground cover. He felt the sticks and dirt through his gloves as he grasped the virtual ground. Finally, he felt the hilt of the sword. He seized it and jumped to his feet.

...and fell back against the computer chair.

The pebbly landscape gave way under him and he clamored to catch himself. He had come too close to the bank. His feet lost ground; the sword flew from his hands and clattered against rocks on the edge of the cliff as he slipped over the side. He reached for a hold as he fell toward the lava stream below. He clutched at rocks along the cliff wall and managed to stop his fall.

Jared used glove controls to climb. The stream bubbled and spit bits of lava while he tried to scramble up the bank. He lost his footing, slipped, and grabbed at the dirt as he fell. Suddenly, his hand wrapped around a tree root protruding from the bank and there he hung.

The gurgling of the lava swallowed up the sounds of battle. What was happening up there? Had the troll gotten away? Had he beaten the elves? Were they slinking away to their own lands in shame? Or, had the elves beaten the bushy eyebrow troll and were they now looking for him!

He couldn't hang there all day. Would his strength give out eventually and would he fall to his death in the hot lava stream?

His muscles were taut. It was disconcerting to feel as though you were hanging on for dear life. He scanned above his head. There was nothing else to use for a handhold and his feet slipped when he tried to climb.

The lava intermittently popped and spewed molten rock into the air. Maybe the other troll was looking for him. Should he call out for help? He wished he knew how the battle was going above him. He didn't dare alert anyone to his location.

"Hang on," said a voice from above. It was the rat-creature. Before long, a thick vine fell toward him. "Grab on. I've got ya."

Jared grabbed the vine and then crawled until he reached the side of the bank. He collapsed at the top, right at the rat's feet. A ripple of lava sprayed toward him, hardening as it cooled on the grass not two feet from his leg. He jumped up and scrambled in the opposite direction. That had been close.

Back in his bedroom, Jared's chest heaved with urgency as though he'd physically exerted himself. This was an intense game! He hadn't been in Lavascape for an hour and he'd already had a duel and a brush with death. Cool.

Jared slipped off the mask, wiped the sweat from his forehead with his shirtsleeve, grabbed a bite of a candy bar from the stash in his desk drawer, and was ready to set off again. He heard his older sister's fake girlfriend-laugh. She laughed differently when she talked to Cam, her first and oh-so-hot boyfriend. Her voice seemed higher…more girly. He preferred hearing those sounds, however, to the ones that followed.

"Have you seen the MasterCard bill?" came his mother's voice, low and intense. "It's huge; how are we ever going to pay that down?" She used the rough whisper when she and Dad were fighting. She must have thought it didn't carry as well as her regular voice, but she was wrong.

Dad's voice hadn't undergone a transformation today. No, he came through loud and clear. "Just pay the minimum."

"We're drowning."

"Oh, don't be so dramatic!"

"What's this charge? Eighty-nine dollars…"

"I don't know. You're the one always buying stuff for the house."

"A tablecloth. The only thing I bought in the past month that wasn't a necessity was a tablecloth."

"Yeah, but last month you got that carpet."

"An area rug. And I thought you said you had some jobs."

"I thought I did. It's not my fault people decide to do their renovations themselves."

"Maybe you need to think about another job."

"I don't have time."

"If you'd quit a couple of your service clubs, you'd have *plenty* of time."

"Why don't *you* get a second job?"

"At least my first job pays!"

"Small businesses aren't easy. I keep telling you. Things are up and down."

"Mostly down. And you're never around when *I* need you."

"Why did you need me? What do you want me to do, now? Mow the lawn, weed the flower bed, or some other job you could do just as easily yourself instead of sitting here mad at me all morning."

"You were at some club thing, again. You promised you'd be home more. Did you mean it or were you just trying to shut me up?"

"I'd do just about anything to shut you up," said his father's voice. Jared heard the door of his parent's bedroom slam and heavy steps moved down the stairs. Was Dad going to mow the lawn or was he heading for his car to get away? He peeked out his bedroom window. It faced the street. He waited and held his breath. His dad's car backed out.

Jared sighed and put the face mask back in place. The sights and sounds of his home were overshadowed by Lavascape. His troll, which had been frozen in place, became animated with Jared's expression. "Thanks," he said to the rat creature. "What happened? Where are the elves?"

"The elves got the other troll and when they couldn't find you they left." The rat led him to the scene of the fight.

"Got him? Is he captured?"

"No. They got him. He's dead." He pointed to where the troll lay in the tall grass.

Jared felt as though a stone dropped in his stomach. Dead? "Was he out of lives?"

"That's not how it works here."

"What's not how it works?"

"You don't get a hundred lives."

"How many do you get?"

"Same as you do in real life, buddy."

"You only get one life?" What kind of game was this?

"Yeah, so take care of yours."

They reached the body of the muscular troll. The elves' axes had done their damage. There were wounds on his face, on his arms, and an especially wide gash on his leg. The graphic torn muscle and bloody injuries struck Jared like a sledgehammer to the chest.

The dead troll's head hung to one side; his grey eyes stared out at nothing. Horror moviemakers gave zombies eyes like these. Jared felt light-headed and queasy as he looked at the bushy eyebrows framing eyes rolled back in his head.

Suddenly, blood appeared on his troll's hands. Jared lifted them to examine in first-person viewpoint, but the image of dripping blood persisted. He yanked off the game mask, flung it on the floor, and peeled off the gloves to convince himself he wasn't really covered in blood. The sticky feeling of drying blood was so realistic. For a second, his hands still appeared to be bloody. His whole body shook. Then the blood was gone but he couldn't take his eyes off his hands, the vision of blood too fresh, too vivid.

A new spasm overshadowed his quivering hands. His stomach! He jumped from his seat and made it to the garbage can beside the desk before he retched, bringing up sour smelling bile that burned his throat. Barf oozed around the discarded paper and candy wrappers in the half full plastic container.

Slowly his breathing returned to normal. What was the matter with him? He never reacted to gore in video games.

Real life, sure. He felt sympathy pain when his older sister, Melissa, broke her arm three years ago, and when his best friend, Monty, gashed open his knee last summer falling off his bike. But this was nothing but a game. It didn't make sense.

He picked up the game mask. Would he have rushed to help that troll if he knew his own Lavascape life was so fragile? His unconscious bravery was useless anyway. The troll was dead.

If he were more skilled, this might not have happened. His willy-nilly, jump right in, style of play was to blame. His carelessness was embarrassing. His lack of skill, unforgiveable. He vowed to do whatever he could to get the skills he needed.

What was the kid behind that troll thinking right now? "Why didn't you help me? What's the matter with you? Why didn't you fight like a troll instead of a little novice hockey player that needs his stick for balance? " Jared had done about as much and been about as threatening as that.

Jared slipped the mask into place and put on the gloves. Lavascape materialized and the rat creature was staring at him. "It really hits you the first time, I know. Are you okay?"

Jared felt comforted by the compassion in the rat's voice. "I think so. I never feel creeped out by video games. I don't get it."

"I know what you mean. But, this isn't like any other game you've ever played. This is a whole other experience."

"Did it freak you out? You know, the first time you saw someone dead?"

"Don't worry. I think we all hurl."

"Really?"

"I think you'd have to be a serial killer not to."

For some reason, that made Jared feel much better. "Thanks."

"I'm a scurry. You can call me Kentucky." He stuck out his hand.

Jared reached out to meet him. He shouldn't use his real name on-line, but he couldn't remember the fake name he picked. "I'm Jerry," he said, feeling the grip of his new friend through the glove.

"Welcome to Lavascape, Jerry Troll."

An hour later, Jared was ready for the annual Father-Son Fishing Derby. He had his spin cast reel and his fly rod, Dad's fly rod (he only fly-fished now), Dad's vest with all the pockets, and the tackle box. They were supposed to meet at the community center in fifteen minutes. Jared paced. He filled up two water bottles and added them to his pile of fishing gear by the door. He looked out the window. Sure, Dad was mad at Mom, but he loved fishing. He wouldn't miss the derby.

The meeting time came and went. Dad knew where they were holding the derby, though. They didn't have to travel with everyone else. After another fifteen minutes, Jared went to the kitchen. He stared in the fridge without seeing. He found chocolate ice cream in the freezer and filled a bowl. He ate it on the front step, watching the street.

The early September light shone on his hands. A quick flash of them covered in blood entered his mind but then it was gone and he noticed dark hair between his knuckles. It was much darker and thicker than he remembered. Of course, you don't go around staring at your hands every day. He smiled. It looked awfully manly.

An hour later, he went in the house and watched TV. He stayed up ridiculously late but Dad still didn't come home. As he drifted off to sleep that night, he thought, *I hope Dad steps on his fly rod when he comes in.*

Chapter Three

"What the heck did you do to your leg? What is that?"
exclaimed Monty pointing at Jared's ankle. Jared was lying
on his back with his knees bent and Monty was supposed to
be holding his feet while Jared did sit-ups. Instead, Monty
knelt in front of him, gaping at his leg. "No wonder you
were complaining!"

It did hurt. It killed. It felt as though a sword had
punctured the skin, stopping with a jolt at the bone. He'd
been limping around all morning. Jared sat up.

There, next to his ankle, was a hard, stone like scab
protruding almost an inch from his leg. The skin around it
was beet red and raw-looking. Jared was shocked when he
looked at it but another emotion quickly replaced it. Fear.
There was something frighteningly expected in what he
saw. Hadn't he been on an adventure last night? Hadn't he
slipped next to a lava stream? Hadn't he witnessed a spurt
of lava escape the confines of the river and hurtle toward
him?

"I've never seen a scab like that," said Monty. "It's sticking out a mile. It's basically round! What were you doing?"

Jared shrugged. 'Playing a video game' seemed a little too much to swallow, even if it was the truth. Nobody came away with 'ol' video game injuries' to brag about. Besides this one was a little too freaky, not to mention freshly painful, for flippant comments. "I'm not sure."

Jared touched it. The scab pulled slightly away from his skin. The weight of it was so great it ripped away from his leg and dropped to the gym floor with a clunk. The area exposed was raw and blood formed like a wave moving from the outside rim and flowing toward the center.

Mr. Becker didn't think much of dawdlers. The gym teacher walked toward them. "Is there a problem, boys? Do you remember what a sit up is? Do you need extra practice to get it in your head? You should have switched places by now." Then he saw the blood that was now dripping on the floor in what appeared to be a continuous stream. "What happened?" he yelled but sprinted to his office without waiting for an answer.

The teacher returned with paper towels, a first aid kit, and a somewhat annoyed look on his face. The paper towels were abrasive. Jared had to grit his teeth to keep from crying out when he pressed them against his wound. "Open the kit," Mr. Becker said to Monty. He undid the latches and pulled the lid back.

Mr. Becker grabbed a stack of absorbent pads and pressed them to Jared's leg.

By now, the rest of the boys in the class were gathered around Jared, the sit-ups completely forgotten. Some boys commented with awe, almost admiration, at the amount of blood, as though Jared had done some great thing by producing so much of it. The gauze against the wound was softer but still hurt.

"What happened?" asked Mr. Becker, now that the bleeding seemed under control.

Jared shrugged. The thing he suspected wasn't possible, and he couldn't think of a likely substitute. "I...I...well, I guess I picked a scab," he said eventually. The flat-sided pebble was under his leg now. No one would believe that it had been stuck to his flesh. It wasn't a tough brown scab. It was a rock. Or was it? Maybe there was nothing supernatural about it; it could just be some injury he didn't remember getting.

That sort of thing happened all the time. You'd expect to remember getting hurt, but the adrenalin rush kicks in and you don't realize it until later. Maybe it wasn't so bizarre.

That hope only lasted a moment. Monty was right. Who'd ever seen a scab like that?

"What an idgit!" said Colton, a stocky blond haired boy. "Any kid older than three knows not to pick his scabs, Jare." His tone of voice made it sound like his joke was a friendly jab between friends; but Jared knew better.

All the other guys laughed with Colton; even Mr. Becker chuckled.

"Oh, the little baby was picking his scab. No. No. Bad baby. We have a baby scab picker here, guys." It wasn't an eloquent tag but Jared could see it sticking.

The gauze at Jared's ankle was soaked through and blood dropped to the gym floor again. Colton shuffled away from it and almost lost his footing. Mr. Becker grabbed another inch of gauze and applied it on top of the already soggy bandage.

"Little scab-picker" taunted Colton. He had a way of getting away with things no one else could. Teachers seemed to see his blond good looks and assume he was some sort of little angel, which was nothing near the truth. Colton was one of the kids Jared usually went out of his way to avoid.

"Good one, Picky!" Colton was in fine form. He had a crowd, a teacher ignoring his kind of fun, and somebody smaller and weaker taking it. Colton was painting a target on his chest as real as any spray paint graffiti. A target for future bullying.

He had to do something. Jared thought of turning the tables. Maybe pointing out how Colton seemed to be afraid of blood, stumbling all over himself to get away. But, his mind worked in slow motion and each new laugh brought a new burst of embarrassment that froze this thoughts.

"It was a really big scab," said Jared, weakly.

"I've never seen anything like it," agreed Monty with enthusiasm. "It was huge. It stuck out this far...it was like a second ankle." Mr. Becker left the gauze in place and put a large bandage over the wound.

"So Picky, picked it off!" taunted Colton when Mr. Becker left to put the first aid kit away. "Good thinking." The other boys chuckled. The ridicule from picking the scab overshadowed any awe over the amount of blood.

Colton looked at Jared with steely eyes—eyes the color of Jared's, now notorious, scab. He looked like a lion that had just discovered fresh meat.

After school Jared, Monty, and Katie stopped at Josie's Diner. In the small town of Willow Creek, hangout options were limited, but it didn't matter: they liked the little restaurant, liked that it wasn't part of a big chain. "I was dying to be a troll. What else would I choose?" Jared popped a french fry in his mouth and then regretted it. He forgot to dip it in his runny ketchup and vinegar mixture. It's such a shame to waste a fry like that. Of course, he could just slop up any leftover mixture with his finger but Katie was giving him a look like she could read his mind. Katie was almost as bad as his mother was when it came to manners. That is, back when his mom noticed things like that.

"How about a goblin?" said Monty. "They look so cool with their big bows and quivers full of arrows. Someone at school said something about them being smart. They can figure out all sorts of puzzles and..."

"I haven't heard that. I think they're only as smart as you are." Jared elbowed him in the ribs. "And that's not totally brilliant."

Monty scooted an inch down the orange plastic seat they shared, as if anticipating more flying elbows. "I'm pretty brilliant," laughed Monty.

"How about a human?" said Katie.

"Human? You're a human in real life, who would be one in Lavascape? How boring is that?" said Monty, grinning. "You guys, I'm so excited to have a shot at working on the school newspaper," he said tapping the table with both hands.

"Are you still going to do yearbook?" said Jared.

"Some of the pictures could be in both but I want to move to the paper."

"Cool," said Katie.

"If they'll stop treating me like a little kid, it will be cooler. But Ms. Key, the teacher advisor, said I have a real chance. If I get good pictures and write good enough stories, there's no rule that reporters have to be in high school. "

"Good luck," said Jared.

"You'll have to wow 'em," said Katie. She opened up her backpack and pulled out two bottles of nail polish, hot pink and lime green. She went to work on her left hand fingernails making flowers out of dots—pink around a lime green center.

"That stuff stinks," said Jared. "Put it away before you get us kicked out of here again."

"Josie was smiling when she said that. She'd never kick

us out. Besides, this is a simple design. I'll be done in no time."

"Oh, no elephants beside a mystic pool today?" said Monty.

"Laugh all you like; and I guess they did kind of look like anteaters. But, I'm going to revolutionize the way people think about nail polish. It's an art form waiting to be recognized."

"Ant eaters? I was going to call them big grey blobs." Monty's rotund middle shook with laughter. "Maybe it would be cool if we did get kicked out. That could be a great story for the paper. And I'd snap a shot of Josie hauling Katie out of here by her ear to go with it, a trail of nail polish on the floor like blood."

"I don't think Josie was kidding. She said it nicely but meant every word. Smell that! Not too appetizing." Jared looked back and forth. He tapped his index finger on his temple. "No matter what you think."

"Yes! Do Wishful Thinking," cheered Katie.

"That's so big on YouTube right now," laughed Monty.

"It's trending worldwide," said Katie.

Jared grinned and in his best hillbilly accent he quoted, "I wasn't in the mood for an alien encounter but he didn't care none. He brought his swag over and said, 'Earthlings for breakfast.' And yeah, I'd probably be tasty as vittles but I'm like 'Whoa there Little Feller, put that tentacle back in your neck and back off.' But he took out a sword and yelled 'Prepare to die--rotisserie style,' so I knew it was time for 'Wish-ful Think-ing'." He tapped his temple.

Monty chimed in, "Ding, ding, ding-dong."

"And out of my trusty gun came a short stack of pancakes," said Jared. "Those little grub muffins saved my life."

Katie laughed.

"I like the one where he's chased by a rabid dog and his gun shoots T-bone steaks," said Monty.

"You crack me up with that voice," said Katie.

"You won't be laughing if we really do get kicked out," said Jared.

"She's just used to getting away with everything because she's an only child," said Monty. He smirked. "No one to have to share with, no waiting for the shower every morning, you can do whatever you want."

"I don't know where you get your information. Being the only child means there's pressure to be really good at *everything*. You have to be perfect. There's not another kid coming along behind you that can fulfill their hopes and dreams. It's all on you. Plus there's no one ahead of you to break your parents in. You're on your own."

"Still, you don't have to wait for the shower," said Jared.

Katie shrugged and finished the flower on her left pinkie. "Tell me, what other artist is forced to be ambidextrous?"
"Ambi-what?" said Jared. His voice had a gravelly quality. He cleared his throat.

"Ambidextrous. It means using both your right and left hand." She switched the tiny brush to her left hand and began to create flowers on her right fingernails. Her forehead crinkled as she concentrated on steadying her hand. Her shoulder-length, walnut-colored hair was shiny and the bangs, which were a little too long, fell forward, the hair curving at the sides of her eyes. She shook her head in a little burst to clear her vision. She almost looked girly doing it, but Jared knew she would have stopped immediately if she'd known it. She wore nail polish for artistic expression, not to look pretty.

"Trolls can do that with their swords," said Jared, coming back from the distraction of Katie's smelly art and curling hair. "Fight with both hands."

"They *are* the best with swords, I'll give you that one," said Monty. "I wish I could play it. I don't know why I'm left out just because some people are fanatics. It's because of that stupid group that my parents are so worked up."

Katie snorted. "My mom calls PAL a radical group of fear mongering parents." She put her fingernail polish away.

"What do they really have against Lavascape," said Monty, whining. "My parents say it's too addicting. They act like it's a drug or something."

"They say Lavascape affects people. That there are risks," said Katie.

Jared laughed. "I wonder if anyone has actually heard what sort of 'risks' they're talking about? You can bet it's something bad...they'll say it's 'destructive to youth'...but, give me a break."

"Be glad your mom hasn't joined 'Parents Against Lavascape,'" said Monty. "They'll outlaw smiling next."

Jared crossed his ankles and rubbed against his wound. His smile fell. "I guess," he said. His voice was rougher and lower pitched than normal. The strange scab on his leg was more than painful. It made him uneasy. "Does PAL say anything about injuries?"

"Yeah, but it's so far-fetched that you'd have to be an idiot to give it any validity," said Katie.

Chapter Four

Anna came and stood at their table as Jared, Monty, and Katie munched their fries. She lived out on a ranch and usually took the bus home after school. She never hung out at Josie's. "Hi Katie," she said. "Hi guys."

"What are you doing here?" said Katie.

"Dentist appointment. I have to walk over there and Mom's going to pick me up after."

"You didn't say anything last night," said Katie.

"I didn't know. Mom told me this morning. Like, thanks for the heads up."

Jared chuckled without looking at the girls. Anna could talk about anything and he'd be entertained. He forgot about the sore on his leg. Anna was beautiful. He hardly dared look at her, afraid he'd have trouble looking away and then everyone would know how much he liked her. When she wasn't looking, that's when he stole his glances. Everything about her was perfect. So basically, he did his best to ignore her whenever Katie brought her around. Besides, she was completely out of his league. She had gone out with a guy a year older than them last year, but they had broken up during the summer. She was free but that didn't give Jared any hope. Anna was no more likely to date a guy like him now than when she was going out with that basketball player.

"What were you guys doing last night?" asked Monty.

"Just on the phone," said Anna.

Jared couldn't picture Katie lying around talking on the phone for hours the way Melissa did. Anna's voice was soft but strong. She looked at Jared but then as soon as their eyes met she quickly looked back at her milkshake.

"Sit," said Katie. "Want some fries?" She pulled the plate closer to Anna so they could share. Anna slid in beside Katie.

"Okay. If I'm not interrupting. You guys looked kind of intense."

"We're just talking about video game injuries," laughed Katie. "Please, change the subject."

"Injuries—like your leg?" said Monty, making the connection. "How in the world do you get a scab the size of a quarter that sticks out an inch and not know how you got it?"

"Who did that?" said Katie.

"Jared. Hey, I saw you grab the scab, is it still in your pocket."

"Eww," whispered Katie. "You *kept* the scab?"

Jared reached into the front pocket of his jeans.

"I'm still eating, if you don't mind!" Katie waved a hand over the plate of dwindling fries.

"It doesn't even look like a scab," said Jared, dropping it on the table.

Katie smiled a doubtful, how-gullible-do-you-think-I-am smile. "Very funny."

"What?" said Jared and Monty together.

Katie pushed the plate away. "It may be just a rock, but you've ruined my appetite anyway."

"This 'rock' was stuck to Jared's leg and tore off about 20 layers of skin."

"I'm sure I just banged my leg—" his voice dropped about an octave "—or something."

"Are you catching a cold?" asked Katie. "Your voice is wacky today."

"Did you hurt your leg falling off your bike, maybe?" asked Anna, briefly looking up.

He looked at her lips, shiny with pink gloss. She'd asked him a question. He couldn't stare dumbly at her lips all day. 'Had he fallen off his bike'...that was it. Jared shook his head. Why was he acting like a mute oaf? He turned the stone over between his thumb and index finger.

"—and how does the flat part get imbedded in your leg," said Monty, gesturing with his half-eaten hamburger.

"Lava?" Jared suggested softly.

"Yeah, 'cause there's so much lava around here." Katie rolled her eyes.

"It's very weird," said Anna. Her voice seemed to keep vibrating inside him after the sound was gone. He should ask her out. Someday.

Jared reached for the salt at the same moment as Anna, their hands brushed. "Oh man, I'm sorry," said Jared. "Man? I mean lady...you, go ahead. What a klutz I am! I really am sorry."

"It's okay," sang Anna. "No biggie."

"I only have three fries left anyway. Like I need more salt!" Jared laughed but it was forced and sounded a little like a car refusing to start on a frigid morning. "You keep it. I'm sorry. I should never have salt again." He knew he was rambling but somehow he couldn't get his mouth to stop while he looked at Anna. "Salt's not good for you."

She looked down at her generously salted fries and nodded. Now he'd made her feel bad about the salt content. Was he a total idiot?

Terrance, a boy from their grade, stopped beside their table. His voice was full of awe as he said, "Is it true, Jared?"

Jared faltered. Had he been listening? Did he have salt-related health questions? Or, did he hear the bit about the lava? Did Jared want to make this wild claim to the entire school? Let the bullies have fun with that one?

"Is what true?" said Jared, to buy some thinking time.

"Did Colton get on your case, right in front of Mr. Becker?"

"Oh, that...."

"Colton is such a jerk!" said Monty

"Can I sit with you guys?" asked Terrance. His enthusiasm was contagious but it left Jared feeling a step or two behind.

"Sure," Monty shoved over to make room on the bench.

"This is what I heard," said Terrance. "I heard good ol' Colton was after you and he called you an idiot or something right in gym class and it got worse and worse and Becker did nothing but laugh along."

"That's pretty much how it happened," agreed Monty.

"It's been a couple of years since Colton was always in my face but let me tell you, if a teacher joined in, I'd seriously hit the principal's office with that news. Looking at his pretty boy face and knowing how ugly he is on the inside, made me so mad. I knew no one would believe me back then, but you have witnesses!"

Terrance was a bit of a loner but a nice enough guy. Jared didn't want to feel a bond with him, however. Just because they had both been the brunt of Colton's bullying didn't make them buddies. He didn't want to be lumped with picked-on kids. That's not who he was and not what was happening to him.

Terrance seemed kind of soft. He was a regular kid with a Humpty Dumpty face trying to get along in this world. The sad part was that Jared didn't even realize Terrance had been the brunt of Colton's cruel jokes. Had he seen it and didn't remember?

"It wasn't a big deal today," said Jared.

Monty looked at his watch and jumped in his seat. "Hey, I better get home. It's almost dinnertime.

"You just ate a burger and fries," said Katie.

"Yeah, but I'll eat enough that no one will guess that."

"I better get going, too," said Katie.

There was no way Jared could stay there, almost alone with Anna. They said good-bye to Terrance and Anna, and left. Outside, Jared fingered the change in his pocket. He pulled it out and looked at it. "Hey, Josie gave me too much change."

"Looks like it's your lucky day," said Katie.

"A dollar," said Jared.

"Sweet," said Monty.

"I'm not going to keep it," said Jared, turning back toward the café.

"You're too good, Jared. She's probably short changed you five times before this, you know," said Monty.

"Whatever. See you guys tomorrow." When he finished

returning the dollar to an appreciative Josie, he started home. He was thinking of Lavascape but then he passed the Dollar Store and ducked inside. He paced the aisles. There were fold-up three legged stools, gigantic bubble wands, and thousands of other items. Finally, he exhausted the store, bought a pack of gum, and was back on the sidewalk.

Jared waited at the lights, the only set in town. Troll powers were the best. Too bad Monty's parents wouldn't let him play. It would've been good to join together.

The light turned green and the bright outline of a walking man illuminated. Jared watched for big trucks trying to beat the light, then stepped off the curb. When he was halfway across, a transport truck approached. It was breaking, Jared could tell from the sound, but not quickly enough. He dashed to the other side of the road, his breathing coming in gasps. The truck stopped just before the crosswalk. It was far from hitting him but he was sweating and felt enormous relief to be safely on the other side just the same. One of those semi trailers would flatten him like a bug.

Of course, that wasn't saying much. Half of the guys in the eighth grade could probably squash him flat if they wanted to. Then there were guys like Colton who always seemed to be looking for someone to pick on. He remembered the look on Colton's face. This wasn't over. The fries he'd eaten felt like a solid mass in his stomach.

Melissa's boyfriend's car passed him. Cam drove too fast and always had one arm draped over the steering wheel like he was too cool to actually use his fingers. Melissa's head was a dark shadow on the passenger side. Jared watched them pass with a frown between his brows. The guy was always there in the summer, drinking all the Sprite and taking up the couch. Hopefully Cam would be gone by the time Jared got home. After school, he usually just dropped her off.

Jared turned left onto his street. He squinted. Was Cam's

car in front of the house? It was a block and a half away, and there were too many vehicles on the street to tell if the jerk boyfriend was most likely making himself at home in front of Jared's television and eating his bag of all-dressed chips.

He came closer and finally was sure the road in front of his house was Cam-car-free. He picked up his feet as he covered the final block. Maybe Melissa would want to play video games today. They used to love the racing games. It had been ages since they went head to head.

Jared turned the handle on the front door and pushed against it. It stuck a bit and needed a jolt before it swung open. He had once seen Cam kick the door and it made Jared want to grab him by the sideburns and give a good, hard yank. No respect for property—could add that to his list of flaws.

Today is a phone day, Jared thought when he heard his mother's voice. "And that's not the way things are supposed to be. That's not what a marriage is!"

Jared dropped his backpack on the entranceway. There was another voice, a deep hum coming from his parents' bedroom. She wasn't on the phone blabbing to her friends about her problems. Dad was home early. He checked the kitchen clock. Five forty-five. No, dad wasn't early; Jared was late. Monty was sure to be getting heck right about now.

Melissa was in her room with the stereo blasting. Jared stuck his head in and said, "Do you wanna play..." but Melissa placed her hand over the speaker on her cell phone and cut him off with a curt, "I'm on the phone." Before the door closed, he heard his sister resume her conversation by saying, "Of course he's hot, but sometimes he's so cute, too...."

He started toward his room for Lavascape but his parents' voices escalated another notch and he heard his dad say,

"All that kid does is play some stupid on-line game. Why don't you get him to cut the grass and help out?"

Jared turned and plodded down the steps to the main floor, wondering if he was the only person to gag on the word 'cute.'

He wanted to be in Lavascape not watching mindless TV. However, it did block out the fighting going on upstairs. Around seven o'clock Mom opened a couple of cans of chunky soup and Jared and Melissa sat at the square table by themselves. "Aren't you having any?" asked Melissa.

"I'm not hungry," said Mom. Her face was flushed and her eyes were lined in red.

"What about Dad?" Melissa continued to prod. There was a note of desperation in her voice, as though she was scared to eat at the table with only her little brother for company. Jared knew that wasn't the case, but the dull panic was real. He felt it himself in sharp bursts that he quickly muffled with other thoughts, the way you throw dirt on a campfire that keeps flaring up.

"He has a meeting," said Mom. The way she said the word 'meeting' made it clear what she thought of it. Jared knew it wasn't where she wanted him to be. She always had a better idea of how Dad should spend his time. "When's the last time he had dinner at home?" she asked.

Jared didn't want to scan the past days. He looked at Dad's empty chair at the head of the table. "It wasn't that long ago."

"What about missing the fishing derby! I still can't believe he just forgot."

"It's just fishing. I don't care. I'm getting too old for the derby, anyway."

Mom glared at him, then turned and left the kitchen.

A few moments later, Jared heard the door to his mother's bedroom close. For the next four minutes, Melissa and

Jared ate in silence except for the clinking noise of their spoons on the white glass bowls.

No matter what the commercials say, chunky soup from a can was nowhere near as good as homemade. He used to like it, a lot. But it wasn't a rare treat anymore. Jared concentrated on the tastes—everything too much the same. And, the textures—slightly rubbery carrot, over-soft potato, processed-until-it's-stringy beef. He wondered what Monty was having tonight. He'd be experiencing different tastes and, most importantly, different sounds.

"What meeting is he at?" Melissa asked.

He almost jumped at the sound of her voice. She no longer seemed agitated. They were friends, allies in this mystery of parents. "I don't know. Lion's Club, maybe.

She nodded. "Yeah, maybe."

They were both finished their stew. Jared thought of Lavascape. His troll was ready for adventure. But Melissa said, "Do you want to play Nintendo?" She smiled slightly. She looked young again behind her black-lined eyes and fading pink lips, more like his sister than Cam's girlfriend.

With a bag of potato chips between their beanbag chairs, they passed the next hour in front of the TV in the basement. "It's not fair, I'm so out of practice," said Melissa when they finished a race—Jared in first place and she in seventh. Their hands moved automatically to the bag of chips. When their hands hit, they looked at each other and jumped to their feet. They did three jumping jacks in unison, then a jitterbug jive. Jared was as tall as Melissa now and the octopus arms were easier than he remembered it being last time they did this dance about three months ago. After he dipped her back and they jumped to their feet, they said together, "That burns off the junk, now let's have some more." Their laughter lingered as they settled back into their beanbags.

"Let's play the same course again," said Melissa. "Maybe I'll get my touch back."

Jared laughed. "I can't believe you're having so much trouble with the turns."

"Okay," Melissa took another chip, licked her fingers and then wiped them on her jeans. "You ready to go again?"

Suddenly, they heard Mom and Dad's voices from the main floor. "There wasn't enough in the account to cover the mortgage payment," said Mom. "Yet you think nothing of going golfing and out for dinner."

"Our mortgage is a lot more than I spent at the golf course." Dad huffed. "It's buck-a-hole-night, too."

Melissa looked over at Jared. "They fight all the time."

"It's just a disagreement. They'll work it out."

"But the mortgage—that's the house payments."

"So they'll pay late and maybe have an extra fee or something. It'll be fine. Let's play again. Ready?"

"Same course?"

"Sure."

Jared slowed his vehicle this round and let Melissa beat him by a hair. Her whoops and hollers brought a smile to his face.

"You, Mister Speedy, have just been humbled and I am *back!*" called Melissa. "Best of all, you don't get the upgrade for your vehicle. Too bad, so sad."

"I'll beat you next time," said Jared. Which he did.

Just then, Melissa's cell phone rang. Jared's heart sank as Melissa rolled out of the beanbag chair to get it out of her pocket. "Hi Cam," she said and his fears were confirmed. She glanced at Jared, covered the receiver and said, "Maybe I better quit while I have one win." Then she disappeared up the stairs.

Jared clicked off the video game; he was glad Cam had called. Now he could go back to Lavascape.

Chapter Five

Climbing the stairs, Jared was feeling the effects of his late night in Lavascape the night before. The exhaustion had come and gone all day. He'd been a zombie in math. He had a momentary surge of energy again playing games with Melissa but now the exhaustion was back. Before Lavascape, I have to do some homework, he promised himself. But when he got to his room, his bed looked so inviting he curled in the covers and slept for a full hour. Just as he was getting up, Melissa popped her head in his room.

"Cam's coming over in a bit but we could have a couple more races if you dare face me."

"Anytime."

Jared let Melissa win the first game. On the second one, there was a knock at the front door. "I told him to just come in," whispered Melissa. Just then, there was a loud bang.

"He kicked it," said Jared.

"Lousy door!" Cam thudded down the stairs.

"It's really not that hard to open," said Jared.

Melissa glared at Jared. "He just forgets to pull it toward him first." Cam lowered himself onto her beanbag chair and planted a sloppy kiss on her lips. On the TV, her car swerved off the track and Jared won the race. "Interference." Melissa giggled.

"I better do my homework." Jared left them deciding which game to play and having a hard time choosing with all the kissing getting in the way.

That nap was just what he needed. Math on a tired brain is rough, but when he was rested, all the steps made sense. The computer in his room seemed inviting; he kept looking up from his books to gaze at the gloves and glasses draped over the chair. By the time he finished his homework, it was too late to play Lavascape. He shut off the lights and whispered, "Tomorrow. Lavascape tomorrow."

The next day, however, he had to work on an English essay and that took all night. The game mask seemed to call out, 'Jared!' and 'Hey troll!' as he was working. He wanted to log on just to see what was going on there but essays weren't his favorite thing and he didn't want to risk starting too late.

Now, two days later, he was ready for adventure. The initial sword fight with the elf taught him one thing—he needed practice. He was lucky to have escaped death that first day with his clumsy swordplay. A fleeting image of the troll who'd not been as lucky flashed through his mind. That look had bugged him for days. He couldn't seem to forget it, nor could he ignore that it was at least partly his fault. If he had been a better fighter... if he'd had a better sword...if he'd known how serious failing would be—would it have turned out differently?

He slipped on the gloves, tightened the thin metal chain to cinch them at the wrist, and put the mask in place. Toward the interior of the island, there were nodes of light shining through the trees. He'd heard kids at school mention a troll village. Maybe this was the way. Jared set his hairy troll feet on the path that seemed to lead to the lights.

The forest was dense with vines hanging in tattered curtains. Suddenly, he heard the sound of voices raised in song. It was a jazzy tune with rap in the background. He approached a clearing and was able to see a few trolls dragging carts behind them. Others sat gathered in twos and threes in front of the huts. A group of trolls sang in the center of the clearing. Jared approached and a troll with a golden fohawk met him.

"Welcome, newcomer," said the troll. He spoke with an English accent that reminded Jared of a reserved butler asking, 'Will there be anything else, sir? Grey Poupon, perhaps?' "Are you new to the trolls or new to Lavascape?" It sounded like 'Laahvaah-scape' when he said it.

"Both," said Jared. "How did you know I was new to the game?"

"I'm on the welcoming committee," said the golden haired troll. "I know tons of trolls in Lavascape."

Was he bragging or showing that he was super friendly? Perhaps both. "So, what's your name?" asked Jared.

"Grimball." He seemed pleased to be asked. "What about you?"

He remembered the name he gave to the rat. "Jerry," he said.

"Would you like a tour of our village?"

"Sure. That sounds great."

"The trolls are your new family and the troll village is your home. The most important thing you need to know is dinnertime. The feast is from 6:00-6:15 in the evening. If you miss the feast, you won't have the energy you need."

"You sound like my mom. 'Nutrition is so important'," mimicked Jared.

"Fine, don't believe me? Miss the feast a time or two and you'll see." Grimball walked ahead and Jared had to speed his troll to keep up.

"Where are the other creatures? Goblins, giants..."

"Keep your world small and you'll be happy here. This is the choir; basically they are 'Glee' trolls. Are you interested?" He moved on quickly when Jared shook his head. He pointed out a row of huts on the left side of the clearing with gingerbread-house detailing. "Those are all occupied." He walked toward them rattling off the names of the trolls who 'lived' there. Was Jared supposed to remember all these names?

They came to a larger hut with a flagpole next to the door. The flag was emerald green with a brilliant gold 'T' in the center. An hourglass was on one side of the letter at a forty-five degree angle and on the other side of the 'T', at an angle that mirrored the hourglass, was a large sword with a jewel-embellished hilt. Grimball said, "The troll flag is great, isn't it?"

"Yeah. It's cool."

"It's green now because our king's fohawk is that color. There are many troll villages all over Lavascape. Troll villages, troll training grounds—trolls are very important in this world. And nobody knows how to have a good time like the trolls. Follow me."

Jared followed Grimball into the hut with the flag. Though it was obviously the largest hut in the village, he was still unprepared for what he saw inside. It was huge and everywhere lights flashed, pulsed, or danced across the signs advertising 'Dart Throw', 'Skip it and Win', 'Ring Toss Challenge', 'Obstacle Course,' and many other games whose signs were too far off to read. "What's that supposed to teach?" asked Jared, pointing at the closest skill games.

"Coordination."

"And the obstacle courses?"

"Speed. Agility."

The colors were vibrant and the air radiated with carnival sounds and upbeat music. Intermingled with the bells and whistles from the games was the laughter of trolls having the time of their lives. Jared let the sights and sounds draw him in. Here things were happening. Here there was an escape of epic proportions—total, carefree fun. The game hut was electric, charging him with life.

He followed Grimball through the crowd. At the other end of the hut, large double doors stood open and there were rides visible outdoors. He could explore the rides for days. Jared saw a roller coaster called 'The Fohawk', a log ride called 'Troll tunnel of love', which looked like there was a huge drop at the end, and a ride where carts of trolls spun at the ends of long dragon tails. The carts that spun close to its fire breathing mouth turned red as though they were heating up. This was Disneyland, troll-style. And this was their idea of training! The board of education could learn a few things from this place. Trolls knew how to make learning fun.

They moved into the outdoor area. The bells and whistles of the carnival games faded in the metallic roar of the rollercoaster nearest them. Screams punctuated the scene testifying to the intensity of the rides.

"Pick your poison," said Grimball with a chuckle. Jared raised an eyebrow. "They don't always make you vomit," continued Grimball. "They're an uncertain poison." His English accent was especially strong.

"I'll take my chances." He moved to the line for the Fohawk rollercoaster. It loomed above him. As he looked up, he saw the orange tinged night sky broken by the Fohawk track twisting one way then another.

"Remember your Infinity Suit," said Grimball, handing him a white jumpsuit from a rack by the coaster. "This keeps you alive no matter how epic your wipe out. Your Lavascape adventure's over pretty quick without it." Jared put it on and took his place in the next available cart. There were controls inside. He didn't get to sit back and enjoy the ride. Jared had to control the cart so it didn't fly off the track. Jared splat against the ground repeatedly before getting the hang of it.

The more he played the further down the track he got before splatting, and Jared's coin total rose. He was at it for hours when Grimball met him getting off the ride. "Tomorrow is your Welcome Party, Jerry. Make sure you're here by the feast."

A welcome party. For him. Cool.

The next day dragged. Jared couldn't stop thinking about the Lavascape games during his classes. After school, he attended to his most urgent homework and finally logged in at 5:45.

He had a few minutes to spare so he went to the game hut and joined a couple of trolls playing coin toss. Grimball approached with another troll, shorter than Jared and about twice as thick around. He looked like a sumo wrestler in troll garb and an orange fohawk. "Yo, I'm your hut-mate, Barry."

"Hi," said Jared.

"Do ya wanna check out your new home until party time?"

"Sure."

Barry led the way. As they made their way to one of the huts, Barry called a greeting to everyone they passed, then repeated, pointing with his elbow, "This is Jerry, my new hut-mate." He seemed to know everyone in the village.

There were two distinct sides of the hut. One side had a shelf of trophies on the wall, a comfortable-looking armchair, a table so full of appliances and gadgets Jared couldn't say what they were, and a small white animal curled up in a dog bed. The other side of the room had a single hard-backed chair and that was it. "Guess which side's yours," said Barry.

"The side with the dog?" said Jared, lightheartedly.

"Ha. You wish. And he's not a dog. Come here, Chuck," he said, calling to the animal. That it was no dog became obvious as soon as it stood. The round creature with silky hair took a few bouncy steps on two legs. "It's a mingo," said Barry.

"He's cool."

"I just taught him to fetch."

Barry threw a ball with knobs sticking out all over it and the mingo leapt after it. The ball bounced one direction, then another. It hit the mingo square on the head but then he grabbed it in his stubby arms and brought it back to Barry.

"That's great. Where did you get him?"

"I bought him."

"Where? How?"

"With carnival gold."

"Is that how you got all the rest of your stuff?"

"Yep. You'll probably want to upgrade your chair first. Those nasty wood ones are murder on the butt."

Jared chuckled. Just how would he know the chair was uncomfortable for his electronic troll? He didn't say anything about that to Barry, though.

"Hey, do you want to play fetch with Jerry, Chuck?"

They took turns throwing the knobby ball to the mingo. Chuck sometimes caught it easily and sometimes he bounced off the walls and landed upside down. Once he seemed to forget what he was doing and jumped up on Jared's back.

A gong sounded outside the hut and Barry jumped up. "It's party time. Back to bed, Chuck."

The mingo hung his head as though profoundly disappointed, then toddled back to his bed. Jared needed a pet mingo much more than a comfy chair.

The feast was 'fish and fungus', a breaded trout and fried mushrooms, that somehow seemed very satisfying. At 6:15, the food vanished leaving the tables without so much as a crumb but Jared stayed at the long banquet table chatting with other trolls. Then Jared, Barry, and three other trolls went to the game hut and played dodgeball balloons against each other. Green slime filled the balloons and if you hit your opponent with them hard enough, you sprayed them with the slime. He got Barry right across the face. It was classic!

Another, deeper gong sounded. All the carnival noises went silent. "It's time for your initiation."

"Initiation? I thought it was a welcome? What's going to happen?"

"I'm not allowed to tell. Come on, you don't wanna be late. Believe me, it's worse the further down the line they go."

Jared, Barry, and a few other trolls left the game hut. The music started up again inside after they exited. It had an ominous sound as they moved away. Jared heard two girls' voices coming from trolls behind him. 'At least tell me if it's going to hurt,' said one girl.

'I told you, it does, but it doesn't last long,' the other girl whispered urgently. "Now don't say anything else; I'll get in trouble."

Jared swallowed. If the lava-rock incident was any indication, this could be very realistic. A sign flashed the names of the new trolls and Grimball stood at a podium. "To claim your troll powers you must be initiated into the Troll clan." A fire burst to life and iron handles protruded all around it, hovering mid-flame.

"What's in the fire?" whispered the frightened girl Jared had overheard before.

"If you want to leave now," continued Grimball in his refined voice, "you will go into Lavascape equipped with your sword but you'll be denied entrance to troll training. If you want to leave, do so now." He held up one of the handles. At the other end, immerging from the fire was a circular brand. It had a capital 'T' on it with a sword and hourglass on either side of the letter, just like the flag.

"I won't do it!" yelled a female voice. Two huge trolls came and took the girl out of the square.

"Anyone else like to withdraw?" asked Grimball.

Silence.

Jared was third in line. The first troll stepped forward. Grimball said his name, everyone cheered, and then he lowered the brand already in the air. He pressed it into the chest of the troll. Jared thought he smelled burnt hair. Grimball removed the brand and the troll disappeared.

The second troll stepped forward. Grimball took a fresh brand out of the fire. It glowed red as everyone cheered for 'Frankie'. Jared looked away. A deep male voice cried out.

As Jared approached, Grimball reached for a new brand, his eyes seemed to glow. He heard "Jerry!" in Grimball's accented English and the roar of welcoming trolls. The glowing 'T' came closer. Jared tried to back his troll up. It was stuck.

Jared felt heat in his chest, intensifying with every second it came nearer. He jabbed with the control buttons but his troll stayed exactly in position. The brand touched his troll, Jared sucked in his breath, and a groan escaped his lips. Then an inward scream filled his ears. They were branding him like an animal! Burning the hair, skin and flesh right off his body!

Jared jumped in his computer chair. He felt disoriented. An eerie, otherworldly feeling crept up his arms and brought him back to the moment. Had he passed out? He remembered. He threw off the mask, which was completely blank, clutched the bottom of his t-shirt and whipped it up. His chest looked fine. The girl troll was right. It hurt like crazy, but not for long.

The next morning in the shower Jared washed his chest and the troll brand emerged on his skin, angry and red. He dropped the soap and jumped out of the shower. The brand faded and disappeared. Jared had suds all over, so he re-entered the shower. He closed his eyes and rinsed off. His chest flared in pain but he refused to look.

Over the next couple of days, he started to tell his friends about this 'branding injury' but something always held him back. For one thing, the lava rock on his ankle was right there to see but the brand only showed up in the shower. Gradually, Jared became comfortable with the look of it. It faded from red to white.

One morning he took a mirror in the shower to see it straight on. It couldn't possibly be real. Not if it disappeared as soon as he left the shower. But there it was, reflected back at him.

As he walked to school, he wondered how it worked. How does a troll brand mark your skin from the world of Lavascape? And why could he only see it in the shower? It had to be a mind trick...which might be even freakier than the lava scab. He pulled open the door to the school, and two girls from his grade said, "Hi Picky!" then they left, laughing like they'd just heard the funniest thing in the world.

"Great," whispered Jared. He regularly heard 'Picky' from Colton and his buddies, especially in gym class, and now it had spread.

By the time he got to his locker, kids he hadn't spoken to in over a year said, "How's it going, Picky?" and "Picky is here!" One guy even said, "Hi, Picky-Poo."

Colton came by his locker and elbowed him hard in the ribs. It was such a quick passing gesture that, in a crowded hallway, Colton could claim it was accidental if Jared tried to make an issue of it. Of course, there was nothing accidental about a smack in the back of the head, and that's what he got from Colton between third and fourth periods.

He had to ignore more and more 'Picky' references. Many people seemed to think it referred to picking his nose, judging from the actions that often went with the taunt. There was no point trying to set the record straight. Picking a scab wasn't that much better and he'd look like a major dork if he clarified 'what exactly' he was picking. He tried not to let it show, but it really bothered him. He hoped that if he ignored it, it would go away. That strategy wasn't working out too well. Also, Colton's passing attacks had him on edge every time he was in the school hallways. For a big guy, Colton sure was good at sneaking up on someone.

Luckily, Jared had an escape. Each day he logged on as soon as he got home from school and each day he mastered the skills of the games in the troll village. He watched his coin total rise. Movement was so easy now; he could do the obstacle course with only his body movements, he didn't even need the palm pad. Sometimes, he wondered if he actually moved or if the troll responded telepathically. But, that was dumb. That was just how good he was getting.

He loved the Troll Teaser games that challenged his

agility, and he was even on the high scoreboard! He did wonder why they called them teasers though.

Jared was having a blast in Lavascape. Living with Barry was what it must be like having a college roommate, except instead of studying and going to classes, they headed over to the game hut to earn gold coins.

Lavascape was more than a game; it was increasingly the focus of Jared's social life. He met the trolls from his village as they rode the roller coasters, which had such fantastic graphics that he actually felt his stomach rise and fall when he rode them. They challenged each other in the obstacle courses and other skill games. There were friendly rivalries developing between a few of the huts.

Now Jared's half of the hut had a La-Z-Boy recliner, an ice cream machine and best of all, his own black and red mingo. Jared made a curly top ice cream cone and handed it to Barry. "Here you go, hut-mate." He farted loudly.

"Nice one, dude."

"The shape of the ice cream or the epic fart?"

"Both." They laughed for a solid minute. "But seriously, you're really getting good at it," said Barry. "No one makes a perfect circular curl at the top like you."

"Thanks." Jared made himself an ice cream cone too and then lowered into the dark green recliner. "It's so refreshing," he said. "I don't know how, but it is."

"And didn't I tell you about how your butt would get sore sitting on that rickety wooden chair?"

"Yeah."

"Are Red and Kelsie coming over for a treat, too?"

"There wasn't any answer at their hut. "I'm sure they'll be on-line before long."

"Hey, you don't talk about that," whispered Barry. "Ruins the atmosphere."

Jared nodded, then dumped the rest of his ice cream cone on a pie plate beside the recliner. "Here, Tiger," he called.

The longhaired mingo jumped up from a circular cushion and bounded to Jared's side. When he saw the ice cream, he looked at Jared affectionately and then dug in with both hands. The ice cream melted down his arms and covered his hairy chin but there was no mistaking his gleeful slurping noises.

Barry farted loudly. "You're going to have to give him a bath again."

"He can shower himself. That was quite an explosion; do you need to clean up, too?"

"Very funny."

Jared liked to take care of the little pet. When you gave him a bath, he tried to pop the bubbles in the washtub; when you brushed his hair, he purred contentedly; and when you fed him, he was enthusiastic for the things he liked and made pouty faces over the food he didn't. The funniest thing was the time Jared had fed him broccoli, but Tiger wouldn't eat it until Jared added cheese sauce. There was cheese all over him in the end.

The pie plate was empty now. "Go take a shower, Tiger," he ordered. The mingo looked up expectantly. "Nope. No bath today. Go to the shower." Jared watched the mingo toddle off then he turned back to the troll beside him.

"How many more coins do you need for the CD player?" Barry asked.

"About a thousand."

"You get that and I'll get the snow-cone machine."

"Sounds great."

"We're really moving up in the world."

There was a knock at the door followed by two farts from whoever was out there. Jared opened the door to find two girl trolls framed in the doorway. One had sleek long red hair and the other short brown hair with a red fohawk.

"Hey," said Jared.

Barry pointed at them. "We went to your hut earlier and you weren't in."

"Just got here," said Red, the redhead. "We just made the feast."

Jared had missed the feast once and he'd never do that again. That day he felt like he was walking in a daze of sleep deprivation. His mind seemed clouded and his troll moved like it was treading water. The ice cream from their machine did almost nothing to help.

"Do either of you want an ice cream?" asked Jared.

They both shook their heads. "Naw, we're full from the feast," said Kelsie.

"Maybe later, though," said Red.

"We're ready to rock and roll, then," said Barry. "Let's go."

Chapter Six

Jared and his family sat at breakfast in their usual spots. No matter what the tension from Mom and Dad's latest spat, the kitchen table pulled them together from separate rooms and separate pursuits. There was a stack of French toast and a plate of cut fruit in the center of the table. Melissa said, "Yum. Please pass the oranges." Jared slid the plate toward her. Mom slipped a plate of crispy bacon on the table and took her seat.

"Wow, bacon too," said Melissa taking two strips and passing the plate to Jared.

As he reached for bacon, Jared noticed a 'humph' from Dad.

"We hardly ever have bacon," said Mom. "Besides, it's protein."

Jared farted loudly and unexpectedly.

"Don't be gross!" his sister, snapped.

The morning news hummed in the background. "I did

things I never thought I'd do," said a female voice from the program. "Drugs were the only thing that was important to me. I can't tell you how hard it was to stop. "

The interviewer interrupted her, "How were you able to break away?"

There was a pause and Jared tilted his head to get a better look at the screen. The girl had thick black eyeliner circling her eyes and a face that seemed shrunken somehow. "I was lucky. I wouldn't have said that when I was going through withdrawal, but the truth is, I'd be dead right now. The addiction takes over everything."

Jared's mind wandered. What happened to her?

"Poor girl," said Dad. "These kids don't realize they're playing with fire. Look at the sadness in her eyes. She's had a tough time and she probably started out as some innocent girl who was just led in the wrong direction."

"Or she was some stoner who didn't care about anybody but herself and the next thrill," said Mom. "You can't tell."

"Either way, I'm sure she got more than she bargained for," said Dad. "She's been hurt. I hope she goes home and starts over."

Suddenly the word 'Lavascape' caught Jared's attention. The next feature was about the game. A middle-aged man, with sideburns a little too long for his age, said, "There have been far too many cases, statistically speaking, for a connection not to exist."

"You really believe Lavascape poses a health risk?" said the interviewer.

"I do. Parents-against-Lavascape has documented a disturbing number of young people suffering from unusual ailments. Some, like Michael Newton's are serious. He is sixteen years old and his parents say he was in perfect health until he became addicted to Lavascape."

Jared choked on his bacon. He coughed and sputtered. Then he couldn't breathe.

"Are you okay?" asked Mom. She rose and patted his back.

"That's not what you do," said Dad. He hurried behind him and, with one hand a fist, gave Jared the Heimlich manoeuvre. The piece of bacon shot from his mouth, hit the door of the microwave, and stuck there.

"Are you okay?" Mom repeated.

Jared coughed again, then, in a voice much deeper than usual, he said, "I think so."

Melissa pointed at the bacon clinging to the microwave. "Somehow you always manage to be gross," she said, but she was smiling.

He missed the rest of the interview.

Jared hadn't heard about physical problems before, he'd only heard vague references to 'destructive to youth'. Now here was some hippie-wannabe trying to claim serious health issues. It was laughable! He rubbed his forearms: the hair was standing on end and a chill had crept over him.

The weather report was on now.

"Mom," said Melissa. "I need to talk to you."

"So talk."

"It's...personal...kind of."

"Can it wait?" She glanced at her watch. "I've got to get going soon."

Jared turned to his dad and asked, "Are you free to go fishing this weekend? Since we...you know...missed the derby and everything..."

"Not this weekend." He finished his orange juice. "I gotta go, too. Sorry I forgot about the derby. " Without even looking him in the eye, Dad was out of the room. Mom rose and followed him. The table shook and continued to wobble as they left.

He could hear the whispered, under-their-breaths, conversation at the front door. "You have all the time it the world for strangers but nothing left for us," said Mom.

"It was fishing, not his high school graduation. Give me a break."

"'It would be different if you had to work."

"How do you think you get work? You get out in the community and network. You think this is fun for me? I'm out there selling myself every second. I'm busting my butt trying to find enough work to pay the mortgage."

"It's a waste of time! You need to get a steady job!"

"It's working! I'm bringing in more contracts all the time!"

"Not even close enough. The credit cards are killing us. Twenty eight and a half percent interest!"

"Yeah, you told me. So stop using your card!" He was no longer attempting to whisper.

"Sh. The kids will hear you." The door opened and closed.

Mom came back in the kitchen and took a Tylenol bottle out of the cupboard. "Fundraisers," she mumbled. "How ironic." She swallowed a pill and washed it down with water. "Fishing." She looked heavenward.

Jared wanted to say, 'Stop mom, it doesn't matter, it's no big deal'.... but he didn't.

There was sunshine beyond the confines of the dingy classroom. It shone through the needles of the evergreen outside the window creating jagged lines of sun and shadow on Jared's notebook. Exponents? Square roots? Who cared? The night before, Jared had felt an ache inside as he turned off the computer and now he was aching to get back on.

The teacher droned on, flashing power point slides that meant nothing. Jared's attention drifted. Why wasn't the world like a math question? Perfect squares everywhere. There would be a right answer. No grey zone. We'd all see eye to eye. Sounds like utopia. Math saves the world—who would've thought?

Only, Jared wouldn't be the super hero to conquer evil with math because he didn't have a clue what Mr. Glenn was talking about.

The bell finally rang and though he was still at least twenty minutes from Lavascape-time, he felt renewed energy as he was sprung from his last class. In the mass confusion of the hallway he spotted Anna. She was waving to him. He timidly raised his hand. They would be connected through upraised hands, an invisible current of friendship and maybe even attraction pulsing between them. As he came closer, she burst into a smile, ran toward him, and stopped in front of Katie's locker where Katie was talking with Monty. "I have to tell you!" she squealed, grabbing Katie's hands and pulling her away. "You know Sara and Mike broke up? Well..."

Jared's face burned. She had been waving at Katie, not him. As the girls caught up on the latest gossip, Jared and Monty stood back. Suddenly Jared felt a sharp stabbing pain in his back, just above his jeans, making him jump and spin around. Colton Barnes was a foot away holding a math compass, the sharp metal end, red with blood, in the air. "I just can't get the hang of drawing the circle graphs," he said and walked away. Reg, the goon on his left, snickered.

"Did he stab you?" said Monty.

"Yeah. I'll be fine."

"You should tell the principal."

"It will only get worse, if I do."

"Were you waving to me?" It was Anna and she was standing right in front of Jared.

"Oh, uh..." Jared wanted to die. She'd waved to get Katie's attention and he had waved back at her. "No, I was...uh... just feeling the current."

Anna crinkled her forehead.

"Current?" Katie's eyes narrowed.

"Uh, no not 'current.' The breeze, air currents, you know. I thought a door was left open."

"It's three thirty; people *are* leaving the school."

"Um. Yeah." He couldn't wait to get out in the air currents right now. He felt like he was suffocating.

They gathered what they needed from their lockers, and said 'goodbye' to Anna as she went to catch her bus. Why did she have to be so beautiful?

Katie, Monty, and Jared headed toward home. "Math class went on forever," Jared complained.

"Math is so easy and he goes over the same concept so many times I want to scream," agreed Katie. "I started writing my English essay half way through."

"Is that what you were doing?" asked Monty. "I thought you were taking notes. I thought I was missing something. I wrote down everything he said!"

Jared and Katie laughed.

"Where were you yesterday, Jared?" asked Monty.

"Nowhere. Home."

"I called and your dad yelled for you, then said you must not be home."

"I guess I didn't hear him from Lavascape."

"That's lousy. We went fishing and Dad said I could invite you."

"Crap."

They turned the corner and Josie's was in sight. Jared felt a cold shiver run down his arms. He usually loved hanging out with Monty and Katie at Josie's. It was his retreat where there was good food and good friends and no worries. But today it felt more like a prison. He'd be trapped until he could break free and get to Lavascape.

"So what are you guys going to have today," said Katie. "Last time we said we should try the deep fried mozzarella sticks. If we split it three ways that's pretty cheap." Katie pulled a wallet out of her book bag and looked inside.

"I don't know if I'm coming today," said Jared. There was really no reason to hurry home. No reason...except Lavascape.

"You can owe me if you don't have money," Katie offered. "I'm dying for some marinara sauce."

"It'll be about two seventy-five each," said Monty.

"It's not the money..."

"We don't have to have the mozza sticks then," said Monty.

"It's not that, either. I... I just have things to do."

"What things? It's Friday," said Monty.

Jared dragged his feet. "Lavascape...."

"You don't want to come with us?" Katie didn't look angry; there was something else in her eyes. She must be mad though.

"Don't get on my case! Do I have to go eat deep fried cheese just to make you happy?"

"Calm down, Jared." Monty looked at him through slits of eyes. "What's up with you?"

Was he mad, too? Probably. This was the 'peer pressure' teachers were always talking about. They would make him spend two-seventy-five on cheese sticks and keep him there chattering for over an hour. The ends of his fingers tingled, and another tingle spread from right between his eyes, over the top of his head, and down the back.

"We always hang out on Fridays," Katie said.

"I don't remember signing a contract," said Jared.

"Fine. Do what you want."

"Gee, thanks for your permission. I think I will."

"You don't have to get mad about it," said Monty. "Are you okay?"

"Who's mad?" said Jared. "I'll see you guys later."

With that, he turned away from his friends and hurried to the lights. He tapped his foot. The highway ran through town. He was fast, he was agile, he was a troll, and he could beat the traffic, easy. A semi truck was barrelling down the southbound double lane. Jared sprinted out into the road. The wind chilled his face and the smell of exhaust fumes reached his nostrils. The truck was almost upon him. A horn blared. Jared passed the truck's lane but he hadn't noticed the little sportscar next to the semi. Both drivers slammed on the breaks and the little car skidded and screeched toward him. Jared leapt and rolled toward the curb. Once it was clear that he was unhurt, the man rolled down his window, yelled, and cursed at him. Jared called back, "Gotta live in the moment." He brushed gravel from his hands and hurried on, adrenaline pumping. *That was the way to live life*, he thought. *A little more troll courage would be a welcome thing.*

When he reached his house, Jared pulled on the front door and fantasized about grabbing Cam by the sideburns. He'd probably squeal.

He listened. Was today a phone day? As often as not, Jared came home to hear Mom telling her friends all about how lousy dad is and how much more she wants out of life. It was quiet today, though, except for dishes clanking in the kitchen. Jared followed the noises. He rounded the corner and there was Melissa standing at the counter with a big wooden spoon in her hand and a smile on her face.

"Hi. Want some cookie dough? I'm almost done."

"Yeah—of course."

"Where's Mom?" asked Jared after his second spoonful.

"I don't know. There was a note on the fridge that said she'd be home late; she left us money to go to Dairy Queen for burgers."

"Is there enough for ice cream?"

"I think so."

Jared smiled at the bowl of cookie dough. "I think they have a cookie dough blizzard."

Melissa's smile was forced. "She's gone almost as much as Dad. When I saw her note, all I could think of was chocolate chip cookies. The kind she always made after school when we were little."

They were quiet for a minute. Then Melissa said, "When's the last time she cooked a real meal in the evenings? Sure, she cooks breakfast sometimes, but that's it."

"She's busy, Melissa. And she's worried about...stuff."

"I suppose. I just miss the dinners with a roast and vegetables and everybody there."

"I know what you mean." It was more than the roast beef that Melissa was missing, Jared knew. It was family time.

"Oh, and the note says you're supposed to take out the garbage."

"Blah." Why was it always him? Melissa was certainly strong enough to carry the garbage. Jared gathered the kitchen garbage bag and tied a knot in the top.

"When do you want to leave?" asked Melissa.

"About six-thirty, I guess. I don't want to miss the troll feast. Plus, I promised a guy I'd be there for a doubles match at five."

"Doubles? Is it tennis or something?"

"Kind of the troll version of tennis. You use a sword instead of a racquet and you stab the ball to send it over the net. Me and Barry are running their show. We're top of the leader board."

"Cool."

Jared took the garbage to the bin in the alley behind the house, then went to his bedroom and settled into his game chair. He slipped on the 'gear' as he'd come to refer to the mask, gloves and leg straps. Barry wasn't in their hut. Jared checked the time. It was still early. He played with Tiger and waited. At ten minutes to game time, Barry was still missing. Maybe he'd gone to the game hut without him. Jared hurried over there but Barry wasn't at the doubles court. Jared waited anxiously as the previous game concluded. Their opponents warmed up, knocking the ball back and forth to each other. Jared and Barry's teaser game time came and went and Barry didn't show. Jared had to forfeit the game and now they were knocked way down in the standings. He went to the coaster rides to pass the time until feast.

Suddenly, Barry sat next to him at the feast. "You missed our doubles match," said Jared.

"Sorry bro. Things happen."

That was it? That was all the explanation Jared was going to get? 'Things happen.' One thing didn't happen... they didn't make the leader board. He ate his fish and fungus in silence.

There was a knock on Jared's bedroom door. Melissa popped her head in his bedroom and said, "Do you want to walk or take our bikes?"

"Bikes. It will take more than half an hour to walk there." He left his troll inactive at the feast without another word to Barry.

The wind was cold in Jared's face, except for the center of his hairline. He felt a strange warm tingling there. Melissa panted as they locked up their bikes. Her hair was wild, like a strawberry-blond porcupine. Jared liked it. It was better than the perfectly straightened look she got with all the time she spent in the bathroom every morning.

As they ate, Melissa's phone rang. "Hi Cam...No, I'm not home. At Dairy Queen for dinner...No, just me and Jared... Okay. Bye." She slipped the phone back in her coat pocket. "That was Cam," she said, unnecessarily.

"Yeah, I figured," said Jared, rolling his eyes.

"I don't know why you act like that. He's never done anything to you."

"I can tell just by looking at him that he's some kind of a low-life."

"Why? Because his jeans are torn?" Melissa was defensive already.

"He just seems to be hiding something. Put that guy in a police line-up and he'd get picked every time."

"He'd be innocent!"

"Melissa, he just seems sketchy."

"He hasn't done anything to you," she repeated.

"Yeah right!" Sure he had. Lots of things.... Suddenly 'he ate all the chips I wanted' didn't seem like a federal offense, and complaining about his driving seemed like a minor thing, too. But there was stuff! Jared just couldn't think of anything this exact second.

"Well, we're together, so you'd better get used to him. I may even marry him one day."

"Marry him? You're sixteen." Jared took a big bite of his burger and continued with his mouth full, "Wonderful."

"I love him. It would be nice if my brother got along with him. Won't you at least try?"

"Fine, next time I see—"

"Here he is now."

Cam Kensington strut into the Dairy Queen like a movie star, spied Melissa and Jared, and swung into the seat next to Melissa planting a kiss on her waiting lips.

Great, thought Jared. *Don't mind me over here. Don't mind the thirty other people in the restaurant.*

"Hey Shorty," Cam said when he disentangled his lips from Melissa's; his eyes were red and watery.

Shorty! Jared glared at Melissa. There, did she need more proof than that? Jared had every reason to dislike him.

"Are you about done?" Cam rested his right arm on the back of the booth tapping his fingers non-stop like a professional typist. You'd think he owned the place.

"Yes," said Melissa.

"No," said Jared.

"Well then, I guess we'll see ya later, Shorty."

"Cam, what about my bike?" said Melissa.

"I brought Dad's truck. We can throw it in the back."

"Well, let's wait for Jared to finish."

"You don't want to come with us, do you?" said Cam to Jared.

It was obvious that Cam didn't want to give him a ride home. "Nope, I could use the exercise."

"Good plan, buddy. Build up some muscle." He reached over and felt Jared's upper arm with mock interest.

"We shouldn't ditch him," said Melissa.

At least she felt guilty about it, but the last thing Jared wanted was pity-company. "I'm good," he said.

"There," said Cam with a smug smile. "Come on," he urged Melissa. "Let's go."

Jared finished his burger as he watched through the window while Cam waited for Melissa to bring her bike to the dented, red truck.

Cam started to lift the bike into the truck but he didn't have it high enough and the pedal caught. He stumbled back and dropped the bike. Was he drunk? Or on something else? He laughed and looked at Jared. Where were Cam's superior muscles? Jared flexed his biceps and grinned at him. Cam glared and Jared turned away.

The only place there was any respect was in Lavascape.

Chapter Seven

"Halibut, tuna, shark fin, trout. No wonder I never get tired of fish and fungus," said Barry. "They change it up and somehow it always seems to be just what I was hoping for."

Jared laughed. He couldn't stay mad at Barry. They'd been in their seats waiting for the troll feast for ten minutes and all Barry could talk about was eating.

"The mushrooms have even more variety," added Jared.

"Oh don't get me started," said Barry. He licked his lips. Jared did the same, just so he could see his troll mimic his real actions.

Suddenly, there was a commotion at another feast table. A thin, black-haired female troll with a flaming red fohawk stood on the table. "We can't hide out here in the village forever," she called to all the trolls. "The war goes on and we're just ignoring it."

"It's safe here," someone heckled back.

"It's only a matter of time before they figure out how to get into the villages. Rumor has it that the humans have done it already."

"And that's all it is: rumors. Stop trying to get us all worked up over nothing, Louila," said someone behind Jared.

"I know where the elves' lair is. They just took down a bunch of trolls in a battle in the valley. Their troll captives need our help. I say we attack the lair, catch them at their victory party, and show them what happens when you mess with trolls. Who's with me?" A few trolls called out their assent. "We can surprise them and really make a difference in this war," said Louila.

Barry leaned in to Jared and the other trolls nearby. "One person can't make a difference. She's delusional. And if I've learned anything here in Lavascape, it's look out for yourself. Anything more gets you killed."

A troll across the table from Jared stood.

"What are you doing?" Barry demanded.

"I'm going to join the fight. And you should too, Barry."

"I certainly am not! Think about it, Winston. Why should you stick your neck out for her? It's dangerous out there."

"I know."

"So listen to me and sit your butt back in that chair. The feast is due any second."

"I'll have my feast over there...before we go," said Winston.

"Ignore them" Barry said to Winston. "You've always ignored them before." There was an edge to Barry's voice. "You were the one who wanted to sit as far away from the questers as possible. You said, 'Crazy Adventurers on one side and Good Time Trolls on the other.' You used to laugh at the trolls that got sucked into quests, remember?"

"Maybe we were just putting our heads in the sand."

Barry started to say something else but Winston cut him off. "It's my choice, Barry. Thanks for caring, and I'll miss hanging out in the game hut with you guys, but I see now that there's something more going on in Lavascape." He picked up his plate and walked to the tables on the other side. The feast appeared just as he left.

"Looks like another one's gone over to the dark side," said Barry. "He can't say I didn't warn him." He dug into his food with both hands and emitted a long machine-gun series of farts.

"What's the war all about?" asked Jared.

"Who knows? Look, we're here for a good time. Just relax."

After the feast, the adventurers went to their quests. Jared had no regrets about staying in the village, but he was interested in the war just the same. He went to Grimball; surely the troll who welcomed him to the village knew what was going on. He seemed to have been there forever.

"What can you tell me about the war?" asked Jared.

"There's not much to tell. Trolls battle with giants and elves. We have an alliance with goblins. It's dangerous, messy stuff. Have you tried the capture the flagship game in the hut? It will give you a taste of the kind of thing you're looking for."

"Who says I'm looking for anything?"

"You're asking. Naturally I assumed you are considering going."

"No, no. Just curious about the war, that's all."

Grimball let out a breath. "Oh thank heavens. I thought I was going to have to talk you out of leaving."

"Why would you do that?"

"For your own good."

"Hm. What about the humans, which side are they on?"

"They're unpredictable."

"What about the Scurry?"

"They're stinky and unpredictable."

"What's it like out there, Grimball?"

"Terrible. Nasty. I heard you had a taste before you found us."

Jared remembered the dead troll. He remembered the blood on his hands. "Yes, nasty," he said. "I'm not going anywhere."

Grimball started to walk away.

"But if I want to know what's going on?"

"You don't." The clipped way he spoke annoyed Jared.

"But there must be a way. I suppose I could eat with the adventurers; they'd tell me."

"Stay away from them." Without waiting for a reply, Grimball strode away.

What happened to Mr. Congeniality, Jared wondered, the guy who welcomes every troll to the village.

Barry laughed when Jared told him about his talk with Grimball. "Why that guy's on the welcoming committee, I'll never know. He can be so unsociable."

Later that evening, the girl trolls from next door came to hang out. "Oh, look at your mingo," said Kelsie. "What's all over him?"

"He's been eating ice cream again," said Jared. Tiger was licking the fur around his mouth with his long pink tongue.

"You treat that thing better than you do your friends," said Red.

"Fine, you can have a cone," said Barry, getting up to make one for each of his guests.

While they ate, they chatted with Barry as Jared filled the washtub and scrubbed Tiger's long hair. As he lathered the black strands, his mind wandered. He was feeling more and more at home in Lavascape. The real world was the hard place to be. People don't live happily ever after there. Big people picked on little people. The world wasn't fair. He wished he could go back to when he'd been young enough to believe in Santa and parents and fairness; and even more, he wished the world truly was as good as he had thought it was back then.

An especially large bubble floated out of the washtub and, as Jared focused on it, a vision appeared within it.

A beautiful girl turned, her hands sprang to her mouth. She tried to run but a guy, an obvious intruder in her room, stepped in front of the door, his lean frame blocking her escape. He was talking but Jared couldn't hear him. She shook her head, the long blond locks of her ponytail swinging gently in contrast to the brutality of the intrusion. She fell to her knees pleading with him.

She wore a long white nightgown. A canopy bed with sheer pink fabric was next to her.

The man made a motion with his right hand and two other men, holding swords in front of them, came toward her. The girl jumped to her feet and darted away from the approaching thugs. They split up and attempted to corner her but she scrambled under the bed and out the other side. One of the men swung his sword at her; she ducked and his sword smashed one of the wooden pillars of her bed. The canopy tilted and the wispy pink fabric fluttered to the floor. She ran to a large window and flung back the deep burgundy curtains. The peach hue of the Lavascape sky was revealed. She had one leg out the window when the men grabbed hold of her and jerked her back into the room. There was a gash on her forehead but the men ignored it and bound her hands. The man still stood smugly at the door. He grinned and led the way out. The girl looked over her shoulder as she stumbled from the room. Jared saw her terrified eyes and the blood on her forehead vividly just as the bath-bubble burst, ending his vision.

"Well, are you coming?" It was Barry. He was standing at the door to the hut with their friends. Where were they going? Oh, the games.

"Who was the girl in the bubble?"

"Don't pay any attention," said Barry.

"Did you see it, too?"

"It was probably showing you your quest, but you don't have to accept it. If you do, you leave the village—and the fun. I don't understand why anyone goes. It's dangerous out there; guys get hurt, killed even."

The newscast that claimed healthy kids were getting sick from playing Lavascape suddenly popped into Jared's head unexpectedly. "Yeah, it would be crazy to leave," agreed Jared.

At the next feast, Jared noticed the adventurers were louder than usual. "Hey, Louila is looking pretty happy over there," he said to Barry. "I wonder if she rescued those trolls she went to save?"

Barry shrugged and popped a deep-fried mushroom into his mouth.

"I'm going to go ask them."

Barry dropped the fish he'd been holding by the tail. "What? Why?"

"I'm interested in how it went."

"They'll just give you a hard time for being a villager.

There's a reason the adventurers sit on one side and the villagers sit on the other. We're different."

"We're all trolls. They can try to talk me into joining some quest, but they're not going to be able to suck me in. I just want to know how that raid went." Jared rose and made his way to the far side of the feast area.

Louila's jet-black hair gleamed in the sunlight. Jared had the thought that shiny hair probably wouldn't be the most advantageous trait in a rescue mission. It might draw the enemy's attention. As he came closer, he noticed how large and expressive her eyes were. Those eyes narrowed slightly as she looked at him.

"Hey," said Jared in greeting.

"Hello," said Louila.

"How did it go? Your mission to free those prisoners?"

There was a long, uncomfortable moment when no one said anything. The other trolls at the table had stopped talking too, and they all turned their eyes on Jared.

"Why do you care?" asked Louila.

"Because...we're all trolls."

"Where were you when we went into elfin territory?"

"Hey Louila," said the male troll to her left, "maybe he's ready to join our forces. Don't give him such a hard time."

"Oh no," said Jared, quickly. "I'm not involved in your adventures."

"Then why ask about them?" said Louila. Her tone was dry.

"I was just interested," said Jared. "Never mind." He turned to go.

"You villagers are really something," said Louila. "You're nothing but a bunch of cowards hiding out in the game hut, ignoring the realities of this world. Then you have the nerve to want to know how it's going! Well, here's the news update—we lost three of my best friends and saved seventeen trolls."

"I was one of the prisoners," said the guy at her left. He had a spiky yellow fohawk, brown hair, and deep-set eyes. "Freedom is the ultimate gift. We won't stop fighting until everyone in Lavascape is free. Don't you want to be part of something big? Join the adventurers."

"Sorry," said Jared. At his answer, most of the adventure trolls went back to eating their feast and talking to each other.

Louila snorted. "I knew it."

The yellow-fohawk troll focused his deep eyes on Jared. "When you're ready..."

"I'm glad you saved them, Louila," said Jared. He made his way back to Barry and the other light-hearted villagers.

"How'd it go?" asked Barry as Jared sat beside him.

"Those guys are intense." He took a breath. "Louila's crew did rescue the prisoners but lost three trolls doing it." Jared remembered the face of the bushy-eyebrow troll that he wasn't able to save his first day in Lavascape. Three more trolls with those empty, dead eyes.

"Now you're looking intense," said Barry.

It felt like an accusation. "Naw, I'm fine," said Jared.

Chapter Eight

A week later, Jared plopped in his computer chair ready for another party in Lavascape. After the feast and a couple of hours in the game hut, Jared saw Grimball standing by the gate. He was on the welcoming committee and had to know more than he was telling. Jared approached him.

"I want some answers."

Grimball backed up. "Just keep earning gold coins. It's all about the stuff you can get." Grimball turned and hurried away from him.

Jared followed, cornered him against the side of the 'Slime Shot' game booth, and demanded, "Tell me what it's like outside the village. What's really going on?"

"We *are* at war with the giants and elves, you know that." Grimball said in answer to Jared's question, his English accent sounding scholarly. Then Grimball suddenly punched his fist into an oval orb that floated toward them. "Giants are thick in the head and elves are scum," he said. So much for scholarly. The number 25 glowed in the spot the orb had been, then the orb ricocheted around the room and another three trolls each jumped up to punch at the roaming punching bag as it floated past them too. One said, "Giants pick their noses," as he punched the bag. "Elves are jerks," said another. Each time they punched the bag and insulted giants or elves a number appeared over the balloon-like punching bag, sometimes 10, sometimes 15, and sometimes 25.

"What are the numbers?" Jared asked.

"Gold coins, of course."

Jared nodded. The orb was a distraction but he refocused. "How do the quests fit in with the war?"

His guide huffed and again he seemed annoyed. Instead of answering Jared's question he said, "You get coins for your hit and coins for your insult. They are our enemies." Grimball swerved around Jared and left the hut.

"But are the quests part of everything?" Jared persisted as he followed Grimball, leaving the carnival music behind.

"Some yes, some no," said the guide as though resigned to answer the question. "And some become involved in the war while they have more personal quests. But the war is always in the background. It's a war that's always been and always will be. If you'll take my advice, you'll leave it to those who want to go into training and—"

"Training! Isn't that what I've been doing?"

"The Teasers aren't training...not real training." Grimball shrugged and walked away.

Jared wandered into the center clearing. The feast tables were gone and the Glee trolls had called it a night. Out of the forest a vision appeared. Jared could see the same beautiful young woman from his first vision. She was in a stark room of concrete with only a hard little cot in one corner. She rose from the bed and came closer to Jared. This time there was sound in his vision. The girl said, "My name is Sparket and I'm being held captive. My uncle plans to marry me to the prince of another kingdom. He hopes this forced marriage will bring peace to our lands, which have long been at war. The prince is a cruel, heartless beast and will make me miserable every day of my life. I refuse to be traded like a sack of flour, and they've given me two months to change my mind before they send me to the gallows. Please help me, Jerry Troll."

The princess returned to her cot and looked toward the single window that was her only light. She faded away and a shrivelled little man with green eyes filled the area of the vision. "Do you accept this quest?" he asked.

Everything was quiet in Lavascape as the man waited for his reply. There was a noise coming beyond Lavascape—a high pitched, intermittent sound. Jared's clock-radio alarm was going off. He ignored it.

Jared didn't want a quest to save a girl. He didn't want a quest at all. If she'd just been captured, that would be one thing, but this was so much worse than that. There was something about her. She was beautiful, and she needed him. Where was the justice in the world, even the world of Lavascape, if girls were kidnapped and forced to marry? *I'm not some mushy romantic,* he thought, *but that's just slavery.*

The man's green eyes seemed to intensify.

Jared told himself that Sparket's situation wasn't real. It wouldn't be any different than the trolls held prisoner that Louila and her gang had gone after. But, the fear in Sparket's eyes seemed so real. If he'd seen the faces of those other prisoners, maybe he would have joined those rescuers, as well.

Ten minutes earlier, Jared had been happy to while away his time in the troll village, but now everything had changed. The beautiful girl had set his heart on a new course. The injustice spurred him on. This girl faced the same bone-crushing bullying that brought the weak under someone meaner and stronger everywhere he looked. The victims were left hoping for mercy from the merciless. Today, here in Lavascape, he wasn't one of the weak; he could be her rescuer. Jared felt pride in himself. He was willing to fight the good fight.

The decrepit old man was still waiting.

"I accept the quest," Jared announced.

The man nodded and faded until he was gone.

High thrills and adventure awaited him.

Wait a second. The alarm was still ringing. Jared removed the mask and stared at his alarm clock in disbelief. It read 7:00. It was seven o'clock in the morning. Time to get up for school...and he had yet to close his eyes in sleep.

Jared moved through his day snatching moments of sleep when he could—at lunch; in class, when he was supposed to start the math homework; and when he rotated off the court during volleyball in Phys. Ed. He got home and felt fine.

When he got to Lavascape, he felt even better.

Jared sold all the things he'd accumulated back to Grimball, in spite of the grumbling from Barry as he watched all the items removed from the hut.

"Come with me," said Jared. "Aren't you tired of troll teaser games and eating ice cream and snow cones every day?"

"I'm not tired of living the good life. How do you get tired of fun?"

"When something else is more important, I guess. I'll be back for feasts."

"See you around, then. Good luck."

"Thanks," said Jared. He tucked the money into a pouch and started out, with Tiger following close behind.

"You're taking your mingo?" Grimball called after him, as Jared passed the gate to the village.

"Sure. He's my little buddy."

"That's not a good idea. Believe me, your pet would only be in the way on any quest. I'll give you seven gold coins for him."

"Maybe Barry wants him. Tiger and Chuck are friends." He turned back to Barry. "Well?"

"How much do you want for him? I know you paid ten gold coins." He looked down his nose at Grimball, who had been getting a few too many good deals.

"You can have him for free if you'll take care of him until I save the princess. Then I'll be back."

"You won't be back," said Barry.

"Maybe I'll surprise you."

"I hope so."

Jared passed a boulder and a young evergreen that seemed a little too familiar. Was he walking in circles? The trees were a mixture of evergreens, poplars, and oaks and the jungle-like blue bushes. They weren't thick, but Jared stayed alert, listening as much as watching for others. Where was the Troll Training zone? Grimball's lousy directions were to blame. Grimball probably didn't want Jared to find it. Grimball probably hoped Jared would turn around and come back to the village, tail between his legs. Then Jared realized: Grimball had never been to Troll Training; he'd never left the troll village.

Jared rounded a lava boulder, still glowing red from its core, and saw another troll heading toward the lava stream, the blue fohawk he sported visible against the pink mist.

When *all else fails, ask for directions,* thought Jared. He quickened his pace and caught up to the stranger.

"Where'd you get the sword?"

"Troll training," he replied. "Where do you think?" The troll trotted off, clutching his sword.

What did he have to do to get a little help around this place? Jared faced the direction from which the troll had come and started walking. About a hundred yards further on, he saw an oak tree with two flowing cursive T's on the trunk. At last, a sign. The tree marked a path, and Jared set off on that course.

Eventually he came upon another tree with a low branch that stuck out like a lever on a slot machine. The top of the tree was a mass of small leaves—yellows, oranges, and reds. Fall colors, Jared noted, wondering if it changed with the seasons. The trunk had a convoluted design of brown bark and sea-green leaves etched into it. He came closer and written on the branch were the same letters: 'T T'.

This looked promising. Jared pulled the branch down. It swung as though on a hinge and the dense trees to the right lifted their branches to form a pathway, the canopy of leaves above forming a tunnel. Jared entered.

As he moved along the path, the foliage changed. The short palm-tree-top bushes disappeared and fuller, denser, bushes took their place, along with more of the trees with fall-colored leaves. Evergreens abounded, as well. The intense colors became hazy, as fog rolled in.

A strange feeling overcame him. Suddenly he was worried. He didn't see anything threatening but an ominous feeling settled on him and, for an instant, it was so strong he almost took off the mask. He felt he was entering an area of great importance; that his life would never be the same again.

The fog intensified. He paused and placed his hands on his hips. He stood like that for a full three minutes staring at the scene. "Don't be silly," he eventually told himself. "It's just a game." He had certainly played games that were more terrifying than Lavascape had been so far.

But Lavascape was different. He thought back to the questions when he set up his account. What kind of video game delved so deeply into your personality? And then there was the little issue of the scab on his ankle that wasn't a scab at all, and the mysterious brand. "Don't get freaked out over nothing," he chanted. "It's just a game."

Jared continued forward along the path. Almost immediately the fog cleared. He heard the faint rumbling of far-off thunder and felt the earth shudder under his feet.

The path widened and in glowing letters carved into a slab of granite on the cliff wall Jared read, 'Welcome to Troll Training, Jerry.'

At that moment, he was distracted from the game by the sound of a door slamming. Jared tried to ignore it and focus on the game, but the voices that had started shouting were too loud. It was like a car accident. You know you should turn away but the wreckage is too spectacular not to sneak a peek. And you always want to know just how bad it is. So with an ache in his chest and morbid curiosity taking over, he left Lavascape and turned off the computer.

"A golf membership! Really? That's a business expense?" Mom yelled.

"When that's where the deals are made, you bet it is!" Dad sounded smug in his logic.

Jared opened his door. They were in their bedroom. The door was closed but could have been made of paper for all the privacy it provided.

"And what deals have you made? Where are the contracts? Nothing but a new pair of golf shoes to show for it. Another business expense, I suppose."

"I can't look like I'm not getting enough work to have decent shoes. They have to be able to trust me."

"You're *not* making enough to pay for a pair of shoes. I'm doing everything!"

"Oh, here we go! 'My life is so awful. Poor me!'"

Jared's curiosity turned to disgust. He had to get away. He descended the staircase, slipped on his shoes, and went into the backyard. The neighbor's dog, a terrier-poodle cross, rounded the house with a tennis ball in his mouth. There was a row of bushes at the back of the yard. How the dog got out of his own yard was a mystery but how he got into Jared's was not. There were no less than three gaps large enough for him to gain entry and he found his way into their yard at least once a week.

"Oh alright, Lewis. Bring it here." As he threw the ball repeatedly and watched the little black dog chase it down with enthusiasm, Jared made a plan. Tomorrow would be a better day. He would cook dinner and they would all sit around playing board games just as they had when he and Melissa were little.

He got home from school the next day and things were already off to a terrible start: Cam was there, sprawled across the couch in front of the TV. Jared made hamburgers (there were frozen burgers in the freezer) and he put one on for Cam because he showed no signs of leaving. Thankfully, Cam did leave just as Mom came home.

Mom had talked to Cam civilly. She must be a good actress. Surely, deep down she wanted to ban him from their house.

"Jared! You cooked! Thanks honey." She smiled. It seemed he hadn't seen her smile in a long time.

Melissa grabbed a slice of dill pickle and popped it in her mouth.

"They're almost done," said Jared. "I want to play games after dinner. It's part of the deal. You eat my food; you play my game."

Jared put the patties on a plate and set it on the table with the other hamburger fixings. Dad still wasn't home.

"We don't want them to get cold," said Mom. "Let's start." They were half done eating when Dad finally walked in the door.

After dinner, Jared brought out Monopoly but everyone complained that it took too long so he got Pay Day instead. Dad played for two rounds, then claimed he had to go to a meeting. Mom clenched her teeth, then said, "See ya." Jared had to keep reminding Melissa it was her turn because she was texting Cam the whole time. Mom moved her red dollar sign game piece with enough force to leave little dents in the board. Her mood sapped the rest of Jared's enthusiasm. "Never mind," he said, finally. "I'm done with this game, too. I'm going to Lavascape."

The phone rang just as he reached his bedroom. "It's Monty," called Melissa.

Jared picked up the phone in Mom's room, "Hey."

"Want to go over to the school and shoot some hoops?"

Lavascape was calling to him but Jared knew he hadn't hung out with Monty for quite a while, plus it might do him good to get completely out of the house after the miserable failure of family night. "Okay. Meet you there in ten."

The next day, Jared reviewed the game night in his head as he walked to school. Maybe he had called it quits too soon. It's true that Dad had left early on, but Mom and Melissa were still there, even if they hadn't been putting their best efforts into the whole thing.

"You're not usually here this early," said Katie, coming to his locker.

"What time is it?"

"Twenty after eight."

"You're right. I don't usually leave 'til now."

"What's wrong?"

"I didn't look at the time when I left, obviously." Katie just looked at him, waiting. "Yeah okay, there is something." He and Katie sat on the floor in front of his locker. "I tried to organize a family night with dinner and even a board game." Jared elbowed his locker door. It rattled with a satisfying clank. "It was kind of a disaster."

"What happened?"

Jared wished he hadn't said anything. "Never mind."

"Come on. What?"

"Dad left early, Mom was grumpy, and Melissa texted Cam the whole time." Jared sighed. "It was a stupid idea. We haven't played board games for years. But, I did cook."

"Impressive."

"Just hamburgers. Don't be impressed."

"Oh. I thought you made chicken cordon bleu or something."

Jared smiled. "Yeah, I considered that. It was either blue chicken or hamburgers."

"Sorry it didn't work out how you wanted."

Jared crossed his arms. "They fight so much. Any ideas that might work better."

"Do your parents have any old photo albums?" Katie said after a moment.

"Yeah, I think so."

"Pull them out. Find a picture where they look really happy together and leave the book on the coffee table open to that page. Maybe they'll want to look through the whole book and it will remind them of good times with all of you together." Jared shrugged. Katie continued, "It's worth a try. I know my parents get all smoochy when they look at their old pictures."

"Really?"

"Yeah, it gets so gross I have to leave the room sometimes."

Jared chuckled. "Thanks. I'll try it."

Chapter Nine

Troll Training had a giant hourglass as big as a troll in the center of the clearing. The glass was filled with glistening sand that could have been tiny diamonds. Decorative wood encased the top and bottom of the glass, and three swirling pillars of wood connected the top to the bottom. Around the hourglass were three flat stones each large enough to step on with both feet. On them were the words, 'Retina Reading,' 'Sword Skill,' and 'Hyped Hearing.'

"Quite the smorgasbord," whispered Jared. 'Retina Reading' sounded intriguing so Jared went to that stone first. As soon as his large, hairy foot made contact with the stone, he was transported through the hourglass to another clearing.

Jared looked at a list of Retina Reading game titles on a vertical granite slab. "I guess I have to learn it all," he whispered and laid his hand over one of the names at random.

His view changed to first person. A grid of faces appeared

on the screen of Jared's mask. Then the faces changed to identical flowery designs, like the backs of playing cards. "Match the faces," said a voice in Jared's ears. He reached his gloved hands out and tapped one of the squares. A face appeared. He touched another square and a different face materialized. No match. It was the card game 'Memory' only with facial expressions instead of numbers. Some of the differences in the faces were so subtle that Jared really had to concentrate. When he matched the similar faces, the tiles would disappear with a gentle bell tone and a voice would proclaim the correct expression: 'distress,' 'excitement,' 'dishonesty,' 'desperation,' 'cunning,' 'joy' along with the more generic emotions of 'sad,' 'frustrated,' 'interested,' and 'happy.' He learned to read trolls, giants, elves, scurry, and even humans. It was a challenge, but the longer he played the better he got at noticing the traces of emotions.

When he told Monty about the game at school the next day, Monty asked, "Sounds kind of boring. Just matching faces? Wouldn't you rather be in the sword fighting zone?"

"No. Don't you get it? The game trains you to judge emotions. It's like reading their minds, knowing what they're thinking and feeling. It will help me know what they're going to do next."

"They're going to stab you, and you won't know how to fend it off 'cause you spent too much time playing games instead of learning how to fight."

"You don't get it," Jared repeated.

He jumped into another Retina Reading game, as soon as he got home from school. Jared had to identify the fleeting emotions that came and went in a creature's face. The 'emotions' became more specific, as he progressed. Which face was someone withholding information? Which was showing relief at your arrival? Which was smugly waiting for unseen comrades to arrive? Jared thrilled to think he'd be able to 'see' these things. It would be such an advantage in future combat.

He trained to be observant of surroundings. He was shown a scene and then another almost identical one and had to note the differences. There were no multiple-choice answers to choose; he had to remember and describe everything aloud. As he moved from one level to another the amount of time to view each scene grew shorter. His mind seemed to be expanding as the scenes themselves became more complex. Battle scenes or the layout of a building, he never knew what sort of things he'd need to remember; he had to remember it all.

Then he went on to the most difficult tasks yet. They dealt only with eyes. "Choose a companion" was the instruction and he had to choose from a line-up of eyes.

"This is stupid!" he told the game.

"Choose a companion," the trainer repeated.

The first few times he made random choices. Then he started to 'read' things. He chose the eyes that belonged to 'The enemy with a terrible secret', 'the friend with insecurity issues,' and so on. The list seemed endless and the longer Jared tried to determine which set of eyes revealed this fact or that temperament it seemed to actually make sense. There were almost imperceptible differences that showed a great deal about the person behind those eyes. There was less luck involved and more judgement and knowledge required. It reminded him of math problems—the story problems that seemed impossible to figure out until you knew the right language for picking out what was plainly there. Retina Reading wasn't impossible; there were simply clues to look for and reasoning to follow.

He skipped Josie's the next day. It was too much Lavascape time wasted to hang out with Katie and Monty. Now, he was getting all kinds of compliments from the trainers for his quick progress and intuitive choices.

On Saturday, Jared trained in Retina Reading from the moment he got up until deep into the night. He didn't realize he hadn't eaten any dinner until he woke Sunday morning with intense hunger. He felt like a hollow drum inside. Melissa must have gone out for dinner with Cam the night before and who knew what Mom or Dad had done about dinner. There were no leftovers in the fridge and no one had called him away from Lavascape. He ate four bowls of cold cereal and three frozen waffles.

Where was everyone? Off doing their own things? His mind returned to earlier years and happier times. Maybe Katie was onto something. He went to the basement shelf where all the photo albums were standing in a row. He grabbed three of the oldest albums and took them to the kitchen table. He flipped through each in turn until he found a shot of a happy, smiling family together. He left the books open. "Remember the good times," whispered Jared.

Then he spent the day back in Lavascape. When he finished with one exercise, the game would bring the next one faster if he grunted loudly. He was perfecting a great 'troll grunt.' Jared hit high scores on some of the Retina Reading training exercises. He was celebrated and decorated with symbols of his achievement. One trainer said he was a 'marvellous specimen' and the most recent one called him 'an elite troll among the most special.' When he tried to thank the trainer for an award he said, "Don't be thankful. If you've earned something, you did it yourself and you deserve it. Simple as that."

He left Retina Reading. A trip through the hourglass, and Jared was learning all the Sword Skill of the trolls. He felt right at home. The sword felt like an extension of his arm. He was picking up moves like it was second nature. Eventually he realized that he was again on his way to another all-nighter, and broke off to collapse into his bed.

The next morning he dragged himself out of bed. A wave of dizziness crashed against him and he lay back down for several minutes. His eyes focused on the clock. He had to get to school. He was still wearing his clothes. He pulled off his T-shirt and replaced it with one from his dresser. In the stillness of the house, the walls seemed to close in on him. He opened Melissa's door. Her bed was a crumpled mess, her bedspread mostly on the floor, but she was gone.

He ate cold cereal while he put on his shoes. When he grabbed his coat, the clang of the metal hanger against the rod echoed in the empty house.

Half way to school, he leaned against a light post and closed his eyes. The Lavascape terrain came to mind. He wished he was there. He pushed himself into motion and arrived ten minutes into his first period class.

It wasn't until Monty exclaimed, "What's with your hair?" when they met for lunch that Jared considered his morning. He had skipped his shower, of course, gobbled down cold cereal, grabbed his backpack with the reading assignment he'd forgotten to do, and headed out the door. He hadn't so much as glanced in a mirror that morning.

"Geeze, how bad does it look?" he asked, brushing his hands through his hair. "I must have major bedhead if even you notice it."

Monty didn't have a chance to respond. Katie, Anna, and Terrance joined them at the lunch table and the girls were talking so quickly and in such a high pitch that Jared chuckled.

"It's going to be great," said Katie.

"What is?" asked Monty.

"They're having a talent showcase at the dance," said Terrance. "I'm going to play my guitar." How someone could have so much guts and still seem shy was a mystery to Jared.

"And sing," said Katie. "And we have at least 8 other people willing to bring stuff for the display tables."

"Can I bring some of my pictures?" asked Monty. "I'm so

tired of yearbook, and the school newspaper still hasn't printed any of my shots. I talked to the advisor and she said she'd look at my stuff, but I think she plays favourites. I have some great shots from the last volleyball game."

"She can't ignore good pictures," said Katie. "It'll happen soon."

"When's the dance?" asked Jared.

Katie looked at Jared through narrowed eyes. "It's been on the announcements every day for two weeks. Her tone was grumpy, but Katie's eyes held a different, unreadable emotion. Maybe he needed to work a little harder on his Retina Reading. Girls were complicated.

Why didn't he hang out with her and Monty at Josie's anymore? It doesn't take that much time and they always had fun together. Lavascape was the ultimate cool game, but he hadn't been with his friends outside school for quite a while.

"Who listens to the announcements? What dance are you talking about?"

"The Homecoming Dance," snapped Katie. "It's next Friday." She cleared her throat and changed her sharp tone. "It's going to be fun. This is really going to be better than other years where people wander around and only occasionally dance."

"Last year the boys just ate brownies and ran around the school," said Anna.

"Oh yeah. I remember those brownies," said Jared.

"Mmm," agreed Monty.

"So, you better start thinking about a date." Katie still had a somewhat agitated look in her eyes but she looked pointedly at Jared. Jared felt his face get hot. Anna was less than two feet away, and these girls were talking about dates.

"You don't have to have a date," said Anna. "People can just come. Everyone should come."

"Tell them what you're doing for the talent showcase," said Terrance to Katie. Jared could have given Terrance a hundred dollars, he was so thankful for the change in the conversation.

Katie smiled and lifted her hands to show off her nails.

"You're going to walk around and show people your fingernails?" said Jared.

"Nope. I'm going to take pictures and blow them up. It will be a side-by-side two picture set, one of the left hand and one of the right."

"Oh yeah, the ambidextrous art form," said Jared.

"How did you know?" Terrance asked. "That's what she's going to call it."

"It could look really cool with your artsy shots next to my action shots—Sports Illustrated style," said Monty.

They ate their lunches, sharing with Jared who had forgotten to grab something to eat as he had rushed out the door that morning. The chocolate bar he had found in his coat pocket had been inhaled in seconds, so he gratefully accepted their offerings, then did his homework at the lunch table. It was difficult to concentrate with Anna so close, however. Maybe he should ask her to the Homecoming Dance. His face warmed simply from the thought. He focused on his homework.

School and troll training were both supposed to prepare him for what was coming in life. Troll training seemed to be doing the better job. How he'd ever need this math was a complete mystery. When he had asked, "When would you ever use this?" last math class, Mr. Glenn got red in the face and clenched his teeth. Jared could read in his eyes, "I wish this kid would shut up and do his work." But anyone would have guessed that one.

"So, I have things for the tables but not many people willing to get up on stage..." Katie looked at Jared meaningfully.

"What?"

"Everyone would love to hear your Wishful Thinking impression."

"You must be joking."

Katie simply looked at him wide-eyed and hopeful.

"I'm not a performer."

"You could be." She smiled encouragingly.

There was a fluttering feeling in his stomach. How could he disappoint her? "Oh okay, Katie, but if I make a complete fool of myself it will be on your conscience."

"Thanks Jared." Katie's smile was warm.

Jared punched her shoulder lightly. "What are friends for? Besides, now you owe me a big time favour." Jared suddenly farted. It shook the bench. "Excuse me," he whispered.

"I could overlook that little production. That would be a big favour." Katie smirked.

When the bell rang, they cleaned up their area. Just before Katie left, she turned back to Jared. "By the way, what's with your hair?"

Melissa stood in the front entranceway of the middle school with Cam at her side. As Jared approached, he saw Cam leave with Mr. Reynolds, the industrial arts teacher. "What are you doing here?" asked Jared.

"Cam is getting some paint stuff for Mr—Jared? What did you do to your hair last night?"

"I just slept in this morning."

"Yeah, but what did you do to it? Does Mom know?"

"That I slept in and didn't wash my hair? Do you really think she's going to care?" Lately Mom hadn't even noticed when Jared missed eating for a day.

Melissa came forward and held up strands of his hair from the top and the sides. Jared brushed her hands away. "Stop it." All he needed was for someone to see his sister running her fingers through his hair.

"Mohawks just look ridiculous," said Melissa.

"Mohawks?"

"Well, it's Mohawk-ish," said Melissa. "Did you cut it yourself?"

"Of course I didn't cut it."

"Well, I can't imagine you got a stylist to do that."

"I didn't go to a stylist."

"I figured."

"What?"

The late-bell rang but Jared ducked into the boys' bathroom instead of class. He stood in front of the row of white porcelain sinks and stared into the mirror.

What he saw was nowhere near a Mohawk, but he could see why Melissa had compared it to one. The sides of his hair were laying straight against his head, but the top, about a two-inch strip down the middle, was rumpled and stood up at strange angles, some even straight up in the air. Since when does hair defy gravity without a ton of hair gel?

Is that how Lavascape designers got their troll fohawks? They woke up with bed-head and thought, *Hey, I like it.* "No more skipped showers," vowed Jared.

He ran to his Science class.

The next Friday afternoon, Jared tried to skip Josie's and head home to Lavascape but Monty and Katie poured on the guilt. Monty straight-out asked if Jared liked his computer buddies better than them. In the end, Jared sighed, "Don't be ridiculous," and followed them to the cafe.

Now they sat and shared a plate of fries and Katie had several questions for him. Personal questions. Questions that no guy in the eighth grade wanted to answer.

"Who do you like?" Katie said, in a false casual tone.

"Nobody," said Jared. He moved his backpack off the seat to make more room. He dropped it on the floor and kicked it under the table.

"There must be somebody." She had her backpack on the seat beside her. She always got to sprawl her junk on the whole bench, while Monty and Jared shared a side.

"I like everybody," said Jared. "I'm a very friendly guy."

"Monty told me," said Katie, smugly.

Jared gave Monty a murderous glance.

"Not about you," said Monty defensively. "I told her who I like."

"Who do you like?" Jared asked, feeling more than a little betrayed. How could his best friend tell his deepest secret to Katie and not to him?

"Carrie."

"They're going to the Homecoming Dance together," said Katie, proudly. "I set it up myself."

"Wonderful," said Jared. There went his brownie-eating partner. Carrie was a tall, thin girl who must be at least two inches taller than Monty. Had he thought of that? He'd be looking at her neck when they slow danced. She was nice, though, and kind of pretty; but what was Monty thinking getting a date without even checking with Jared first!

"What about you, Jared? Are you going to ask someone? Jared didn't need Retina Reading to know Katie was excited. Yeah, the dance was a big deal to girls.

"No."

"Really?" She swallowed audibly. "I can help you get a date, then."

"I don't want your help."

"Oh, don't be so stubborn."

"I'm not being stubborn. I'm not going to the dance. It will interfere with my training."

"Training? What training? Did you join the football team or something?" asked Katie.

"Football?" said Monty. "Do you have a death wish?"

"It's not football," said Jared. "It's Troll Training. I'm really into Retina Reading and Sword Skill. And ya wanna hear something weird? Since I'm standing and wielding the sword, which has some weight to it, and parrying back and forth, I'm actually getting exercise. I think I must be quicker than I was before, too, because when we were playing volleyball in gym yesterday, Chris asked why I didn't try out for the volleyball team," Jared laughed. "At the beginning of the year, I would have been laughed out of tryouts, but I was doing okay in gym, hustling after the ball."

Monty had a relieved look on his face. "That's cool. I'm glad it's not football, my friend."

Katie rolled her eyes. "You can't seriously think of skipping the dance for Lavascape."

"I'm thinking about it, alright," said Jared. "Especially if my best friend isn't there to hang out with."

"She talked me into it," Monty said, defensively. "Besides, I've always liked Carrie and Katie said she likes me, so…"

"So you have a date," finished Jared.

Katie looked at Jared expectantly. He searched her eyes but things seemed jumbled and he couldn't make out anything there. He gave himself a shake. Of course not, we're not in Lavascape. "I know somebody who likes you, too," said Katie, softly.

The bait was set. Even though he knew it was just her tactic to get him interested, Jared couldn't help but wonder who it could be. He looked into Katie's eyes again and all of a sudden he knew: Anna. But there was something else. Something he couldn't quite read. He dismissed the mysterious part and focused back on Anna. Could it be true? Was she actually going to say that Anna liked him?

He remembered Anna's hurried response at lunchtime, saying everyone should come. She was so sweet. "Probably some loser," said Jared trying his best to sound casual.

"I don't think you'd think that," said Katie. "In fact, I'd bet on it."

They sat in silence for a full minute. The plate of fries was only half gone but it was forgotten. "Okay. Tell me who," said Jared.

"Just Anna," said Katie. "But if you think she's a loser, I can tell her you think so."

"No."

"No? No, you don't think she's a loser?"

"Of course not."

"But you're too busy training to go out with her?"

Jared squirmed. "I suppose I could make it to the dance."

"I thought so," said Katie.

"We could make it a double date," suggested Monty.

Jared turned back to Katie and asked, shyly, "Will you talk to her for me?"

"What are friends for?" said Katie.

"What about you?" Monty asked Katie. "Do you have a date?"

"That's right," said Jared. "You have to say who you like, too."

"I'm busy with the talent displays and everything. I don't have time for a date."

"Yeah, right," said Monty. "You're too chicken to tell us."

"Come on, Katie," said Jared. "Maybe we should set you up." It was good to have this particular shoe on the other foot.

"Terrance is going to help me set up the talent stuff," said Katie, refusing to act embarrassed. "That's as close to a date as I think I'll get that night."

"You better get a haircut before Friday," Monty said, turning back to stare sceptically at Jared's hair.

"What does everybody have against my hair?" His voice dipped lower partway through his sentence and his tongue felt thick.

"Are you getting sick?" asked Katie.

"I'm not sick." He farted loudly. A high school couple a few booths away laughed and the girl held her nose even though there was no way she could smell anything...not yet anyway.

"While your friends are in 'giving-you-advice' mode... watch what you eat before the dance," said Katie.

"Probably not a bad idea." Jared laughed.

The second he got home, he bounded up the stairs to Lavascape. Last time he'd been training with a Master Swordsman. Now the game put him back to Intermediate because his time logged wasn't at a serious level.

Jared yelled, "What? I'm totally serious! And that's a stupid rule!"

The Intermediate swordsman shrugged. "You aren't ready for the Masters, apparently."

"I got an award for excellent timing!"

The trainer shrugged again. "Tough luck. Prove yourself and you'll get to move on."

How could Jared have wasted valuable Lavascape time at Josie's? Why didn't Monty and Katie see how important this was? He was back to Intermediate! Urg!

Chapter Ten

Five days later, the yelling got going about four-thirty in the afternoon and went on strong for over an hour. Jared and Melissa sat in the living room listening to their parents in the room above their heads. Many of the words were muffled but most were completely discernible. Terribly discernible.

"You have no ambition," said Mom.

"I have plenty of ambition. It's not like I sit around on my butt all day long!"

"You might as well for what you get paid for it."

"In case you haven't heard, we're in the middle of a recession! What do you want me to do, break into people's houses and demand they hire me for renovations they can't afford?"

"You could do something other than spend half the day playing golf!"

"You say that like I'm out enjoying myself. Do you think

I *enjoy* listening to Somerset's so-called jokes? He disgusts me! That I *enjoy* having to lose to that moron Adams? I'm out there busting my butt chasing work. Because playing golf and sucking up to those guys is how you get contracts in this town!"

"What contracts? You haven't had anything other than handyman work for eight months! You're not a contractor if you never have any contracts! Stop deluding yourself and go get an *actual* job to support your family."

"What job? There are no jobs! Recession, remember!"

"There are jobs if you're not so picky."

"I'm not taking a job at Wal-Mart! I'm a contractor, not a greeter!"

"You're not a contractor! You're an unemployed bum!"

A door slammed, and the words overhead became muffled again.

"I think this is going to be it, this time," said Melissa, softly. "He's going to leave."

"Everybody's parents fight sometimes," said Jared.

They had dropped naturally into their roles. Melissa voiced their fears and Jared minimized them.

They knew that after their parents fought, they would each be listening for the sound of one of the cars leaving home, perhaps for good. Once the neighbour had started up his lawn mower right after an awful fight and Jared had heard Melissa burst into tears in her bedroom. He had gone to her room and found her with a pillow over her head and frantic tears flowing. It had taken him almost half an hour to convince her that their parents were both still home. Dad had slept on the futon in the basement that night, but he was still in the house.

Now Jared wished he and Melissa were up in their

bedrooms. His dad was coming down the stairs in a huff. "I can't live with this anymore," he said.

"He's going to leave," whispered Melissa.

"No, he won't."

Their mother was right behind him on the stairs. "Well then leave!" she shouted. "It's not like you're contributing anything now! You seem to think bills pay themselves! And you're so caught up in your clubs that you don't even know what your own children are doing."

They were in the living room with Melissa and Jared now. Melissa seemed to sink another inch into the back of the couch, as though bracing herself for what was to come.

"You're so controlling. You'd like to schedule every minute of my day. Just hand me an itinerary I could follow like some puppet."

"I know what I wouldn't schedule—every charity club in town and two rounds of golf," she said, sarcastically. "Tell me, do you even know the name of Melissa's boyfriend?"

The seconds of silence that followed seemed endless. Poor Melissa. Why drag her into it? Why shine the light on the father/daughter relationship and expose the flaws? Both Jared and Melissa wanted to disappear into the shadows when it came right down to it. Melissa only voiced their fears with the understanding that Jared would refute them.

Mom was waiting. Finally, Dad said, "Oh, that proves everything, doesn't it? I'm a terrible father because I can't remember the name of whoever Melissa's dating this week!"

"She's been dating Cam for months. And when was the last time you spent any time with Jared?"

Now it was Jared's turn to sink into the couch. He wanted to be anywhere but his own living room in the middle of his parents' argument. He tried to ignore his parents and think of Lavascape. 'Hyped Hearing' was up next. What sounds would he be able to discern when his training was complete? A whispered conversation across the room? A ladybug munching on a leaf? An elf sneaking up on him?

Dad turned away from the couch, his gaze resting on the large evergreen visible through the bay window, but Mom kept after him. "You know, I've thought about calling the Big Brother's Association. Jared needs to have a father figure in his life. If you're not going to be part of this family, just say so, because what we get from you now is next to nothing."

"Yeah, well maybe I'd be home more if you weren't always on my case..."

"Oh real mature! That's it, make this about you. But the truth is you sleep here and sometimes eat here. This is just a place to keep your clothes, a place where someone else will do your laundry so you can look fresh and clean at your next meeting. That's not what being a family is about."

Dad turned and faced her; his eyes were suddenly hard, like a stone statue in a museum, staring blankly into eternity. Jared's breath caught in his throat. The past five days his Troll Training skills had improved like crazy and he knew what was behind his father's stare. 'He's imagining life without us,' Jared realized. He felt numb. He was lost in his father's stare. How could Dad imagine such a thing? Why would he even consider it? He should be fighting back, explaining why what he's doing is important. Or, he should be apologizing, agreeing that he'll focus on time with the family more, get a job, take care of them. But, the hard eyes revealed their mystery—he imagines that life without us might be nice, peaceful.

"That's it, I'm gone!" shouted Dad. He left the room.

"Go then," yelled Jared. "Get out." He jumped up from the couch. "Here, I'll help you." He sprinted up the stairs, grabbed a suitcase out of his parent's closet, and started emptying his father's side of the dresser into it. When he came to the underwear drawer, he paused. He slammed it shut: no, no underwear. He pulled dress shirts off hangers and stuffed them in the case instead. Then he carried it to the stairs. Dad had his shoes on and was slipping his arms into his brown leather business coat. He looked up as Jared thundered down the stairs with the suitcase. Dad's eyes showed hurt.

Good.

Jared pressed the case into his stomach. "There—be gone, then, if that's what you want!"

Dad snatched the handle and stepped back, taking the case from Jared's shaking hands.

"Get out of here!" Jared yelled.

Dad clenched his teeth, his eyes flashing with anger.

"We don't need you, either!" Jared shouted.

Without a word, Dad opened the heavy wooden door and flung the screen door wide ahead of him as he strode out of the house.

Jared watched from the open doorway, his feet planted in that spot. Dad opened the back door of the sedan in the driveway and threw the suitcase on the seat. He looked back at Jared, as the screen door clicked closed under its own power. Dad nodded once, walked to the other side of the car, opened the door, slid behind the wheel, and started the ignition. Jared heard Melissa cry out at the sound. Jared slammed the wooden door but could see in his mind the car back out of the driveway and head down the street.

There was a moment's silence as Jared tried to think of something to say. "I shouldn't have packed for him," he said. "I pushed him out. I'm so sorry, Mom."

"He was already determined," said Mom. "He was going anyway." When she raised her eyes, Jared saw a desperate need for comfort. She wanted a hug. Jared was uncomfortable; they weren't a huggy family, not even when things were good. He stepped forward and Mom rose to meet him in an embrace. She pulled Jared in tighter. Then she stepped away, climbed the stairs, and Jared heard her sobs as soon as she was out of sight.

Tears streamed down Melissa's face. "Dad's gone," she said. "You said it wouldn't happen. Then you made him go!"

He wanted to reassure her, at least to mention how he had packed with a lack of permanency. You couldn't stay away long without a change of underwear.

Jared put his hand awkwardly on her shoulder. "They'll cool down," he whispered. "He'll be back." He didn't believe it, not after what he saw in Dad's eyes, but he had to say something. Melissa turned and hugged him tight. Then she sniffed loudly. "I'm all snotty," she said and hurried to the bathroom.

Jared sat in the living room feeling shell-shocked. Eventually, he went up to his bedroom. Melissa was crying in her room, Mom was crying in hers. It was like his heart was split in two, one part reaching out to each of them. He had to hear them, to be sure they were real, to somehow give them support. He went to Mom's room. She was pacing back and forth like a caged tiger. "I have to think things through, Jared," she said dismissively through her tears.

Jared went back to his room. The sobs from both sides seemed to echo in his head. He heard Melissa go to Mom's room. He didn't hear much of their conversation but he did hear Mom say, 'This is how it's going to be from now on. You'll just have to get used to it." Melissa didn't stay long but returned to her own room.

The phone rang and Jared's hopes rose. But it wasn't Dad. It was Cam on Melissa's phone. 'Cam,' the name Dad couldn't remember, the name that proved how little he knew about Melissa's life. If he had a more common name like 'John' maybe Dad would've remembered.

Jared had to block out the sounds or go mad hearing the anguish in his mother's sobs and his sister's voice.

He made it to the feast. That was lucky; he hadn't been watching the time at all, of course.

"Hey Barry," he said sitting next to his former hut-mate.

"I thought you were eating with the adventurers again today."

"No. I was just late getting here." Why couldn't he keep friendships with the villagers just because he'd accepted a quest? After eating two salmon steaks in Cajun spice and sautéed mushrooms, Jared felt strengthened.

"Barry? How do we know we're on the right side in this war? The trolls fight alongside the goblins just because we're told goblins are our allies. The giants and elves must have some bad stuff to say about us too, or kids wouldn't fight on that side, right?"

"It's a war. We all want to win. Besides, we have the hourglass."

" Hourglass? There was a big hourglass at Troll Training."

"The hourglass is the root of everything," said Kim, another village troll with eyes that always looked tired. "The giants and elves say we stole it from them, but it's ours fair and square."

"How do you know about this?"

"History games in the game hut. Don't you play those?"

"No. They sounded kind of boring," admitted Jared.

Kim shrugged. "I guess they are compared to the coasters."

"Why don't we just give it back? It seems that would solve a bunch of problems."

"Are you crazy? We can't give that up."

"Why not? What's it good for?"

"Haven't you ever wondered why your Troll Training works so well? The mystic hourglass is responsible for accelerated learning. It gives trolls power quicker."

"*Did* we steal it?"

"No, but as long as the giants and elves keep telling all the new people that we did, there will be eternal hatred between us. They think of it as cheating, but it's not. It's part of troll culture. Deal with it! The goblins understand. They have their talismans, we have ours. And so have our enemies. It's not our fault their talismans aren't as good as ours.

After the feast, Jared went to Hyped Hearing and trained hard with all sorts of sounds unrelated to money, service clubs, what makes a good marriage, the names of jerk boyfriends, slamming doors, and starting engines.

Best of all, Hyped Hearing came with the option of training in 'white noise' to increase the efficiency of the outside noise-cancelling headset. There was a warning, "Turning on white noise will block out your mother calling you for dinner, a teakettle whistling, a fire alarm, or a door to door cookie salesman." Jared clicked "accept white noise". It worked great. Mom and Melissa were completely blocked. He breathed a sigh. He would turn white noise off periodically to check on things, but it was a relief to be removed for a while.

The first stage of Hyped Hearing involved hearing different sounds and being able to recognize them and tell where they were coming from. The snapped twig was the hardest; it seemed to rebound from everywhere. Footsteps and whispered voices became easier and easier and pretty soon he mastered the basics. His high percentages garnered praise from the game. He seemed to have an aptitude for Hyped Hearing.

The volume of the sounds changed too, until Jared was

sure he was discerning sounds quieter than he'd ever heard before. It was wild.

He turned off white noise and moved on to isolating certain voices. The game provided crowd noise but now that he could hear household noises again, he could clearly make out the sound of Melissa talking to Cam. They must have been on the phone for hours.

In the middle of one of the hearing challenges, he heard Melissa say, "Goodbye," and the click of the line disconnecting. Her tears started afresh. It was two hours later that she eventually stopped crying, thanks to the miracle of sleep.

Jared left Lavascape and started his homework in the perfect stillness of the now too-large house. Not perfectly still. No. There was the faint whoosh of air from deep exhausted breathing coming from Melissa's room and another strain that shuddered in shallow troubled breaths coming from Mom's room.

Chapter Eleven

"A pop quiz! How can that be legal?"

"Legal," said Katie with a laugh. "I doubt there's legislation about teachers giving tests. Besides, it was just a small one and it was just like the homework. Didn't you do your homework?"

Jared and Katie were sitting on the two railings facing each other outside the south doors of the school. "I did the homework," said Jared, defensively. "Apparently I did it wrong, but I did it."

"Did you really do that bad? You didn't fail, did you?"

Jared tightened his lips. So far, he only admitted that he did lousy, not what his score was. Lousy used to mean anything in the B range. "Yeah, I failed it," he said. "Zero percent is a fail."

Katie's eyes opened wide for a second. "What are your parents going to do? No wait, it won't be on the report card and won't be worth much. Don't worry." She jumped down and paced. "I know you must feel awful; I feel like crap when I don't do well."

"Math is so hard this year."

"I thought it was hard at first, too, but I'm starting to understand. Maybe I could help you out. "

"Where is Monty?"

"He was talking to Carrie at her locker when I came out."

"Hm."

"Are you excited for tomorrow?"

Jared paused. What was happening tomorrow? Then he remembered. The Homecoming Dance, of course. "Sure," he said.

"Well Anna's a little more excited that you seem to be. Are you picking her up or meeting her there?"

Good question, he thought. Katie was so efficient and capable. She always thought of everything.

Anna lived on a ranch out of town and Jared hadn't arranged anything. He could ask Mom to drive him out to pick her up, but that was tomorrow and he hadn't asked Mom yet. Maybe she was busy…or a basket case over Dad. Between Mom and Melissa, Jared was lucky he didn't drown in his sleep at night. He figured Dad would be back. This was just a new stage to their fighting. The I'm-mad-enough-to-walk-out-the-door stage. "I guess I'll meet her there."

"Maybe you should tell her that."

Jared didn't say anything. The thought of picking up a telephone and calling Anna made him break out in a sweat. He'd rather take pop quizzes.

Mr. Shaw, the boys' volleyball coach, came out of the school. "There you are," he said, pointing at Jared.

"Hi," said Jared, wondering if Mr. Shaw was also the

teacher responsible to crack down on anyone who got a zero on sneaky pop quizzes.

"I watched you in Phys. Ed. the other day. A couple of the guys on the team said you were pretty good. They were right. You have good timing and a nice touch." He slapped Jared on the shoulder. "Have you thought of coming out?"

"Aren't tryouts over?"

"Yup. But we have a short bench and could use another guy or two."

Jared shook his head. Not only was he far from competent enough, these guys practiced all the time. His time logged in training would plummet too far to maintain his standing. "I don't have time."

"You have a job?"

"No."

"Then why not?"

"I'm just too busy."

Mr. Shaw's eyes showed disappointment. Did that mean he really thought Jared could be a good player? "Maybe next year, then," he said and walked away.

Monty finally came through the school doors. "Sorry I made you guys wait," he said, slinging his backpack over his shoulder. His lips spread into a huge, silly smile.

"Yeah, you look all broken up about it," joked Jared. Monty had the right idea. Talk to the girl casually at her locker or in the lunchroom. He'd ask Anna tomorrow at school if they could meet at the dance. No telephone.

"Do you want to go to Josie's? We can help you with your math there," said Katie.

Lavascape was calling but zero on his quiz swayed him to Josie's. Jared had an image of himself. He was Jared Thompson: quirky sense of humor, good friend, and honor student. Now it seemed he might have to erase that last identifier. But, he liked being one of the smart kids. He couldn't give that up.

When they settled into a booth with a large plate of deep-fried veggies, Monty said, "Have you been lifting weights or something, Jared?"

"Who has time for that?" he said, picking out one of the deep fried mushrooms and dipping it in thick ranch sauce.

"Well, you must be doing something. Look at your arms. What do you think, Katie?"

Katie smiled. Her face turned a light pink color. "I don't know." She took a deep-fried zucchini stick.

"Flex," said Monty.

Jared did and, wow, he was amazed. His biceps were almost the size of baseballs. How do you go from ping-pong ball size to baseball size without trying?

"Well?" said Monty.

"Yup, looks good," said Katie shortly. "Monty, did you do okay on the quiz today?"

"It was easy," said Monty. "I got a hundred." Monty pulled open the zipper on his backpack, rummaged around for a minute, and then set his quiz on the table.

After a mere five minutes of explanation, Jared had to admit it wasn't hard at all. He had been completely clueless. Why did he have so much trouble? Then he remembered that he started his homework pretty late; in fact, it had been ridiculously late.

"You don't want to start the year off like this," said Monty.

"Start? We're almost halfway into October," said Jared.

"We could all get together to do our homework. That way we can help each other out," continued Monty.

Jared shook his head. "Our homework would take

the whole evening if we did it together. We always get distracted."

"So? It just means we get to hang out and have a good excuse for doing it 'on a school night.'"

Jared smiled at Monty. They'd been friends forever. "It'd be fun, but I'd never finish my troll training that way."

"I wish my mom hadn't banned me from Lavascape," said Monty longingly. "She seems to think that every kid who plays a game with fighting will turn into a mass murderer. She's paranoid. When it comes to fighting games, she doesn't get it."

"Maybe your mom's right." Katie wrinkled her brow. "Not about them turning into killers, but it's easy to get too carried away with those games."

"Okay, I'll do my homework before I play Lavascape, *Mom*." Jared stretched out the 'mom' in a whiny tone.

"I wasn't talking just about you."

"Do you guys mind if I have the last mushroom?" Jared asked.

"You're the only one who eats the mushrooms," Monty answered.

"Well, what about your hair?" said Katie.

"I have messy hair one day and I never get to live it down?" Jared laughed and elbowed Monty as if to say, *What's up with that?*

Katie and Monty looked at each other. Their expressions seemed to ask each other, *Does he really not know?* Finally, Monty said to Katie, "Do you have a mirror or something? Girls always have makeup mirrors."

"I don't do makeup...at school," said Katie, defensively.

Jared put both of his hands on his head. He didn't need a mirror to know what his friends were talking about. The strip down the middle was sticking up again. "Oh, come on! I combed it the same as I always do and it looked perfectly normal before I left for school!"

"You're really not doing it on purpose?" said Monty.

"Of course not!"

"Then you didn't dye it?" Monty continued.

"Dye it?" Jared jumped up and ran to the men's room. He waited for an elderly man to finish washing his hands, which seemed to take forever, and then he looked at his reflection. There was his fohawk of raised hair and, yes, it was a different color! The fohawk hair was a lighter shade of brown, a reddish brown. Red?

He could hear Katie's voice beyond the bathroom door. "Go see if he's alright. He looked freaked out."

"I'm not following him into the men's room."

"Please Monty, I'm worried about him." They sounded right outside the bathroom. Jared pushed open the door to confront them but his friends weren't there. They were back at the booth and Monty was just now sliding out and making his way to the back of the restaurant.

Jared's breathing quickened. They had sounded right next to him. How had he heard them talking way over there? Had he imagined it? When Monty reached him, Jared said, "Did Katie tell you to come after me...did she say she was worried about me?"

Monty stepped back. "Are you okay, Jared?"

"Just tell me!"

Monty's eyes showed he was anxious. "I had to go to the bathroom. That's all," he added.

"Oh," said Jared. His shoulders relaxed. He must have imagined the conversation. "Good."

"And your hair?" asked Monty.

"It's weird. I don't know why it's growing different lengths. And it lightened from the sun, I suppose. I just need a haircut."

"Yeah, that's it," agreed Monty.

They walked toward their booth together. "You didn't need to go?" Jared said indicating the men's room.

"Naw. Later. Why do girls worry so much?" said Monty.

"Are you talking about your mom, again?" asked Jared. "No...Katie."

She was watching them approach. Her eyebrows knit together.

"Katie's not really a girl. Well, of course she is, but you know what I mean," said Jared. "It's not like trying to talk to Anna."

"He just needs a haircut," Monty said to Katie. "Let's get going before Mom comes to Josie's looking for me. She threatened to do that if I'm late for dinner again. She doesn't let me breathe. I swear, one of these days, I'm going behind her back and joining Lavascape. "

"Family!" exclaimed Jared. His was hopeless. He was fine without them. "Family just isn't that important."

Jared's dinner was a bucket of take-out chicken and a too-vinegary coleslaw salad. He, Mom, and Melissa dished out of the cardboard containers onto paper plates. "Where's Dad?" asked Melissa.

Mom cleared her throat and, in a business-like tone, said, "He's at his friend's, Donald Wilson's place. You can call him there if you need to talk to him."

"Is he ever coming home?" Melissa blurted out.

Jared felt every muscle in his body tense up.

"I don't think so," said Mom. "He won't be back." To Jared

it felt as if Dad had instantly vanished from his life, never to return.

Mom pushed her chair away from the table, picked up her paper plate with half a mound of coleslaw still on it and went to the sink. She dumped the plate in the garbage. Then she left the kitchen. As soon as she was out of sight, a sob escaped her lips. It was loud enough that both Jared and Melissa jumped at the sound.

"She doesn't think so...but maybe," said Jared softly, taking up his optimistic role.

Tears streamed silently down Melissa's face. "He's gone for good."

Jared didn't eat any more. How could he eat when it felt like his throat was cinching closed with a drawstring?

Melissa took her cell phone into her room and Jared went even further away: Lavascape.

A couple of hours into his advanced sword training, Jared progressed to the final sword upgrade. The weapon was so sleek and beautiful. The hilt included a thin strip of gold that circled his hand for both protection and beauty.

Jared finished a duel, bowed to the training hologram, and took a break. He removed the gear and went to the bathroom. He saw his reflection in the mirror. His hair had never stuck up like this in his life. It always fell super flat against his head. When Mom used to cut his hair, she'd complained that it had to be perfect because Jared's hair lay so straight there was no curl to hide an uneven snip. Now he'd developed a wicked cowlick.

He ran the water over his hands and pressed the wild parts of his hair down. It sprang back the moment he removed his hands. He scooped up more water and plastered the fohawk down. The center strip of hair seemed to repel the water. As it began to rise again, Jared turned the faucet on full and stuck his head under the tap. He shut off the tap and stared at his reflection.

"What's happening to me?" He enumerated the other bizarre things he'd experienced since joining Lavascape. The lava scab, the shower-exclusive brand, the conversation between Katie and Monty that he was now sure he'd actually overheard. There was also the hair on his knuckles, his lower voice, and an abundance of gas he couldn't account for with bean burritos. Each consideration seemed to tighten a noose around his neck. He could hardly breathe. He opened the window and stuck his head out. The cool night air was a blast in the face. Anything else? Yes, hadn't he looked in someone's eyes and known what they were thinking? Katie had been thinking of Anna. The hair on his arms rose and he gasped in breaths like he'd been suffocating. And then there was Dad. Dad had been imagining life without his family. The anger and hurt boiled up from the depths of Jared's soul. In a rage, he picked up a jar of women's face cream sitting beside the sink and chucked the glass jar out the window as hard as he could.

It hit the sidewalk with a crack that echoed up the street. The light pink cream formed a little geyser in the center and a smattering of blobs like a lava stream spewed forth.

He looked down at his leg, half-expecting to see a small creamy gloop of pink, but there was nothing there. He rubbed the scar where the lava rock had been. Of course it hadn't splattered on his leg! It broke yards from the house... but he'd looked...he'd actually looked. He lowered the toilet lid and sat. His breathing slowed. "What's really real?"

Jared went back to his room and slipped his hands into the game gloves. "I've got to quit this stupid game. It's not going anywhere, anyway." The great thing about online gaming is playing against other actual people. "Where are my player-to-player competitions? How many more weeks of practice before that happens?"

He wanted to click the 'Training Suit' button that made him invincible and really go at it.

He reached for the mask but his hand brushed his

backpack as he picked it up. He had math homework. The zero on his last quiz was in thick red ink, so round it could've been traced around a quarter. His thumb rubbed the edge of the mask. He clenched his jaw and tossed the mask on the computer chair and peeled off the gloves.

He pulled out his math homework and the instructions for an English essay that was due next week. He had to analyze a short story. Why did some short stories seem so long?

He ripped one of the pages in his textbook as he flung the math book open to the right spot. Jared reached back into his pack for his coil notebook. He didn't have a pencil, however.

There was one in his desk drawer, the desk by his computer chair. The mask hung over the armrest, where the duelling ring in the forests of Lavascape was waiting for him. He had left the game paused. He got off his bed and opened the top drawer of the desk. There was an assortment of pens and pencils. He reached for a stubby green pencil, but before his fingertips touched it, the computer emitted a sound he'd never heard before. It was like chimes from a church tower. Jared slipped on the mask. There were the words, 'Player-to-Player Challenge'.

Some actual person, somewhere in the world, was challenging him to a sword fight. Finally! It was just what he'd been waiting for, exactly what he wanted. Exactly. A shiver ran the length of his spine.

"Do you accept or decline?" asked the trainer. How could he pass up his first real fight? He kicked a shirt on the floor out of the way, and said, "I accept."

The duelling ring opened and there was his opponent, a troll with a yellow fohawk protruding from light brown hair. Each of them wore a protective training suit. "Ready for your date with doom?" asked his opponent.

Jared was taken aback—somebody was taking this a

little too seriously. "Bring it on," he said. They raised their swords. The holographic referee began the fight by smashing two stones together with a resounding 'crack'. Jared and the other troll came toward each other. His opponent moved smoothly and was good at seeing when a short jab would do the most damage. However, Jared's 'round-about-stroke' where he spun around to gain momentum, was also very effective. The wins alternated between them at the beginning. After seven or eight matches, however, Jared was clearly the superior fighter.

After each match, Jared and his opponent exchanged a few words. Jared learned that the 'blond' troll was from Montana, he had been in Lavascape a few weeks longer than Jared, and his quest was an ancient sundial with magical properties.

After the eleventh match, in which Jared made a fantastic stroke that the training suit scored as if he had severed his opponent's right leg, the blond troll asked, "How would you like to join my quest? You have a real talent for fighting. I'd like to work with a guy like you. What do you say?"

Jared considered it. Companionship, a common goal—it sounded good while he was alone in his bedroom. The blond troll seemed like a decent fellow but what about his own quest? Sparket. "Sorry, I better stay on my own course. Any chance you'd like to save a princess?"

"Naw. But good luck. One more duel?"

Jared removed the game mask and looked at his bedroom clock. He couldn't believe the time, so he got closer. The digital numbers said 3:45 am. "Sorry, I better get some ZZZ's," Jared said.

As soon as the computer shut down, a wave of exhaustion hit him squarely in the chest. He had felt fine while he was in Lavascape. If he hadn't looked at the clock, he would have gladly accepted another duel. Now, he could hardly make it to bed. His math homework was lying open on the quilt. There was no way he could concentrate on it now.

He slipped the open books onto the floor, and crawled into bed. There was something happening tomorrow...or rather later today, but Jared couldn't think what it was. He'd remember tomorrow.

Chapter Twelve

"Have some breakfast," said Mom.

"I don't have time." Jared walked to the table to check out the offerings anyway.

"I'm tired of you strutting through the house like a weight lifter with a chip on his shoulder," said mom.

"What are you talking about? I do not." He looked at Melissa who was sitting at the table. "Do I?"

She shrugged. "Kind of. Your walk is different than it used to be."

"You swagger!" said Mom.

"*Me*? What about Cam? He walks like he owns the world and would happily crush anyone under his feet.

"Don't be ridiculous. You're reading an awful lot into the way he walks," said Melissa.

"That's what you're doing to me."

"Not at all. It's just an observation. You've been walking... differently."

"With a swagger?"

Mom nodded and Melissa said, "Kind of, yeah."

"Well maybe that's not so bad. I walked like a timid hamster before."

Melissa smiled. "Maybe you're right. Just don't let it go to your head. Your walk reminds me of that conceited gorilla of a quarterback."

"I hate it," whispered Mom under her breath.

Jared had seen the quarterback walk with ultra-confidence around the halls at school—he wouldn't mind having a bit of that.

The phone rang. Mom answered it and dove into a 'phone day' session of complaints against Dad. She took the cordless phone and headed to her bedroom.

Jared snapped. He took the stairs two at a time and barged into Mom's bedroom.

"What's the matter with you?" said Mom.

"Yacking to your friends about Dad isn't going to help. They agree with you, blah blah. "

"I've heard enough out of you! You don't understand anything. Now, get out. I'm on the phone."

He closed the door and heard Mom say, "He's been acting so cocky lately. It's driving me crazy."

Jared went back downstairs.

Cam was there, staggering slightly. Melissa appeared with a glass of water and handed it to him. Cam's eyes were bloodshot; it looked like he had light red eye makeup surrounding his eyes.

Melissa took his glass back to the kitchen and Jared followed her. "What's he on?" he whispered.

"Nothing. What are you talking about?"

"Cam. Look at his eyes, he's on something."

"He's not feeling well, that's all."

"Really?"

"Yes, really."

She hurried out of the kitchen and past Cam. "My homework is upstairs."

As soon as she was gone, Jared looked pointedly at Cam. "She says you're not feeling well, but I think you're feeling a little too good."

Cam chuckled. "You want a little something, Jare Buddy?"

"What kind of something?"

"Nothing too strong. Just enough to give you a bit of energy."

Given how tired he was, Jared wasn't sure he'd get through this day on his own. Cam reached in his pocket and pulled out a little pill. He dropped it into Jared's hand. Melissa bounded down the stairs, and she and Cam left.

Jared looked at the pill. He went to the bathroom and filled a glass with water. What would be so wrong with getting a little help from a drug?

Then he threw the pill in the sink and washed it down the drain. "What I really could've used was a ride to school," said Jared. But, who rides with someone like Cam? Melissa was crazy.

He walked to school and it seemed to take every ounce of energy in his body. He was such a zombie in class that Mr. Glenn asked if he needed to go to the infirmary. By the next class, he wished he had gone. Maybe they would've let him sleep.

He bought a hot dog at the noon fundraiser and then crashed in a corner of the lunchroom with his head on his science textbook. He had really done a number on his hair again after that though, judging from the strange looks he got on his way to class.

The entire day he felt one step behind. When the final bell rang, it seemed like he'd lived through a 48-hour school day.

Katie appeared at his locker. "I have some things to set up in the gym so I won't be walking home with you guys today."

"What things?"

"What things do you think?"

Jared shrugged.

A strange look crossed Katie's face. Jared saw something sad in her eyes. Disappointment, that's what it was. Then he saw more clearly. The talent showcase! The pictures she was going to take of her fingernails! It was more important to her than Jared realized. He reached out and grabbed her wrist as she turned away. Then he turned her hand to see the fingernails. "They're not still done up?"

Katie's expression changed in an instant. "No."

Jared dropped her arm and said, "Can I come see the pictures then? An early look before the dance?"

"Okay."

The gym was busy with a decorating committee bustling about with balloons and streamers in their school colors, blue and white. Katie led him to the front where two areas on either side of the stage made up the talent showcase area. There were tables with an assortment of artistic projects and various drawings hung on the walls. There was an intricate drawing of an owl in a matted frame, and eight or nine of people Jared felt he almost recognized.

"Self portraits, I think," said Katie, when she saw where he was looking. "I remember doing that in art last year."

"Why didn't you use the stage?"

"The DJ will be up there, remember?"

"Oh yeah. Where's yours?"

Katie led him to the other showcase area. There was a sports table with a couple of plaques and a trophy, a pair of football cleats that were so worn the sole was lifting off and the tongue was hanging by a thread, and a hockey goalie mask. Behind the sports table were photographs, one of Willow Creek at either sunrise or sunset, Jared couldn't guess which, and then there were Katie's two pictures. They were at least 11" X 14" and zoomed in on her fingernails so they were several times their normal size. It actually looked pretty cool. "I like them," he said. Then he added with a smile, "It looks a lot more like an elephant, this time."

"You jerk," laughed Katie. "That's a cat."

Monty's voice called out from the middle of the gym. "Jared! Katie! I've been looking all over for you guys."

"I had to see the elephant before I left."

Monty glanced up at Katie's photos, took a double take, obviously searching for the elephant, and then said, "Well, did you see my shots?"

They were next to Katie's pictures. There was a great game shot of one of the volleyball players smacking a ball down. "Yeah cool! Man, those guys can jump!"

"Hey, I thought you were going to get your hair cut before the dance."

"Yeah, I guess I should. Maybe I'll head over before I go home, see if they can fit me in."

"Oh that reminds me," said Katie. "You owe me a thank-you." She looked at Jared.

"How come?"

"You didn't say anything to Anna about tonight, so I told her you'll meet her here."

Jared reached over and gave Katie a thankful hug. "Katie you really are terrific. I love ya." Jared swallowed hard and stepped back, suddenly feeling very awkward. Why did he say that? It must have been a carryover from recently comforting Melissa and Mom.

How had he forgotten to set things up? He'd had a crush on Anna for the past four years and now that he finally had a chance with her, his brain was freezing up on him! "You're right, I do owe you," said Jared. "Thanks a lot."

Jared started to walk away.

"No problem," said Katie. Her voice was small.

Jared headed for the front doors of the school. Just as he pulled open one of them, he felt a sharp pain in his upper arm. His head snapped to the right and there was Colton with a wickedly sharp pencil in his hand. He cackled and pushed ahead of Jared.

Half an hour later, Jared was asleep in one of the soft padded chairs in the Andrew Salon's waiting room, dreaming of lead poisoning. They'd said they might be able to squeeze him in when he'd mentioned the dance that night.

He was so soundly asleep that the stylist had to shake his shoulder to get his attention.

"You here for a haircut?" she asked. "Rise and shine."

She made a few startled comments about his hair while she cut but Jared was too groggy to pay much attention. No, he didn't want the top strip left longer; yes, he'd had his last haircut there; no, he didn't want her to use the buzzers around his ears; yes, he was going to the big dance tonight. It seemed she had an insatiable thirst for knowledge.

Walking home, Jared was still exhausted. He wasn't even going to be able to stand on the dance floor tonight if he didn't get some sleep. He warmed up two pizza pops in the microwave, set his alarm for seven o'clock, and crawled into bed. The dance was supposed to start at eight. He would have plenty of time to get there.

When the alarm went off, Jared was confused for a minute. What day was it? Was it morning? Then he remembered. It was seven at night not seven in the morning. He switched the alarm off and climbed out of bed. The two-hour nap had done the trick. He felt rested. He felt wonderful. He'd probably even have time to play a little Lavascape before the dance.

Anna's angelic face filled his mind. "Get ready first," he said, aloud. "Then, if there's time..." But, there was plenty of time. "I'll even set my timer." With the clock set to ring in twenty minutes, Jared logged on to Lavascape. He'd missed the feast but decided to visit Barry before going to the training zone. He was in luck. Barry was still at the hut. When he walked in, Tiger came bouncing up to him. "He remembers me," said Jared.

"Sure. Mingos are smart." Barry called Chuck to come say hello, and the other mingo bounded into the room, too. Barry patted both mingos on the tops of their heads.

"It looks like you're taking good care of Tiger. Thanks Barry."

"My hut mate went to round up people for a new game. It's basically paintball. Want to stick around and play?"

"Better not. I wanted to do a little training."

"Sure. Okay." On the surface, he didn't seem to mind but there was an undercurrent. Jared said goodbye.

Soon Jared was duelling with a troll from British Columbia and really scoring well. They were both at the Masters' level, too! The Troll Trainer entered the ring at the end of their second match to declare, "Jerry has reached all-star status." Trumpets blared to celebrate and the trainer placed a crest on Jared's wrist that indicated he possessed the highest, gold-level skills.

The celebration was suddenly blocked out by a bubble, hazy at the edges. Sparket was in the same cinderblock room she had been in last time. She listened at the door on the far right for a moment, and then went to the bed. She pulled the thin sheets off and tied the top sheet to the bottom sheet. Then she tied the blanket to the sheets and hung them out the window. Jared's view changed to outside. The makeshift rope was still several feet from the ground. She looked out and shook her head. Then she smiled. Her small hands worked quickly. She pulled a long portion back up, made a loop at the end, and swung it through the window toward the parapet above. It missed its mark and she tried again. This time it caught. She pulled to test its strength and climbed out the window toward the roof. Her foot slipped over the stones but she held tight and regained her footing. When she was safely at the top, she unhooked the bedding rope and threw it to the ground below her window.

Sparket followed the roofline. On the other side, there was an oak tree near the building. She carefully climbed on the parapet in her gown, then leapt for an outstretched tree limb. Her hands caught it. She swung in an arc for a moment, hanging there. Then she inched along the branch, grabbed the trunk, and climbed down until she was safely on the ground.

The sound of barking dogs erupted as she turned toward the forest of evergreens. Three large black dogs came around the tower and raced toward her. They formed a semi-circle and with lips pulled back in snarls over dripping fangs, their throats rumbling with deep growls, forced her back toward the base of the tower. She tried to break away several times, but one or another of the dogs was always there to block her escape. Soon she was up against the stone wall. One dog lunged at her. Its teeth caught the bottom of her dress and dragged her to the ground. Jared gasped and then winced as another dog snapped at her arm.

A young man in a hooded black cape helped her up only to grab her by the chin and force her to look into his face. The hood fell back. His eyebrows arched at different angles, the right one pointed in the middle. "Welcome home," he said, his mouth looking remarkably like the dogs'.

"Antonio!" she said.

The vision began to fade. Jared scanned the surrounding landscape for clues that would help him know it again when he saw it. As it faded, Sparket looked out into his eyes for an instant before she was gone.

A choice was before him. "Continue Training Exercises" was written on one of the buttons, "Leave training and seek the princess" was on the other.

There wasn't time for either option. Jared clicked the exit button instead.

"Are you sure you want to exit?" asked the game. "If you leave now your time log will not be sufficient to keep gold crest status." The buttons available now read, 'Exit, anyway' and 'Continue.'

Jared's hand hovered in the air. Then he clicked the game glove sensor over the word 'Continue'. Now he had the other question before him. Sparket was going to get herself killed. "Seek the princess," he said.

Melissa opened Jared's bedroom door. "Cam is late. I'm going nuts. Hey, what are you doing? I thought you were going to the dance."

He slipped the mask down and looked over the top. "I am."

He put the mask back in place. He began down a new path that opened up to his view. "I can play while I get ready," he whispered, "just enough to keep my gold status." He wanted that crest. He also wanted to go out with Anna, he silently reminded himself.

A cloud of hairspray billowed in with Melissa. He pulled the mask down and peeked over the rims. She wore a skirt and sweater. "Do I look okay?" she said, stepping further into Jared's room.

"Sure. I don't know."

"You're very helpful," said Melissa, sarcastically and left.

Jared looked at the time. Anna! He was already late. Did his alarm go off? He couldn't remember. Maybe he set it wrong. "I have my own damsel in distress," he whispered. "At least she'll be in distress if I don't get a move on." He removed the mask and gloves but left the game on. Hopefully, he could come back to the game and keep gold status this way.

Jared found his dark blue dress pants. They were a little snug in the thighs, which was surprising. They were also really wrinkled. His blue dress shirt was going to be a problem. It was more than two inches too short in the arms. He slipped on the mask and travelled the path while he rolled up the sleeves of his dress shirt so no one would notice they were too short.

There was a quick knock at his door and Melissa pushed it open. "Cam's here. Do you want to ride with us since you're late? My gosh," she said looking at his clothes. "You *are* planning to iron those things, aren't you?"

"There's no time. Do you really think I have to?"

"Definitely!"

Melissa's eyebrows suddenly came together. "Hair…"

"Yeah, I got a haircut today."

Melissa stammered for a second then took her brother's arm and led him to the bathroom.

"It stinks like your stupid hairspray in here," he complained.

"Since when do you have dark bushy hair...?" She turned him to the side and continued, "On your ears?"

Jared couldn't believe his eyes. "What the heck...!" He leaned toward the mirror for a better look. On the top of his ears and all along the sides were large tufts of dark brown hair. Was this new? Or had that been there for ages, revealed now with the haircut? His ears also seemed to stick out further than they had before.

He found Melissa's reflection in the mirror. "What am I going to do?"

A giggle escaped her lips but she quickly pursed her lips together and became serious, again. "Shave it, maybe." She thought for a second. "Or you could use a hair remover cream."

"A what?"

Cam's impatient voice came suddenly. "Melissa! I thought you were so worried about being late! What are you doing?"

"Be there in a minute," she called out the door, then she turned to Jared. "Here, move out of the way."

Jared stepped away from the sink and Melissa opened the cupboard underneath and moved bottles around. He never thought he'd actually need anything besides toilet paper from this mysterious cavern in his home where Melissa's girl things were scattered into every cranny.

"Here it is," said Melissa. When she straightened up she had a small, pink, somewhat teardrop shaped bottle in her hand. The teardrop seemed especially fitting. "You might have to do it a couple of times to get it all." She touched his ears and made a clucking sound with her tongue. "It's so darn thick. Well," she put her hands on her hips, "do you think you can handle it?"

"Absolutely not," said Jared. "I don't know how this stuff works. What am I supposed to do with it?"

"I'll tell Cam to wait on the couch and I'll be back to help you in a second."

"Thanks!"

Jared winced at his reflection. Since when did he have hairy ears? That was something reserved for little old men who were too blind to see what they'd become, not someone in junior high. With little Yoda men, it was always a less shocking grey color, too.

Melissa returned. "Now you probably want to be careful not to get any of this stuff actually in your ears." She glanced at the label on the back of the pink bottle. "The likelihood of it specifying 'Do not put product in ears' is too slim to waste time reading the small print," she decided. "Give me your shirt. I'll iron it while you do this. Put the lotion on the hair and leave it for five minutes, then rinse it off. Here," she said handing him a razor and scissors. "Try to get it a little shorter first."

Melissa disappeared with his shirt. Jared snipped what he could, then shaved little strips on the top of his ears. He nicked his ear, grit his teeth, and threw the razor on the counter. He twisted the lid of the hair remover and poured the lotion into the palm of his hand. It had a strangely antiseptic smell and a texture that reminded him of paste, though much thinner. With his index finger, he scooped up some remover and doused the offending hair with it. How much did he need? He reapplied the pink substance and looked at the clock in his room to begin timing the five minutes. He stared at the digital numbers in disbelief. The dance had started almost half an hour ago, and here he was with gooey blobs of hair remover on the tops of his ears. He looked like an amateur clown, ready to push a flower on his chest and send a stream of water into someone's face before bounding off in bright red over-sized shoes. It was a far cry from the cool image he was hoping to exude on his first date with Anna.

May I have this dance? Or would you prefer to cruise

*around the gym in my miniature fire engine? I'll pedal it
and you can spray the chaperones.*

The lotion dripped down his neck. He grabbed some
Kleenex in the bathroom and attempted to stop the flow.
Melissa popped her head into the room. "Did it work?"

"I was just going to wash it off."

"Stick your head over the tub and I'll spray it off for you."
She had pulled her robe on over her dressy clothes. Jared
knelt at the edge of the tub and she got the water going. "I
can't believe I'm going to be late for the dance because my
brother needs help shaving his ears." As she sprayed, she
pulled at the hair tufts. It came off in patches. Sometimes
she tugged on a section that was firmly rooted, however.
Jared yelled "ouch" and she mumbled "sorry."

As they examined the result in the mirror, Melissa had
trouble controlling her smile and eventually burst into
laughter. "Now you look like a troll whose going through
chemotherapy...a little cancer patient-troll."

"Wonderful. I was kind of hoping to not look like any sort
of troll, let alone..."

"You're a troll in your game. Maybe it's rubbing off."
Melissa interrupted, laughing hard.

Jared didn't laugh. In fact, Melissa had come very close
to voicing his true fears and he was a little taken back
hearing it out loud.

"Melissa!" It was Cam calling up the stairs.

"I better go. Use the razor on what's left. It'll be fine."

"If you see Anna or Monty, tell them..."

"That you're home shaving your ears?"

She looked so funny trying to hold in her smirk that Jared
laughed with her. "Tell them I'm coming."

"Troll prep in progress." She patted the top of his head.

"You better comb this before it dries like that." Washing away the hair remover had wet the hair around his ears. He looked even more troll-like with the dry strip down the middle.

Melissa left and Jared struggled to shave where he could hardly see. Twice he cut his right ear with the razor and had to stop the blood with toilet paper. Then he rummaged around in the same messy cupboard that had produced the hair remover until he found a package of band-aids. He used two of the extra small size. They looked ridiculous folded over his ear. It would be bad enough if he had cut himself shaving his face...in fact, since Jared had shaved his moustache a grand total of two times, he figured a cut from shaving his chin might even be cool, but what kind of freak was late for a dance because he was shaving the tops of his ears? Maybe the bleeding would stop by the time he got to the school. And expose the cuts? Augh!!

He'd think up some kind of excuse along the way.

He quickly dressed in the shirt Melissa had left on his bed, freshly pressed. "Thanks Mel," he whispered. His pants were tight over his upper thighs but it would be dark in there. His dress shoes were small and uncomfortable but they'd have to do, too. He was a troll squeezed into formal wear sized for a scrawny human.

The light from the game mask caught his eye. He was still on the forest path in Lavascape. He picked up the mask and then the gloves. He meant to exit right away. But what he meant and what he did were very different. There was a fire flickering through the trees on the left of the path. He had to check it out. What if the princess was right over there? With sword drawn, he approached.

When he saw an axe swing in an arc and fly into a nearby tree, he knew he'd come across elves. When he heard "Nice shot, M," he knew they were the same ones he'd encountered before. There were just the two elves. The blond one said, "Life calls. I'll see you tomorrow."

"Life, smife," said M, the elf with blackspringy hair, laughing.

A feeling of patriotism for the trolls swept over Jared. How dare this elf laugh when he had killed the troll Jared had fought with? One of his brothers. The indignity was worse because Jared didn't even know the name of the troll with the bushy eyebrows.

Jared emerged around the boulder that had shielded him from their view. M pulled his axe from the oak tree where it still hung.

"You killed my troll brother," said Jared.

"You're that troll that ran away!" taunted M. "I'll give you a head start if you want to do it again. But it won't help."

Jared advanced and M's axe met his sword stroke. Jared hit again and again. Mostly, M was able to block him but one stroke hit his left shoulder and another, his right arm. He soon had M retreating around boulders and through the trees. "Who needs the head start," Jared muttered to the elf.

With renewed strength, the elf came at Jared. Jared started to worry this impulsive challenge wasn't going to end well for him. He wanted to leave the game. He tried to exit. 'No wimpy exits,' said a voice.

Jared accepted the rebuff and fought harder. Soon he had M backing away. Eventually, the elf broke into a full run. Jared saw him dive into the crevasse of a stone wall. Now he had him.

He thought of the troll he would avenge. He thought of the dead eyes under those bushy eyebrows, the feelings he felt then crept over him now. He called to the elf. "You're trapped."

"Please." The elf didn't say more.

A chill skittered over Jared's shoulders. Did he want to be responsible for causing those empty eyes? "If I spare you,

you have to promise to spare the next five trolls that come under your power."

"Really? You'll make a deal? I promise!"

"Make sure you keep it." Jared circled back to the path and exited. Power felt good.

Jared looked at the clock. That took longer than he thought. He left the house running, straddled his bike, tore down the road, jumped curbs and hurtled through the traffic to eventually arrive at the dance two hours and ten minutes late. Not bad for a guy who had to deal with last minute troll transformations...and then the game.

Chapter Thirteen

Monty was indignant. "Well, I'm telling you, if a stylist clipped my ear not once but twice in the same haircut, I'd be looking for some compensation!"

"That's exactly what's wrong with the world," said Carrie who was sitting next to Monty on the hallway benches. "She made a mistake. Who knows what's going on in her life? Jared survived."

"I bet Andrew carries insurance for times like this. Why should it go to waste? Jared barely escaped that place with his ear!"

While Carrie and Monty enjoyed their debate, Jared simply wished they'd stop saying the word 'ear' repeatedly. He was self-conscious enough without the constant reminder. Besides, Katie wasn't back from the girls' washroom and most likely, that meant Anna wasn't coming out.

"Has she been in the bathroom for two hours?" Jared asked, his feet tapping alternately against the tile floor.

Monty wrinkled his nose, thinking. "At least an hour." He looked to Carrie for confirmation.

"She thought you stood her up." She might as well of said, 'duhhh' next.

"You were in there for a while with her," said Monty to Carrie.

"How was she?" asked Jared.

"Hurt, embarrassed. She was in tears. Who wouldn't be? She was here all dressed up and her date was AWOL."

"But, I sent word. Didn't my sister tell you guys I was coming?"

Suddenly there was Anna standing in front of him. She looked like an angel in a white skirt and a navy blue sweater over a silky white top. Her eyes were rimmed in red but her complexion was flawless.

"You look nice," said Jared.

She acted as though she hadn't heard him. "We got the message from your sister...eventually, but why were you late?" Her arms were crossed and she leaned to the left with her graceful hip out to the side.

"Maybe we should let them talk," suggested Carrie rising and waiting for Monty to join her. Katie went in the gym with them. Jared felt as though he had been deserted in enemy territory. Anna didn't look sad; she looked angry.

"Let's walk," said Jared. The hallways with lockers were closed off during the dance but the main hall was accessible, so that's where Jared led. "I'm sorry I was late."

"Why were you late?" Anna persisted.

"I had to get ready."

Anna took in his wrinkled pants and raised an eyebrow.

"I had a haircut after school, and then I needed a nap so I slept for a couple of hours. When I woke up, I played a little Lavascape, and then I had to iron my shirt." He didn't mention that Melissa actually ironed his shirt and he certainly didn't mention the hairy ears ordeal. "It all took longer than I thought it would."

"Lavascape?"

Anna latched onto the thing he could have easily left out to get there on time...or at least a lot less late. "I thought there was time."

"You know what Jared? We make time for things that are important to us. For you, that was sleep and video games. I really liked you..."

Jared didn't like the past tense.

"But I deserve a guy who likes me back," she continued.

Jared wiped his sweaty palms on his wrinkled pants. "But," his voice caught in his throat. Why did he have to say it out loud? "I do like you, Anna."

"Not as much as Lavascape," she threw back at him.

She was slipping away. He had to stop her. Jared reached out and took her hand. "Anna, please don't be mad." It seemed his heart was crawling up his throat. "I've liked you for a long time. Years. I know I messed up tonight, but give me another chance."

"Lavascape, Jared." Her clipped words felt like a slap even though her tone was soft.

Jared let out a fart: a loud, long stream like a freight train clacking over the tracks. "Sorry," he said and his voice dipped low and growly. Could his body do anything else to destroy him? This wasn't the suave, love-struck hero he wanted to portray.

Anna shook her head. Then she turned and walked briskly down the hallway toward the beat of the dance. The way her white skirt swished from side to side was mesmerizing.

She was so beautiful. Everything she did was graceful and classy...even the way she dumped him.

Jared walked much more slowly toward the dance. He found some of his friends on the bleachers. He sat next to Monty who had his digital camera and was reviewing the shots of the dance he'd already taken.

"How did it go?"

"I don't want to talk about it. For yearbook?" asked Jared pointing at the camera.

"School newspaper. I could get the front page, if it's good enough. Then I'd really show those year-book guys who looked down their noses at me."

"Who did that?"

"It doesn't matter. I mean, I know the yearbook is more enduring—people save their yearbooks their whole lives and newspapers come and go. I don't care, I want the paper."

"The faster pace is up your alley," said Jared. "Your pictures are good, and you can write. Don't worry about those cross-eyed jerks looking down their noses."

Monty laughed. "Thanks."

Katie was with some older guy on the dance floor, who walked her back to her seat when the song ended. Anna sat next to Carrie on the other side of Monty. Terrance was on the dance floor with a pixie-like girl from seventh grade.

"I love this song," said Carrie as the next tune began.

"Let's go," said Monty. He and Carrie hit the dance floor.

Jared scooted down the seat and sat next to Anna. She straightened her back. "Wanna dance?" he asked.

She smiled cryptically and nodded. "Yes—two hours ago." Her eyes were still a little red. "Just don't, Jared." She rose and seemed to float down to the floor. A guy from their grade asked her to dance and they disappeared into the dimly lit mass of swaying dancers.

Jared moved next to Katie. "I've blown it." It was a matter-of-fact comment, an observation.

Katie shrugged. "What did you think was going to happen? That she wouldn't mind waiting around? That she'd smile and lead you to the dance floor when you finally showed? You didn't even talk to her about meeting up here—I had to do it. And, you were two hours late! By the time Carrie found her crying in the girls' bathroom, it was already an hour and a half into the dance. She got stood up on her first date!"

"She wasn't stood up!" He wished they'd all stop saying that. He wasn't that late. He thought he'd done quite well under the circumstances. He deserved a second chance, didn't he? Regret bubbled up inside like a spring of muddy water.

When the song ended, a spotlight appeared to the right of the DJ, who was tucked into the far left of the stage to leave room for the talent show performers. Katie hurried into the spotlight and spoke into a microphone. She wore black pants and a dark purple sweater. She looked nice. "Our next talent showcase will be a sports spotlight." Another circle of light illuminated the sports table. "Take a look at those worn out cleats. Rodger Livingstone wore those in the final game last year at provincials!" A cheer arose from the crowd both on and off the dance floor. Katie was such a natural when it came to public speaking. She was great.

When she finished with the sports spotlights, Jared met her at the bottom of the stairs and said, "Good job."

"Thanks."

They didn't speak for several seconds. Then Katie asked, "What's happening in your Lavascape game now?"

"I had a duel with the elf I met the first day. He schooled me then but today I dominated. It's such an amazing feeling to wield that sword. If Anna could just try it, maybe she'd be more understanding."

"Yeah? I don't think so. Think about it, Jared! Stood up! Besides, she doesn't get video games, never plays them." The music continued to blare, then Katie said, "But in Lavascape, you feel like a real warrior?"

Jared smiled. "A warrior in training, more like."

"What about Sparket?"

"I'm starting the quest. I could train forever but at some point I have to say, I'm ready."

"Hey you're quite a bit taller than me, now," said Katie. "Remember in elementary school? You were always so short." She laughed. "In fourth grade, you wore that brown and tan striped shirt for pictures two years in a row."

"Did I really?"

"Yeah, I was looking through the old class pictures the other day."

"I'm sure I looked much more mature in grade 5."

"Hardly, they could have been taken the same day."

While they talked, Jared noticed Katie's hair. It was longer than she'd had it for a long time, years. It also seemed shinier in the near darkness of the gym.

"I don't think that shirt fits anymore. I won't make the mistake of wearing it on picture day again."

"You do look older now."

"So do you. You don't look so much like a boy anymore."

"Aw!" She pretended offense.

"I just mean your long hair is...nice."

"Well, thanks." After a silent moment she said, "And it's not just outgrowing *the shirt*. Your face is different. Your forehead...

Suddenly Colton Barnes loomed in front of Jared. It was like facing a bear in the woods that reared up on his hind legs. On either side of Colton were faceless menacing figures, like shadows. Did those guys have names? Colton summoned Jared with a gesture. "Sorry, I need to use the washroom," said Jared and ditched Katie on the edge of the dance floor.

He followed Colton to a dark corner of the gym. "I want you to do something, Picky," said Colton. The dimly-lit gymnasium seemed to close in on Jared. "You'd love to do a little favour for me." Colton slung one of his thick bear arms around Jared's shoulder. It was the shoulder that still ached from the jabbed pencil lead.

"What?" asked Jared, his voice thinner than he wished it sounded.

"Get Terry's guitar for me."

"What? Why?"

The Bear pulled back his lips in an angry grimace. "Get it and meet me outside the front doors." The paw on his shoulder clamped down hard. "You have five minutes." The Bear lumbered away and the Shadows followed him.

Jared counted the assaults. He had endured four smacks in the back of the head, three trips in gym class warm up, one hip check in gym basketball, a math compass poke, a jab with a pencil lead that also broke the skin, and getting more people than ever to forget his real name.

He was tired of it. Maybe it was better to join with the bullies, feel their power instead of his helplessness. What would it be like to have the respect and fear the bullies commanded? One look from Colton and he had hurried to his side. He wanted that power. Right now! He didn't have the power to help himself and he certainly had no power to help his family.

Katie and Monty joined him. "Jared, do you think my fingernail pictures look stupid?" asked Katie.

"I don't think anyone even looked at them," said Jared, distractedly.

"Oh, probably not," said Katie. Her face fell and she walked away.

"That was kind of harsh," said Monty. "It is pretty dark but.... It's not like you to be so...insensitive. She was all worried they looked dumb and didn't believe me when I said they were great so I said, 'Ask Jared.'"

Carrie appeared at Monty's side. "I love this song."

"Tell her they look good," said Monty. Then he and Carrie headed toward the dance floor.

Jared felt alone in the noisy, festive gym. Colton was waiting for him. There was Terrance's guitar case on the bleachers. He walked toward it. Surely, someone would see him if he took it out the door.

What did Colton want with it? If he stole it, Jared could always tell the police. No one would have to know he helped. He could give the cops an anonymous tip—maybe through crime-stoppers.

The deejay cut the lights and an erratic strobe light flashed. The dancers' movements seemed broken, disjointed, isolated. Jared sat in the bleachers next to the guitar.

Colton probably wouldn't steal it. Not permanently. Maybe he just wanted it long enough to keep Terrance from doing his number. Jared might actually be doing Terrance a favor. If his song was bad, he could easily become a worse outcast than he already was. Taking his guitar might be an act of kindness.

Jared's hand reached out, the movement intermittently illuminated. His fingers closed around the strap.

The strobe light stopped flashing and circles of light danced around as the disco ball overhead spun. Colton was going to go ballistic if he had to wait any longer. Jared rose, slung the guitar case over his shoulder, and left the gym. He didn't look to the left or the right but made a beeline for the front door and stepped into the night air.

Colton and the Shadows were waiting. Questions lodged in Jared's throat; words he dared not utter. Colton grabbed the guitar and pushed Jared so hard he stumbled back and fell. "You're late. Next time I tell you to do something, Picky, I expect you to hustle your butt."

There was no camaraderie with the bullies even though Jared had stuck his neck out for them. In his nervousness, Jared farted two loud bursts. Colton said, "Hey guys, I think we scared the crap out of him." They laughed. "They haven't even brought out the treats yet. Now get out of here before I give you a punch for every second you made me wait."

Jared scrambled to his feet and hurried back to the school where the brightly lit hallways seemed inviting. He drank from the water fountain and the cold water seemed to numb his throat and knot his stomach. He returned to the gym and sat where he'd been three minutes ago. Before he had joined with the bullies. Before he had become a terrible person. The jarring music seemed accusing.

Katie sat next to Jared on the bleachers. "Have you seen Terrance? He better not chicken out." Katie's eyes scanned the dim dance floor. "What about you?" said Monty, joining them.

"What about me?" said Katie.

Jared saw something in Katie's eyes just then. She was scared. Scared or sad or something else entirely. She was so hard to read sometimes.

Monty jabbed his thumb toward the art table. "I haven't heard you point out your fingernail photos. Jared's right, they're in the dark; you need to spotlight them."

"They're right there for everyone to see."

"Right," said Monty. "And those football cleats were hidden in a box."

"Whatever," she said, rolling her eyes.

"They are good and you have them hiding in the dark," continued Monty.

"Fine. I'll point them out if it makes you happy."

Suddenly Terrance was with them on the bleachers. His eyes had a frightened, anxious quality.

"Good, you're here. Are you ready?" asked Katie.

Terrance shook his head. "I can't do it. Not in front of Colton and those guys. I thought I could but...no."

"I heard you practicing," said Katie. "You're really good. Don't let Colton Barnes decide if you play your guitar or not!"

"Grab some troll courage," suggested Monty, elbowing Jared.

"Easier said than done," said Terrance slowly.

Just then Colton walked in front of the bleachers. "Terry, you missin' a banjo?" he yelled. "Cause I saw one out in the mud."

Terrance flew down the bleachers and for one horrifying instant Jared thought he'd tackle Colton from behind. Instead, he ran toward the door. Jared, Monty, and Katie followed. Outside it was dark; the wind was cold and sharp against their faces.

"Where is he?" asked Katie, pulling her hands up into the sleeves of her sweater.

They started to circle the school and found Terrance on his hands and knees, digging. Sticking out of the ground, reaching heavenward as though pleading with the forces of good to save it, was the long thin neck and half of the acoustic area of the guitar. Jared dropped to his knees beside Terrance and helped dig. Monty and Katie were quick to follow.

Terrance whispered, "Troll courage."

"And sometimes you really need a sword, too," said Jared.

That comment made Terrance look up. He smiled. "Yeah, sometimes."

Finally, the guitar was free. Surprisingly little mud had penetrated the instrument and simply shaking it upside down left the inside near perfect. "I'm ready to play now, Katie," Terrance said, slinging the filthy guitar strap over his shoulder.

They followed Terrance into the school. Katie brought a pause to the dance and introduced Terrance. There were a few gasps and muffled comments when Terrance entered the spotlight and it was obvious how dirty both he and his guitar were. He strummed the guitar and started to sing. His voice was shaky at first but then turned bold and deep.

"This isn't the song I heard him practicing," said Katie.

'I'm happy who I am' was a common line in the song and all that seemed to be missing was '...in your face, Colton Barnes.'

Colton let out a 'Boo' but he was quickly silenced as others began clapping along with the country/rock beat. How many guessed the reason Terrance was covered in mud was impossible to know, but the fact that this song was more than a talent showcase was obvious to everyone. Jared felt guilt like acid in his stomach.

When Terrance finished, applause erupted from the crowd. He jumped off the stage instead of taking the stairs. He came toward Jared and said, gripping his guitar, "This was my sword tonight."

"That was the best fighting I've ever seen," said Jared. Terrance had won this round. Maybe it didn't matter that Jared had helped Colton.

After washing his hands and face, and making a trip outside to brush off, Monty passed Carrie's dirt inspection and was acceptable enough for a dance. Jared tried to laugh at him for following her every whim but his heart wasn't in it. He would have gladly done as much and more if Anna would only say the word.

"Can't you say something to her?" Jared asked Katie. He'd sat on the sidelines like a lump for half an hour. "Tell her I'm not so bad. Can't a guy make one mistake?"

"I'll try," said Katie. She came back to his spot on the bleachers a few minutes later.

"Well?"

She shook her head. "She's really mad that you chose a video game over her. She says she 'just doesn't like you anymore'...Sorry to have to tell you that."

"You wouldn't be like that, would you Katie? You'd forgive me, right?"

"That really doesn't matter. Anna won't." They were silent while the music bounced off the walls, then Katie said, "If it makes you feel any better about your game, Troll courage seemed to be just what Terrance needed tonight."

"Yeah. Lavascape isn't all bad."

"I think Terrance has achieved semi-star status," said Monty joining them and pointing Terrance out on the dance floor.

"What do you mean?" asked Jared.

"He's absolutely filthy and nobody made him clean up before they'd dance with him."

Carrie rolled her eyes.

"The perks of fame," said Katie. The song ended. "Oh, I better announce the treats are set out."

Jared and his friends walked to the hall table. "Where

did these brownies come from?" Katie asked one of the other organizers. "I collected everything from the food committee. I don't remember brownies." The other girl shrugged. The goodies disappeared off the table as dancers turned ravenous.

Treats. Why had Colton said something about the treats? It was when Colton had said they'd scared the crap out of him after his ill-timed farts.

"Oh no!" yelled Jared.

"What is it?" said Katie.

"The brownies. I bet Colton put Ex-Lax in the brownies."

"Why?" asked Monty.

"Something he said earlier makes me wonder; no, I'm positive! We've got to do something."

"Should we tell a chaperone?"

"I don't have any proof," said Jared. Besides, Colton would wrap those massive paws around his throat and squeeze the life out of him if he squealed.

"I'll get rid of what's left on the table," said Katie quickly moving away. Jared and Monty scanned the students in the gym. Many carried the white dessert plates with a few squares on them.

"Are you up for a 'brownie snatch'," asked Jared.

Monty grinned mischievously. "Let's go."

The lights went down and the music blared again after the break, which was good and bad. It was easy to take the brownies but harder to see them in the first place. As Jared reached for a brownie on a plate held by a short, angry sort of girl from an older grade, she turned to face him. "Were you going to take my brownie?" she asked.

Jared farted. It was one of those SBD's —Silent, But

Deadly. "I think the brownies smell bad. I told you but you didn't hear over the music."

"It does smell bad," she said bringing the plate to her nose. "Take it."

Jared was able to snatch two more without being noticed but then he saw Mr. Bernard. The teacher held the large square brownie an inch from his lips. Jared hurried over to him and said, "Hey Mr. Bernard, I was wondering if you played basketball in high school." Mr. Bernard was tall but had a large belly.

"Actually, I did," he said. The distance between his mouth and the brownie increased.

"I bet you were a force under the basket."

He smiled obviously reliving a good basketball memory. "Sometimes."

"Bet you were in amazing shape back then."

"I was much thinner then and could run the court all day," he agreed.

"Did you follow a strict athlete's diet?"

The brownie to mouth distance widened a few more inches. "Yeah. I ate a lot of protein...." The pudgy ex-basketball player turned and threw the brownie and the rest of his plate of goodies in the garbage. "You don't get to be an athlete eating that stuff," he said.

"Thanks for the tip," said Jared.

Jared, Monty, and Katie met up on the bleachers. "I think we got most of them," said Monty. "What did you say to Mr. Bernard?"

Jared told them and they laughed hysterically.

"That was cruel," said Monty.

"After the next song, I'll introduce you," said Katie to Jared.

"Introduce me to who?" Jared stared at her blankly for a moment, then he remembered—Wishful Thinking. "I forgot my gun," he said.

"I thought you might. I have a Super-Soaker up on stage for you."

"Oh no, I'm going to miss it," said Monty, looking at his watch. "Dad's picking me up at eleven and it's five minutes to eleven now."

"I don't think you'll be missing much," said Jared. "But why eleven?"

"I know; ridiculously early, right! He can wait a couple minutes. I have to see this."

"I...I didn't practice," Jared said to Katie.

"Just wing it."

"Erg! The things I do for you!"

Katie went up on stage and introduced him.

Just as Jared took a step toward the stage, Colton approached. He gave Jared a playful punch in the shoulder about a tenth of the force he used for his frequent passing attacks. "Thanks for stealing Terry's guitar. We couldn't have done it without you."

Terrance was standing about a foot away. Jared looked at him. Terrance stared wide-eyed and said nothing. Katie arrived in time to hear, too. She whispered something under her breath. Monty started to deny it, but stopped when he noticed Jared's face. Colton chuckled, said, "It was one nasty looking banjo," then he turned and walked off.

"I'm sorry," said Jared. Terrance refused to meet his eyes. "I didn't know what he wanted with it. And he was going to murder me if I didn't get it for him. I knew he wouldn't steal it forever. I was thinking of calling crime-stoppers."

"And reporting yourself?" asked Terrance.

"I'm so sorry."

Someone in the gym yelled, "Come on, already! Either take the stage or put the music back on."

Jared walked on stage. He gave himself a shake. At least he wouldn't let Katie down. He slung the Super-Soaker over his shoulder by a strap and in his hillbilly voice began, "I wasn't in the mood for an alien encounter but—as so often is the case with these bully critters—he didn't care none." He glared at Colton. It was pure genius or a suicide attempt; he wasn't sure which. He had a message for Colton Barnes. Jared may have joined him in his bullying tonight but never again. He had become the thing he hated most. But, he'd also ruined Colton's Ex-Lax plot. These jerks weren't nearly as clever as they thought they were. "He brought his swag over and said, 'Earthlings for breakfast.' The bigger species always thinks they get to do whatever they want...take stuff that ain't theirs, be a literal party pooper, even.

"And yeah, I'd probably be tasty as vittles but I'm like, 'Whoa there Little Feller, pull that tentacle back in your neck and back off. Pull your leg in and stop trying to trip guys, put away your pencils in the hallway, and buried guitars ain't no joke...oh, and neither is Ex Lax.'" He could feel the water sloshing in the tube of the gun. There was water in the gun. Katie had actually filled it with water! Colton neared the stage, daring him to continue. Jared swallowed hard when Colton stopped in front of him, right next to Cam Kensington, Jared's second favourite person in the world. Melissa was a few feet away. She'd been talking with a friend and stopped to watch Jared.

Jared stalked around in a circle until he faced the crowd again. "But then he said," Colton mouthed the words with him. "'Prepare to die.' So I knew it was time for..." Jared wasn't a singer but monotoned the 'Wish-ful Think-ing.' He swung the Super-Soaker into his hands and held it to the ceiling. "And a short stack of pancakes saved my life... with syrup." He lowered the gun and shot a strong stream of water at Colton and Cam. Cam sidestepped the stream and only got a bit wet. Colton, however, got hit right in the face and became an enraged bull...but an immobile enraged bull...dancing in place and taking the full force of the gun.

It was short and sweet. Especially sweet.

As he passed Katie, she said, "I like that version."

The chaperones met him as he came off the stage, those that weren't already holding a struggling Colton Barnes by the arms.

"Come with me," said one of the parent volunteers.

As he passed Terrance, Jared said, "I'm such a spineless idiot. I'm so sorry."

Terrance clenched his teeth but nodded.

Monty, standing beside Terrance, still had a look of disbelief on his face. Over his shoulder as he followed the chaperones out, Jared said, "I didn't know what he was planning."

"I know," said Monty. It was a weak concession. Jared knew that no matter how understandable it was to cave to Colton, he'd still messed up, big time, and Monty was disappointed.

Jared stood outside for a long time listening to the chaperones take turns lecturing him as if he were the bully. Then, after promising to give the principal a full report, they told him not to come back in the school that night.

Melissa and Cam appeared as soon as the chaperones re-entered the school. "I guess you could use a ride," said Melissa. The three of them walked toward Cam's car. Jared looked back at the school. The front door was open and a large boy was silhouetted in the frame.

Chapter Fourteen

Mom grounded him for the rest of the weekend when she heard about his behaviour at the dance, which would have been fine with Jared if he'd been able to play Lavascape, but she made him work in the yard all Saturday afternoon raking leaves, bagging them, and dumping them in the compost area in town. Every hour of manual labour was worse because all he could think about was getting to Lavascape. Finally, he was done. He ate, showered, and made it to the feast.

After the feast, Jared moved to one of the teleportation platforms. Now that he'd left the training, the platforms would take him to wherever he was at his last session. They were square stones large enough for several trolls to stand side by side. He stood in the center and exited the village like someone out of *Star Trek*.

Lavascape grew dim as Jared walked into the shadow of the trees, but the memory of the beautiful girl who needed his help was bright in his mind. Perfect. It was a perfect quest. All he had to do was rescue the fabled damsel in distress. It was classic.

He wished he hadn't lost his temper at the feast today but Grimball had been showing off, acting like he knew everything, just because he welcomed new trolls to the village. Jared hadn't been able to take it. He had told everyone within hearing that Grimball had given him terrible directions to Troll Training; and then Jared had accused him of purposely keeping them in the dark about the world of Lavascape outside the village. It had gotten kind of ugly. Grimball had lost his refined tone and quite a lot of his accent as he had attacked Jared with insults about Jared's coordination, sense of direction, intelligence and odor. Jared had actually felt sorry for him.

Now Jared was lost in the trees. If only he could get to higher ground maybe he could see some fortress that might be hiding Sparket.

The ground under his feet trembled and two giants came from the dense trees to his right and were almost upon him when he spotted them. They looked like professional basketball players wearing two-foot tall platform shoes and sporting about three times the muscle. Jared turned and ran two steps before large hands took hold of him and the next thing he knew he was lying on his back staring up at the pink Lavascape sky. The smaller of the giants threw him over his shoulder and carried him through the brush. Branches slapped against him and he bounced against the giant's back.

How could he be captured so soon? He'd out manoeuvred the elf M the night before only to be unceremoniously snapped up by giants! The giants walked on until they came out of the trees. Jared hit his captor's back but he didn't seem to notice.

The giants stopped when they reached a waterfall. Jared thrashed about, and yelled, "Put me down. Afraid you can't beat me in a fair fight?" the giant ignored both his words and his struggling. The giant's hand pinned Jared's sword sheath to his thigh. It was impossible to retrieve his sword. What happened if you died in Lavascape? Did a big 'Game Over' sign come on the mask? Did you have a heart attack and die in your chair? He might be about to find out.

The giant holding Jared stepped into the water and walked through the waterfall. Jared held his breath, but then they were through. On the other side was a large cave with a high ceiling. Giants were coming and going from tunnels at the back. The front seemed to be reserved for prisoners, however, with several cages there made of huge bones. Most of the cages were empty but the giant carrying Jared approached a cage that held a single occupant, a scurry. The giant held Jared in front of him and waited while the other removed a padlock as big as Jared's head from the cage. He opened the door that seemed comprised of the ribs of a dragon, or some other, equally intimidating animal, swinging on a hinge. The giant shoved him in the cage. Jared landed on his elbow and the pain shot up to his shoulder. Jared gasped.

The larger giant cackled in a deep, unpleasant way. "It won't be much fun logging in to Lavascape every day to sit in a cage. But we just exchanged prisoners, so it's not likely we'll be doing it again any time soon."

"No, it's not fun," said the light brown scurry with ropes around its ankles and wrists. There were no knots in the ropes, just two unbroken loops holding him tight.

"Let's look north," said the larger giant. "We haven't patrolled there for a couple of days. Maybe there're more trolls wandering around just waiting for us."

"Those guys are jerks," grumbled the scurry when the giants were gone. They were silent for a moment, then the scurry said, "So, Troll, do you have any friends? Anybody who might rescue us?"

"I know trolls at training and others in the village," he said, hopefully. "If we could get a message to them..."

"That won't help us. You must know what the villagers are like. And the trainers never leave the training zone; I doubt most of them are real."

"You mean they're generated by the game?"

"That would be my bet. You trolls are much better prepared than the Scurry, though. I got *zip* help. It was 'choose your side and good luck'. Even if I wanted to join their side, these giants wouldn't believe me."

"Would you really..."

"Side with them? Did you see the size of them? And the fact that they've captured me and thrown me in this skeleton-like cell is pretty persuasive."

"Could I side with them?"

"You're a troll."

"Yeah, so what?"

"So what? So trolls and goblins have an alliance; giants have an alliance with elves."

"Who's going to stop me?"

"I don't know. But all the groups have their leaders and I don't think they'd have any qualms about executing a traitor if they found one."

Jared remembered his pouch of coins from the troll village. Perhaps he could buy his way out of here. "Do you think they can be bribed?"

"Nope. If I had the treasure chest I'm after, I'd give it a try, though."

"I met a scurry who was on a quest for the same thing? Is that what all the Scurry are after?"

"Hey, Eager Newbie? Is that you?"

"Kentucky Scurry?"

"Hey! Cool! How are things going for you in Lavascape? Every time I see you, you're in trouble."

"Things are good. I have my quest to save a girl," said Jared. "She's really in trouble." He considered his own troubles now. "How long have you been here?"

"Two days. Hey, you've got a sword!"

Jared withdrew his weapon. Sure, he had a sword, but how was that going to help them get out of this cage.

"Cut me loose," said Kentucky Scurry.

Jared positioned the sword between the scurry's paws and, with tiny movements, sawed through the cords.

As soon as the rat-like creature was free of his bands, he shuddered, stretching his arms and legs at odd jerky angles. Jared watched with a dropped jaw as the scurry changed shape. He became tall and oh so thin. His snout was a little bump protruding from the rest of his rope-like body. He easily slipped between a couple of the bones. Once the scurry was outside the cage, he hid behind a wooden barrel and eased back into his normal shape.

"Thanks, N00b."

"What about me?" whispered Jared.

"Relax. I'm looking for a key or something."

There were barrels and baskets on the stone floor and jars on shelves along the wall. The scurry poked his snout into each and rummaged around. With every noise, Jared jumped and expected one of the giants deeper into the cave to come charging up there. None came, however. They all seemed busy doing something else.

Drops of water sprayed from the waterfall toward the scurry. "Oh no. Here they come," said Jared. The scurry chose a basket and climbed inside. It was far too small, his head and shoulders were above the edge, but in the next second the scurry changed shape and was perfectly hidden inside.

The smaller giant hurried to the cage. "Oh great, now we've lost our scurry."

"Didn't you take his sword?"

"Scurry don't have...."

"Not the scurry, the troll."

"Oops."

"Oops? All you can say is oops?" He smacked the smaller one in the back of the head.

"I forgot." He kicked him back. "Everybody makes mistakes!"

"I've never forgotten to disarm a prisoner. What a dummy."

The smaller giant came close to the bone bars. "Give us your sword. Hey troll, if you have it, hand it over."

Couldn't he see the sword hanging at Jared's side? No, he probably couldn't. Jared had heard that giants have heightened senses in all but sight. "The scurry stole it," said Jared.

"I can smell him, he can't be far," said the bigger giant.

"Can you? Oh wow, I got it!"

"About time!"

"It's kind of a wet dog smell."

"I'm surprised you can pick it out over your own stench."

These giants sounded like a couple of brothers after a week of rainy days.

"Let me out," called Jared.

"Never," said the bigger one. "And don't start yapping or you'll regret it."

"Do you think the scurry's still here?" asked the smaller giant.

"You'll never catch him," said Jared, looking toward the waterfall exit.

"We'll see about that," said the larger giant. Grabbing the smaller giant by the elbow, he dragged him away from the kegs he had been sniffing and into a lumbering run towards the waterfall and the forest outside.

Once they were gone Jared whispered, "Kentucky, get me outta here."

The scurry returned to normal shape and approached Jared. "I don't have a key; don't know what you think I can do."

Would Kentucky take off and leave him there? It smacked of betrayal and maybe that's what he deserved after what he had done to Terrance. "Wait a second. You can change shape. Here," he held up the padlock on the cage. "Try to pick it."

The scurry transformed one of his front paws into a shape that would accommodate the opening, and began fidgeting around inside the lock. In five minutes, he removed his paw, put it back to its original shape, and pulled. The padlock opened. Together they eased the lock off and opened the door as quietly as possible.

Jared was free. "With talents like that, why did you need my help? Why didn't you just change shape and slither away?"

"I was tied up too tight. I have to be able to move for it to work. When a scurry is bound up tight, he's pretty much helpless."

They made their way to the mouth of the cave and as Jared moved toward the waterfall, a vision burst upon him. He saw the lovely princess in her stark cell. The sight of her face caused his chest to feel warm and jittery. *This is probably what love feels like,* mused Jared. Then he dismissed the idea.

His field of vision broadened and he saw that the fortress that held her was on an island. The rocky skyline resembled the curve of a shark's mouth with the teeth stretching heavenward. He hardly had time for this now!

Jared came through the waterfall. The scurry was already a quarter of the way across the river. "Come on," he said. "What were you doing?"

Without taking time to answer, Jared hurried into the water. So, there were regular water streams along with the lava ones.

"Look out," called Kentucky. "They're back." He arched his back and began a transformation. It seemed every muscle in his body stretched to its maximum before changing shape. Suddenly the scurry plunged under the waist-deep water and was gone.

Jared drew his sword and splashed toward the far shore. The giants were returning to the cave but changed their course when they spotted them. Their long legs covered ground quickly, while Jared's went at a painfully sluggish pace slogging through the water.

Did trolls know how to swim? How would he do it? Suddenly, Jared was jerked beneath the surface of the water and in utter amazement his view changed to first person and he watched as the blue-green water flooded past him. The wiry limbs of a water plant caught on his arm and then his face. He pulled it off; it felt slimy.

Fear gripped him. Was the switch in point of view a sign he was going to die?

Just as abruptly, he saw his troll-self lying on the sandy edge of the river, Kentucky beside him, retracting what appeared to be flippers. Jared's head was spinning. What was happening? The giants were coming through the river now!

Kentucky was already scrambling up and moving toward the forest. "Come on!" he yelled. Jared stood and hurried after him. He was taller than the scurry and had more trouble with overhanging branches. They turned down a stone-paved trail and made better time...but so would the giants. "We'll never outrun them," yelled Jared. The ground shuddered. "Hide!"

Kentucky arched into his metamorphosis, which left him snake-like among the stones in the path. He stretched thinner. He had become the mortar between the bricks. The giants would walk right over him and never even realize it. It was a brilliant move.

Jared looked around. He whispered, "Under a bush? Up a tree?"

"Up a tree," said Kentucky. "Hopefully they'll look down not up."

It seemed like good reasoning. Jared went to the nearest tree and easily ascended ten feet or so. Trolls were good climbers when they weren't hanging over a cliff. That was good news.

The giants slowed. "Did you hear something?" asked the smaller giant.

"Definitely," said the other.

Jared held his position. They left the path and walked straight toward the tree where Jared was hiding. From his hiding place behind a branch, Jared could see straight into the bigger giant's eyes. Retina Reading gave him a wealth of information. The giant was angry at the world and desperate to prove himself, which made him mean.

Kentucky grabbed a stone and threw it into the trees on the other side of the path. It was a classic distraction and it worked. "This way," called the larger giant and he and his companion disappeared into the greenery on the other side of the path.

For what felt like a long time, Jared stayed in his tree and Kentucky stayed between the stones. The vision of Sparket returned displacing Jared's view of the forest. She sat on her bed, the sheets all pulled off to one side. She grasped two sides of the material covering the mattress and pulled in opposite directions. The fabric ripped revealing foam padding. She ripped the thin layer of foam, carefully tucking any loose pieces back inside the mattress. The metal springs were visible. There was a sound at the door. Someone was unlocking the cell. Sparket threw the sheets and blanket back in place.

A man walked in. He had a chubby face but a lean muscular body.

"Did you bring me food?" asked Sparket.

"Yes." He opened a pouch and brought out a napkin bulging with food.

"Thank you, thank you! I eat and eat at the feast but I'm always so hungry when I get here. You're a life saver, Yonis."

"The pre-game show has its rules, too, you know. I'd be in trouble if anyone found out I was sneaking food out. If Antonio knew I was doing this for you, he'd probably have my head."

"I know and I appreciate it so much. If I am ever rescued, I'll remember you."

"What about when you marry Antonio?"

"*If* that day comes, you can count on me to get you the positions you want in the army." She picked up a peach. "As much as I appreciate the fruit, do you think you could bring me meat next time? Protein is so much more filling."

"I'll see what I can do. Give me the napkin."

She placed the napkin in his hand and he left the room, locking her back in.

The vision faded.

Eventually, Jared and Kentucky ventured out of their hiding places. "Thanks a lot. I owe you big time," said Jared. "If there's anything I can do for you, just ask."

"I was hoping you'd say that," replied Kentucky.

Chapter Fifteen

It was a long, terrible day. The talk with his parents would be etched in Jared's memory forever. It was the day the speculation was over. Mom and Dad didn't need a little time apart, they didn't need a break to realize how important their marriage really was, they weren't going to go for counselling—Mom and Dad were getting a divorce. They each had a lawyer. And, 'so sorry it may affect you kids,' but they just couldn't live together any more.

May affect them? May? Yeah right, Dad. Tearing their family apart had the potential to, maybe, affect them!

Mom wasn't much better. She wanted Dad back, but only if he agreed to change enough to her liking.

What happened to their vows? Didn't they have 'to have and to hold... at least a bit everyday' in their vows? Did they have 'for richer or poorer, in good times and hard times'? Surely 'till death do you part' covered everything they were going through.

Jared simmered as he listened. Melissa sat in the rocking

chair perfectly still like a sculpture and Jared stood opposite her, his arms resting on the back of the matching rocking chair, his hands in tight fists.

It was hard to hear what his parents were actually saying, when their eyes were shouting so loudly. Dad cleared his throat and looked as though he were preparing to address his fellow lodge members about a promising fundraising project. "Once I have a permanent residence, we'll work out a custody arrangement." He could have been reading from a manual —'How to destroy your marriage in three easy steps: first, secure a permanent residence; second, work out a custody arrangement (you have to, it's the law); and third, get on with your real life.'

So Jared and Melissa would be shuffled around between Mom's house and Dad's house according to some agreement. Jared felt like they'd just stolen his sense of belonging. He'd never feel completely 'at home' no matter which residence he was at now. It would be Mom's or Dad's but never his.

"You know we'll still love both of you." Dad's voice was stiff. Another line from the manual.

"Almost half of marriages end in divorce," said Mom. She clutched the cushion of the couch on either side of her body. The material of her blouse vibrated with her ragged breathing.

"We're in good company, then," said Jared. They were in the front room. The formal living room—not the family room.

Dad glared at him. "Sometimes people are happier and better parents when they're not together." He cracked his knuckles and shifted his weight from one foot to the other.

Jared nodded.

All the time they spoke, Jared could see into his parents' eyes and read everything they weren't saying, the anger, the pain, the disappointment, and the hatred. But, even all that wasn't as bad as what he saw in his sister.

Melissa's face seemed to drain: the result was a shallow, pale, well of despair. She could have been watching a television program for all the reaction she showed her parents. They only saw the stoic, slightly distant expression—they couldn't read deeper. Surrounded by her family, she felt lonely, lost, loveless.

Jared was having trouble taking in how suddenly your world could change and you had to alter your image of yourself. He became the son of two very separate people instead of a married couple. He had a story but not many wanted to hear it, and he wished it was fiction.

He was the child of a broken home. He was surprised how alone he felt, too. How permanent it seemed. There was no hope left. No one talked of mended homes. This kind of broken didn't get fixed. People had to move on and start over.

Later, Melissa was in her room with her cell phone melded to her ear. She'd broken her silence and Jared was glad. Maybe talking about things would help. Melissa had Cam, but Jared couldn't talk about it. It wasn't the guy way to handle things.

Besides, his friends would know soon enough. Other kids came through divorces okay, didn't they? Jared and Melissa certainly weren't the first or the last kids in their school to have their parents break up...but it felt like it just the same.

Monty phoned. "Hey Jared, you should see the pictures I took at the dance."

"Why? Did they turn out?"

"Yeah and I have a great shot of Terrance singing. You can see Colton at the side of the stage dirty and peeved. It's classic and it's going to be in the school newspaper."

Jared felt Monty avoiding the fact that Colton hadn't done his bullying alone this time. Nice of him. Jared couldn't muster any enthusiasm for Monty, though. Things at home were on a completely different scale. "Good," he managed.

"Hey, are you tired or something?"

"Yeah."

"Okay. Well, I'll talk to you tomorrow."

It was after ten o'clock and Jared stared at the stippled ceiling as though it held answers, somehow, to all his problems. If only he could find the clues in the random pattern, he could rest with enlightening knowledge washing over him.

Melissa raised her voice but not high enough for Jared to understand her. Jared strained his hearing, remembering his troll training. Then, all of a sudden, he could hear Melissa perfectly. "It so unfair! Dads shouldn't just leave. Parents should have to work out their problems. Whenever me and Jared fight, that's what they tell us. Why doesn't that apply to them?" Melissa paused and Cam must have been talking. "Well, that's what they tried to say," she continued, "but I don't buy it. It's not going to be okay. How can it? How?" She was crying again.

There was too much pain in her voice. Plus, it was hard to hear his sister express his feelings out loud, feelings he didn't want to examine. She was bang-on with everything. How could his parents let this happen? Why was being a contractor the only thing Dad was willing to do? Why did Mom treat him like a bum because work was slow? When did their frustration boil over into something else? When did they stop loving each other? The problems weren't insurmountable. It was a bump on the road of life. Why had they stopped climbing?

He could use some climbing right now. Exertion that required all his effort would help clear his mind. He saw his computer sitting as though eager for him to return to it. Climbing and hiking around the forests of Lavascape would have to do.

He logged on. He had missed the feast today, of course. Life changing events got in the way. Kentucky met him in the forest. "What do you want me to do to help you out?" asked Jared.

"Coin games," said Kentucky. "The richest scurry is always the leader. So if you'll collect coins and transfer them to me, we can call your debt paid. Literally, ha ha. About a thousand coins should be good."

Jared considered the coins he brought with him from the troll village. He had a start toward that thousand but maybe he'd need money later. He'd work the Scurry games and hang on to his stash. "You got it."

Jared sampled the coin games and was soon captivated by the tennis-like game where the ball bounced off the walls of the room and could be hit innumerable times on the same side without penalty. He played through his exhaustion. Missing a troll feast was like missing three normal-life meals. Somewhere in the back of his mind, he thought of Sparket and the time limit. But, a deal was a deal. He'd help Kentucky and then get on with his quest.

Sometime in the quiet of the night, he went to bed. Jared woke while it was still dark. His instep itched. His feet felt weird as he scratched. Was something stuck to the bottom of his feet? He drifted back to sleep but in the morning the itchiness returned. He sat on the edge of his bed and stared at his feet alternating from left to right. There was hair in his instep. It was short but thick. Who had hair on the bottom of their feet? Besides trolls?

On Monday, Jared mostly avoided Colton, and got elbowed or sucker punched when he didn't. The strength behind Colton's 'attention' was up a notch after the dance.

Tuesday, he completed a fantastic round of 'Scurry like a Scurry,' a game that required jumping to moving platforms and ducking to avoid rolling or bouncing boulders. He paused to catch his breath. The mask must be made of one advanced material because it never fogged or felt stuffy no matter how hard he was working. It was as if the mask was permeable, air easily moving from one side to the other. He got into a ready stance and was about to click the game glove to begin the next round when a vision of Sparket appeared.

She was speaking with a brawny female guard. "I know it's too dangerous for you to help me...unless you come with me, that is..."

"I've told you 'no'," said the guard. "I like it here, except for the rulers."

"Deliver a message for me?"

"I'm not telling them where you are."

"I know, I know. It's not that. They're going to be slaughtered when Antonio puts his plan into action. If I can warn my captains that Antonio will be splitting his army, it will save many lives."

"Write. I'll deliver your message. For a price."

"What do you want?" asked Sparket.

"Fifteen hundred gold coins per message. That's my price."

"Done. Give me paper and I'll sign the directive."

Sparket spoke as she wrote:

"Do not be deceived. Antonio will march by the city Zoric with a small number of soldiers to try to lure you out of the strongholds. A larger army will be waiting to occupy the city if you leave it sparsely protected.

"Please pay the bearer of this message fifteen hundred gold coins for her service.

"Your ever devoted Princess in captivity,

"Sparket."

She pressed her thumb into the paper for several seconds.

A faint imprint of her thumb remained. She rolled the paper and handed it back to the guard.

The vision faded.

"That's it! Go Sparket," cheered Jared.

He excelled in his games that day, racking up coins. Unfortunately, even at this rate it would take forever to reach the thousand that Kentucky wanted. He sent Kentucky a text message, 'Chat?'

A couple of minutes later, Kentucky answered with audio chat. "How's it going?"

"Good...but..."

"'Good' sounds good," said Kentucky. "Is there a problem?"

"Well..." Jared lost his nerve. "No," he said. A problem? *Besides the fact that there's a princess locked away who is trying to save her people with smuggled messages while I'm playing games—no problem at all,* thought Jared.

Two days later, right after feast, Jared talked to Kentucky again. He told him how many coins he'd earned and then gathering his courage he said. "So what are you going to do to pay *me* back for cutting you loose, in the first place?"

"Yeah, right," said Kentucky with a laugh. Then he wished Jared luck in his games and left to play his own.

Our escape was a team effort, thought Jared as his finger hovered over the button that sent him on another long night of gaming. A thousand coins was a so much bigger debt than he realized. He sighed and clicked the button. He was completely focused, as once again time seemed to stand still in Lavascape. Jared finished one round of the tennis game, Super-Digs, and was about to advance to the next level when he was given a view of Sparket.

She was alone and still captive in her cell. What he saw in her eyes was dwindling hope. She turned to look directly at Jared, and pursed her lips together before she spoke.

"The man I'm expected to marry visits regularly now. The guards unlock the door and in he comes as though he was here to save me, but every time he leaves, they lock the door behind him. He claims to love me, but it's fake. He wants the power he gains if I agree to marry him. I hate the politics—is the misery of one an acceptable price to pay for the safety of my people? I can tell you that when you are that one, the cost is monstrous. And I will not pay it. I'd rather die...and I'd rather kill.

"I know you are out there somewhere, my dear troll friend, and I know you seek to help me, but I also sense your distractions. I have nothing to distract me. I have no diversion for my mind. There is only the decision and the consequences I face. And I roll them all around in my mind until I'm sure I'll go mad." She reached her hands out to Jared. "Don't forget me."

As her image faded, Jared looked at his 'total coins earned.' He had 540.

Sparket needed his help. She was getting desperate and spoke of killing. Rash plans would surely get her hurt. What was he doing playing Super Digs for hours?

Paying off a debt, he reminded himself.

Sparket had never spoken to him quite so directly before. Her feelings and frustrations seemed to settle on his mind like a thick blanket of snowflakes. This most recent vision put them on a much more personal level. He got a sense of her strength, her sweetness, and yes, her desperation.

Her eyes showed her lack of hope. If she knew he was back on track instead of playing around with coin games, perhaps she wouldn't do anything stupid.

He closed the Super Digs game after saving his progress. Then he clicked the communication box in the bottom right corner of his screen. His list of contacts was a single name: 'Kentucky-Scurry'; and Kentucky was on-line.

All the village trolls were inaccessible while he was away from the village.

"Kentucky, hey," said Jared.

"Hold on," Kentucky answered a few seconds later. He must have been in the middle of a game. It was a couple of minutes before Kentucky said, "What's up? How do you like the games?"

"The games are good," said Jared. "But I have my quest and I'm only half way to the thousand coins you wanted."

"Half way, already! Wow that's great. Keep up the good work."

"The thing is..." He felt like such a heel trying to go back on a deal but what else could he do? His quest was for someone's liberty, not treasure...but would Kentucky understand this or just think he was a welcher? "...the princess really needs me right now."

There was no reply.

Jared hoped he wasn't making an enemy in Lavascape. "I'll do my best tomorrow but I'll have to call it quits soon."

"Your princess is still going to be locked up safe and sound whether you go after her tomorrow or the next day or next week."

"I suppose," said Jared. He totally felt like a welcher. He threw himself back into the scurry games.

He didn't feel tired, not while he was in Lavascape, only when he paused to look at the clock. Then the exhaustion crashed over him like an ocean wave. He earned another 100 coins before he finally dropped into bed for an hour's sleep. He was almost too tired to sleep. He tossed and turned in his bed. When he closed his eyes, he saw scurry games. His throat was parched. He got out of bed and as he descended the stairs to the kitchen, he noted how normally when a person is over-tired, their reflexes and judgement suffer but Jared had come to recognize that that wasn't the natural order of things in Lavascape. There, the longer he played, the more he plunged onward despite drooping eyelids or a growling stomach, the more quickly his skill seemed to progress, and the more endurance he seemed to develop.

The game rewarded him for his dedication with the experiences he wanted. At least, Jared suspected this to be true. He thought back over his weeks of play. The game seemed to entice him to keep him involved. It was a bribe, in a way. If he kept playing, he could have the player-to-player battle. If he kept playing, he would get more visions to help with his quest. If he kept playing, he'd become a 'Master Swordsman' or an 'Advanced Retina Reader.' The game did everything to keep him in Lavascape.

Jared wondered, what if Lavascape was tailored to each player in more ways than he first realized? What if it was more than an individual quest? From the first time you logged in, maybe it was getting to know you. Why did the game want to know him? Would it use the information against him? Try to sell him stuff? Give his personal information to marketers? Or suck him in a little bit more by understanding what makes him tick. The climb back up the stairs seemed longer than it was going down.

The next day he was so tired he almost slipped up twice and walked by Colton's locker while he was still there. When he spoke to his friends, he repeated himself incessantly. He couldn't concentrate in class. The teachers seemed to be speaking extra quickly and he was hearing in slow motion. The school day was a hundred years long. And all the while, he longed for Lavascape. Was Sparket okay? Would she forgive him for his delay? What would Kentucky say if he transferred his coins? Should he give Kentucky his coins from the troll village? There were so many decisions.

At lunch he waited until Anna left for Earthcare club, then spoke to Katie, Monty, and Carrie about it. Monty's opinion was that Jared had to finish earning the coins he owed, before rescuing the Princess or no one would trust him again, and he might need allies in the rescue. Katie's opinion was he should save the princess first, because she was in immediate danger, while Jared could pay off his debt at any time. Carrie's dismissive opinion was that he was far too involved in this dumb game. Great, three different answers! Very helpful!

Lavascape was more than just a game to Jared, though. Sometimes, he felt like he was more in sync with his friends in Lavascape than at school. Plus, there were so many elements that crossed into reality. The hearing: he was sure he had heard a dog whistle on his way to school that morning. He saw a man blowing a little silver whistle and a Yorkshire terrier came running. No one else on the block seemed annoyed by the high-pitched noise. He was reading his friends' eyes, without even trying. Katie was the only one he occasionally had a hard time reading. He saw conflicting emotions and often something unexplainable came into her eyes. Katie was complex. Like how can someone be a fingernail artist but not super girly?

Jared ate the last of his barbeque flavoured potato chips. His jeans felt too tight over his thighs today. He pulled at the outer seams to try to stretch them a bit. The tight jeans were only a mild inconvenience compared to his feet, however. His new shoes were already too tight. The big toes pressed against the end of the shoes even when he was sitting down. After lunch, he put his shoes in his locker and walked around the school in his socks.

By the last period, Jared was little more than a zombie. Just get through this day, he told himself, live in this humdrum world and then you can go to Lavascape. Or, he could go to sleep. But somehow he figured he'd feel just as rested if he got to the cyber-world. When he got off the game, he'd crash, he knew that. But, Sparket needed him now. He had to get out of his debt. He felt like he was a slave to Kentucky Scurry.

Jared skipped the stop at Josie's even though Monty and

Katie were up for it. Instead, he made his way home in a mental fog and stumbled to his computer as though it held the oxygen he needed to breathe. He logged into Lavascape and immediately felt better. The exhaustion lifted. His mood changed. Lavascape felt like home. Home like it used to be. He felt refreshed. He had his second wind.

The phone rang and rang. Finally, Jared paused the game, went to his mom's bedroom, and answered it. "Is your Dad home?" came the male voice on the line.

It was an innocent question but Jared's heart fell. He mumbled through the conversation, even writing a note for Dad. As soon as he hung up, he ripped the note to shreds. Why should he give him a message? Then, he stumbled back to his computer, sighed, rewrote the message, and tacked it on the note board in the kitchen. He'd done his part.

Chapter Sixteen

Jared was so into the coin games he almost forgot about the feast. His jumpy nerves reminded him, however. He and Barry stuffed themselves.

"It's so good today," said Barry.

"That's so crazy," said Jared. "True, but crazy."

Suddenly, a group of adventure trolls passed by them. One of them was Louila. "I know it's a war, but there should still be some decency," she said.

"Haven't you heard, 'all's fair in love and war?'" one of her companions replied.

"I've heard it...I just don't want to believe it. What was the point of slaughtering them? They had already surrendered!"

"I know. They are so brutal sometimes."

"The elves aren't much better, if what we heard is true. They're keeping slaves."

They moved out of earshot. *I'm glad I'm on the right side of this war,* thought Jared. As soon as he left the feast, a vision opened before him.

Sparket had both hands around one of the springs in her mattress. She twisted it around and around. There was sweat dripping down the sides of her face. "Come on. Come on," she hissed at the spring. A loud bang on the wooden door brought Sparket to her feet. She threw the blanket to cover the spot where she'd been working. A young man barged into her chamber. He was slender, and his face was all rugged angles. The uneven eyebrows seemed to mock her. He was the guy from the dog attack, the young suitor.

"Sorry, did I scare you?" His unpleasant smile showed he hoped that was the case.

"Your manners could use improvement," said Sparket. "But if you scared me, I'd have married you already."

"It just shows you have no idea who you're dealing with."

"Oh, I know all I want to."

"Ignorance isn't bliss in Lavascape. It gets you... conquered." His tone made Jared's mouth go dry.

"Very funny," said Sparket. There hadn't been a shred of humour in his words.

"That's right, I am. One more reason for us to team up. You'll enjoy spending all your time with me."

"You think so?"

"Of course."

"Then let me choose for myself without a death sentence hanging over my head."

"You've already turned me down."

His expression seemed to ask how she would dare do such a thing. Jared found it a disturbing reflection on the kid behind this character.

"If you've changed your mind, say so," the prince continued. "Shall I call the guard and have a priest summoned?"

"I don't think so, Tony."

"I told you to call me Antonio. My whole kingdom calls me Antonio; some wimpy little princess from another kingdom can surely show me that much respect!"

"But I don't respect you." Something in his face made her step back.

"Don't be so stubborn." He stopped in front of her and looked down. "Think of how great it would be to join forces and rule together. The power we command will be incredible. Nothing will be able to stop us. We'll control all of Lavascape."

Jared saw clearly. For Antonio it was all about power; and he liked having this power over Sparket, too.

He continued. "Strength is all there really is, Sparket. If we have to, we'll fight the giants and all the others who get in our way. I'm building a wonderful army. I have creatures deserting their own groups every day and joining my force. Plus, there are all the warriors from the conquered nations that are forced into my service—it's great. *I'm* the winning side of Lavascape, Sparket. You have a chance to join me. You won't be a slave. We'll rule together. I promise."

"I've told you before but you just don't seem to get it. I'm not into this whole 'world domination' goal. Why would I want to be dragged into a quest that's..."

"How about to stay alive?" interrupted the prince. "And to keep your people from being slaughtered."

"They're strong. There will be losses on both sides. We humans are supposed to be free agents, choosing the side of the battle we want to support, but you don't want to join with anyone, you want to dominate them all. And, am I supposed to trust the promise of a murderer?"

"We're at war!"

"You're at war."

"We're all at war. There's no way around it. We might as well win it and rule Lavascape. Think about it. It will be... fun." His smile reminded Jared of the wolves growling and snapping at Sparket when she had tried to escape.

"More fun than sitting in this room, perhaps," said Sparket, looking at the dark stone walls.

"We'll expand our kingdom, build new cities."

"New cities in place of the goblin ones?" asked Sparket. Jared could see from her eyes that this was a verbal blow. "What would you call this rebuilt city? Slaughter Heights?"

"You know about that?" he actually stumbled back a couple of steps. Then he straightened and clenched his jaw. "Not all of them were killed. I have a few prisoners, too. Those willing to fight for me or build my new cities will never have to die."

"I hate it all."

"You wouldn't tell me your quest, but I think I can guess. World peace? Is it world peace, Sparket? Ha ha ha. Now there's a goal that's bound to fail. That's it, isn't it?" He fluttered his hand at his throat. "You and every beauty pageant contestant in the world wants...world peace." He laid his hand over hers. "Rule with me! Once we rule it all, there *will* be peace!"

Sparket's mouth was a hard line. The prince continued. "I will get what I want. I don't care how many creatures I have to defeat to make it happen." His voice shook. "You're time is running out. You have until the next full moon. I'll take your kingdom the hard way or the easy way. The easy way—you and many more of your people get to live."

He went to the door and knocked twice. The door swung inward and, with a final glare at her, he was gone.

Was she considering it? 'More fun than sitting in this room everyday'. Jared jumped from his computer chair, flung his mask to the floor, curled his right hand into a tight fist, and punched a hole in his bedroom wall. Then he stared at the hole. Had he actually done that? His throbbing hand testified to it.

He would make his quota and leave the scurry behind.

Melissa burst into his room. "What's going on in here? Are you okay?"

Jared pointed at the hole in the wall and shook his sore hand.

"I was almost asleep. You scared me half to death!" Melissa fumed.

"Sparket might join with those stupid humans if I don't rescue her soon."

"Really? *That's* what this is about? It's just a game, Jared! Calm down." She regarded Jared for a long moment, as if trying to figure him out. "You better hang a poster over that, until you can fix it," she said, pointing at the hole. "Mom will have a conniption if she sees it."

Chapter Seventeen

At the troll feast the next day, Jared talked Barry into eating closer to the adventurers. "They have more interesting conversations," he said.

"It's only interesting if you're interested," Barry said, but he followed Jared to the table bordering the villagers and adventurers.

"There," said Jared as he started chowing down on the sautéed mushrooms and sushi-rolled fish, "the best of both worlds."

"If you're trying to get me excited about life outside the village, you're wasting your time," said Barry. "Just so you know."

Jared shrugged. "I just want to hang out with you and hear any news at the same time. You question my motives?"

"Totally."

Jared laughed.

A loud voice from the adventurer side of the feast caught their attention. "They don't care if they ruin the world, as long as they forge their axes and clubs."

"Elves and giants are notoriously messy," said another troll.

"Messy is one thing," said the first speaker, "pollution is another. This could affect us all. Who knows if these fumes from their armouries could hurt us? We're in this world. We breathe here." He held up a greasy mushroom. "We eat here."

"Let's see if we can get a closer look at the factory. We might find something."

They moved to one of the teleportation platforms and were gone to their quests.

Soon Jared said goodbye to Barry and did the same. In the moments of teleportation, he saw a vision of Sparket. Antonio grabbed one of her hands and then fumbled for the other. He pulled her closer to him. Except for the dog-like jaws, Antonio would be a lot of girls' definition of 'hot'. The way Sparket was held by his eyes reminded Jared of groupies hanging around rock stars.

"So, what do you say Sparket?" Antonio asked. "Ready for fun ruling the world?"

She looked up with a dreamy expression and said, "I certainly am not!"

"What?"

"You heard me." The fake adoration was gone. Her confidence came through in her tone. "I won't be bullied or romanced into joining forces with you. I'll get out of here or you'll kill me, but I won't help you."

"You're so dumb," huffed Antonio. He stomped out of the prison cell and slammed the door behind him.

After he left, Sparket snickered. "Dumb? I guess I can add

'immature' to your faults. " Then she walked to the single window and her expression turned hard.

Jared slipped off his game mask and yelled, "Yes!" As he jumped, he knocked over the chair. It banged the desk as it fell.

Melissa opened his door as he pumped his fist in the air. "What now?"

"Go Sparket, Go Sparket," he chanted.

"Really? This again? Jared, it's only a stupid game." But Jared grabbed her hand and spun her around still chanting "Go Sparket. Go Sparket" until she laughed and joined in.

"Did she escape?" asked Melissa dropping down on his bed, then scooting down to the carpet. There was a bag of tortilla chips and a bowl of salsa on the floor. She dipped a few chips and ate. Jared joined her and leaned against the bed, also eating.

"No, nothing that good happened. But, she isn't fooled by that jerk." Jared thought of Cam and hoped Melissa would be just like Sparket—brave and independent and not fooled by a guy. I think Sparket actually made him think he had charmed her into marrying him—then she stomped on him.

"Your game girl's got grit," said Melissa, laughing.

"Yeah, she does."

Melissa's phone buzzed. She had it on vibrate. "Text from Cam," she said, rapidly typing with her thumbs. She snapped the keyboard closed when she was finished. "You better save that girl," she said.

Jared nodded. "I know."

Melissa's phone buzzed again. She rose and walked to the door chanting, "Go, Sparket, go, Sparket." She turned and they smiled together before she left.

Sometime into the night, in the middle of a round of

Super Digs, Kentucky interrupted Jared. "Hey Jerry, you out there?"

"I'm here," responded Jared. "Hold on." When he finished that round he said, "I just rolled over 600 coins. But, I've got to tell you, Sparket, the princess, is starting to get restless." He remembered her determined look after she turned Antonio down. "You said something about how she's locked up safe and sound, but she's not safe," said Jared. "She has a deadline at the gallows and I don't know how to find her. I have a feeling that she's desperate enough to do something rash. I've got to help her."

Kentucky was quiet for what felt like a long moment. When he finally spoke he said, "I was such a jerk the other day. Sparket's in trouble and you do need to help her. Tell me more about her."

Jared explained Sparket's situation, captured, with Antonio forcing her to marry or die. Jared described Sparket's long blond hair and delicate, angelic face. He told Kentucky about the desperate feelings he was picking up from her and disturbing comments that showed she was nearing the end of her rope.

"Where is she?"

"All I know is the shape of the skyline and I haven't seen anything like it in Lavascape yet," said Jared.

"You need to get to higher ground," suggested Kentucky.

"Where's higher ground? I've been in the forest most of the time and all I see are trees. The waterfall at the giants' cave wasn't much help since we were running for our lives at the time."

"What does the skyline look like?"

"An open sharks mouth. At least that's how I think of it. There's a flat area and then it's like half of an oval with the jutting 'teeth' spaced along it. Then the skyline goes flat again."

"I know of a hill. I'll take you there, if you'd like."

Why was he so helpful all of a sudden? "That would be great," said Jared. "But aren't you too involved in your own quest?"

"You put yours on hold for me. If I can't do the same for you, what kind of friend am I? Besides, I'm sorry about the way I acted when this is a girl in trouble."

Jared exited the game room and he was back in the forest. He turned in a circle. There were dense evergreens in every direction except for the paths that criss-crossed through them. Suddenly Kentucky was at his side. "Let's go," he said.

They walked along, jumping lava balls and logs that came rolling down the path. Jared's foot caught one of the logs and he landed on his shoulder, leaving him with an ache he rubbed as he fell asleep that night.

The next day when he got to Lavascape, there was a feeling in the air like the calm after a storm; Jared tread lightly. Before long, the path was plagued with fallen logs, scrap metal, stones, bits of vegetation, and charred planks of wood. "It's like trekking through a garbage dump," complained Jared. "What lives in this part of the forest? Pigs?"

"Not pigs." said Kentucky. "Goblins."

An arrow whizzed through the air, ripping a piece of Jared's tunic as it skimmed by. "What the heck?"

"Hands in the air," said a confident male voice.

"I haven't met any goblins," whispered Jared.

"How do you like 'em so far?" asked Kentucky.

Further down the path, Jared saw a creature a little shorter and slimmer than himself. It had a large nose with two ski-hill bumps down the bridge. The goblin was holding a bow with the string taut and an arrow ready to fly.

Goblins and trolls were supposed to be friends but this fellow was acting mighty unfriendly.

Jared spoke. "Whoa! We come in peace. We're just looking for some higher ground to get our bearings and find our way."

The goblin's hands shook, the bow and arrow jerked up and down. "Who are you?" he demanded.

"I'm Jerry Troll and this is Kentucky Scurry."

"You returning to the scene of the crime?" With that, the goblin let loose another arrow. Kentucky hit the ground. It whizzed past Jared's head and lodged in the tree behind him.

"Hey! Hold on! We haven't done any crime!" yelled Jared.

"What are you doing with him, troll? You can't trust a scurry!"

"Hey! We're friends," said Kentucky.

"Do you trust him?"

Jared hesitated. Did he? Why was there the sudden change from collecting coins to helping Jared with his quest? The goblin was waiting for an answer. Kentucky had saved him. "Yes, I trust him."

"You do know about scurry, don't you?" They pick and choose and change their alliances at the drop of a hat." He placed a third arrow in the bow. "I'm warning you."

"Okay," said Jared. "Calm down."

"Where were you the last two days!" he demanded.

"Gaming," said Jared. "Earning coins."

"What about you, Scurry?"

Kentucky spoke through clenched teeth. "I was gaming, too."

The goblin was passionate, if misguided. With the goblin/

troll alliance, it would be great if he could get this goblin to stop threatening him and help him out—then he'd know he had someone he could rely on a hundred percent.

"What are you doing here, then?" asked the goblin.

"We're looking for a skyline that looks like an open shark's mouth. Can you tell me where I might find it?" asked Jared.

The goblin lowered his weapon for the first time since they'd come upon him. "I know the view you mean."

"You do? Where is it?"

"Not on this island," said the goblin. "I've seen it from the shore. It's the skyline of the island Lorava."

"How can I get there?"

"The ferryman is the only way." The goblin was leaning on his bow now. He was apparently convinced they weren't a threat. Jared could breathe again.

"Come with us. Be our guide!" said Jared. "I'm on a quest to find a princess."

"Your basic damsel in distress," added Kentucky.

"There's nothing basic about her," said Jared. He wasn't sure that was true, but from looking in her eyes when he received those personal glimpses of her he felt the kind of person she was. The messages she sent him, the desperation in her communication, it all gave her an individual aura. There was no way she was a computerized person...no, she was definitely a real person. A computer person would be content to wait to be rescued. Sparket was not. Something bound him to this trapped girl.

"If she's a princess, she must have gold," said the goblin.

"You can forget about that," said Kentucky, briskly.

The quickness of his reply made Jared think. Kentucky was so concerned about the golden coins; maybe he saw this quest as a way to really cash in. Not that it really mattered. Jared was here for the princess; Kentucky could have the gold. Or the goblin could have it; it didn't matter to him.

"I've been in Lavascape a long time," said the goblin. "But something tells me you two are new to the game. You didn't even know you were heading into goblin settlements did you?"

"I figured," said Kentucky.

The goblin went on. "I know things about the Lavascape life that you two couldn't even imagine. I've served in tons of missions and I know this island like the back of my hand."

"Then why would your big mission at the moment be to guard a path?" asked Kentucky. "Sounds like peon work to me."

"Humph! You sure have a big mouth for someone with so little upstairs. You have no idea what we've been through."

Suddenly, the rubble around Jared looked a lot more like a tragic battle scene than a garbage dump. As Kentucky and the goblin spoke, Jared let his mind wander. The goblin knew the island, he knew the sharks tooth skyline, he had insights into Lavascape—Jared wanted him on his quest. "Would you help me save the human princess?" asked Jared.

"A human, eh?" His voice revealed keen interest.

"What are you doing?" asked Kentucky. "We don't need him." Then to the goblin he said, "Just point us in the right direction and we'll be fine."

"Tell me more about this princess," the goblin said.

When Jared was finished, the goblin said, "I've always wanted to fight the humans. He was quiet for a very long time.

"If I'm going to become the best warrior in all of

Lavascape," the goblin finally continued, "I need experience with humans." He spat out the word 'humans.' "Hmm." He looked at Jared and Kentucky until Jared felt very uncomfortable. "Alright, I'm in."

"But you don't care about the princess..." said Jared.

"No, I don't. Not particularly. Is she cute?"

Jared didn't answer at first but the goblin was waiting. Finally, he said, "Yes, she's beautiful."

"All the better. I'd hate to risk my life for a homely princess. Oh, and while we're talking about the particulars, I'm going to need a fair share of any gold that comes our way as a reward."

"Sure," said Jared.

Kentucky was silent.

"And if we have the pleasure of killing the tyrant holding her captive, I want to do the honours."

"Why you? I hate this guy," said Jared.

"Experience fighting the humans." The goblin waited.

In the heat of the conflict, surely whoever could kill Antonio would do it. It's not something you can claim like calling shotgun to ride up front in a van. The goblin was so insistent, however, that it would be easier just to agree. "All right," said Jared.

The goblin pushed a button on his wristband. "Hey, Riven here. I've got myself a little detour. Send someone else down to route G?" He paused for a second, apparently receiving a message from higher ups.

"Okay, I'm good to go," he said turning to face Jared and Kentucky.

"Walkie Talkie's, how high tech," sneered Kentucky.

"It also sends arrows if I run low on ammo or a new bow if mine goes missing. It's high tech enough."

Chapter Eighteen

Melissa and Cam came in the front door. Jared could hear their voices. He had just signed out of Lavascape and climbed into bed. It was almost one o'clock. That was mighty late for Melissa to be getting back from a date, especially on a school night.

Where was Mom? Was Melissa going to get reamed out in front of Cam or would Mom wait until Cam left? Jared listened but there wasn't a trace of his mom's voice. Had she gone to bed while Melissa was still out with Cam? That was unheard of. Mom always said she couldn't rest until her children were tucked in their beds. Of course, that was before. Now that Dad was tucked in elsewhere, maybe a kid out late didn't bother her so much.

Jared could hear their voices perfectly.

"Melissa, it's no big deal. It just loosens you up so you can have some fun."

"I don't know, Cam. I'm starting to hear things even when I'm not smoking it."

"Well, you're a downer when you're not high."

"Why? Because I'm sad my mom and dad are getting a divorce."

"You don't need a boyfriend. What you need is a really good shrink."

"I can't just listen anymore," Jared said to himself. Troll courage emboldened him. He burst out of his room and took the steps down to the entranceway two at a time. He stood nose to nose with Cam. "Hey Jerk! I think you've said enough."

Cam pushed Jared's chest and Jared took a step backwards. His temper flared. The adrenalin rush was intoxicating. "I told Melissa you were a loser; thanks for proving that I'm *so* right. Now, get out of our house." He grabbed Cam by the back of his jacket. "Here let me show you the proper way to open the door." He shoved Cam out into the night. Was it the adrenaline or was he really stronger than ever?

Cam lost his balance then caught himself. He swore and started to back away from the house. "Your brother's crazier than you are!" Jared slammed the door and flipped the deadbolt. He turned to Melissa.

Instead of appreciating his help, however, she screamed, "Jared!" and hit him twice in the chest. Then she stumbled up the stairs and flung open the door to Mom's room.

Mom bolted up in bed. "What?" Her eyes were wild.

"Jared's completely out of control! He grabbed Cam and shoved him out the door!"

"You let him talk to you like that!" yelled Jared.

"It's none of your business."

"He was a jerk to you!"

"That's how people talk. We have a good relationship. You're too young to understand."

"It's one o'clock in the morning!" screamed Mom.

"At least, we *had* a good relationship. What if we break up, now?" Tears ran down Melissa's face.

"Sounds like a reason to party to me!" said Jared.

"Mom! He's ruining my life!"

"Shut your mouths! Both of you!" yelled Mom. "I can't believe we have to have screaming teenage drama in the middle of the night."

"But Cam..." whined Melissa, swiping at tears and jumping up on Mom's bed. "He's my life."

Mom grunted.

"You could do so much better," Jared mumbled.

"No, I have to have Cam!"

Jared winced. She sounded so pitiful.

The next morning, Jared fell out of bed when his alarm rang and he bumped his head on the night table. The alarm seemed to be set especially loud this morning. He rubbed the side of his face and checked the volume. It was set at number 4, same as always. *Must still have my troll hearing on,* he thought.

Melissa was hunched over a bowl of corn flakes when he entered the kitchen. "Hey," he said. "You okay?"

"Great," was her sarcastic reply, followed by a slurp and crunching of a mouth full of cereal.

Jared set his own bowl on the table and went to the cupboard for another brand of cereal. Was she drowning her sorrows in huge bites of cereal or was she really okay? Jared thought he'd better test the waters a bit. "Then, you're okay?"

He waited but she continued to slurp her cereal. "Things are going to be fine," she said finally.

"There are a lot better guys than Cam out there."

"Don't say that. He's a great guy. We had an argument... and I'll apologize for what you did."

"I heard you talk about smoking...something."

"Mind your own business."

Her words felt like a slap. Jared clenched his teeth. Surely she could see it; why wouldn't she admit it—Cam was bad news.

Chapter Nineteen

Jared enjoyed the troll feast; the breading on the fish sticks was about three inches thick. He heard snippets of rumours from the adventurers, but Barry seemed to deliberately draw his attention away. Words about attacks in the goblin villages made his ears perk up, however. He had seen the devastation those attackers had left behind, first hand. No one seemed to know who was to blame, giants, elves, or humans.

After the feast, Jared jumped into his quest. There was tension in Lavascape, though, as Riven led the way through goblin territory. Other goblins looked their way, staring suspiciously, then disappeared into the brush or small homes. One old-looking goblin approached them, talked with Riven, and repeatedly glared at Jared and Kentucky. Riven assured him Kentucky was Jared's friend and the goblin finally let them pass. But Jared could see more... the old goblin's mistrust wasn't only directed at the scurry. Jared was under scrutiny just for keeping company with Kentucky. Who would ever choose to be a scurry, Jared wondered. It was like choosing to be a social outcast. Was shape-shifting worth that?

The debris in the path intensified. There were more detours around boulders, and more fallen trees to climb over. The ruins of demolished huts lay in heaps on the land.

"What happened here?" asked Kentucky.

"The war, of course." Riven seemed hardly able to choke out the words at first, but then he cleared his throat, got control, and continued. "This was a recent attack. We weren't expecting it in this quarter so we were unprepared. We won't make that mistake again. We don't trust easily." His gaze found Kentucky and his eyes narrowed. Riven pointed at a cluster of what used to be houses, and now were piles of wood and metal. "I used to live there."

"Giants?" asked Jared.

"Not this time." He walked several more steps then spit on the ground, a gooey green glob. It looked disgustingly cool and Jared made a mental note to try to spit sometime.

"Are we almost there?" asked Kentucky. "How long do we have to waste our time just walking and walking and walking?"

Riven walked a few steps ahead but didn't answer.

"He thinks we need him," said Kentucky in a whisper to Jared. "We'll find that skyline with or without him. Let's ditch him and get out of this hurricane zone."

They were at the edge of the damage caused by the battle. "The going won't be so slow now," said Jared. "Besides we don't know where to find the skyline and he does. He also knows about the ferry."

"He told us about it. Now we know about the ferry, too."

Riven stopped and faced them with his hands on his bow, the arrow aimed at Kentucky's heart. "You were whispering!" he yelled. "You, Troll, and your rude little scurry are thinking about attacking, aren't you?"

"What a paranoid..." began Kentucky.

"I wasn't talking to you, Scurry!"

"No one is going to attack you," said Jared. "At least, we're not."

"I should be able to trust a troll...."

"You can trust me," said Jared.

"Then what were you and the scurry talking about behind my back?"

Jared was silent for a long moment then he said, "About whether we needed you to find the ferry and the island we're after. We decided that we really do need you."

The goblin spit on the ground again. "We could lose the scurry, Troll. But if we're going on this quest together, there can't be whispers."

"Okay," agreed Jared.

"I want to hear it from the scurry, too!"

"Okay, okay," said Kentucky.

"We need to make an official pact," said Riven. "You and I, Troll, have the alliance and we have the same goal, although for different reasons. If I'm going to see this through, I need to know that I can count on both of you. In the middle of the battle, I don't want you to decide the girl isn't worth the trouble and leave me to my death. And as for the scurry, I don't know what he's in it for, but I don't want him switching alliances whenever he feels like it."

"I think my goal is a little more compelling than yours," said Jared. "I'm trying to save a person and all you're doing is trying to gain fighting experience."

"And gold." Riven pointed at Kentucky when he said it.

"Yes, of course, the gold," said Jared. "If there is a reward. I can't make promises."

"Now what about the scurry? What do you want, Scurry?"

"Call me Kentucky."

"Why are you part of this mission," he repeated.

"Well..." Kentucky had a note of embarrassment in his voice. "We're friends."

"You have an identical quest?"

"No. But we're friends and we help each other out. And I don't think we need you." Kentucky seemed to be bristling, his fur even stood out from his body menacingly.

"Stop it, Kentucky," said Jared. "We do need him!" The constant bickering, the tension, it all felt a little too familiar.

"Shall we make a pact or go our separate ways? Decide now before somebody gets killed," said Riven.

"I'll make a pact," said Jared.

There was fierceness in Riven's eyes. He was more devoted to this quest than someone who only wanted fighting experience....and it wasn't the gold; the comments about the gold were just to get under Kentucky's skin.

"Okay," said Kentucky. "I'll make the promise."

"For what it's worth—the word of a scurry—but just the same here's the pact. The goblin set his bow at his feet, raised both hands above his head. The sky began to swirl around them, the clouds from the sky elongated to thin ribbons that glided around the goblin and then enfolded Jared and Kentucky, too. Riven said, 'In our mission to save Sparket, the princess, I will fight to the death for the quest and for my companions.' Now you guys say it."

Jared felt the solemnity of the pledge he was about to make. He laid his sword next to the bow like an offering on a sacred alter. Then he repeated the words of the pact. Kentucky had no weapon to lie down but he repeated the words quickly when Jared finished.

When the ritual was complete, Jared felt a new bond, a new devotion to the goblin and even to Kentucky. His desire to save Sparket was also intensified. It was a powerful vow.

A vision of Sparket opened before him. She was speaking with a remarkably short man, presumably a guard. "That's what I told your captain," said the man. He leaned in closer. "Why don't you beg me to reveal your whereabouts to your army?"

"I know you won't do it." Sparket answered quickly, perhaps too quickly.

"Hm. I wouldn't expect you to assume that. I've broken vows of loyalty left and right."

"Are you offering?"

"No. Even I have limits. I was simply curious about why you weren't trying harder."

Jared saw in her eyes....she knew there were rescuers coming...Jared and his companions. The trust in her eyes was familiar, he wasn't sure why. The guard left and Sparket took a napkin filled with dark red cherries out from under her bed. She ate the cherries and placed the pits back in the napkin. The vision closed.

"He saw a vision," said Kentucky. "That's the look he gets when he's seeing the princess."

"Nothing new," said Jared. Nothing except that she had placed her faith, her freedom, and her life, on their little band.

They followed Riven over logs and through narrow paths. Jared saw the goblin wipe a tear. That was taking the mirroring feature of the game to another level. Jared mentally fumbled for something to say.

Kentucky was having a hard time keeping up in this terrain. Jared whispered to Riven, "Are you okay?"

He shook his head. "I had it so good for a while. I took it for granted. She was so...cool."

"Who?"

"I had a wife," said Riven. "My Lavascape girlfriend....I miss her...terribly." He paused and Jared wondered if the conversation was over, then he continued. "When I think of what happened, it makes me crazy with hate. I will have revenge!" His voice was like acid. "When the humans and their allies attacked my village, they were ruthless. They came without warning. They didn't fight fair; they have no honour. They were inhumane!

"They barged into huts and smiled at the fear in the women's eyes. They killed everyone in their path. She was in their path." Riven bit his quivering lip.

"That's awful," stammered Jared. Riven was taking the game so...literally...like someone was really hurt. He was actually mourning the loss of his goblin wife! Jared had compassion but also awe over how deep he was into Lavascape.

"I thought she'd sign up and start over and I'd see her again before too long, but it's been over a week." He took a deep breath. "We're almost there. Follow me."

The goblin adjusted the bow slung over his shoulder. The foliage seemed to close in on them as they traveled. Tree branches, thick with leaves, almost obscured the sky overhead. Finally, the brush grew thinner and the sky seemed to expand.

Then, there it was: the view from his vision. "Shark's teeth," said Jared.

"Look," said the goblin. Down an embankment was the shore and floating a short distance into the churning lava was a ship. "The ferryman is here. He's the only one who can cross the lava."

"I see the boat but I don't see him," said Kentucky.

"He's there if the ferry is," said Riven.

"Then what're we waiting for?" asked Jared. He sidestepped his guide and hurried to the slope.

"Wait!" yelled Riven, but Jared was already slipping and then tumbling down the hill.

Chapter Twenty

Jared turned down the hallway at school and saw Colton at the other end with his left fist filled with the front of a white cotton t-shirt, and in that stretched t-shirt was Terrance. They both looked Jared's way as Colton dragged him into the boys' bathroom. Crap, this wasn't good.

Jared hesitated. He could turn away, let Terrance take his punishment, and maybe be safe walking through the halls of this school or he could report Colton to the nearest teacher and have to look over his shoulder every minute for the rest of his life.

Jared made his way to the bathroom door and listened. He heard an 'oomph' as Terrance's body took a blow. What could he do? He could walk right in to the principal's office and say, "Hey, you know that grungy bathroom by the drama room…well it's going to have a ghost haunting it if you don't get down there and stop a murder. And then can I have a body guard or I'll be the next ghoul to haunt that place."

Jared heard a noise that could only be a punch to the stomach. Surely, one of the teachers heard that and would come running to see what was going on. No one came. Then he heard more banging and realized that some of it was coming from the drama room. These teachers probably heard all sorts of noises that would cause alarm in any other part of the school, but were common place here. No one else would come to the rescue. If Terrance was going to get any help, it was going to have to come from him.

'He's not even that good a friend,' whispered a voice in his mind. 'Are you going to get yourself killed sticking up for this guy?'

When was a friend a good friend and when did you go out on a limb for him? How long did you have to hang out together? How many plates of fries did you have to share? "None," whispered Jared. "He's my friend and I have to do something."

Jared pushed hard against the rusty door. This bathroom seemed to have existed much longer than the rest of the school. The white sheath around the pipes was covered in graffiti and all the stalls but one had missing doors. The urinals looked as though they might fall off the wall at any moment. Today he didn't notice any of these things, however. He faced a much more frightening sight.

Colton Barnes.

Colton looked as huge as the giants of Lavascape and dripping with as much hostility. A moment of fear passed through Colton's dark, mean eyes when the door opened, but that disappeared when he saw who the intruder was... Jared! Terrance was on the floor now and a big goose egg was starting to form on the left side of his forehead. Colton let go of Terrance and lunged at Jared but Jared ducked into the stall and locked the door.

Colton kicked the door twice and Jared couldn't breathe as he stared at the old lock praying it would hold. "Gotta come out sometime," laughed Colton. Jared looked through the crack around the door. Colton turned back to Terrance who was on his feet. Colton's hands clamped on his arms like a vice. Terrance kicked but Colton jabbed him hard in the left arm.

Terrance swung and connected with Colton's jaw. With a movement so quick Jared wasn't sure he really saw it, Colton bounced his fist into Terrance's face. The result made the movement undeniably real. Terrance's lip split and blood ran down his chin.

Jared looked away. The graffiti around the pipes from days gone by caught his eye. 'Frank was here' was ancient. Some Neanderthal with a knife had carved MK into the material seven feet up. *Maggie is hot* was more recent and covered fainter declarations from earlier times. An artistic depiction above praise for Maggie held Jared's focus, however. It was the classic hangman game with the caption *Kilroy was here* printed over it. An arrow pointed to the hung stick figure identifying him as *Roy*. Someone else had added. *Who cares? We never liked him anyway.* A shiver ran up Jared's spine.

The lights flicked like a strobe light at a dance. It gave a disjointed, unreal feeling to the scene. The tiles on the floor were scuffed up brown and who could say the last time they'd been cleaned well? The swish of a janitor's grey mop couldn't touch this filth. The real sign of neglect was the grunge that held the tiles together. The place smelled like rust, plus the sweet acrid smell of blood and fear. Jared's eyes moved from the floor and he pushed the bile that was climbing his throat back down. He had to do something. He snatched up the end of the toilet paper roll and began to unravel it.

"You thought you were so clever," Colton said to Terrance. "You dug up your sissy guitar and sang your stupid cowboy song. Everyone must have felt sorry for you, 'cause they didn't laugh you off the stage. Big man, aren't ya!" There was the sound of another punch. Colton chuckled. "Power is everything."

Jared had a huge pile of toilet paper in his hands. He dipped it into the toilet water and arranged it on his right hand. The sodden fibers clung to him. There was a cowardly force encroaching on his mind that wanted him to stop, for-heaven-sakes-stop, and imagine what lay down the road if he continued on this course. A greater force shone from deeper inside, however. Compassion and courage bubbled up as though fed by an underground stream, a geyser stronger than fear. Jared flung the stall door open. There was Colton standing next to Terrance, hefty and intimidating. Jared stepped forward and, with a windmill swing, he launched his soggy weapon. It smacked into the side of Colton's face, a white cow patty molded to his cheek. Small splatters were in his hair and across his forehead. For a moment there was only surprise in his eyes. He released Terrance and clawed the goo from his face.

Terrance wasted no time backing away from his attacker and he and Jared ran out of the bathroom. Instead of going back to their classes, they exited the nearest door. It was probably the dumbest thing to do. That's just what Colton would want...to get a hold of them off school property. Colton didn't follow, however.

They stopped under the bleachers at the football field. Terrance sat cross-legged and Jared followed. "Wow, you're lip's still bleeding hard," said Jared.

Terrance touched it with his index finger. "I kind of forgot about that one. I was thinking about my forehead." He used the bottom of his shirt to blot his lip. "Thanks for coming to help."

"I'm scum for taking so long. Don't thank me." Jared couldn't look at Terrance's face, bloody and swollen, so he looked at the sky. You could get lost in the sky; forget about terrorizing bullies and girls with pretty eyes and parents with problems...but only for a moment. Jared was soon fully back under the bleachers with a kid who was bleeding all over his t-shirt. "Did he punch your forehead?"

Terrance shook his head. "No. He banged it into the sink. For a second I thought the sink was going to come right off the wall."

They sat in silence for a minute then Terrance continued, "He's the biggest jerk. I hate guys like that. Where's their conscience? How do they turn off their humanity like a tap?"

"I don't know." Jared thought of his own decency faucet. Could he have shut it off, turned away and left Terrance to his bloody fate? He stole his guitar and handed it over to that scum. He envisioned the tap like the one on his kitchen sink, a lever you pulled up and swivelled for hot and cold. He would never again be that heartless, spineless guy who could turn his off. He imagined lifting a huge rock high above his head with two hands and bringing it down on the silver lever, snapping it off and letting the waters flow freely.

"I would've been scared to come, too," said Terrance. "Colton Barnes scares the crap out of me."

"Me too," said Jared.

Terrance touched the bump that was now a ping-pong ball above his eyebrow and winced. "How's my eye look?"

"You'll have a shiner tomorrow. But, that bump on your head is going to be legendary."

"I feel like my brain is pulsing like some creature out of a horror film, ready to break out and fend for itself."

The two boys laughed but Terrance cut his short with a wince and a hand placed gingerly to his stomach. Terrance got to his feet and Jared followed. "You should get to your last class so you don't get written up. I'm going to head home."

"Then you'll be written up."

"Better that than have the teachers know I've been fighting."

"You weren't fighting. Colton was whaling on you. That's not fighting."

"Hold on a minute. If anybody asks, tell them I was fighting," corrected Terrance. "Don't you dare say otherwise. I've gotta hold on to some pride, no matter how small."

"You've got nothing to be ashamed of."

'Tis better to have fought and lost than never to have fought back at all.'"

"How poetic," said Jared, awkwardly shuffling his feet.

"Go on, get to class."

"Maybe I should help you get home."

"I'm fine. Don't treat me like a loser!"

"Okay." He admired Terrance. He didn't want pity or even sympathy—just to be treated with respect.

As Terrance walked away, Jared noticed there was a slight limp in his step, compliments of Colton, no doubt—that scum-sucking pig. He wiped his hand on his jeans for about the tenth time. He had the heebie geebies, big time. There was toilet water on his hands, and in any bathroom that would be gross; in the forgotten drama room bathroom, which may not have been cleaned since 1973, he could have enough germs in one spot to cause an epidemic.

Jared entered the school. The vice-principal, a woman with round features, saw him and walked toward him. "What are you doing out of class?"

"Well... I went to the washroom."

"I saw you come in the outside door. Nice try."

"There was a fight in the bathroom."

"So, you peed outside?"

Jared gaped. Was the administration allowed to say 'peed'?

"You think it's fine to walk the halls during class?" the middle-aged woman continued. "That shows a lack of respect for both your teachers and other students. Do you think it's polite to disturb other students?"

She hadn't asked anything about the fight in the bathroom. "Glad you are so concerned with polite behaviour. We wouldn't want one student *impolite* to the others."

"You don't need to speak in that tone."

"Whatever!" He started to walk away.

"I think we better see you at detention this afternoon."

"What a joke," he muttered. Jared went to class and made a mental note not to touch anything except perhaps bullies...until he got himself to some Lysol.

Chapter Twenty-One

"Whoa, save some for the rest of us," said Barry at the troll feast.

"I can't help it," said Jared. He'd gorged himself on the mushrooms today and it still seemed he couldn't get enough.

"I know we're trolls, but hey, learn some manners."

"You snooze, you lose," he said, grabbing the last mushroom from the platter.

"What's your hurry?"

"New people to meet."

"What new people?"

"I kind of fell into their laps—hard enough to knock the wind out of me before I exited. Later."

As soon as Jared left the feast, a vision greeted him.

"How is my peace-loving little fiancé today?" said Antonio.

She sat on the edge of her bed, silent. He waited for the guard to close the door to Sparket's cell before he continued. "Ready to make a deal? Ready to see reason? Ready to make a difference in Lavascape?" She shook her head, but before she could speak he put his palm in her face. "Before you give me your pat answer, there're a few things you should think about." He lowered his hand.

"What? How fun it would be to rule the world?"

"How good it would be to have a say in how brutal this war gets? Without your restraining hand, there would be nothing to stop me from conquering the way we did the goblin villages. "

Sparket stood. The dent in her little cot remained in the thin mattress after she rose. "You'll spare the conquered people—the conquered creatures—if I hand over my kingdom to you?"

"Hand over your kingdom? That makes it sound like blackmail. I'm not talking about anything so base. We'll be merging our kingdoms, Sparket. Joining them through marriage—and all our people will rejoice with us."

"And then follow you into battle."

"But it will be a more humane battle, a kinder victory."

"My husband—the kind conqueror."

"Now you're getting it. You have the ability to save hundreds of lives, from people to giants to elves and everything else."

Sparket paced the small room. She said nothing, but paced from one side to the other and back again three times. *She is always thinking,* thought Jared, *always planning, always weighing things out. She's clever.*

Finally, Sparket stopped in front of Antonio. She looked ready to embrace him, but she didn't. "If I could believe the things you've said, I would consider joining with you. But I can't trust you."

She poked her finger into his gut. "I was a fool to even consider it. You are a murderer. And it's not because of how many lives you took in battle, but what I can see inside your heart. You delight in killing. You will resort to killing me if you don't get your way. Murder is just another way to get what you want. I won't have any influence over your battle plans; I won't save the lives of the creatures of Lavascape. All that would happen is I'd hand over my armies to your command and then you'd be unstoppable in this world."

Antonio closed the small gap between them. Their noses were almost touching. "I'll be unstoppable anyway. Your cooperation simply means I don't invade your land. They will be subject to me, eventually. Your way, there will be fewer of them still alive to fight for me." Sparket stepped back. Then he was gone.

The vision began to clear and Jared had the thought, *Colton was right: power is everything.*

Faces came into focus in the air above him. He was lying on his back in a clearing by the shore. Trolls and goblins, all holding torches, were looking down on him with angry eyes. Not only angry, but worried, panic-stricken even... but the ruling emotion was mistrust.

"Is he part of your council?" asked one of the goblins.

"I don't know him," said a troll with an emerald green fohawk.

"How much did you hear," demanded a goblin with a razor sharp nose. He jabbed his torch toward Jared.

All Jared could think of was the vision he'd had. Should he tell this strange little band of creatures about his quest? "I don't know," said Jared.

'I don't know' wasn't the right thing to say. The creatures pulled him to his feet and pushed him toward three thatched roof huts, two small ones on either side of a larger one, all about a hundred yards from the shore.

"Wait," came Riven's voice.

The mob of creatures didn't falter but jostled Jared onward. In front of the center hut was a troll in stocks, his head and wrists protruding from the wooden device. His blue fohawk was all Jared saw at first but then he looked up. "Hey Troll. I know you. Tell them you know me. I'm not a traitor. I wasn't going to give anyone their battle information. I'm a troll. You can trust me."

"Do you know this troll?" asked the troll who seemed to be the leader of this band.

Perhaps a word from him would free this poor creature. But who was he? Was he someone Jared had met at troll training? He didn't think so. There was no information from his eyes.

No, he was sure he didn't know him. And someone locked in stocks was not the sort of company he wanted to claim as he was being led forward by a suspicious mob.

"No," said Jared. "I don't know him."

"But he does know us," Kentucky said, pointing at Jared. Kentucky and Riven had come down the hill and just now caught up with the mob.

"Is this true?" the same emerald-fohawk troll asked Jared.

"Yes, they're my companions. I have a quest."

"Well then..." said the troll, and the mob grabbed hold of Kentucky and Riven, too. While they moved forward, a group of trolls and goblins brought another set of stocks forward and pounded it into the ground next to the lying troll.

The prisoner sneered at Jared. "You should have stuck up for me. Now you'll join me, instead." He laughed and his crazed laughter followed them into the hut.

Jared was amazed at the dimensions inside the hut. It was huge inside. The round ceiling made him feel like he was in a cathedral. There were smaller rooms along the sides. Some were standing open and Jared could see chains on the walls. A shiver ran up his spine.

"Let the trial preliminaries begin," intoned the emerald-fohawk troll. Was he the king?

Jared couldn't face the trial that day. He left the game and went to bed. He hoped he'd miss it and would show up tomorrow with everything worked out.

As he drifted off to sleep he murmured, "Lavascape doesn't work that way."

"You have detention, again?" asked Monty, at school the next day. "Yesterday wasn't your fault, with Colton and Terrance; I know you had to do something, but what happened today?"

"Math's what happened."

"Math?"

"Yeah, I stuck up my hand and said, *The problem with math is we all have to find the same answer. Someone already knows the answer—ask me to think up something original. Really! It's so stupid.*"

"And?" said Monty.

"Well, I didn't leave it at that and kept chirping a bit more, and refused to go to the office, and..."

"Hence, detention," said Monty.

"School lacks practicality in life—contrary to troll training which is crossing over quite nicely."

Monty shook his head. "Another opinion you might want to keep to yourself."

Chapter Twenty-Two

Later that night, the group of friends gathered at Monty's house. They were in the basement family room that looked like it was frozen in 1975, wood panelling and geometric indoor-outdoor carpeting. Jared ran his fingers over the tops of his ears. He'd used Melissa's cream hair remover again when the stubble started to come back and he was presently praying his hair would grow over his ears soon so he could stop grooming a part of his body he'd never thought about before.

Katie said, "Do you care about people or just trolls and goblins?" She leaned back on the sofa and folded her arms briskly.

"Sparket's a human," Jared said.

Katie rolled her eyes. "Yeah, she's all you've been talking about for weeks. So, are you going to try to meet her in real life?"

"Lavascape is real."

"It sounds like you really have a thing for her."

"I do have a thing...it's called a quest."

Katie snapped up several pretzels and crunched them loudly.

Anna folded her arms and said, "You are far too involved in this game. It's taking over your life. It's all you do!" There were unspoken undertones. Would she ever forgive him for the Homecoming Dance? At least they spoke now. "Quit altogether, that would be best."

"It wouldn't be so great for Sparket."

"Sparket sounds hot," said Monty."

"She's the only girl for me," said Jared, laughing.

"Wonderful", Katie groaned. "I hope you'll be very happy together."

"Really hot," repeated Monty.

"What about me?" asked Terrance.

"Yes, you're very hot," said Monty, rolling his eyes.

"No. I mean, aren't I human? Jared helped me."

Katie licked her fingers and chuckled. "Okay, you have a point. He sometimes cares about humans." She took a rippled potato chip and sank it into the bowl of dip. Jared noticed red marks around Katie's wrists.

"How did you get that?" he asked.

"I must be allergic to the metal in the bracelets I was wearing earlier."

"Oh." He didn't remember seeing her with bracelets on.

"You were great, Jared," said Monty.

"Yeah," admitted Anna.

Terrance laughed. "That was the biggest, gooiest spit ball

I've ever seen in my life. And in fifth grade I made some pretty impressive ones."

"I wish I'd had enough spit," said Jared popping a chip in his mouth and continuing to speak with his mouth full. "But honestly my mouth was bone dry. Lucky there was a full toilet bowl right at my feet."

"Eww, do you have to remind us of that part?" said Anna.

"I want you to know, I'd stick my hand in a grungy toilet for any one of you guys." Jared laughed, feeling very troll, very I'll-do-the-dirty-work like.

Monty pulled cans of soda pop from a plastic ring and handed them to his guests. When he had his open, he raised it in the air. "Here's to Jared," he said.

The rest of the group raised their cans. The toast was followed by gulps and root beer burps from all three boys.

Anna giggled, then proclaimed their immense immaturity for a good five minutes afterwards.

Monty opened a packet of pictures and laid them out on the table. "Shots from the dance that didn't make the paper," he explained. In one, Colton's pants were covered in mud. He had a look of distain on his face. They passed the pictures around.

"What's with this one?" asked Katie. "Jared, is that you talking to Colton?"

"Did you have to bring that up?" Jared's voice grew loud as he felt a surge of aggression. "Is it too much to ask for your friends to understand you might have been bullied into something stupid?" He smashed his hand down on the coffee table. The girls jumped. Katie's eyes seemed twice their normal size.

"Sorry. Just acting like a troll."

"How do you *act* that way without *being* that way?" asked Katie.

Another wave of anger rolled over him. *Down Troll*, he said to himself. "Sorry," he said aloud, carefully moderating his voice. "I wish you hadn't reminded me, is all. Now I feel like an even bigger jerk, since you toasted me." He swallowed hard. The troll-anger subsided. "I really am sorry about that, Terrance."

"You made up for it," he said, but his lips were a straight line and Jared could see there was still hurt in his eyes.

Pretzels, chips and jube-jubes began to disappear. "The real question," began Katie.

"What real question?" said Monty. "No one mentioned a fake question."

Katie began again, unfazed. "The real question is how we're going to keep Jared alive come Monday morning. Colton Barnes isn't likely to forget he had a toilet water spit ball the size of a baseball blindside him in the face."

Monty chuckled. "Wish I could've seen it..."

Monty's party was a celebration of Terrance's deliverance, but it was also about Jared. He was in danger. "Look," said Katie, "Jared's a dead man if we don't think of something."

"Gee, don't sugar-coat it," said Jared, weakly.

"She's right," said Monty. "You need a plan. You got through today because Colton wasn't at school. "And you'll have the weekend to hide out. Hey, would your parents consider hiring a bodyguard for you?"

"They don't know about it. And I'd like to keep it that way, especially from Mom. I thought of calling Dad at his place but he's never home." Suddenly Jared realized that the room had gone extremely still. Then like a jolt from lightening, he realized why. He hadn't told his friends about his parents' break up. Now he saw surprise and sympathy in their eyes. It's just what he had been afraid of.

"Why didn't you tell us?" Monty dropped the chip he was holding. It landed dip-first on the carpet, but he ignored it.

"How long have they been separated?" asked Katie.

"A while."

"So that's why Melissa has looked so sad lately," said Katie. "I saw her with a friend in the drug store the other day and she really looked...well, just bad."

Jared shrugged. That could be about mom and dad, or her relationship with Cam or maybe even drugs. His friends didn't need to hear any more sob stories today. "Hey, people's parents get divorced every day. It's no big deal." Jared had said this to himself so many times he was beginning to believe it.

No one said anything. They all knew it was a lie, deep down, even Jared. It was a big deal, it was a huge deal, it was the biggest deal in the world; aside from the fact he may get beat to death the next time he saw Colton Barnes.

"Your dad is coaching my brother's club basketball team," said Monty.

Jared nodded. It was news to him.

Katie's eyes were the only unreadable ones in the group. Instead, however, she seemed to read Jared's. "No one is going to hire a bodyguard," said Katie, "so we better think of something better than that." Jared gave her a thankful smile for changing the subject, and she returned it with her eyes.

With her eyes? Jared was so surprised his mouth actually dropped. Katie's eyes were the hardest to read. The Retina Reading in real life was a phenomenon he was getting used to, but he was also used to not seeing as much in Katie's. This was different. She had voluntarily sent him a smile through her eyes. He was struck by it, but before he could ponder this new mystery, Monty brought him back to the Colton problem.

"Think people, what can we do?" said Monty.

"He could tell Principal Hayes what happened," suggested Anna.

Jared's shoes pinched his toes. He took them off and stretched his over-sized troll feet. The toes seemed unusually wide.

"I'll make a list," suggested Katie. "Just brainstorm." Katie grabbed a sheet of paper out of the nearby computer printer and a pencil from a mug next to the monitor and wrote as she and her friends thought out loud:

Tell Principal Hayes.

Pretend to be blind and go to school with an attack dog posing as a guide dog.

Always have someone with him.

Bribe Colton with candy, money, or homework services to leave Jared alone.

Hire a taxi to pick him up and take him to school.

Buy dog spray to use in an attack.

Buy Raid to rid the world of insects like Colton.

Never go to the bathroom at school.

Volunteer to head an anti-bullying campaign.

Get Colton a girlfriend and give her a good strong leash.

By the time they finished their list, they'd laughed a lot and eaten every last bit of food, including the remnants of the dip that Jared scooped off the bottom of the container with his finger.

"Alright," said Katie examining the list. "What do you guys think would actually work?"

"I don't know if I really believe it would work, but the anti-bullying campaign has potential," said Terrance. "Everyone knows it goes on but no one wants to get involved. They're afraid they'll be the next target. If Jared took that view, I'd look a heck of a lot worse than I do right now." He lifted his sandy-coloured bangs to let them have a good look at the huge purple and black bump above his eye.

"I think we should make sure Jared is never alone," said Anna. "Colton won't bother him, especially if he's with a girl." She looked at him from under her eyelashes. Was she flirting? Did this mean she forgave him for the dance fiasco?

He ran his fingers through his hair. He felt stubble on his ears. Man! Not already! That hair remover stuff was garbage. He pulled on the hair above his ears, willing it to cover better. Jared looked at Anna again. She was still beautiful, of course, but for some reason she seemed less appealing to him.

"She's got a good point," said Katie, somewhat reluctantly. "I'll take turns, too." She kept her head down and eyes on the paper.

Jared noticed Katie's bangs in her eyes and the flush in her cheeks. He was so captivated by the little dark line of her eyeliner that he agreed without thinking. He'd just agreed to be escorted around like a six year old!

Monty added. "That may help with the immediate situation but I think Terrance is right. We need an anti-bullying movement. These guys need to understand, no one thinks they're cool, and no one's going to let them get away with this."

"It's not just guys, girls bully, too," said Katie. "They do it with nasty rumours, turning your friends against you, laughing at your clothes, and making you look dumb. Sometimes they send mean messages to your e-mail or Facebook account and stuff like that. Girls can be just as cruel."

"Fair enough. But we need to think about Colton first," said Jared. "I could take mean e-mails a lot easier than his fist. What if I have to go to the bathroom during a class where you guys aren't with me?"

"Don't go during class," said Monty. "Go at lunch time when there's lots of people coming and going. And stay out of the drama room one, it's always empty and it's scary at the best of times."

"I'll be available after school..." began Anna.

Katie cut her off, "Yeah, okay, we got it."

They worked out Jared's schedule and who would be with him when. "I feel like I need a babysitter," Jared complained.

"Think of me as your bodyguard," said Katie.

"Gee, I feel worlds better. I have a bodyguard three inches shorter than me who has no fighting skill but does have seventeen layers of pretty nail polish on her fingernails. "

"For strength," said Katie brandishing her nails like a claw.

Chapter Twenty-Three

It was a thirty-five-minute bike ride to the gym, much of it up hill, so Jared was sweaty along with angry by the time he got there. The sound of basketballs hitting the hardwood echoed through the gym. Jared eased in and sat in the bleachers. There were only two parents in the seats. It was just a practice.

There was Dad. He held a clipboard and drew out a play or a drill for these younger boys. Jared hadn't seen him for over two weeks, but here were a bunch of boys he had made time to coach. He watched for fifteen minutes. His dad got right in with the boys, showed them how to dribble around a defender, demonstrated the best shooting form. Jared couldn't take it any longer. Every part of him seemed to ache from the inside out. He glared at Dad and then sprinted from the gym.

Jared bent over the porcelain water fountain on the wall. He drank in gulps.

Dad was behind him, holding the clipboard to his chest, when Jared turned around. "How are you?" Dad asked.

Jared wanted to scream. Instead he hissed, "Where were you when I was learning to play basketball?" Then he read it in his dad's eyes: he thinks he can start over with kids he hasn't hurt yet.

"There's a big contract up for grabs and one of the most influential members of the board asked if I would help him coach. I just finished the coaching clinic. Jared—."

He didn't want to hear (or read) anything else. He turned his back on his father, and strode out of the school. Then he raced his bike toward the comfort of his room and the escape waiting for him on the Internet.

As he burst into the house, he almost ran into Melissa sitting on the bottom step that led to his room. "Hey," she said, raising her head from her folded arms resting on her knees. "Did you go jogging?"

"Bike." He stepped around her and took the stairs two at a time.

"Jared?"

He stopped at the top and looked down at her. "What?"

Her eyes looked especially round. "Do you want to play the racing game?"

"You should join Lavascape. It's so much better." When she didn't answer, he went on, "Be a troll, they're the best." Finally, she nodded and Jared rushed to his room.

Jared made it to the last few minutes of the feast. "How's it going?" he asked Barry, approaching the table far from the adventurers.

"Okay. I'm about done though."

Jared sat beside him anyway. "What are you planning today? Did you get the table hockey game for the hut?"

"Look Jared. We got along great when we were hut mates but..."

"But what?"

"Well, some of the other villagers aren't too happy we still hang out at the feast every day."

"That's stupid. Who cares?"

"They're starting to drop me from the group-play games. I can't find teams to take me. They're afraid I might take off on an adventure with you half-way through the tournament."

"Oh."

"Maybe we shouldn't hang out all the time."

"Yeah. Fine."

Barry got up and left the table without another word. Jared finished his meal alone. Then he went to the portals and was back in the hut near the lava sea.

Amidst the crowds in the spacious hall of the center hut, the emerald-fohawk troll and the goblin in the cloak stood to the left side and conversed. Jared strained to hear them. "He ran away. He's scared: he must be guilty," said the goblin, his nose even sharper than Jared remembered.

"We won't know until we interrogate," said the troll.

"Indeed," said the goblin.

Jared felt weak, sensing he was standing before the king. Where were Kentucky and Riven? He was surrounded by six other trolls dressed as soldiers, each with a sword at his side, like the one Jared possessed. But they had other weapons, including long spears that were presently all pointed at Jared's heart.

"All hail, the kings of the alliance," said a goblin in a gold tunic. A cheer arose as the two kings moved to the front of the hut and sat in thrones with identical gold waves and lightning bolts on tall back rests that rose a foot above their heads. A row of red jewels, each as big as a fist, adorned the top curve of the thrones. The arm rests were also gold, but a thick red pad on each made for a comfortable-looking position from which they could decree those to be placed in stocks, those chained in the side rooms, and those to go free. The troll's throne had smaller replicas of the training zone hourglass holding up the armrests while the goblin's had bows and arrows in dazzling metals doing the same job.

The troll raised his left hand and made a circular motion. The guards in front of him shifted to give him a clear view of the kings.

"What is your name?" asked the troll king.

"Jerry."

"Who desires the information you've come for?"

"What information?"

"Answer the question!"

"Just me," said Jared. "Well, and the scurry and goblin with me."

"What will you do with it?"

"My quest is to save the princess, Sparket."

"What is your role in the war?" asked the troll.

"Nothing."

The troll leader rose. He seemed displeased with Jared's answers. "Really? Have you declared your citizenship?"

"What? I don't know what that means," said Jared. "Was I supposed to do that when I filled out the questionnaire?"

"One's "citizenship" is the alliance one makes sometime in the Lavascape adventure. It is your declaration of where your loyalties lie. More and more creatures change their stripes. Did you complete your troll training?"

"Mostly," said Jared, suddenly not sure of anything in the presence of this awesome leader. "I received the gold level."

"Have you been recruited by any other group?"

"What do you mean?"

"Stop playing dumb!" snapped the king of the trolls. He was obviously agitated and the time for explaining things nicely appeared to be over. Somehow, Jared had given him the impression that he was being difficult. "Are you working with anyone to overthrow our civilization? Are you true to the trolls?"

"Of course I'm not trying to overthrow your civilization. I told you. All I'm interested in is saving Sparket, she's a princess..."

"A human princess?"

"Yes, that's right."

"Antonio."

"What?"

"Have you met anyone in Lavascape named—Antonio?"

"No." It was the name of Sparket's prince and captor but Jared had never actually met him. That wasn't a lie, was it?

"Do you know what meeting you interrupted?"

"No," said Jared. "I didn't hear anything." The king arose and came toward Jared. All the spears still pointing at him came an inch closer. "When you were asked if you heard anything you said, 'I don't know.' That's not the same as 'no', is it?"

Jared didn't know how to get out of this. They weren't going to believe him. Would they lock him in the stocks where he'd rot away while Sparket needed him?

The king stopped in front of Jared. "You've been caught in one lie. Where there's one, there's bound to be others."

"I'm not lying."

"You interrupted a war council, a secret strategy meeting. That's not the sort of thing a leader can overlook. You are an unknown troll claiming to have a quest intricately involved in the war, but not actually part of it. You can see my dilemma."

"Here's a war strategy for you, fight your enemies not your friends."

The king was quiet while he stared at Jared. "Trolls don't read each other as well as they do others. It's such a pity when it comes to interrogation. Take him away."

At spear point, Jared was herded into one of the stone rooms with chains imbedded in the wall. There, his arms and his ankles were shackled. The door closed with a metallic bang and he was alone.

The next day, Jared heard the king's voice on the other side of his cell. "Bring the goblin again."

Jared heard footsteps.

He tried to struggle free but it did no good. What was going on in the throne room? Was Riven going to help or hurt things?

Concentrating on his troll hearing, Jared could just make out what they were saying beyond the metal door. The goblin leader had taken over the interrogation.

He heard Riven's voice. "I have plenty against the human. Antonio is the reason my village was destroyed; I want revenge." So it was a personal vendetta against this particular human. Of course! That's why Riven was so interested in Jared's quest and had joined them so quickly.

Kentucky's interrogation included bribery, underhanded deals to try to get him to change his alliance, and threats. Then the guard returned and dragged Jared out of the room, jolting him to standing position as he came before the emerald-haired troll again. Riven and Kentucky were already standing before the throne.

"We need to be sure of your loyalty," said the troll king.

"It doesn't exactly build loyalty in your subjects to chain them to the nearest wall," said Jared.

"We know you've heard of Antonio, Jerry. He captured your Sparket." The king paused and let the force of the concealed information settle. "Antonio, the human, is gathering dissenters from among all the other creatures. Even if you had citizenship, we'd be suspicious of your intentions after the lies. As it is, you have no citizenship card, nothing to reassure us but a claim to a noble quest. If you want to leave this compound and gain access to the ferryman, you must accept a mission to prove your devotions."

"But what about the princess? She needs my help!" Jared burst out.

"Help her by doing what's necessary to move on in your quest."

"Very understanding," said Jared. "What do we have to do?"

Chapter Twenty-Four

More disturbing than cheap-shot punches in the gut, more ignorant than bestowing a nickname that had half the grade believing he picked his nose, Jared's worst Colton Barnes moment occurred in the cafeteria. Colton sat next to Melissa and she actually talked to him. Melissa's red watery eyes and blank stare were focused on the worst person in the world.

"This is crazy," Jared hissed to Monty. "How can they be talking?"

"Doesn't she know—?"

"I haven't told her, but can't she see the kind of guy he is?" Jared strained his ears to hear them.

"Cam doesn't like me, anymore," said Melissa. "He says I'm letting myself go. He says I'm too clingy, a blood-sucker. But..." She shrugged her bony shoulders.

"I heard him," said Colton. "My sister married a jerk.

Don't hang out with a jerk." Colton was hardly a good judge of what did and didn't make someone a jerk!

They lowered their voices after that and Jared couldn't hear. Colton said something, and Melissa shrugged and smiled. He chuckled and placed his hand on her arm. Jared clutched the side of the lunch table.

In the hallway after lunch period, Colton came up behind Jared and purred, "You know you're dead meat, right?"

"I think I'm kicking around pretty lively," said Jared "And you can stay away from my sister; the last thing she needs is a Neanderthal like you."

"Are you going to protect her from me, Picky?"

"Yeah. I will."

"You see, that's the problem. The little wimpy guys are the ones that end up protecting the girls. And, they're terrible at it. They get mowed over and the girl is left to get hurt, knocked around, busted up."

Jared's throat went dry. Was Colton threatening Melissa?

"And then what becomes of her?" Colton continued. "She's a cripple. Knife wounds and she's still with him."

What? Who was Colton talking about? Who got knife wounds and became crippled? And who was too weak to help her? Then Jared remembered Colton's words to Melissa. 'My sister married a jerk.' Did he hurt her? No, but he hadn't protected her. It all came together.

"Your sister got mugged." It wasn't a question.

"Yeah, with her loser husband right there. He went down after one punch. And she fought for her purse. Stupid purse with eighty seven dollars and a pack of gum in it."

Jared was speechless.

"He's so weak; he's such a jerk."

Did weak equal jerk? Suddenly, Colton's big hands were

on Jared's chest and he shoved him up against a locker. It was so fast that Jared couldn't brace himself. His head flung back against the unforgiving metal. He saw stars swim before his eyes.

"There's no excuse for being weak," growled Colton. He curled his right hand into a fist and gave Jared a jarring jab to the kidney. Then he made a noise like he was disgusted with Jared's absorption of the punch and he walked away, mumbling "You gotta protect the weak."

Later that evening, Jared postponed Lavascape to be with Melissa. She didn't want to join Lavascape; but wanted to race. The racing games were so lame next to Lavascape but they had settled into their beanbag chairs and he had hopes they'd have fun. His hopes were dashed by Melissa's attitude.

"You weren't even trying," said Jared, at the end of a race.

"So what?" Melissa had changed into her pyjamas right after school and to look at her now, lying on a beanbag chair with her hair mussed up, you'd think she just rolled out of bed.

"So? You used to come close to beating me...at least."

"Close?" Melissa's voice was a low monotone. "I used to beat you."

"Well you sure got out of practice quick."

Melissa pushed the game controller away from her. "Play against the computer. I'll watch. I have no coordination."

Jared stared at his sister. "You're going to pout, because you lost?"

She pulled a blanket off the couch and curled up in the beanbag chair with it. Jared continued playing with Melissa just looking on, because it was almost like doing something together. His heart wasn't in it though because the lure of

Lavascape was strong. Why play a racing game when you could be in Lavascape? To help your sister get out of a funk, that's why. At least, that had been his motivation when he asked her to play. She always said she was tired now, and then complained that she couldn't sleep at night. Jared had tried to remind her of the things she had liked to do before Cam came along. It hadn't worked in the slightest.

"I saw you talking to Colton today."

"Yeah. Nice guy."

"You must be joking."

"Why? He was nice. He listened and had some good advice."

Jared took a breath. It was like they were talking about two different people.

"He's in my grade, you know?"

"Yeah, he'd be a little young for me, but..."

"But nothing!"

Melissa pursed her lips together, a sure sign she wouldn't say any more about Colton tonight.

"I haven't seen Karen for a while," said Jared referring to Melissa's best friend. "What's she up to tonight?"

"I dunno."

"So, why don't you do something with your friends?"

"Why aren't you out with yours? You're starting to get on my nerves."

"Monty's parents offered to give us a ride home. That's a pretty strong hint they wanted us to break it up. What's your excuse?"

"I don't have friends anymore. They're gone, Dad's gone, and Mom's basically gone. I want Cam back."

"What drugs are you taking?"

"Nothing!"

"Really?"

"Yes, really!"

She wasn't going to tell him anything. "Do we have any ice cream? "asked Jared. If there was one thing that would cheer Melissa up it was rocky road ice cream.

"I dunno," she grunted. "I'm not hungry. And Mom never goes shopping anyway."

Jared searched the deepfreeze. "There's chocolate fudge," he said, returning to the family room.

Melissa shrugged and dragged the blanket up the stairs. "Goin' to bed," she said. She tripped and fell against the wall. Giggling, she gathered the blanket around her and continued.

Jared went to his room too, but not to go to bed. It was as though he had a Lavascape radar that was picking up a progressively stronger signal, calling to him until he could ignore it no longer.

As soon as he logged on, he heard from both Kentucky and Riven. "Where have you been? We can't leave without you," said Riven.

And, "The council has given us our mission. Let's get going," said Kentucky.

Jared fell into step with his companions and asked, "What are we doing? Somebody bring me up to speed."

"Several trolls and goblins were taken prisoner by the giants: the elves could be in on it too, but they are sure the giants are calling the shots. We need to find the prisoners and rescue them," said Riven.

Jared rolled his eyes at that. Back to the giants' cave? They were lucky to have escaped with their lives the last time they met up with them. Now they were heading back into the danger just to prove they weren't traitors.

"Wonderful," he said.

"Do you remember how to get to the waterfall?" asked Kentucky. "I think I remember but I'm going to need your help to find it."

"When I was running for my life, I didn't exactly take time to look for landmarks! This is crazy! Even if we do find it, how are we going to free the prisoners?"

"We have weapons," said Riven.

Jared looked at the goblin and noticed he was carrying a large brown sack over his shoulder. He looked like a ghastly imitation of Santa Claus. *Presents all around, swords and bows for all the good little kids,* thought Jared.

"When we free them, they'll be able to fight with us," Kentucky explained.

"How are we going to free them?"

"He told me about your escape from the giants," said Riven. "Kentucky, do you think you'll be able to pull your lock-picking trick again?"

"It'll be a cinch."

They climbed the hill where Jared had made his abrupt entrance into the war meeting and then picked their way through the trees. They walked for what seemed to be hours, and may have actually been so: time in Lavascape was a strange thing—sometimes seeming to flash by and other times occurring at real life speed.

They wandered east and then backtracked to the west. They were lost.

"I thought you knew these forests so totally well," said Kentucky to Riven. "You've been here so freaking long, remember?"

"I haven't been in giant territory much, you stinky rat!"

"Do you remember that boulder?" asked Jared, trying to refocus their attention on the job at hand.

"He should," said Kentucky.

"Why don't you touch it and see if you can get any information, instead of giving your snide comments?" Riven complained.

"Touch it?" said Jared. "Why would he touch it?"

When Kentucky didn't answer, Riven said, "Seriously? You two really are green aren't you? You don't even have your powers figured out!"

"What powers does he have?" asked Jared.

"He should be able to touch an object and know who touched it last."

"You're jerking my leg," accused Kentucky.

"Touch that boulder with both hands and concentrate on the feelings you get from it." He grumbled under his breath, "I didn't know I'd have to turn into a scurry trainer."

Kentucky placed his rodent hands on the boulder and closed his eyes. He stayed in that position for a full minute. Finally, he began to murmur. "Interesting. Oh, cool." Then after another minute of silence he yelled, "I got it!"

"What?" asked Jared.

"It was so wild. The longer I concentrated the clearer the image became. This boulder was last touched by a giant by the name of Stallion."

"That's interesting," said Jared. "You might want to get in the habit of touching things every now and then."

"Neat-o," said Riven sarcastically. "I've never heard of a giant named Stallion, have you?"

"No. But we know that giants have come this way and perhaps we've entered their territory," said Jared.

Riven took a stronger hold on his bow and shifted the bag over his shoulder.

"I'll carry it for a while," suggested Jared, pointing to the bag of weapons.

Riven handed over the sack. Jared held it with his left and his sword in his right. It was strange but his body seemed to brace against the weight.

After they walked for several minutes, Kentucky whispered, "I hear water."

"Yes, I do too," said Jared. "Here's the spot we hid. I was in that tree."

"I'll shape shift and slither up to take a look. You guys wait here."

After he left, Riven said, "I think we should follow him. I'm not sure we can trust him. Scurry can side with anybody."

"This one seems to have sided with us," said Jared, matter-of- factly.

"Yes, that's how it seems," agreed Riven," but they can switch alliances at the drop of a hat, too. Come on. Let's go after him. If he switches to the other side, he'll lead us into a trap."

The goblin was moving stealthily through the trees and Jared was left with no choice but to follow or wait alone. "There he is," said Riven and stopped. The scurry was on the bank of the river, curved unnaturally around a large rock in a way no creature with bones ever could. There were at least five guards on either side of the falls. It could have been a hundred and Jared's despair wouldn't have been any greater. How would they ever get by so many guards?

Kentucky slithered through the tall grass and into the trees where Jared and Riven were hiding. The goblin reached out as Kentucky came by and grabbed him.

"There are guards," said Kentucky when the goblin

released him. "Perhaps I can slip by them at night, but there's so many, I don't think I'll go unnoticed."

When they were back in the clearing, they hid together in the brush and considered their situation. "I think you'll have to use your two-faced nature to get in there," said Riven. "And we'll have to trust that you don't actually turn on us."

"I don't have a two-faced nature," snapped Kentucky.

"Perhaps not you personally...but your kind is known for it."

"If you don't trust me, maybe you can take the risks! You be the one to go in after the prisoners. Or let yourself be captured and help the prisoners from the inside!"

"Hey," said Jared.

"What?" said Kentucky. "He deserves everything I'm saying and more. Have I ever given you a reason to mistrust me?"

Jared thought of the Retina Readings he got from Kentucky. They were muddled: sometimes his loyalty was evident, sometimes he seemed to crave power, but other times it was Kentucky's greed that Jared perceived most strongly. Greed could lead to betrayal. Would Kentucky sell his loyalty to the highest bidder? Jared wasn't sure that his first Lavascape friend would always be true to him. Trusting Kentucky, however, was a risk he apparently needed to take.

That wasn't what was foremost in his mind right now, however. Kentucky had given him an idea.

Chapter Twenty-Five

"Listen to me," began Jared. "I think we can use both of your ideas. You should let yourself be captured, Riven."

"Lovin' it so far," he said, sarcastically.

"Then, with Kentucky acting like he's on their side and you on the inside organizing the other captives, we'll have a good chance of freeing them."

"You seem to be rather absent from your plan," said Riven, dryly.

"I'll take the weapons, cross the river further downstream, and make my way back to the waterfall on the other side. Then, when the time is right, Kentucky and I can get the weapons behind the waterfall, and pass them to you and the prisoners in the cage. He can do his pick-the-lock trick and we'll escape the prisoner camp, fighting our way out if we have to."

"It sounds to me like a good way to get a lot of prisoners

killed," said Riven "—unless Kentucky gets in tight with the giants and they leave him in charge or something."

"That's not likely," said Kentucky. "And if they realize I'm the same scurry that broke out of their jail a while ago, we can say farewell right now, because I'm a goner."

"They don't see well," said Riven. "What if you play your cards right, and little by little build up their trust."

"We don't have time for that!" said Jared. "The princess has until the next full moon. My guess is that's less than a week until her execution. "

"Yes, I suppose there won't be much of a fight over a dead princess." Riven stroked the bridge of his pointed nose.

"Don't be such a jerk!" said Jared under his breath. "She's my friend." Could Jared trust either of his companions? Kentucky the scurry could change alliances, and Riven the goblin was too callus about Sparket's possible death to be completely devoted to her rescue. Jared felt very alone with Kentucky standing on one side of him and Riven crouched on a rock on the other.

"Any other ideas?" asked Kentucky.

They puzzled over the issue until nightfall but didn't think of another workable plan.

"I'm off to join the enemy," declared Kentucky.

"And I'll move downstream and hide in the bushes on the north side of the waterfall." Jared stood and picked up the sack of weapons.

"Stay here and I'll make sure you're captured in the morning," said Kentucky to Riven.

"Looking forward to it," said Riven. As they started to move off, Riven called, "Remember the pact." He moved his fist in the vertical line they had performed together as they made their promise.

Kentucky and Jared made the same sign back. It was all

the reassurance Riven could hope for but Jared saw in his eyes that it did little to quench his doubts about Kentucky's loyalty.

Jared followed the shore of the river just inside the trees. There could be guards placed all around the prison. He wanted to play it safe. At last, when he was confident he was far enough away, he came out of the trees, and with the heavy sack over his shoulder, he waded into the river.

He hadn't gone far before the strong current yanked his feet off the riverbed and he stumbled. The force of the river picked him up and carried him downstream several yards. He banged his feet and knees on rocks as he struggled to regain his footing. He struggled against the flow but he went further and further downstream with every step. Finally, he was swept into a calmer part of the river and was able to make his way to the opposite shore. A cut in his right hand was bleeding, and his legs were cut and bleeding as well. He stepped and his ankle gave out. A shot of agony radiated from ankle to knee. Jared fell to the ground. He took a deep breath and forced himself to stand.

Jared removed the game mask and glanced at the clock on his nightstand. It was after four in the morning but he couldn't rest yet. He didn't know how long he had before it started to get light in Lavascape. Nor did he know how early Riven would be captured. He needed to be ready when everything started happening. He had to make it to the waterfall and hide in the brush while it was still dark. It was his only chance, especially now that he was injured. He put the mask back on.

His left arm soon grew too weak to carry the heavy load. He switched arms and discovered a big red bruise on the inside of his left elbow. His right hand throbbed and before long, this arm was tired, too. By switching from left to right when each arm began to fail, Jared was able to carry the load. He limped, but his legs continued to move. The roar of the waterfall got louder. He moved deeper into the trees. His progress was extremely slow now, but he was safer. When Jared finally reached the edge of the waterfall, he sat to catch his breath. With the last of his strength, he crawled, dragging the sack of weapons until he collapsed under a thicket. This was one day when a missed feast would have meant failure. It had been a lonely meal. Jared missed hanging out with Barry and he missed seeing his mingo at the hut. But, that meal had sustained him.

With immense relief, he fell into his bed. He ached all over, but his exhaustion overshadowed his pain and he was soon asleep.

When morning came, Jared's alarm sounded like the thundering of footsteps. "Giants," he said and jumped out of bed. Then he realized it wasn't his alarm at all. The sound was a persistent knock on his bedroom door. He fell back down on the bed. "What? Come in!"

It was Mom. "You're not up yet, either?" she said. "Don't tell me you and Melissa have the same bug?" She placed her hand on Jared's forehead and looked up as she gauged his temperature. "You don't feel especially hot. How do you feel?"

"Tired and achy," said Jared. Which was the truth. Not only was he so tired he felt sick to his stomach, his arms and legs felt as though he'd run a marathon with wrist and ankle weights on.

"Fine, go back to bed. Just check on your sister in a while, would you?"

"-kay," he mumbled.

"I'll call the school." She looked at her watch. "I'll have to call from the dental office though or I'm going to be late." How long had she been back at work? She must have worn out Dr. Dobbs patience in asking for sick days; either that or she realized she needed to get out of the house. Whatever. The point was that Jared didn't have to go to school today and if things in Lavascape were happening as quickly as they seemed, he'd need to be there soon.

After a trip to the bathroom and then the kitchen, he sank into his game chair and logged on. The pinpoints of light like stars in a distant galaxy began to stream toward him. He started to feel better, his limbs less exhausted, his mind less clouded.

Jared was in a densely wooded area. His arm lay in a pool of reddish-brown. He realized it was a pool of blood. How could he have been so careless? He could have bled to death. Instead, while he was resting his blood had clot. His arm ached slightly but seemed to be working fine.

Suddenly, Jared heard Kentucky's voice. "I've had it with trolls and goblins! I'd like to see the whole lot of them wiped out of Lavascape once and for all. They take the best land for their grubby little villages and so much space for their troll training sites. And of course there's the hourglass, too!"

There were grunts of agreement.

"Let me help you with your quest, my giant friends. I guarantee you'll find me a valuable ally."

"How's that," said a deep, resonate voice.

Jared peaked through the branches. Kentucky was talking to three giants who towered over him even though they were sitting.

"I can help round up the enemy. They won't know I'm with you. I can lead them into traps for you. I'm telling you, you definitely need a few scurry working for you.... How many do you have in this area?"

"None that I know of," said the deep voice giant.

"What? How in the Lavascape world have you managed to get this far?"

"How do we know we can trust you? What if we're the ones you're planning to double cross," said one of the giants, standing.

"I can prove myself to you right now, if you'd like."

"How?" said all three giants, together.

"I happen to know where there's at least one goblin. He might not be there right now, of course, but I saw where he made camp for the night. Even if he's moved on, he can't be far."

At the thought of a new prisoner, the three giants whispered eager-sounding mumbles. "Let's go," said one.

"He's probably not alone," said another eager voice.

"We'll be heroes if we fill another cage," said the third.

"And then we'll know if this scurry can be trusted," added the first giant. "I still think he looks like the scurry that helped that troll escape."

"All scurry look pretty much the same," said Kentucky. "It's the fur on our faces." Jared could hear the tremor in his voice. "I can tell you though that I have much higher standards than to hang out with trolls. You may not know this, but scurry have a heightened sense of smell and I've developed mine so it's especially strong—and trolls reek!"

The giants laughed.

"Believe me, I can't even exaggerate it! If I had to hang out with a troll, I'd be barfing all the time!"

"Some say giants are the smelly ones," said one giant, suspiciously.

"No way," Kentucky assured him. "Trolls are much worse."

"Let's go get those goblins before they run off," said the second giant.

"You stay here, Stallion," said the first giant. "Me and Cliff will drag in the goblins."

"I always have to stay behind," Stallion complained.

"This is the first time," said the one who had taken charge.

"Now shut up or I'll give you a rotten job worth whining about."

The two giants followed Kentucky across the river and into the woods. It was a shallow area and even Kentucky was only wet up to his thighs. That was a lot different than the spot Jared had crossed the night before.

How long would he have to wait? The giant left behind disappeared from Jared's view. He may have gone into the cave. Where were all the others? It was a school day; maybe he shouldn't be surprised to find just three giants here at this time of day. Jared sat back on the ground and leaned against a smooth-barked tree.

Back in his bedroom, Jared also leaned back in his chair. The exhaustion he'd felt before he entered Lavascape had returned. He heard a toilet flush. Wasn't he home alone? No, Melissa was home from school, too. Mom wanted him to check on her. He started to rise but changed his mind. She'd just been to the bathroom; if she needed him she would have come to his room and told him so. There was a smell in the air. Was she smoking her 'nothing' at home now? Was he his sister's keeper? His Lavascape family was going to need him far more.

His head rested comfortably on the chair back and Jared was soon asleep. He awoke with a start unable to tell what had brought him to consciousness. He was certainly tired enough to sleep on. He adjusted the mask, which had slid slightly down his nose. Things were happening in Lavascape. Kentucky slithered under the brush in a flattened snake-like form and re-formed into his rat-like shape in front of Jared.

"Kentucky," whispered Jared. "What's happening? Where's Riven?"

"You didn't see them? Man! It was awful. I didn't want to do it."

"What happened?"

Kentucky crouched down. "The giants didn't believe Riven when he told them he was travelling alone. They made me do it, Jared. If I'd refused, they would have known we were in it together. It was the only way."

Jared came closer to the scurry. "What is it, Kentucky? What did you do to him?"

Kentucky didn't answer.

"Is he alive? Is he okay?" insisted Jared, grabbing Kentucky's shoulders.

"He's alive, but he's not okay." Jared saw the fear in Kentucky's eyes. It was so strong Jared could have sensed it on a first stage Retina Reading exercise.

Jared waited and eventually Kentucky began his account of what had happened. "When we came to the clearing, there was Riven, just sitting there like he was waiting to be captured. He wasn't hiding in the trees, he wasn't packing up supplies, nothing, just sitting pretty, 'come and get me giants'. Well they thought that was strange enough, but when Riven didn't have any companions, and when they didn't buy his story about why he was so close to their lair, they turned on both of us. They accused us of an alliance and of plotting against them. We denied it of course but probably sounded guilty. So you see, Jared. We'd both be locked in there if I hadn't done it. You'd never know what had happened, and they would have found you hiding here with your bag of weapons."

Jared felt as though his throat was closing and he was slowly suffocating. "What did you do?"

"The goblins are bow fighters."

"Go on," said Jared, when a long pause followed.

"I cut off his left arm. You can't shoot a bow with only one arm. It satisfied the giants. They thought it was a great trick." Kentucky's voice dropped in volume as he finished. He brought his head to his hands.

"Oh no," whispered Jared. Riven had lost a limb and he'd lost it at the hand of one of his companions, one he'd made a pact with! Was Kentucky really forced to take such drastic measures? Or was this just an excuse to attack the goblin he'd always disliked? Jared felt a blanket of dread fall over his shoulders. Riven and Kentucky hadn't trusted each other before. What would happen to their little band now?

"It was the only way," said Kentucky, pleading.

"It wasn't the only way. I could have saved you both."

"I don't think they would have given us that option. You didn't hear them, Jerry. If they believed we were working together, one or the other of us was going to die out there. Maybe both of us."

"I don't know if Riven will see it that way."

"I know. But *you* understand don't you, Jerry? I was backed into a corner. I had to act and act big. Help me convince him! When he's free, he'll try to kill me. I need your help or I'm dead. I better go. I went for firewood and I should get back. Quick, help me gather some kindling."

Jared scrounged in the woods for sticks and moss for starting fires. Soon Kentucky's small arms were full. "How will I know if you're ready for the jail break?"

"I'll say, 'It's been a great goblin-maiming day.' I'll make sure it's loud enough for you to hear."

Jared shuddered. "Okay." Had that vile sentence slipped out a little too easily?

Kentucky gave Jared one last anxious look and left.

Jared sat feeling numb, shocked by what had happened. Riven was dismembered but alive. Could Riven die from this serious a wound? Would he be able to run away if Jared got him out of there? To fight? Not with a bow, obviously, but what about with a sword? Would his first act with a sword be to run it through Kentucky Scurry?

While he waited, a vision of Sparket blocked out the trees and shrubs. Sparket flung back the blanket on her bed. She grabbed one of the mattress springs. She began to twist and yank it. It broke and she fell back with the twisted metal in her hand, a smile on her face.

Either the time was right or Kentucky wanted to get Riven out of prison before his wound killed him. In any case, Kentucky set things in motion that very night. He didn't use the code words; he simply came to Jared. He wanted to sneak the weapons in two at a time. The clinking sound from carrying the large sack would surely wake the giants who were supposedly sleeping in a room near the prison area. Jared wasn't sure that was possible. Could they stay half in and half out of Lavascape by staying in while they were sleeping in real life? He decided he didn't want to risk discounting the possibility.

"I can carry quite a few weapons," said Jared.

Kentucky started to protest, "But you're a troll."

"If you get caught carrying weapons to the prisoners, it won't matter that you're a scurry or that you helped them capture a goblin today."

"Okay, we'll make one trip," said Kentucky. "We'll take what we can carry quietly and then lead the prisoners to the weapons we'll stash outside the cave. The faster we're out of there the better. They've left me to guard the prisoners overnight, but you're right, everything could change in an instant."

"How many prisoners are there?"

"Three cages like the one we were in, all filled pretty much to capacity."

Jared didn't like the sound of this plan. They would arm so few of the prisoners before they got out of the cave. If the giants confronted them, they'd never have enough weaponry to defeat them. Kentucky grabbed three swords and started off. His arms were ridiculously short. Jared took the remainder of the weapons to the mouth of the cave, then he slung a bow and quiver of arrows over each shoulder, and carried three swords in each hand.

He crept in the cave after Kentucky. As he neared the first cage, he caught sight of Riven. There was a makeshift bandage wrapped around his body and over the spot where his left arm should have been. A fellow prisoner must have donated his tattered cloak to bind the wound. It crisscrossed over Riven's chest several times and ended in a huge knot at his left shoulder. His eyes smouldered with savage intensity and Jared had to look away to keep from being caught up in Riven's sense of betrayal, anger, and hatred. Riven's eyes also showed pain. If Jared's arm ached from his injuries in the night, how much more must Riven be feeling after having an arm chopped off? There wasn't time to read so much.

"I have more just outside the cave," Jared whispered as the prisoners reached for a weapon. He handed the bow and arrows to a goblin next to Riven.

'Adding insult to injury?' whispered Riven.

Kentucky approached Riven. With anguished eyes, he handed the first sword to him.

Riven snatched it with such violence that Jared wondered if Kentucky was right, and killing Kentucky would be Riven's first course of business when he was free.

In a long minute, Kentucky finally sprang the lock on Riven's cage while Jared handed weapons to the prisoners at the back. "Now, single file and quietly," whispered Kentucky. He went to the other cages to open those locks, as well.

It was an impossible request. The captives out first would be the most likely to survive. Jared winced. They were too loud. Within seconds, he could hear footsteps coming through the tunnels near the back of the cave. They grew louder until they were claps of thunder.

Jared hurried toward the cave entrance. The sound of heavy footfalls echoed in the cave.

He ripped open the bag at the mouth of the cave and planted the weapons in the eager reaching hands before him. Soon the bag was empty. It was a meagre store. He barely had enough weapons to arm every fifth prisoner. The ones in the rear were defenceless. The giants thundered through what Jared could now tell were connecting caves.

The trolls and goblins scattered into the forest as soon as they had opportunity. Jared joined them, seeking the protection of the trees.

The first giants appeared. Their feet fell like meteors striking the earth. The newly freed prisoners with swords jabbed at the giants but it was only when three or more were attacking a single giant that any of those massive creatures fell.

Suddenly Kentucky was at Jared's side, but he saw no sign of Riven, the one-armed goblin. "Is Riven in the rear?" asked Jared.

There wasn't time to respond to the question. A giant was bearing down on them. He knocked Kentucky into the branches of a tree and came toward Jared. Jared's sword seemed a child's play-thing next to the brute force of the giant.

He would have few strokes, few chances to bring down this creature. He had to make his swings count. The eyes, nose, and throat were tender spots, but all out of his reach.

Suddenly, he remembered a story he learned in school. It was a Greek myth about a man who was dipped in a substance that would make him invincible and every part of him was super strong except for the back of the heel where he was held. The Achilles tendon! That, he could reach!

Kentucky climbed down the tree and Jared yelled to him. "Go for the leg, above the heel!" The giant kicked Kentucky. Jared hustled to the rear of the giant. He slashed twice over the tender area. Kentucky was at the other leg a moment later, his sharp teeth gnawing at the tendon. The giant roared and fell, face first, to the forest floor, taking a couple of thin-trunked evergreens down with him. "Stupid idiot morons!" he bellowed.

Kentucky and Jared scampered out of his way and sped through the forest.

Chapter Twenty-Six

"Kids wear a lot worse things to school, Mom," screamed Melissa. "If you're going to make me go when I'm deathly ill, the least you can do is let me be comfortable."

"You're wearing your pyjamas!" Mom yelled back.

"Tell her," Melissa said, appealing to Jared who was eating his breakfast cereal and wishing they weren't so loud. His temples were throbbing. "Tell her kids wear everything to school."

Jared only shrugged.

"Tell her!"

"I suppose," said Jared.

"You have always been meticulous about your appearance, sometimes too meticulous. What's with you, today? Now you are willing to fall out of bed, put on a pair of shoes, and walk out the door?"

"I don't care."

"Why not?"

Jared saw the dejected look in Melissa's countenance. Her face muscles seemed drawn into a deep frown, too heavy to pull up. Her eyes said she was hovering above rock bottom. Jared forgot his headache.

Mom took a ravenous bite out of the croissant she was holding, chewed vigorously, and swallowed. "You look awful." Her clipped words seemed to tear at Melissa's beaten-down ego.

"Say it a hundred more times, Mom. It's really making me feel good."

"And we need to have a talk, Jared," she said turning on him. "Could you really not hear me last night?"

He shook his head. "When?"

"You were totally zonked out." Mom ate the rest of her croissant and threw back her orange juice to finish off the glass. "Your math teacher called me at work yesterday. Your grades are terrible and if you don't pull up your socks...." She left the room and came back with her purse. She pulled out a slip of paper. "If it's laziness, get on the ball; if it's not, here's the number of a good tutor. One of the girls at work gave me her number." She laid the paper on the kitchen table and gave Jared 'the eye.' "And you need a haircut," she added as she left.

Jared shook his head. She didn't suggest she or Dad could help him. It's eighth grade not rocket science! And, his hair was finally long enough to cover his hairy ears. He wasn't about to reveal them anytime soon. That hair remover hardly worked at all with the thick hair he had to deal with.

"She doesn't understand anything," said Melissa when they heard the front door close. "She doesn't even try. She's as gone as Dad, really."

Were those the words she said to Colton? "Well, she

doesn't understand when a guy actually needs a haircut," said Jared. "I can't ever show my ears in public again."

Melissa didn't even crack a smile. Jared thought for sure a reference to his hairy ears would bring a comment from his sister, but she continued to look blankly ahead.

"Are you going to change your clothes?"

Melissa wrinkled her mouth as though considering it. Then she shook her head. "Nah." She sounded unbearably tired, as though the very act of changing would require more energy than she could muster.

Ever since he found out about Dad coaching basketball, Jared knew the truth. He had no one to blame but himself for his family falling apart. He wasn't the kind of son a Dad likes to hang around with, show basketball moves to. Dad loves strangers' kids more than him.

"I still can't believe they're getting a divorce," said Melissa. "Why...."

Instead of comforting her and taking up his optimistic role he said, "Things are changing. It's crappy, but we have to face it, suck it up. We'll be okay."

"No! We won't be okay, not if we're not together. No."

When they entered the school, Jared hurried to his locker and left Melissa to dawdle to hers. Cam didn't pick her up anymore. She didn't want to talk about it.

Katie was suddenly behind him. "Where were you yesterday?"

"Home."

"You can't let Colton scare you like this, Jared. You have friends, you know. And, I talked to Principal Hayes about an anti-bullying campaign. He's all for it. This school has a zero tolerance when it comes to bullying, he said. Well, I told him that may be the case but nobody is going out of their way to find it when it's right under their noses." Katie seemed to realize that Jared hadn't said anything. "Are you okay?"

"A lot happened yesterday," he said. While he was busy freeing prisoners in Lavascape, Katie was at school fighting the battle of the bully. "You're great, Katie," he said. "Thanks, I really mean it."

Katie's face was pink in an instant. It intrigued him. He'd rarely seen Katie embarrassed in all the years they'd known each other. She looked away from him. "Hey, you're welcome." She tried to sound nonchalant but it didn't quite come off that way.

The bell rang and Katie said, "Bye."

Colton came by and hip checked Jared into his locker. "What? Didn't you see that coming? Aren't much of a hockey player, are you Picky? Keep your head up."

"I guess that makes you a goon." Jared braced himself for retaliation. How had he let that slip out?

Colton's eyes flared and the pupils darted back and forth. "You don't know anything!"

"I know you don't like your sister's jerk husband but you don't mind acting like a jerk yourself." Surely Colton wasn't so dense he couldn't see the resemblance.

Colton pushed Jared against the cold metal locker. His voice was clear and low. "It's his fault as much as the mugger's." He threw Jared to the floor. "So weak." Jared wasn't sure if he was talking about him or the brother-in-law.

Jared stumbled to his feet and went to class. He found it difficult to concentrate on the teacher, however; Katie's pink face kept coming to mind. At lunchtime, he found Katie and Anna in the corner working on a poster for a Social Studies project. They had it on the floor and scattered around them were pencil crayons and markers.

"Need some help?" asked Jared.

"Sure," said Anna. Then she added softly, "Mr. Spitball King." She was definitely flirting with him.

"You can trace those letters for us," said Katie handing him a dark blue marker. Katie's pink face had returned to its regular shade and Jared was surprised to realize he was rather disappointed. He found it intriguing. He didn't know what it meant and he wished he could figure it out. It was gone, however.

He listened to the girls talk as they worked on the poster. Anna was more talkative than Jared had ever seen her before. Who had Jared walked to school with? Would his sister be with him when he walked home again? She went on and on.

Finally Katie said, "Anna is asking if she should walk home with you after school...for your own protection."

Anna smiled gratefully at Katie and then went on to explain how her parents wouldn't mind if she was home late and her dad would probably even pick her up on his way home from somewhere he had to be.

Anna made several references to his bravery, which Jared suspected gave him his own pink-tinged face. After one such comment about Colton, Katie elbowed Anna in the ribs and whispered, "Shh". There was Colton Barnes walking toward a table with his lunch, he had only one shadow today—Reg. Jared couldn't take his eyes off the big lumbering kid. Was it his imagination or was Reg limping? They stopped in front of a partially full table. "Well, move over," said Colton.

"Stupid idiot morons," said Reg.

Jared's mind returned to the battle with the giants in Lavascape the day before. The giant he and Kentucky had battled—he said 'stupid idiot morons' in the same tone—and they had attacked his legs. "The Achilles tendon," Jared whispered.

"Huh?" said Katie.

Jared noticed his hand first. It was shaking and he lifted the blue marker off the poster before he made a bigger mess. It wasn't just his hands. His whole body shook. He had been on his knees leaning over the poster, now he sat cross-legged and tried unsuccessfully to steady himself.

Anna sputtered something under her breath about Jared not being too terribly brave at the moment. Then she giggled and said, "Just kidding."

Katie laid her hand on his arm. "What is it, Jared?"

Jared could hardly breathe. "Katie. It's Lavascape. I need some fresh air."

"I'll go with you," said Anna. But Katie was already at his side.

"You'll see him after school," said Katie. "I'll take the poster home and finish up whatever you don't get done."

Anna's lower lip protruded, but Katie and Jared left the lunchroom without her. Once they were in the crisp fall air, Jared took quick shallow breaths until Katie put her hand on his shoulder and said, "Slow down. Just breathe."

A couple of minutes later, Jared felt better.

"What was all that about? Colton?"

Jared leaned against the bricks of the school's exterior. "I don't want to tell you. You'll think I'm crazy. I'd think I was crazy if I were you. You could have me committed."

"If I promise not to drag you off to the psych ward, will you tell me?"

Katie's smile was reassuring. He took another deep breath before he began. "It's Lavascape. It reaches out into the real world, Katie. Remember that scab I had, the one that was like a rock? Well, it was rock. It was a blob of lava from Lavascape. Don't shake your head. Just listen! It wasn't a scab."

Katie looked sceptical but simply waited for Jared to say more.

"There's the way my hair has started to grow funny. It's longer and spiky down the middle."

"I thought you were doing that on purpose, gelling it or something."

"Since when do I care enough to style my hair?"

Katie shrugged and Jared continued. "So my hair is looking like the troll in the game...and trolls also have hairy ears and big feet." Jared lifted the hair over his ears for Katie to see the transformation."

"Wow," said Katie. "So, when you were walking around in your socks...?"

"My new shoes are too small. I've been wearing an old pair of Dad's I found in his closet. They're three sizes bigger than I used to wear."

"Why were you shaking all of a sudden?"

"It was Reg."

"Don't worry, Jared. We're going to stop those bullies. The principal is going to help. He said they'd patrol the school better, bring in a guest speaker for a special assembly, there's going to be a poster contest and, well I don't know what else, but I'm working on it."

Katie had done a lot of planning in the past couple of days. Jared had his doubts whether it would work. Bullies were bullies, you can't change them; but her effort was nice just the same. "It's not the bully he is in real life that got to me. It's what happened yesterday in Lavascape. I'm sure Reg is one of the giants. He sounds like him and he goes around calling everyone a 'stupid idiot moron'. Nobody else says that, do they?"

Katie shook her head. "They could, but it's redundant and I haven't heard anything close since kindergarten."

"Well, to make a long story short, yesterday me and a Lavascape friend escaped Reg by hurting the backs of his ankles, here in the Achilles tendon." He lifted his jeans and showed Katie where he meant. "Then, when I saw Colton and Reg walking in the lunch room, Reg was walking with a limp."

"That's freaky…but it could be a coincidence."

"I know it could be, but it's not. The more I think about it, the more I recognize the voice."

His conviction made Katie's expression change slightly. She believed him. Lavascape had affected reality, again. Her voice was soft. "I'm scared of that game. I think it has a power we don't understand."

"You have no idea. I've only told you the big things, there are a hundred smaller things that Lavascape seems to do."

"Like what?"

"While you're playing, it can make you feel perfectly fine when you're dead tired. You don't notice time, you don't notice exhaustion—it changes your body. Then, if you can break away and turn it off, you're left to yourself again. I've been so tired I thought I was going to barf."

Katie bit her lip. "You gotta stop playing."

"I don't know if I can."

"Of course you can."

"I have a quest. I have a mission. I feel the draw, the call of Lavascape, all day long, if I'm being honest. I want to play it right now. I want it the second I walk in the front door of my house. In fact, as I'm walking home, every step I take brings me closer and I feel it stronger and stronger."

"Okay, okay." Katie waved her hands as though she were erasing an invisible chalkboard in the air. Her eyes held a new message, gone was the aura of belief; doubt and scientific thinking dominated now. "Let's be logical. You're just obsessed with Lavascape because it's so fun. And everyone loses track of time when they're playing a video game. There's nothing supernatural about Lavascape, Jared. The scab and the hair and Reg limping—they could all be coincidences. Let's not let our imaginations run away with us."

"Yeah right, it's harmless," said Jared with a grunt.

"I didn't say that. I do think you should stop playing. Give it a rest."

"Easier said than done. Besides, what about Sparket?"

"She'll be fine. Promise me."

"Okay."

Chapter Twenty-Seven

A rest was exactly what Jared needed. The last class of the day ended and he had a plan. He would take a nap before dinner and then catch up on some homework assignments. Katie had helped him map out his evening, an evening that would be so scheduled that he wouldn't have time for Lavascape. Katie hadn't actually scheduled the nap but he added that to his plan as he headed out the school doors. He felt as though he was forgetting something, but he shook off the feeling. It was probably from actually having his homework with him...a delayed reaction from all the days he had gone home without it.

As he walked he considered, if he had time for a nap, he certainly had time to play Lavascape. He didn't have to play long. He could go there for just a half an hour or so.

No. He had to be strong. Katie would ask him tomorrow and he didn't want to admit he had so little self-control. She'd be disappointed in him.

His report card marks were going to be a nightmare, but

if he finished some assignments maybe he could avoid his mother having an aneurysm and lecturing him for hours. That would be hours sitting in a living room chair instead of playing Lavascape.

Was that all he could think about? Lavascape was the problem. It was...Jared got goose bumps up and down his arms...Reg was definitely limping at lunch today. Lavascape was eerie.

As he opened the front door to his house, the guilt hit him full force. There were people in Lavascape counting on him. Kentucky and Riven were helping him with his quest. Was he going to go missing in action? They had made an oath. What would happen to Sparket? She had less than a week to live. She was depending on him. He could quit Lavascape after he saved Sparket.

Nap, said another part of Jared's mind. He'd promised himself a nap. Nap first and then Lavascape.

The Lavascape force seemed to lighten its fierce hold on him ever so slightly when he gave himself permission to play. Jared slipped off his shoes and climbed the stairs to his bedroom. He fell into his rumpled sheets and pulled the quilt up to his shoulders. There was no rest this close to his computer, however. He hadn't turned the computer off the night before. He could see the screen saver on the mask flickering, casting shades of light and dark. The fan in the computer seemed especially loud. It churned not only the air, but the thoughts in Jared's mind.

Each thought came on the stage of his mind, lingered, and then was blown away by the next thought: Reg limping through the lunchroom; Sparket glaring at the power-hungry man she had to marry; Kentucky Scurry's eyes after dismembering Riven; the lava scab falling from his ankle; Retina Reading Dad's eyes before he left them; Mom emerging from the dark hole she seemed to have been in; Colton's face splattered with the toilet paper spit ball; Terrance's guitar buried in dirt; Melissa rolling up in a beanbag chair like it was her own dark hole; Riven's wife slaughtered in an ambush; Sparket's beautiful face; a rough grey rope around Sparket's neck...he sat up with a start.

Had he been dreaming? Not quite. He was on the verge of sleep in the zone where real and make-believe merge. He swung his legs over the side of the bed and was surprised to find himself immediately in his computer chair. He didn't make a conscious choice to go there. Sparket needed him now. How could a self-respecting troll withhold his aid?

Jared hesitated. He'd promised Katie. He had a plan. He had homework. He had to use his will power. But Katie didn't understand. Lavascape was more than a game. It was another life. Jared put on the gloves and mask and clicked the button to return to Lavascape. A feeling of release filled his body, followed quickly by hazy yearning for more.

He went to the feast but he was too early; he could sit and talk or go to the forest and return to the troll feast at six o'clock. Barry came and indicated they sit together at the nearest table. They sat. "How are things going?" asked Barry.

"You're talking to me? I thought I was interfering with your popularity for teams."

"Yeah, but it's been such a long time since we've hung out. Plus, I'm pretty secure with the team I'm on now."

"That's nice." There was an uncomfortable pause. Jared didn't know what to say to Barry now. The games weren't important; he couldn't act like they were. They were two old friends who took different paths and didn't know each other anymore. "Look, you were right before. You can't be a fence sitter and neither can I. I have an adventure; I don't belong with the villagers. Sorry." Jared rose from the table.

"Where are you going?"

"Adventure."

"Don't forget to return for the feast," said Barry. His eyes showed concern and something more. Jared focused his Retina Reading; trolls were hard, but he thought he saw envy.

"I won't." Jared went to the adventure portals.

He teleported to the forest outside the giants' lair. Kentucky was by his side. "You're here finally," said Kentucky. "I've been going crazy checking every few minutes."

Before Jared could answer, a vision burst upon him as though it had been waiting for him with as much anxiety as Kentucky showed.

Antonio grasped Sparket by the wrists and flung her to the floor. Her chin came down hard on the stone floor. Antonio towered over her, glaring at this obstacle to his complete power. Then he swung his leg and the toe of his boot smacked into Sparket's stomach. She grunted and rolled into a ball.

"Think about what I've said." Antonio gathered his belongings from a pile by her bed. "I'm losing my patience with you, Sparket. Don't ever call me Tony again. He stomped his foot. "The next time I come will be the last. Be prepared to marry me or have a lot more of this." He kicked the side of her head. Bright red blood trickled from her nose. She brought her arms over her face for protection.

He stepped over her, knocked for the guard, and left her there, semi-conscious on the floor.

"Sparket needs us!" said Jared when the vision faded. "He's beating her! I'm going to tear that guy limb from limb. Do you understand what I'm saying, Kentucky? He's not just holding her captive. I don't have time for war strategy and gaining trust of this or that council. Sparket..."

"Calm down," said Kentucky. "We'll save her."

"What's going on? Are the giants still after us?"

"I think they've given up."

"Where's Riven?"

"I haven't seen him. Maybe he was re-captured."

Jared wanted to scream. He didn't have time for this! "We better go back for him."

"Back into giant territory? Are you crazy? He's probably dead by now."

Just then there was a blur and Kentucky slammed against a tree. Jared gaped. It was Riven the goblin and he had Kentucky pinned to the tree with his left knee. In his right hand he held a knife to Kentucky's throat. "Don't move or I'll make this a lot more torturous. I may not be skilled with a blade," said Riven, "but I think I can figure out how to drive it through your neck."

"Wait, stop," pleaded Kentucky.

"You'd like to believe I was dead or recaptured, wouldn't you, you lying rat. Then I'd be out of your way."

"I've never lied to you! I only did what I had to do. I didn't want to hurt you."

"You didn't look all broken up about it, dude. In fact, there was a bit of a smile on your face like you were thinking about your gold reward and not having to split it with me. I'll give you a taste of a different metal."

Jared called out. "Don't do it, Riven!"

The goblin paused and looked over his shoulder at Jared. "You'll deny me revenge? You better stay out of the way, Troll."

"He did what he thought he had to do," said Jared.

Still holding Kentucky at the point of his knife, Riven said, "Would you feel that way, if you were the one he mutilated? If he crippled you so you couldn't use your weapon, would you be so forgiving?"

"I don't know," admitted Jared. "I think he made some

bad decisions and you were the one to suffer for them, it's true."

"You have no idea!"

"I'm sorry," screamed Kentucky as the knife quivered.

"But his heart is good," said Jared. "He thought if you were both captured, it would be the end for all of us."

"There were other ways!"

"I agree," said Jared. He moved so he was next to Riven. "But remember, neither of us knows how to pick a lock. We needed Kentucky for that."

"You could have cut him loose, again," Riven fumed.

"*If* they let me live!" yelled Kentucky. "I had to come up with a plan, fast."

"It was a terrible plan." Riven glared at Kentucky. "Brutally, unforgivably terrible. Jared was free! He could have saved us. You wanted to do it!" The blade came closer to Kentucky's throat.

"No! I was desperate!"

"Riven! Don't!" said Jared. "Let him explain."

"It all happened so fast," said Kentucky. "There were so many giants guarding the main cave and more in the other caves. I didn't think we'd make it if we were both trapped, Riven. I'm sorry. "

"He is sorry," said Jared, gently. "I see it in his eyes."

Riven lowered the blade from Kentucky's throat. He stepped away. For a long time he stared at Kentucky. "Low-life, stupid logic, Scurry!" He paused. "Stupid, but not traitorous." He sheathed his knife at his waist and turned away. Kentucky finally dared move.

Riven walked ahead, into the woods. "Let's get back to the war council. I'm interested to see if they think we passed or failed. None of us may live 'til tomorrow, anyway. Then it won't matter if I can use a bow or not."

Jared considered thanking Riven and Kentucky for their parts in the effort but he didn't. Jared was the only one who actually did what he was supposed to without rising suspicion or turning on his companions.

"Where are we?" asked Jared. "Do we know which way to go to get back to the council?"

"Follow me," said Riven.

"Do you need a new bandage?" asked Jared.

The goblin didn't respond but started out to the east. There wasn't a trail; he picked his way through the forest. They swerved one way and then another. Just as Jared was beginning to wonder if Riven would lead them somewhere even more secluded and use his knife on them, they came to a trail. Jared suspected that Kentucky had similar fears because when he saw the trail he looked at Jared with relief.

"It's the trail that leads to the ferry, right?" Kentucky asked.

"Yep," said Riven. "It leads to the beach where the ferryman docks. And also where the troll and goblin leaders have set up their war strategy headquarters, apparently. It makes sense. This way they can see everyone who enters or leaves this island. There's only one ferryman, so it's essentially the gate in and out unless someone else figures out how to sail lava."

The goblin ducked under a low branch. He pulled it back and let it snap into place, knocking Kentucky off his feet. "Rotten luck, Scurry," he said before moving on.

"Jerk," said Kentucky.

"You cut off his arm," Jared reminded him. "I'd say he's taking it remarkably well."

Kentucky examined the scrape across his chest another moment before moving on.

The trail ended at the shore of the lava sea. There was a sign with an arrow pointing to their right. In a shaky scrawl was the single word, 'Ferry.'

"Written by the finger of the undead, himself," said Riven. Jared and Kentucky followed the goblin as he took the turn indicated by the arrow. "Better check in with the council, first," said Riven, stopping.

As they turned and trudged over the rocky beach of magma, Jared was suddenly distracted from the game as his bedroom door opened. He slipped the mask off. There was Melissa. "Hey. Do you want to have these CDs? I know you like them." She was in the same pyjama pants she wore to school that day and her eyes were glassy.

"Sure. Thanks," he said.

She set them on his bed.

"Don't you like them anymore?"

She shrugged. "Just lightening my load. Besides, I know them backwards and forwards." She left.

Jared put the game mask back on. Riven and Kentucky had pulled ahead of him. The huts on the beach were in sight. He tripped over a rock, fell, picked himself up, and quickened his pace to catch up.

A troll with a boring brown fohawk saw them approach and blew into a curved horn. A few seconds later, the troll king emerged from the thatched hut. His emerald green fohawk was regal and impressive, especially next to this guard. Suddenly, instead of one guard there were several each holding a long spear. They advanced on Jared and his companions, surrounded them, and herded them into the hut. The king had disappeared.

"What's going on?" demanded Jared. "We did our best! You can't do more than your best."

They were back in the courtroom. Trolls, goblins, and a scurry or two pushed them to the front before the thrones. They each chanted a different chant that mingled until they were nothing but a roar of enthusiasm. Riven turned to Jared in the throng of creatures and said, "It's judgement day, friend. Salvation or damnation. What's your guess?"

It was impossible to tell. Jared concentrated his Retina Reading on a few goblins—they were happy. One of the scurry made eye contact with him. He felt pride for Kentucky.

The troll king, his emerald hair glittering in the torchlight, took his seat at the front of the courtroom, and the goblin king, looking magnificent in golden robes, tied with a red sash, sat next to him on the similar throne. Immediately the room became quiet. "Relate the tale for all to hear," demanded the troll king. "You, Troll. Stand and report."

Under the scrutinizing eyes of the crowd, Jared told how they had reached the giant's cave near the waterfall. He outlined their plan and described the trouble that had unexpectedly come along. He extolled Riven's bravery in being willing to be captured, and the terrible price that he had paid. He told of Kentucky's cunning in joining the enemy. The two scurry in the company seemed to grow an inch taller as they listened. He glazed over his own trouble traversing the river with the entire stash of weapons, and the now seemingly insignificant injuries he'd sustained. He told of Kentucky's skill in picking the locks of the prison doors and the mayhem that had followed when the giants had learned of their escape and pursued them into the forest. He declared heartfelt sadness for those who surely must have died in the rescue attempt, but expressed hope that many had escaped the giants and would return to this council. He acknowledged that mistakes were made but that they had each done his best in the heat of the conflict.

When he had finished the account of their mission, the crowd erupted in loud cheers. Jared stepped back between Kentucky and Riven.

Both the troll and the goblin kings rose. "Heroes step forward," commanded the magnificent goblin.

Did he mean them? Were they really welcoming them back as heroes? The three companions stepped forward. Riven went down on one knee and Kentucky and Jared followed his lead. The kings approached. They placed a medal around their necks, a purple crest on the left side of their chests, and a pouch of coins in their hands.

When the presentation of these emblems was complete, the mass of creatures erupted once more. The crowd moved in and suddenly there were hands of all varieties patting their backs and touching their medals. Some of those in the crowd were thanking them; obviously some of the prisoners they'd set free. Others were admiring and still others seemed envious.

Jared made his way to the front of the courtroom chamber. When he finally reached the two kings, he knelt before them and said, "We request passage with the ferryman to the island to the north."

"You're needed in this war," said the troll king. "You can't leave now!"

The entire room went deathly quiet. Those who had been cheering them a moment before now looked at Jared and his companions as though they were traitors.

"We've proved we're on your side," said Jared.

"Then continue to fight at our side," replied the troll king.

"I'm dedicated to my quest," explained Jared. "When I've completed it, I'll be free to join other causes and fight other battles. Right now, a girl needs me desperately. My companions and I have made a pact to see this mission through. We must get back on this course before it's too late to save her. And I trust you won't hinder us further."

After a long pause, the goblin king spoke softly. "Ah yes, the human princess, this may be your role." Then to everyone else he said, "There have been human attacks. Perhaps their quest will help our efforts more than we realize."

He reached into the deep pockets of his robe and pulled out three cards, each the size of a bank card and handed them to Jared, Riven, and Kentucky. "These are your citizenship cards, they allow you access to the ferry and can be used to show your alliance should you find yourself in a war zone."

The troll king said, "May the fates be kind."

They left the hut and the troll in the stocks called to them. "How much is in the bags? Enough to buy my freedom, I bet. You won't need it—not where you're going."

Kentucky tossed his coins to the unfortunate troll, who caught them and uttered undying thanks. Jared stared. Kentucky, the one who wanted money more than anything, gave up his reward?

"You may be the king of stupid decisions," muttered Riven.

Climbing over the lava rocks toward the ship, a new vision took over Jared's view. It wasn't Sparket. It was a pudgy man with a crooked nose and tiny eyes. "I have an offer, Troll," said the man. "I will trade the ultimate troll power—the Mind Probe—for your quest."

"What's the Mind Probe," asked Jared.

"With this talent, you can see the past actions of any entity in Lavascape. You'll know their quests and the desires of their hearts."

"What will happen to Sparket if I accept?"

"You'll never know."

Jared didn't like the look in his eyes. He was asking him to choose between love and power. Love? No, of course he didn't love Sparket. Between duty and power. "No deal."

They reached the beach and sat in an area for gathering. There were three logs placed roughly in a circle around a fire pit. "I can hardly believe we got metals," said Riven. "It was a disaster! And not just for me."

As he spoke, Jared noticed Kentucky take a few coins from Jared's pouch he'd set behind the log. Maybe Kentucky was regretting the impulse that made him give his away. Jared found the two actions very baffling. *It's as if Kentucky has two sides and they're warring with each other,* he thought. Jared caught his eye. "The coin debt I owe you..."

Kentucky looked sheepish. "Paid in full."

Riven looked in his money pouch. "They didn't cheap out on the reward," he said.

"What's the money good for anyway," said Jared. "I know you can spend it in the villages but out here what's it for?"

"If you miss a feast, sometimes you can find a vendor willing to sell you some food at ridiculously high prices," said Riven. "It's never as good as feasting though, no matter how much you buy. Money is more for status," he said.

"The richest scurry is always the leader," said Kentucky.

"Is that what you want? To be the leader?" asked Jared.

"It's what every scurry wants...eventually. It's the only way to get any respect."

Were all scurry a bunch of outcasts looking for respect? Jared puzzled over the possibility as they speculated what the troll in the stocks had done and why he could buy his way out of a treason charge. It was still in the back of his mind when they decided the ferryman wouldn't appear that night and said, goodnight. And it continued to disrupt his sleep long after he went to bed.

Chapter Twenty-Eight

Jared watched the remnant of the troll brand disappear from his chest after his shower the next morning. He looked in the mirror. His hair was basically a Mohawk. There was really no point hiding it. He took some of Melissa's hair wax and played it up—literally. It was bold. He liked it.

He got some looks at school but if Jared was 'reading' those right, most of his classmates were more interested in him, some were afraid, and some liked the hair. *Works for me,* he thought. He strut through the halls and he caught the attention of two of the most popular girls in his grade.

As he walked on, he heard one of the girls say to the other. "His name is Jared Something, he's been here forever."

"Weird hair but kinda cute," said the other girl.

Troll hearing was fantastic. He'd hear stuff no guy ever did.

Jared saw Katie soon after he overheard the popular girls'

comments. She was stretching up to get a book from the top shelf of her locker. She stopped, rubbed her forehead, and then traced circles on her temples with her middle fingers. She took a swig from a water bottle and noticed him. "What's that look about?" Katie asked as she watched him lean against the locker next to hers.

"Some girls think I'm cute." The word cute didn't seem quite so gag-worthy today.

"That right?" said Katie.

"I just heard a couple of girls talking about me."

"Don't let it go to your head. There aren't enough nice guys around as it is without you falling from their ranks with a giant ego."

"Nice *and* cute? Hmm." He smirked at Katie then went to his locker. He heard them talking as he walked away.

"Don't go overboard, Jared," said Katie, under her breath.

"He *is* more attractive since he stopped acting like he's invisible," said Anna.

After school, Jared came into Josie's cafe and felt like the world was at his feet. Josie's reminded him of the game hut in Lavascape, full of people he knew and lots of activity. Jared's arms hung at his sides, but with attitude. He flipped out his elbow to acknowledge Terrance at another table. *That's so—troll,* he thought, considering the gesture.

Josie herself brought out the heaping plate of fries that he, Monty, and Katie planned to share, along with Jared's tuna sandwich and order of deep fried mushrooms. "I thought you three dropped off the edge of the earth," said the large woman with blond curls. "I was ready to put up missing person signs."

"Jared's been missing in Lavascape," said Katie. She rubbed her temples.

Josie gave them a blank stare.

"It's an Internet game," said Jared. "It's no big deal."

"Except that it is," muttered Katie. She pinched the bridge of her nose. "I've got such a headache. I don't suppose you could give me a Tylenol, Josie?"

"No chance. Sorry." Josie placed the fries in the middle of the table. As she set the sandwich and mushrooms in front of Jared she said, "I don't think I've ever seen a teenage boy eat a tuna fish sandwich when there were hamburgers."

"I like fish."

"Fine with me! Hey, it's better for you, too. It's good to see you kids again. I was starting to think there'd been a lovers' quarrel of some kind. Though I can never quite decide which one you like best," she said directing her comment to Katie. Before Katie could launch a protest, Josie continued, "I know, I know, you're just friends." She winked and left the table after patting Monty on the shoulder.

"Speaking of dating," said Monty, "how was your escort home? Or should I say, 'your bodyguard'...that was hilarious. Like Anna would be any help at all if you did have a run in with Colton Barnes or one of his goons. "

"It didn't happen. I didn't see her."

Katie interjected her own evaluation as though she were a simmering pot that was suddenly boiling over, "You mean, you forgot and left without her."

Jared shrugged.

"She was searching the school for you after last period. She waited outside the main bathrooms and sent some other boy in to look for you. All day today she was down over it and you didn't even have the decency to at least apologize."

"I forgot. It's no big deal."

"Obviously not to you." Katie dipped a fry in the pile of

ketchup rising from the edge of the plate. "Why are guys like that?" she continued.

"Me?" said Monty. "I treat Carrie super-good. I would never forget if we have any kind of plans. "

"Well Jared, this is the second time you've done this to her. Twice you've stood her up! It's the ultimate insult. Why are you being such a jerk to her? Katie slapped her open palm on the table, "Guys want a girl around when it's convenient for them, if they want to have a date to a dance, if they want to go to the movies and be seen with someone pretty. They don't see them as real people that they might want to get to know."

Jared felt like she'd slapped him across the face—shocked and hurt. It wasn't regret about how things turned out with Anna. That just *was* what it *was*. Fine, he'd move on. But the thought that Katie was disappointed in him—that was awful. "That's not true," said Jared. "You're a real person. I don't treat you like you're not real. And besides, I've been busy."

"Busy with what, Jared? Your beautiful princess in Lavascape?"

"Yeah."

Under her breath she said, "Would you risk your life if she weren't so pretty?" Then she hurried on in a louder tone. "What about your promises the other day? You agreed there's something freaky going on and yet you won't stop playing it. It's like an addiction. It's like a drug."

"Don't you think you're blowing this a little out of proportion?"

"You've been acting different. Kind of jerky. You strut around the school, make rude comments, and then ditch us for Lavascape."

"Now I'm a drug addict because I play a little too much Lavascape. Man!" He looked at the clock on the wall. "I've got to go meet my math tutor." He spit out the words. Jared slid out of the booth, slapped ten dollars on the table for his share of the food, and stomped away.

Jared looked over his shoulder and saw that Monty looked stunned for a second, but another, thoughtful, look quickly replaced it. Thanks to troll hearing, he heard Monty say, "Why did you set Anna up with Jared?"

"I don't know...they liked each other. It's what they both wanted." Then, Katie munched her fry and said nothing more.

He saw his reflection in the glass door as he approached. The gait of his walk, the Mohawk-styled hair, the thick forehead of the reflection made him think of his Lavascape troll-self. For a fraction of a second, he had to remind himself that this was real life, not video reality.

He left the diner in a huff. Why had Katie gotten him a date to that stupid dance in the first place? Now he was stuck feeling guilty because he had forgotten Anna's stupid little plan!

Anna would get over it, he thought as he walked. He'd tell her 'sorry' tomorrow. Katie needed to lay off. Lavascape was great. He felt at peace there; he had a purpose there. It was larger than life. It was better than life.

A part of his brain noticed a hulking figure in the alleyway as he passed and noted that the figure eased itself away from the brick wall where it had been leaning but he didn't register any alarm until he heard the sound of quick steps behind him. Strong hands took Jared by the shoulders. He was too startled to yell for help at first, and when he could have done so Colton had already planted his fist in Jared's stomach. His knees gave out under him and he sank to the gravel with a grating crunch.

Colton's foot came barrelling through space. Jared covered his face with his arms. His stomach took the brunt of the blow. He rolled on his side away from Colton and struggled to a standing position.

"Where's your rescuer?" taunted Colton. "Your friends don't stick up for you the way you do for them, I guess. Nobody hiding in a bathroom stall out here, is there Jared? Just you and me and a fair fight."

How he could consider an ambush from behind a fair fight was the least of Jared's worries. Colton wasn't just tall; he was muscular. He came toward him with his strong hands in tight hard fists.

Colton's right fist snapped forward and landed squarely on Jared's left cheek. He stumbled backwards and fell to the ground again. The pain exploded in his face. It was almost blinding. The world became a light grey blur.

Colton stood over him now. He was laughing and babbling but Jared couldn't make out the words, the rushing sound of his breath and the screams of the pain in his ears blocked him out. Colton's legs were within six inches of him. Then suddenly Colton was standing on one foot and the other was raised high in the air over Jared's head. Did he actually mean to stomp on his head! Jared rolled as the foot came crashing down toward him, just grazing his head.

Colton stumbled, regained his balance, and came toward him again. This time Jared grabbed Colton's standing leg but he didn't budge. Could Jared use the same strategy that had saved him in Lavascape? It was his only hope now. He lifted Colton's jeans to expose his ankle and bit into the back of his leg. Colton yelped and fell on top of him.

The wind was knocked out of Jared. He gasped for breath.

"What's going on, you two?" came a voice from the street. An old man in a Smart Car leaned out his window. "Do I need to call the cops on you two?"

Colton scrambled off Jared and hobbled away, cursing in the worst way Jared had ever heard.

Jared could breathe but with each breath, a new wave of pain hit him.

"You okay, kid?" The elderly man from the street approached him.

"I think so," said Jared.

The man helped him to his feet. "I don't suppose I could give you a ride home? Kids don't take rides from strangers these days. At least, smart ones don't." He took a cell phone from his pocket and held it toward Jared. "What's your phone number?" Jared's cell was in his backpack.

"My mom's probably not home, but I'll try." Jared took the phone and punched in the number. Melissa answered, sort of. Her 'hello' was soft and only the 'o' was audible. "Where's Mom? Is she home yet?" His face hurt when he spoke. One of his eyes was throbbing and tearing up. "I need a ride home from Josie's," he said.

"It's not that cold. Walk."

"I kind of got hurt on my way home."

"Call Dad. He has that cell, now," she said and hung up.

Where was the sisterly concern? thought Jared.

"No luck?" asked the man.

Josie came out of the diner at a run. She hugged Jared. It hurt but it was also the nicest feeling in the world. "A man came in, said a kid with spiky hair was getting hammered, I knew it was you."

"Do you know this kid?" asked the old man, obviously pleased with the prospect of pawning off his hurt acquaintance on someone else.

"Yes, of course." She led Jared back into the diner. Katie and Monty were nowhere to be seen. They must have left right after he had.

Josie brought a baggie of ice for his face. When he revealed his pummelled body she said, "Come on. We're going to the Emergency Room."

Chapter Twenty-Nine

"You're not playing that computer again until you tell me who did this to you. Was it the same kid from the dance?"

"Mom, I can handle it," said Jared in a panic. How could she think of taking his computer away? She was totally serious, however, and was down on her hands and knees right then unplugging the power bar. When it disconnected from the socket, Jared felt a pang as real as the ache in his chest. "Okay, okay I'll tell you." She straightened up and waited for Jared to go on. "Yeah. It was Colton." He told her the whole story.

"A water gun is one thing! This!" She could hardly speak she was so angry. "You say that Katie has gone to the principal about this boy and nothing has been done about him?"

"They've planned lectures or an assembly or something."

"Lectures?" She was red in the face and her teeth clenched so tightly that Jared could see the muscles of her jaw straining. It was obvious she wanted to launch into a full-blown lecture of her own. "I'm calling him at home! I can't believe no one bothered to tell me! And, that includes you. Rest tonight."

"Okay Mom."

As soon as she left, he climbed out of bed and plugged the computer back in. The pain in his ribs exploded when he bent down but he felt better to have the computer connected. It was as though he'd been holding his breath, though it was actually coming in shallow gasps.

There. He'd go to sleep and would check in on Lavascape later. Jared gingerly climbed back into bed and closed his eyes. Though his body ached, he couldn't stop thinking of his adventure in Lavascape and the deadline that could end in a death if he delayed. What if Kentucky and Riven were on-line waiting for him right now? The thought wouldn't leave him alone.

His cracked ribs alternated between sharp pain and ballooning ache but his mind seemed to weave around the words 'log on, log on, log on.'

Jared climbed out of bed as carefully as he could, which was still painful. He told himself he needed a drink of water; his throat was dry. That was his reason for getting up. As he passed the computer his gaze turned to the game gloves and mask on the chair. There was an escape from his present discomfort...in Lavascape. He could become the troll who was in perfect health. He always had energy in Lavascape. He'd feel better if only he could log on. Log on, log on, log on.

Jared forgot about his dry throat and eased himself into his computer chair. Mom had unplugged the computer while it was running so it took longer to boot up than normal. Finally, Jared was on to the Internet. Whew, it was like a warm blanket settled over him. Now things would be all right.

The sun glittered on the shore of the lava sea when Jared arrived. His two companions were nowhere to be seen. He walked toward the shore and found Kentucky and Riven around a small fire on the beach. Riven was drawing in the black sand with a stick. "If we were to light a fire here and here," he made x's in the damp sand, "then the elves would be forced into this area and then our army could attack."

"Hey," said Jared. "How's it going?"

"We've been here for an hour already," said Riven. "We're helping with strategy."

"In the war," added Kentucky unnecessarily.

"Shall I make arrangements with the ferryman?" asked Jared, anxious to get on the right mission.

"Sure," said Riven. "While you do that, I'll give the troll king my idea."

"You mean *our idea,*" said Kentucky.

"That's what I said."

"No it's not."

Jared realized he should have logged on as soon as he got home. Now Kentucky and Riven were distracted from the real quest. He'd be lucky if he didn't lose them to a new mission. He could see the large barge docked on the shore. Some movies showed a ferryman in a little rowboat. This was as big as a pirate ship. "He's there now," said Jared, pointing at the ferry.

"We'll be quick," said Kentucky as he and Riven set off toward the huts.

Jared trudged through the black sand until he reached the ferry. There wasn't a sail or motor and Jared wondered how it was propelled. He hesitated; he couldn't see anyone on board. "Hello," he finally called. "Is anyone up there? I'm looking for the ferryman."

"I may be dead, but I'm not deaf," said a voice behind him.

Jared spun around and there was a man in a black, hooded cloak. Only the outline of his face and his dark green eyes were visible. He stood several inches taller than Jared and was thin enough that, as he looked out over the lava, the bulge of each of the vertebrae of his spine protruded, each forming a bump in the back of his tight cloak.

"Are you the ferryman?"

"Indeed."

"My friends and I need a ride to that island in the distance. Can you take us?"

"Us? Yes, I can...but that's not the question."

"What is the question?"

"The question, little troll, is whether I will." His gaze became sharp. "Hmm. So you're the troll."

"What are you talking about?"

"I can take you to the island. I have the ferry; I know the way to go to avoid the dangers of the deep; I could give you safe passage. But why should I?"

"Because there is a princess in danger and my mission is to save her."

The ferryman yawned and wide-spaced crooked teeth became visible. They also seemed to give off a stench. "People die every day. I've done it myself. It's not so bad."

"The troll king said you'd help me."

"Did he now? That was presumptuous of him. I don't ferry everyone who comes a-calling. It's a dangerous journey over this lava. I don't take those risks for just anyone."

Kentucky and Riven were on either side of him now. Jared breathed a sigh of relief. He was starting to wonder if he would only be begging passage for one.

"Oh, so you do have companions."

"Did you think I was lying?"

"I thought you were knocking on insanity's door."

"Calm down, Jared," Riven whispered. "He's not someone you want mad at you when you're travelling the lava."

"He's not going to take us, anyway. He says it's dangerous and he doesn't take those risks for just anyone."

"Are you just anyone?" asked the ferryman.

Jared, Kentucky, and Riven were silent for a moment. "We're heroes," said Jared pointing to the crest on his chest.

Then Kentucky pulled out his citizenship card and showed it to the ferryman.

The hooded man nodded and pointed to a spot on the ferry and a rope ladder appeared. It hung over the side of the deck.

Of course, their cards! He knew he needed the citizenship card to use the ferry. He'd almost died in a plot against giants to get it! The fight with Colton must have jumbled his brain. Fight? Hardly a fight, it was just an attack.

Jared made his way to the ferry, showing his own card. The ferryman pointedly looked in the opposite direction when Jared presented his card, as though it wasn't what he was waiting for all along and showing it was some kind of insult.

"Thanks, you guys," Jared said as they all climbed to the top of the ferry. "I was talking in circles with that psycho. He said something strange about me. Something about me being 'the' troll, like he'd heard of me already."

"We are heroes," Kentucky reminded him.

"I didn't see him at the party," said Riven.

Jared laughed. The image of this skinny hooded creature celebrating anything was impossible to imagine. "Certainly not," he agreed.

They reached the deck and there was the ferryman standing at the top. He moved to the helm, a long straight oar in his hand. The fingers that protruded from his drooping sleeves were hairy, green, and bony. The knuckles stood up like rounded tombstones in an unkempt graveyard.

The three friends huddled on a single bench that put them in the ferryman's direct line of vision. He could have been the figurehead on the ship for all the movement he made. Jared ignored him and watched as the island that had been his Lavascape home grew smaller as they sailed away.

After a time, the ferryman snorted and suddenly the mists in the lava became thicker. The island became a foggy outline and then disappeared altogether. The ferry halted in its journey and bobbed on the lava waves.

Uneasiness crept into Jared's heart. They weren't moving. He was trapped on a ferry in the middle of a lava ocean completely at the mercy of the unnerving ferryman.

"Does this happen often?" Kentucky called up to the ferryman. "Do we have to wait for the fog to lift?"

"That's not what we're waiting for," he answered. His face turned away from them so the outlines of his vertebrae were visible like a snake down his back. Then abruptly his gaze returned to his passengers and he said, "And yes, it does happen often. Very often." His eyes glowed brighter.

"What happens?" said Jared.

The ferryman didn't answer.

"I've heard tales," whispered Riven. "Some say there are creatures that live in the lava...blood-thirsty creatures... and they say...."

"You're telling us this now?" interrupted Kentucky. "'Oh, by the way, there are monsters in the lava and there's a good chance we'll be their lunch!'"

Continuing to whisper, Riven went on as though Kentucky hadn't said anything. "But they say it's the ferryman that controls the monsters and to keep the journey safe for most travellers he sacrifices a few to the monsters."

"Quaint little arrangement...unless you're the sacrifice. Man! And you were on his side, Jared! He's brought us out here to die."

"This would have been good information to share!" agreed Jared. "How could you know and not warn us?"

"He's the only way across, we didn't have a choice. I rode with him once before and we didn't see monsters," said Riven.

"I can hear you," said the ferryman, suddenly seated on a bench that appeared directly in front of the little group.

"Well, are the stories true?" said Jared, boldly.

The green eyes in the hood seemed to glow even brighter. "You should hope you don't find out," he said. "To know is knowledge you don't possess long in this world." His gaze became less intense and took in Riven and Kentucky as well. "But perhaps you'd like to discuss something else."

"Gladly," said Kentucky.

There was silence for a moment and then the ferryman said, "Misery loves company. And I'd like some company." When the silence following this strange statement stretched out, the ferryman pointed a bony finger at Jared. "I'm most interested in you, Troll. Tell me of your misery."

"My misery?" Jared began. "Well, I told you before that there is a princess who's depending on us to save her. I saw her get beat up. She's been captured by..."

The ferryman was shaking his head. "No. Tell me about your misery. Yours."

"Mine?" said Jared. He was hyper-sensitive to all the sadness in his life.

"Real misery. I *feed* off misery."

"What do you mean by real?" Did he expect Jared to talk about things from his real life? You just don't do that on the Internet. 'Never give away personal information,' a policeman had said about a hundred times in a school presentation. He didn't want to offend the deathly ferryman, however.

The ferryman feeds on misery? Jared closed off his heart. He let out a snicker.

"What?" said the ferryman.

"From the looks of you, everyone you've met must be supremely happy."

Riven and Kentucky laughed. The ferryman simply stared with his green eyes and waited. The Retina Reading told a story Jared didn't want to know. Yes, it was real life misery that this vile creature wanted to hear. Jared wanted to shout at him to either throw them to the lava monsters and be done with it or take them to the island. This talk of misery brought too many emotions to the surface, emotions he was avoiding by coming to Lavascape in the first place!

"Come on, Troll, what's your misery when you're only partly a troll—" prodded the ferryman.

Jared wanted to throw off the game gloves and say 'Forget this, you sadistic jerk.' He shifted uncomfortably in his padded chair. The movement brought fresh pain. Here was a bit of misery that might appease the ferryman.

"If you must know, I got in a fight with someone, and now I'm in a lot of pain. I got punched in the stomach and kicked, too. My ribs especially are killing me. The doctor says two are cracked." There that should do it. Feed on that, creep.

"Who was the 'someone' who hurt you?" asked the ferryman. "An enemy, a friend, or someone in your family?"

"An enemy, of course!"

"An enemy," scoffed the ferryman. "Then, that's pain, not misery. I'm sure you can do better than that."

"Oh come on," said Riven. "Getting beat up isn't enough for you?"

The ferryman glanced at Riven and then turned away without comment. His emerald eyes went back to Jared. "Everyone comes to Lavascape with misery. It's our unifying principal. It's our common thread."

Jared thought back to the first day he joined the Lavascape world. It had been an exciting step. He'd contemplated the various creatures and decided to be a troll. He was happy about it. This ferryman had it all wrong. Maybe some people here were unhappy, but that didn't have anything to do with why he joined.

"Not everyone," he said. "I was excited to be a troll. I was looking forward to adventures. There was nothing miserable about me coming to Lavascape."

"Look deeper," said the ferryman. "Let me know when you're ready to face the truth."

"It hurts every time I breathe," said Jared, and noticed it was true. "Do you want an inventory of the aches and pains? How about a play by play of the fight—how he ambushed me from behind? You should be delighted with that!"

"That's still just pain, not misery. Physical pain is only one level," said the ferryman. "And not a very interesting one, most of the time. Give me the other levels when you're ready". The tattered skin around his mouth spread into a gruesome semblance of a smile that made Jared recoil inside.

The ferryman was suddenly back on his perch with his hands wrapped like springs around the single oar but he didn't row with it and they didn't move. A guttural sound came from his throat.

The lava waves grew more violent. They snapped into

the mist like the ends of whips. The ship was brought high on the back of an angry red wave, then it fell. Jared was jolted off the bench and Riven and Kentucky sprawled on the opposite side.

Jared scrambled for something to hang on to as the violence of another wave lifted the ferry up again. For a split second, he was able to see the outline of the shark's mouth island before the ferry plunged down again. Frustration was swelling inside him like the rocking waves. Sparket needed him and he was floundering in the middle of the lava because misery loves company and he hadn't been good enough company.

"Jared! Please!" called Kentucky.

"I can't," Jared said back. He'd meant to say 'I don't' and was going to continue with 'have anything more to say' but that's not what came out.

Bits of the whips of lava broke free now. Snippets of molten rock slapped against the deck and burned red.

Riven crawled toward him and clutched the side of the ship. "Try." said Riven. "You have to give him what he wants or we'll be thrown into the lava." Just then the ferry tilted. Riven lost his grip and rolled away from Jared, crashing into the bench.

Jared's mind raced. How could he appease this insane ferryman? He could lie. He could make up some story the wicked creature would like to hear and save them all.

"It wasn't an enemy," Jared called out. Immediately the storm calmed. The ferryman pointed to the bench. Jared, Riven, and Kentucky all crawled over and filled their vacated spots. Kentucky had an angry red circle of exposed flesh on his left arm. It steamed still at the edges. Jared knew its source immediately. Kentucky had been touched by a lava ball. A shiver of sympathy pain moved through Jared's body as he wondered if Kentucky would take this wound to the real world.

"Go on," said the ferryman, patiently.

"It was an uncle who beat me up. My favorite uncle. He turned on me in a drunken rage and..."

Jared heard the lava churning to his right. "What's that?" he asked the ferryman.

"What?" said Kentucky.

"I hear something—something swimming this way." Jared rose and looked over the edge of the ferry. Troll hearing was right on. The sound came from the churning of a single, strong tail, like a crocodile but larger and stronger.

A moment later a triangular head almost a third the length of the ferry emerged from the rippling lava. The creature's eyes were wide, green ovals surrounded in deep red scales. A portion of thick muscle under those scales formed into peaks over each eye. Its mouth was like a crocodile, a predator whose sharp eyes had locked on Jared.

Jared spotted a barrel and sped toward it. He crouched behind it and felt foolish in his tiny hiding place. The creature saw him. There was no way out.

"This one loves liars," said the ferryman, calmly.

Jared looked around the barrel and there was the lava monster stretching its sinewy neck toward the ferryman, awaiting a caress from the skeletal fingers. They knew. Somehow, they knew.

The way he'd declared his injuries to be the result of an enemy in the first place had surely undermined this attempt. But was that all? Was there really some way for the ferryman to see inside him? Of course not. That's just ridiculous. He didn't know anything about him.

Jared rose and came around the barrel. He was out in the open, exposed and vulnerable. The monster could snap him up in a second. He was hardly breathing.

"Are you a liar?" asked the ferryman.

"I was."

"And now?"

"Now I'll tell you about my misery."

"Misery laid bare. Oh yummy," said the ferryman.

"I came to Lavascape to escape my parents' fighting." Jared paused. It would be insufficient. The ferryman needed details to satisfy. But just saying those words had opened up a cavern inside of him. He was empty, ragged, raw, and exposed. No one knew how deeply he was hurt. No one would understand. "Now my dad has moved out and doesn't seem to care about...." Jared couldn't go on. His eyes filled with tears that wouldn't be blinked back. Jared's tears wet the front of his t-shirt. The sobs that escaped his open mouth were a shocking sound in his ears. No—he made himself stop—he was fine. "He doesn't care about me. He was here one day and then he was gone and none of my friends can understand, nobody knows my pain, nobody now but you. Dad's happier without us. He likes his life better without us.

"My sister was always talking to her boyfriend. She used to be my friend. You'd think that she'd want to talk to me about Dad but it was always her boyfriend." His heart was throbbing in his chest. One more emotion, one more misery revealed, and it would probably explode.

"The ferryman snapped his hand toward Jared and clutched his left wrist. "Describe what you see in your parents' eyes."

Jared shook his head.

The monster appeared again. Its eyes focused on Jared, closing the distance between them. Jared swallowed hard. "Mom...Mom looks at me without seeing me. And in dad's eyes, I see...relief."

"But you talk to Dad a lot, don't you?

"No." Jared's voice caught on the word.

"Every time the phone rings, how do you feel?" Both the ferryman and the monster leaned closer.

"Why did you ask that?"

The ferryman grinned. His breath seemed rancid. "When the phone rings..." the ferryman prompted.

"I always think it's going to be him and then it turns out to be one of Mom's friends or some stupid telemarketer who won't shut up." Jared took half a step back from the eager, misery-loving eyes glowing green. "That's it." He tightened his lips and they stopped quivering.

He told himself again how this happened to someone every day. He was tough. He could handle it. But, he wasn't handling anything, and his mode of escape had its own price. He finished with, "That's my misery and that's the truth." The monster backed off.

"And now you hate them all?" asked the ferryman.

"I don't know."

"Everyone abandoned you: Mom and Dad who are always supposed to be there; your sister who was once a good friend. It's time for you to say, 'Who cares about them. I'm all that matters now.'"

"Maybe so," said Jared.

"It's the way out of misery," said the ferryman.

"No," whispered Riven.

Jared's chest constricted at the thought. Would hate mend his heart? It was so shattered at this moment he wanted anything that would help the pain go away. This pain was deeper than his wounds from the fight with Colton and sharper than fading memories of better days. If hate would heal it, he'd hate alright! He hated this ferryman first and foremost, hated him but liked him just the same. He had forced him to open his heart, and though it pulsed like a hazard light on an abandoned vehicle, at least he could see it clearly for once.

"There isn't any good in the world. That's the stuff of fairy tales," said Jared. "Everyone has evil inside and you don't have to dig very far to find it." He thought of Katie. She called him a jerk. "Even your friends turn on you when you make them mad. We're all alone with only the flame of hatred to keep us warm."

"Do you hate them?" the ferryman asked again.

"Yes," said Jared. His innocence was gone. "There's no one you can trust, no one to depend on."

The waves quieted. The ferryman released Jared's wrist and returned to the oar. The lava monster responded to the ferryman's signal and sank into the lava. It swam toward the red sun, churning the lava in graceful circles as it went.

The ferryman dipped his oar and the ship instantly moved back on course toward the shark tooth island. The ferryman's face was as focused as it had been before the calm, the raging waves, and the outpouring of misery.

"Thanks for talking about it," said Riven. "You saved us."

"How nice my pain was good for something."

"The ferryman's right," said Kentucky. "We all have our misery. At least, I know it could have just as easily have been me he chose."

"Well you don't have to tell us about it," said Riven. An uncomfortable silence followed. Eventually, Riven continued. "Maybe we'll need to hear it to get back across the lava when we're finished saving the princess. Just keep it to yourself for now." It sounded like an afterthought.

They sailed in silence for a time. "Sorry about your parents," whispered Kentucky even though the ferryman seemed to hear all whispered words anyway. "And I'm really sorry about beating you up."

Jared took a second to process Kentucky's words. It wasn't sorry you got beat up—it was sorry about beating you up.

Colton? Colton! He looked in Kentucky's face. The resemblance was there! Jared jumped off the bench and faced the scurry. "Crap! I don't believe it! Colton?"

Kentucky nodded.

Jared swung at him and Kentucky fell backwards off the bench from the force of the blow.

Kentucky scrambled to his feet. "We're friends here!"

"What's with you guys?" yelled Riven.

Suddenly, the ferryman appeared in front of them again. "You have enemies, Troll. I don't see any way I can spare you."

Chapter Thirty

"Not spare me?" Jared was stunned. Hadn't he passed the misery test? Weren't they home free now? The ferryman interrupted these thoughts with an inhuman roar. "I must honor my agreement," he called. Then he erupted in a string of gibberish shouted at the heavens. Another creature emerged from the lava. This one was much smaller and was as blue as a June sky on a perfect beach day, but there was the end of the resemblance to peace and joy. This monster's head was serpentine and the snake was dripping with slimy, orange strings like the inside of a pumpkin. A glob of orange venom seeped from one of its fangs and sizzled on the deck. It glared at the three ferry passengers with anticipation.

The ferryman pointed at Jared. "You could have been interesting," he said. "I hate to kill you."

"I'll tell you more," screamed Jared. "Anything. I'll tell you about the shoes. I wear my Dad's shoes, and it's only partly because mine are too small." Jared fell to his knees before the ferryman. "How can someone be so hard-hearted, so totally selfish, that he can't call his son to see how he's doing, see if he needs some advice about girls or a few bucks for something? I hate him. You were right. Hate is the only way..."

A whisper came unexpectedly at that moment. It was from Riven. "No, it's not."

The ferryman pointed at Riven and yelled out his garbled words. The slimy snake creature slithered onto the deck of the ship. Jared, Riven, and Kentucky scattered. Jared drew his sword and the ferryman laughed. "You *will* be interesting to the very end."

Jared scampered to the barrel he'd hidden behind earlier. It may have been a terrible hiding place but it was a great shield. The monster's forked tongue jabbed at him a couple of times, snapping at the sides of the barrel.

Suddenly, it caught sight of Kentucky. The ease of prey in the open, drew it away. It slithered back and forth so quickly it was almost a blur. It pinned Kentucky against the bow of the ship with nowhere to run. The blue creature with deadly intent was about to strike. Jared stepped out from behind the barrel and sprinted forward, his sword ready. He stabbed at the nearest part he could reach, the slimy tail end. He punctured it deeply.

The monster let out a howl that seemed to fill the immensity of space. It was the call of a wolf in agony; nothing Jared ever imagined would come from something so snake-like. Of course, this was no ordinary snake. This was a creature of twisted nightmares that took orders from a misery-loving fiend.

The snake turned on Jared. Its mouth opened wide. He could see two drops of glowing orange venom at the tips of its fangs. Suddenly, an arrow struck the monster in the side of its head. It howled again. Jared searched for the source of the arrow. Riven stood in a proud stance at the stern of the ship. How had he done it? Jared watched in awe as Riven lifted his left leg, held the bow gripped between his toes and fired another arrow that flew wide. Riven's strength was amazing, to say nothing of his balance and unconquerable spirit.

The ship rocked more wildly. The ferryman had his arms spread wide. The black cape he wore whipped in the wind. His hood flew back and exposed his face. Only the top of his head was a smooth white skull. There was putrid brown and green skin hanging in tattered ribbons from his cheekbones and jaw line. The resemblance to the pumpkin-slime that hung from the snake monster was unmistakable. He was festering, oozing, decaying. The emerald bright eyes were far too alive for this gruesome creature. One of the brown strips broke free and slapped across Kentucky's eyes as he ran toward the snake. He fell to the deck, clawing at the putrid blindfold.

An arrow flew a few inches from Jared's head. Alarmed, Jared turned to Riven. The bow was on the deck and Riven was retrieving it with his right hand. Then he wedged it into place between his toes. He grabbed an arrow from the quiver on his back. The bow slipped and he repositioned it. He clenched his teeth as he took aim. This time the arrow hit the front third of the snake. The creature thrashed.

Kentucky, now free of the ferryman's skin, jumped on the creature's scale-covered back, his claws scraping along and snagging in the cracks to keep astride. He started to slip and grabbed a scale with both paws. His claws must have punctured the tender skin underneath because a geyser of orange erupted from the spot. Kentucky screamed when it touched him and large chunks of fur burned up instantly. Jared smelled the stench of burnt hair as Kentucky scrambled toward the head.

The ferryman called his gibberish louder and Jared gasped. The ferryman's eyes were on the horizon. He was calling more monsters! There would be no escape unless he could destroy the ferryman.

Jared left the monster and approached the ferryman.

There was no way to sneak up on him. He faced the ship from the prow with his eyes alert and his arms spread. Jared held his sword ready. "I'm dead," laughed the ferryman. "You're sword won't touch me in my after-life."

Jared's mind raced. There had to be a way to defeat him. The ferryman threw his head back and laughed thickly. Then he went back to muttering into the tainted sky. In the distance, Jared could see a series of fins break the surface of the lava. The monsters were coming! This would never end. Unless he could get the ferryman to stop calling out to them.

That was it!

Jared threw off his tunic and dropped to the deck. He jabbed his sword through the woven material about a quarter of the way from the bottom, cut to the edge, and slid the sword back in its sheath. He pulled at the tear and a neat strip ripped off. The ferryman laughed. "Don't you get what it means to be dead?"

The ferryman smiled with tattered lips and waited for his latest creature. Jared heard it a moment before its head broke the surface of the lava. "I've got it in sight," yelled Riven. The ferryman turned to look. Jared dove at him and dragged him to the rough wooden floor of the boat. He struggled on top of the ferryman's bony frame. Jared's skill with movement hadn't prepared him for someone so scrawny. It was like trying to pin down a jumble of bewitched bones. He shifted his knees so they held the ferryman's arms down, then he clutched the piece of torn material in both hands and held it hard over the ferryman's mouth. Bile rose in his throat as bits of oozing flesh came loose and clung to his hands.

Without the use of his voice, the ferryman went wild and thrashed about trying to throw Jared aside. Jared twice came completely off the deck as the ferryman bucked. The ferryman's wrists came free once and Jared had to release the gag to pin him again. Then he quickly held the cloth even tighter in place.

Kentucky and Riven were suddenly at Jared's side. "Help me tie it," yelled Jared. When the ferryman was securely gagged and his wrists tied in front of his frame with another piece of Jared's tunic, the three comrades caught their breath. "We killed it," said Kentucky, pointing at the snake-like monster.

The wide-eyed look on Riven's face made Jared and Kentucky spin around. Above the surface of the lava two monsters had emerged. The multi-fin monster let out a gulping, haunting growl. Left without instructions from the ferryman, its eyes were trained on the floundering ship; a large green gob of drool fell from its jaws, exploding at it hit the lava.

The other monster had a thick, boney forehead, which he immediately used to ram the ship. Jared was flung to the deck in the jarring momentum.

"They're going to sink us," yelled Riven, as he dropped his bow and it slid away as they were hit again.

"They probably want to eat. Let's give them something to eat!" yelled Jared pointing at the huge snake monster on the deck. They worked together to lift the carcass of the sky-blue creature they'd defeated and throw it over the side. The two new monsters churned the lava and tore the carcass apart as they feasted. Then they sank beneath the surface.

Kentucky and Riven cheered but Jared raced to the ferryman's post and took the single long oar that had propelled them through the lava. The ferryman was silent but thrashing against the restraints. The shore they were seeking was in sight. Though all the ferryman seemed to do was dip it into the lava, Jared's attempt left the ferry bobbing on the lava as though it were anchored. Kentucky and Riven each tried the oar but without success. "We're going to have to row," said Jared. He pulled the oar through the thick lava as fast as he could and the ferry slowly moved forward.

They took turns.

It moved frustratingly slowly. Jared felt the anguish of the princess more strongly as they neared the island of her prison. "Almost there," said Riven, coming to his side as Kentucky was at the oar.

Jared hung onto the edge of the ship. They couldn't get there fast enough and each moment Sparket was distressed sapped his strength. "It feels like forever."

"We did it. We beat the ferryman. Nobody beats the ferryman."

Jared nodded and forced a smile.

Riven continued, "It's a good thing lava monsters are cannibals." He laughed.

"I'll make sure there aren't more coming." Jared walked to the other side of the ship. The lava waves weren't enough to hinder their progress and there wasn't the hint of another monster. He clenched his teeth. Of all the people to hear his misery—why Colton?

Finally, the shark's tooth outline towered over them and the ferry ran against the shore.

"What do we do with him?" asked Kentucky pointing at the ferryman as they prepared to disembark.

"Bring him to the beach and leave him like that," said Riven. "Or he'll never take us back when we're done." The ferryman sank down on the black sand, shaking his head and trying to speak.

Jared could read in the ferryman's green eyes that he had something to say Jared would want to hear. They were on shore now. They were safe. And if he started to summon a monster again, Jared could jam his mouth shut with the gag. He pulled the cloth down.

"The money," said the ferryman. "I'll have to return the money."

"What money?"

"The money I was paid to take care of you, Troll. I'll never be trusted again if I don't return the money."

"I'm really not that worried about your reputation," said Riven.

"Someone paid you to kill me?" asked Jared. "Who wanted me dead?" Jared demanded.

"Antonio, the human."

"He knows we're coming?" said Kentucky. "That can't be good."

A hunk of brown flesh fell from the ferryman's jaw. Please! Don't leave me to rot on the shore," he wailed.

"You're pretty much decomposed already," Riven snickered. "But none of the other creatures will be able to cross the lava if we keep him here."

"I don't care," said Jared. "His price is too high. I'm doing them a favor."

"Untie me and you will have my service whenever you need it," said the ferryman.

"Is it true? Will we have your service any time?" asked Jared.

The ferryman nodded. "As long as you live."

Riven looked more serious. "It would be good to have passage at will with what we're going to face."

Jared couldn't feel anything but raging vengeance. The way the ferryman had grinned at his misery, forced out those humiliating sobs in front of Riven and Kentucky. He wanted him destroyed. Jared shook his head.

"He'll be indebted to us," said Riven. "It's your call, but I'd free him."

The ferryman looked optimistic. "Yes, free him, free him."

"You do it," Jared said to Kentucky. "I hope I never have to rely on him again. But I won't hold you two back."

Kentucky untied him and the ferryman scampered on hands and feet toward the ship, his spine jutting out from his robe like a round version of the shark tooth horizon. Jared, Riven, and Kentucky turned and walked away.

The next day after school Monty and Jared waited at the south door for Katie to join them. Katie had asked about his injuries and even though the conversation was strained, she expressed sympathy. Later, when he apologized to Anna for forgetting and joked he'd paid dearly for it, Katie actually smiled at him.

It was interesting how Anna had changed in his view. He'd been crazy about Anna and now those feelings were flat. Did it have something to do with Sparket?

Monty said, "I'm going to do it! I don't care what they say; I'm joining Lavascape. If you were starting over, would you still be a troll?"

"Don't do it, Monty," said Jared. "Video games are a stupid waste of time."

"Did Katie get to you?"

Jared shrugged. He noticed his hands shaking and put them in his pockets. "That game's not right," he said. "Don't laugh, but it's..." He left the thought unfinished. What was he going to say, 'evil'?

"I won't get involved in anything heavy duty. I just want to have a good time, learn the games and skills, hang out."

"You sound like Barry."

"Your hut-mate? Hey, is that hut still open? I could room with him."

"I don't know...but really Monty, find another game. You're not miserable enough for Lavascape."

"Miserable? What's going on?" Monty's face was dead serious and it rubbed off on Jared."

"My life is falling apart."

"Your *parents* are falling apart. You're going to be okay."

Chapter Thirty-One

Jared sprinted the last block home from school. The jarring hurt his ribs and his knees ached from the bruises and scrapes as a result of holding down the ferryman but he was compelled to hurry. He couldn't wait to get back on-line. Sparket was waiting and he was so close. He flung open the front door. His shoes were off in a second, his eyes already halfway up the stairs. He almost ran into Dad.

Dad sat on the carpeted steps holding a piece of paper, a torn envelope beside him. Just sitting there reading the mail like it was the most normal thing in the world.

"Hi," said Dad.

"What?" said Jared.

Dad set the paper beside him and rested his elbows on his knees. "How're things going?"

"Things are great." Jared's tone was dry.

"Really?"

"Of course not! But, like you care!" Jared exploded. "I haven't got so much as a telephone call from you since you walked out on us. Are you coming back home?"

"No."

"Just here to get your mail? Well, you should really arrange to have that forwarded."

Dad rose from the step and Jared was surprised to see he was a smaller man than he remembered. "Look Jared, just because I can't live with your mom anymore doesn't mean I don't love you and Melissa."

"You have a funny way of showing it." Dad started to say something but Jared interrupted him, "And don't try to lie to me. I could see it all in your eyes. You were happy to be rid of us...all of us. Well, that's fine. I don't need you, either."

"I'm sorry I haven't been in touch sooner."

"Yeah, whatever." Jared pushed his way past his father and bounded up the stairs to his room, throwing himself into the game chair and strapping on his gloves. His ribs were on fire but in seconds he was back in Lavascape, threading his way through the crowds of trolls. It was too early for the feast but they were already gathering.

He saw a girl troll sitting alone. Her head was down and when Jared caught her eye she turned away so quickly he wondered if she'd seen him. She was timid and most likely needed a friend. He sat next to her. "Hi, I'm Jerry," he said.

"My name's Sass."

"Are you new?"

"Yeah."

She was anything but sassy. In fact, she looked sad. Jared smiled at her. "Be sure to try the fried mushrooms; they're good."

"Thanks," she said. "Where's the best place to go to meet

people? I don't have a hut mate yet and everyone seems to have their friends already."

Jared didn't need troll training to see she was lonely. "Let me give you some advice." Jared lowered his voice. "Get out while you can."

"What? Out of where?"

"The whole game," Jared said with insistence.

"Why?"

"It's not safe. You'll be happier in another game, or joining a club at school, or anything else."

"Aren't you having fun in your Lavascape quest?"

"It's intense Sass, but, no, not fun. Trust me. Get out before it drags you under." He looked into her eyes and hoped he was conveying all he wanted to tell her. "It will try to..."

A vision of Sparket interrupted his conversation. Jared saw Sparket, he heard Sparket, and he read her eyes, which told him all the rest. She was desperate, crazed even. The vision opened wider.

Antonio stood in front of her, his hands on his hips. "This better not be a waste of time."

Sparket adjusted the white shawl around her shoulders as though she were cold. "What if I was willing to enter into a contract with you instead of a marriage?

Antonio shook his head.

"Just listen. I would be willing to appoint you Chief Captain of my armies. And, as long as you adhere to honourable practices of war, you can have free reign. Consider it," she said. "You still get what you want and I get out of here."

He pursed his lips twice. Jared focused on his eyes. Sparket's proposal was tempting but he wanted more. He wanted the marriage. Jared tried to read deeper. Why?

What does the marriage give him? He's obviously not looking for the kind of companionship Riven had with his goblin wife.

"What's to keep you from breaking the contract?" said Antonio.

"We'll do it legally. I'll be bound by the conditions."

Jared thought, *And so will he. Maybe that's what's holding him back. He doesn't want to use honourable tactics.* Then Jared saw more in his eyes. He wants to kill Sparket. If she died after they were married, he would get control of everything in her kingdom. The marriage contract had a much greater reach, not the least of which would be a more willing army to command, as long as her people didn't find out he was responsible for her death. Jared felt biting cold creep over him as though it was moving through his bloodstream. Antonio was going to kill her either way!

Sparket backed away from him and clutched her shawl tighter. Jared saw she had a plan and it involved this article of clothing. What was she planning? To strangle him with it? That would never work. He'd alert the guard outside the door and Sparket would be dead in less than a minute.

"I have armies stationed all over Lavascape," said Sparket. "There are battalions that you don't even know about. I have a network of communication better than anything you've dreamed up."

"You mean spies?"

"Scouts. We never go into any conflict unprepared for what we'll be up against. Their training is superior. Not just the scouts, but the soldiers also go through intense training before they see a real battle. Each soldier is a marvellous fighter, strong and terrifying."

Antonio was all but drooling at the description of the army. Sparket let go of her shawl and it dropped to the floor beside her bed. She bent to retrieve it, reached under the bed, and pulled out a cord of metal shaped into a 'V' with a handle. The bed spring! There was a hair elastic between the prongs of the 'V'. She fit a peach pit in the elastic and pulled back. Antonio was approaching as she let the pit fly. It struck him in the neck and he stumbled back. She took another pit from her pocket and this one found its mark in his forehead. He fell under this blow. She fit another pit in her make-shift slingshot but Antonio grabbed her ankles and she fell before she could shoot.

He pulled a dagger from a sheath against his thigh and jabbed at Sparket. The blade sliced her hand as she raised it for protection. Sparket slashed at his face with her slingshot. He yelled and held his face where a long gash appeared, while she scrambled back and jumped up. She fit another large pit into the elastic. This one looked like a brown egg, an avocado pit, maybe.

Antonio was on his feet and coming toward her, the rage on his face a terrifying sight. He had the dagger pointed at her heart. She let the pit fly. It hit just above his left eye. He fell and hit his head on the stone floor. He lay still for a couple of seconds and she grabbed the dagger. Then he started to stir and she stabbed his leg. He yowled in pain.

The guard must have heard him. At the sound of a key in the lock, Sparket hurried to the wall where the hinges would soon swing the door of her cell open. The guard rushed in the room toward Antonio who was pushing himself to a sitting position and bleeding all over his tan pants. "Get her! Behind the door!" yelled Antonio, but the guard was already running toward him and by the time the words registered with the guard, Sparket had slipped out the door, closed it behind her, and turned the key still in the lock.

Sparket shuddered and leaned against the door. She took a breath and wiped her hand on the shawl. Then she ran down the stairs and pushed open the door at the bottom. Outside her prison, the lava ocean bubbled. She held the dagger in one hand and her sling in the other.

She turned away from the shore and made her way through the tangled mass of the forest. There were shouts behind her and she ran blindly deeper into the woods. "I need you more than ever, my troll friend," she said.

When the vision ended, Jared jumped over the table and cut in line to the next available teleporter. Riven and Kentucky stared at him when he arrived on the island. "What is it?" said Kentucky. "What did you see?"

"Sparket." Jared was stunned. Sparket who hated war and violence had stabbed Antonio. Jared said, "Sparket escaped; but they're already after her."

"Where are the humans?" asked Riven "I can't wait to get into it with them."

"I'm sure you've met humans," said Kentucky. "Maybe not in Lavascape but in your other life."

"Ha, ha...you're so funny, Kentucky. What a clever kid—not!" said Riven.

Jared's feelings for Kentucky were a swirling, unrecognizable mass. He was his best friend in Lavascape; he was his biggest enemy in Willow Creek. Instead of sorting through it, he spoke to Riven. "It's not humans you want, it's Antonio."

"You bet I do! You saw what was left of my village. He's heartless," said Riven. "He asked for a surrender. We were outnumbered. It seemed like the only way we'd survive. Once our weapons were lowered, Antonio raised his white-gloved hand and they fell on us without mercy. Our king and a few of his royal guards were the only survivors." He cleared his throat.

They were quiet for a minute. Finally, Kentucky said, "Hopefully this princess of Jared's will be a gold mine. It takes money to rebuild."

"That would be great." Riven's eyes were troubled. Jared could see that money was the last thing on his mind.

Kentucky reached into his vest and pulled out a fist full of gold coins. He held them out to Riven. "My contribution to your cause."

Riven didn't say anything for a long moment. Then he accepted the gift and the transfer was made. "Thanks."

"Here's mine, too," said Jared. He gave Riven most of his money. After the transfer Jared said, "I think she's real."

"What do you mean 'real'?" said Riven.

"I mean, she's not computer generated. She's a real person, playing this game and her real fate may be in our hands."

Riven nodded. "It depends how invested she is."

"What?" asked Jared.

"Some invest heavily right from the beginning, others invest a little more each time...they die."

"How do you know?"

Riven cleared his throat. "When I died, I've never been so sick in my life."

"Like, in real life?" asked Kentucky.

"Yeah. Throwing up, stomach cramps, fever—it was awful."

"And then when you came back..." prompted Jared.

"I had to be more invested to return. It's time for the feast. See you guys in fifteen."

"Make it ten," said Jared.

After feasting, they searched for signs of Sparket until Riven said he had to go. Jared had been so pumped but they didn't find a trace of her.

Mom had talked to a lawyer about suing Colton for assault or battery or something. Jared felt it was almost worth getting beat up, to see her in action. He had given her a cause to fight for and her mothering instincts overpowered her depression over Dad.

Jared tried to talk to Melissa about the way Mom seemed so much better but she mumbled, "Do you think so?" She was laying crossways across her bed with her head leaning against the bedroom wall, her hair full of static and clinging comically to the light blue paint.

"Of course. She's like her old self!"

"Hmm." Melissa picked up a teen magazine from a messy pile on her bed. It was the longest conversation they'd had in weeks.

The lawyer costs and lack of witnesses (who knew who that man that saw them in the alley was) meant nothing was going to come of it. And Jared was glad. Could he sue Kentucky? But Mom had changed, and for that he was grateful.

The phone rang and Melissa reached toward her night table and answered it. "It's Dad, for you," she said holding out the receiver.

He took the phone and, trying to sound casual, said, "What?"

"I want to take you to dinner tomorrow. Are you busy?"

"Yes."

"Come on, Jared. We could go to Luigi's Pizza, your favourite."

"Really Dad? That hasn't been my favourite since I was in sixth grade."

"You pick the place, then."

"I don't have time to go with you."

"What's going on?"

"I'm meeting a math tutor." He paused but Dad made no

comment or offer to help. "Bye Dad." He hung up. Jared hadn't called the math tutor to set up another session since he missed the one when Colton beat him up in the alley, but he probably should.

Chapter Thirty-Two

Jared, Kentucky, and Riven searched the forest for Princess Sparket. Their tempers with each other were short as they searched longer and longer without finding her. Jared couldn't help but notice the Colton resemblance in Kentucky's features. He took an opportunity to shove Kentucky into a boulder.

"Watch it," said Kentucky.

A few seconds later, Jared hip checked him into a tree. It caught him off guard and the 'oomph' he emitted was a satisfying sound.

"Things are different here!" yelled Kentucky.

"We are the same!" Jared yelled back.

"What's going on?" asked Riven

Jared waved an open palm toward Kentucky, "Meet the guy who beat me up."

"No way!" said Riven.

"I said I was sorry. What do you want me to do?" asked Kentucky.

"How about, find the princess?" said Jared. "Are you even trying? She must have touched something in this forest. Pick up a trail! Unless you're planning on switching sides—then just take off now!"

"I won't switch sides. I'm trying to save Sparket."

"You do that, and I'll call us even."

"Look, we're wasting our time," said Riven. "She escaped on her own. She's free—hooray for Sparket; you didn't get to rescue her—tough luck. Let's go back to the tower and track down Antonio. And if they're long gone too, we join the war. Antonio has probably given up on Sparket, and may be back to terrorizing peaceful goblin villages right now."

"I know you want Antonio dead as badly as I do, but I think we should stay here. Sparket's out here by herself. Touch the trees over here, Kentucky."

He did. "Nothing," he said.

Jared couldn't believe they'd come this far and now Riven wanted to turn back. "She needs us. She's not safe. You saw the lanterns in the night yesterday. Her captors are searching for her. She's probably in more danger now than ever before."

"I'm starting to wonder if there will be any reward for helping her," said Riven. "Wouldn't she have someone out here from her kingdom eager to take her home? Is she all alone? Who's going to reward her rescuers?"

"It's time for feast," said Jared. "Meet back in fifteen?" Both Kentucky and Riven nodded. They needed a break as much as the nourishment. Jared looked for Sass at the troll feast. She wasn't there. Was she lost in the crowd or had he convinced her to quit the game?

When he returned to the forest, Kentucky and Riven were

waiting. "Let's go find that creep," said Riven. The break had done them all good, it seemed. As the evening grew late, Kentucky brushed against a boulder and exclaimed, "This one's fresh! The princess touched this rock. She can't have gone far."

"Finally," said Riven. "The trail has been so cold; I was starting to wonder if she was dead!"

"This way," said Kentucky after running his hands over the bark of a poplar tree and the outreaching branches of an evergreen beyond. They travelled with renewed excitement.

Jared heard a scream. "They've got her," he said. The hairs of his fohawk felt like they stood at attention.

"How do you know?" asked Riven.

"Didn't you hear her scream?"

"I didn't hear anything."

"Me neither," said Kentucky.

"He's the one with the super hearing," Riven reminded Kentucky.

"Wait," said Jared. He heard a male voice shout, *Yes! We've got her.* A horse grunted as though its reins were suddenly pulled back. "This way!" said Jared. He struck off in the direction of the noise.

The sounds multiplied and intensified as Jared moved through the dense forest.

"I can hear the horses," said Kentucky. "Maybe they haven't caught her yet."

"At last...the men," cooed Riven.

The sounds began to fade but a light appeared in the forest. Then a series of unevenly spaced cracks split the quiet. "Chopping wood?" suggested Riven.

They followed the light. As they approached, they moved with caution. The men had set up a camp in the forest.

There was a fire in the midst of the camp and around it were twelve men in dark clothing and one beautiful girl in a white shawl. *The shawl probably gave her away,* thought Jared. *It helped her escape and then hindered her freedom.*

Sparket sat tall and proud on the log she shared with two other men. "Why are they just sitting there," whispered Kentucky.

"You could slither down and see what you can find out," suggested Jared. "We have to know what's going on."

The scurry changed shape and with a lizard's stealth began to slink toward the clearing.

"That's just creepy," said Riven.

Jared ignored him.

It took a long time for Kentucky to return. "Maybe he's defected," Riven suggested. "They may have more gold to offer him than the princess."

"Stop it," said Jared. "He's our friend." He swallowed hard...he is my friend.

Eventually Kentucky returned and changed back into his scurry form. "They gave her the time it takes to build the gallows to change her mind," he said. "And the gallows is almost done."

The sound they'd thought was chopping wood was really hammering nails. They weren't going to hang her from the nearest tree. They built a gallows...nothing too good for the princess.

Kentucky smiled. "She poisoned their dogs with rotten meat. Antonio was ranting about it. You're right, Jared, she's a feisty one."

Jared was pulled from the game by the sound of Melissa's

voice. He removed the mask. Whispers came from Melissa's room. "I think I'm too stoned to pack," she said.

Cam's voice responded. "You have enough."

Cam? He was back in the picture? Crap!

"It's going to be so wonderful to be together all the time. So romantic," said Melissa.

"Better than being trapped here in this crappy little town and the city has a lot more people to sell to."

"Don't smoke that stuff in the house."

"What do you care? You won't ever be back."

There were frantic words from his Lavascape companions; Jared could hear the intensity through the mask on his lap. He slid it in place. "We could ambush them!" Riven said.

Kentucky's reply was quick. "There's too many of them. We could each take down one or two in an initial attack but that would still leave six or more with a moment of warning. We'd be dead."

"But we'd go down in glory."

"I don't want to 'go down' at all. I'd like to get the girl, get the reward, and get gone."

"They'd give you a new mission," said Riven.

"What?" said Kentucky.

"Oh, there are consequences. I told you how sick I was. It all depends on how invested you are, how much of your soul is on the line. As long as you're willing to keep playing, the game will give you more. I was dead in battle before I found Grace, my girlfriend. Then after Antonio's attack, I joined you two and I was on to a new quest. Is this your first adventure?"

"Yes."

Jared interrupted their conversation. "I don't want a new mission. I want to win this one, save the princess..."

"And live happily ever after," finished Riven. "There is no happily ever after, here. Grow up, Jerry. There's no happy now, no happy tomorrow."

Jared felt a wave of compassion. "What's your story, Riven? What would you have told the ferryman?"

"He's heard my story. On another mission."

"And..." said Kentucky.

"It's nobody's business. I told you about my goblin wife..." He said it in a calm tone but Jared's troll hearing told him the anger behind the words. Riven was so agitated with his hurt and his hatred, all he wanted was to destroy something. "Look, are we going to go out in a blaze of glory tonight or what?"

"No, we need a plan that might actually work," said Kentucky. "We don't want Sparket to get hurt." Of course, the girl in trouble! That's why Colton joined his quest. He had a spot in his heart for girls like his sister, girls in danger.

"I'm telling you, it won't make you happy," said Riven. "There is no happy."

The blanket of gloom Riven draped on their shoulders was thick and scratchy. "Things are working out for me, not in Lavascape, at home," said Jared. "My mom is pulling herself together, she's getting stronger and she's going to be okay. Hate isn't the way to freedom. The ferryman is a liar." There was hope. Jared couldn't abandon it completely. There was hope for Mom and for him and even for Melissa. Melissa!

He removed the mask and held it several inches from his face. He turned his hearing to Melissa's room. "Will you carry this one?" she said to Cam.

"Fine," said Cam. Jared heard kissing noises. "You said

you'd do anything for me. You'll sell the stuff, right? We'll need the money."

Jared started to rise from his chair. A trumpet played in the Lavascape forest. He replaced the mask. Sparket was in position to walk down an aisle between the armed men. At the other end, Antonio stood beside a short man in a black cloak with a high white collar.

The trumpet was better suited to inspire men to war than to set the mood for a wedding but in this case, perhaps it was fitting. It had been a battle.

She'd given up. After all her efforts, Antonio would win. Jared's heart ached. How this must defeat her, how it must break her heart. And all Antonio wanted was control of her armies. Once he had that, he would kill her.

"We can't let her do it," said Jared. He was half-standing at his computer chair.

He slipped off the mask and called, "Melissa." There was no answer so he called again, louder.

"I'm in the bathroom," she returned. It took his most focused troll hearing to be sure she was there.

Jared sat. Princess Sparket walked toward Antonio, his face looking especially dog-like in the shadow. One of his legs had a bandage above the knee. Sparket's fate would be bad with this man who surely hated her more than ever. Another of the men had a goose egg above his left eye. Sparket must have got at least one good shot with her sling before she was captured.

"Follow me," said Jared. He crept forward with Kentucky and Riven on either side of him. Jared took a rock in his hairy hand and tossed it into the giant thick ferns on the other side of the wedding.

The groom held up a hand. The trumpeter stopped playing. Sparket halted. Four men on the side of the rustling ferns went to check it out. They returned after a time with the report of 'nothing unusual.'

Something unusual happened to Sparket, however. She gazed in the direction of the disturbed ferns with more affection than she would ever show the man who would be her husband. There was a change in her. Her chin rose. She walked through the lines of her enemies and stopped next to Antonio. She had regained her spark.

"Will you take this man to be your Lavascape husband, to rule or serve forever?" the minister said and waited for her reply. The groom looked impatient. The 'guests' moved hands to swords and raised bows.

Sparket lunged forward. She grabbed a small dagger from the minister's hip and came at the groom with all her force. "I'd rather kill!" she screamed.

All her force was not nearly enough. Antonio held both her hands away from his face and glared at her. "Then, you're going to die."

Jared lifted the mask when he heard the bathroom door open. "Okay, I'm ready to go," said Melissa.

"Good." Cam's voice was a whisper.

The front door opened and the night sounds reached his ears now. "When's it ever going to be about me!" Jared fumed.

The mask showed the men leading Sparket to the gallows.

"Are you ready for brute force yet?" asked Riven with a gleam in his eyes. "This is your chance for personal glory, guys!"

Kentucky spoke next. "Let your arrows fly. I'll attack those on the gallows, and Jared, you get the princess.

The executioner slipped a rough noose over Sparket's head. It lay around the base of her graceful neck.

Melissa was making a terrible mistake. Cam was using

her. Jared stood with such force that his computer chair flew upside down. He threw the mask on his bed, leapt for the door, then turned back and dove at the mask. He heard the trumpet play again. He brought the mask in front of his face and dropped into the chair. Then he heard the door close. The front door of his house. He couldn't worry about Melissa. She was the older sibling. She could take care of herself. Lavascape wanted him. He had to save Sparket. She deserved his help. She needed him.

But Melissa. His sister. His family. He grabbed his homework binder and flung it at the wall. The papers ripped from the rings and scattered. Then a wail in his mind broke out as though a dam broke. 'Lavascape is the only place I'm happy! Right now it's about me, what I want for once!'

He kicked the chair lying on its side. It smashed into the computer desk and the blank monitor crashed to the floor.

"My sister!" yelled Jared.

"Now!" said Kentucky at the same moment. With that signal, Kentucky and Riven were in motion like they were shot from cannons. Jared exited, peeled off the gloves and leg straps, dropped the mask, and raced out of the house.

"Melissa!"

"Don't worry about me. I'll be with Cam," said Melissa. She staggered down the driveway.

"You can't run away with this guy."

Cam chomped on a wad of gum. "This doesn't concern you. She's not doing anything she doesn't want to do. Right, Baby?"

"I love him," said Melissa in a giddy voice. She got in the little car.

"You're drugged!" yelled Jared. He turned on Cam. "If you hadn't filled her mind with garbage, maybe she could think."

Cam laughed.

"You can't take her," Jared yelled.

"It's a done deal. She's coming with me. Take off, little bro." He opened his car door, threw Melissa's bag in, and sat behind the wheel.

Jared slid over the hood of Cam's car and yanked him out on the pavement.

Melissa screamed. "Jared, don't..."

"You're not going anywhere with this drug-dealing scum!" He slammed his fist into Cam's face.

Cam reared up and hit Jared in the ribs. It felt like his ribs exploded. He couldn't breathe. He fell backwards. Cam straddled his chest and ploughed his fist into Jared's face. Jared's arms were pinned at his sides.

"Cam stop!" screamed Melissa. She jumped out of the car and ran to the struggle on the asphalt. Cam pulled back his fist. Melissa grabbed his arm but he shook her off. She clutched at him again and scratched his face.

Cam turned from Jared, rose, and pushed Melissa hard. She fell and her head snapped back against the car. "You crazy witch!"

Crying and yelling indiscernible curses, Melissa got up, rushed at Cam, her arms flailing. He backed away from her wild slaps.

"You're hysterical. Get in the car," he said.

"You beat my brother."

Cam grabbed her arms. "He came at me first. You saw it."

She struggled to free her arms. "Let go!"

"Can't trust you yet."

She kicked his shins and he released her arms. She ran to Jared and knelt over him. "Are you okay?"

Jared gasped but nodded.

"Get in the car," Cam hissed.

"Jared's hurt! I'm not going now!"

Cam took a step toward them. His fists looked ready for more action. "It's now or never, Babe."

"No...Cam," said Melissa.

Cam went to the car and threw Melissa's suitcase and backpack on the sidewalk. "I wouldn't take you across town, wacko!"

His tires squealed as he sped away.

Chapter Thirty-Three

Melissa got an icepack for his face and Jared and Melissa talked and cried for an hour. Mom came home. She opened the door to Melissa's bedroom and found them sitting on the floor. They told her what had happened and she joined them, hugging Melissa.

Jared moved away to make more room for Mom. He noticed the way Mom's and Melissa's eyebrows arched the same and the narrowness of their noses. His chin dipped to his chest and he slumped against the side of the bed. He replayed the events in his head while he held the icepack against his forehead.

The next day he found Colton at lunch period. He took the seat across from him. "What do you want?" The hostility in his voice smacked Jared in the face.

"I had to leave. It was an emergency."

"Yeah? Whatever!" He grabbed his food and left.

It was the next day that Jared succumbed to the call

of Lavascape. After the feast, instead of going to his adventure, afraid of what he would find there, he stayed in the troll village. It seemed small. He went to the game hut. The lights bombarded him, sending his eyes darting first one direction then another. The noisy atmosphere was overdone—even for a game world. It seemed designed to catch him and keep him there as sure as any snare.

On the next day he went from one adventurers' table to the next, searching for news about Princess Sparket. "She was at the gallows, rope around her neck. Have you heard anything?"

"Sounds like that's the end," said someone at Louila's table. "What does this mean for her territory?" They began talking war strategies so Jared moved to another table.

"She might have been cut down in time. There was a scurry and a goblin there, too, trying to save her," he continued as it appeared those at this table heard him at the last one.

Louila followed him. "Go back to your adventure. You owe her that much."

"You don't understand. I'm sorry...and I'm not sorry."

"Yeah. It's just a death. Why have remorse?" She turned and rejoined her table.

The next troll branding would be starting soon. Jared rubbed the center of his chest. The newcomers were gathering and talking in hushed voices.

He had to know. The teleporter took him to the forest clearing. The circle of the campfire was visible, the gallows a pile of broken wood. There was no sign of Sparket, Kentucky, or Riven.

The ferryman entered the clearing. Jared's gut wrenched. The ferryman's countenance was wicked yet inviting. Jared was fascinated and he hated that he was. "Looks like some nasty business went on here," said the ferryman.

"What happened to Sparket?"

"If you cared, you'd already know that answer. But you only need to worry about yourself. I approve."

"It's not like that."

"Sure it is. Take care of number one. I'm docked this way." He walked away. Jared followed him through the forest. The lava ocean was violently beating against the shore. The ferryman left imprints in the silt of the lava beach. There were bits of green flesh in some of the footprints. Jared stopped. All the muscles in his body seemed to freeze. He couldn't move.

"Climb aboard," called the ferryman from the prow. "I'll take you to a troll adventure in progress."

"The trolls—my family." The words echoed through his mind. Lavascape had what he needed. The welcoming feeling, the excitement to be back in the game, the sense of belonging, and a calm acceptance of the ferryman seemed to soak into him.

"You can start again. I'll set you right."

A new adventure. He grabbed hold of the rope ladder that led to the deck of the ship. He looked up. The ferryman's decaying features were visible. He stopped. "You feed off the misery of others. What kind of sick, parasitic lowlife enjoys other people's misery?" He swallowed hard. "Why would I let you direct my path?" He wanted to leave. Leave for good! "I'm done with you and I'm done with this game!"

"Done?" said the ferryman. "You're barely getting started. Don't you want an exciting new adventure?"

"No! No I don't," Jared snapped back.

"Well then," said the ferryman, "what about your old adventure?"

"My old adventure? What do you mean? How could I have

my old adventure?" Jared stared. "Sparket!" She must be alive.

The ferryman stared for an uncomfortably long moment before he smiled.

Beads of sweat formed on Jared's forehead and then ran down the sides of his face. His heart raced and he felt weak all over. He wanted to go back. See Sparket. Explain.

But she was alive! She would be okay.

No, he wouldn't go back. He wouldn't be trapped again. Not anymore!

Jared took a deep breath and exited the game. He took off the mask, dropped it to the floor, and slowly removed the rest of the gear.

Chapter Thirty-Four

He was free. For a moment, he felt relief wash over him like a comforting fog. His room was so quiet. He gathered the game gloves, leg sensors, and mask and walked to the computer desk. He opened the top drawer, closed it, then opened the bottom drawer and deposited the gear in there. He was done with Lavascape. His quest was unfinished, he had let his companions down, but all that meant little. He had saved Melissa.

Jared rubbed the hair on his ears absentmindedly. He felt the familiar Lavascape tug, the other-worldly draw, but he purposefully pictured the grotesque ferryman full of selfishness and hate and saw him for what he was—evil.

"No!" he said aloud. "You can't have my soul."

The next day he was eager to tell Katie he had quit Lavascape but she wasn't at school again. This was the fourth day of school she'd missed.

He called her house after school. Why didn't she have her own phone! He didn't want to have to talk to her parents—they were nice enough, but it still made him nervous.

"Hello," came a female voice.

"Hi, is Katie there?" Jared asked.

"Who is this?" asked Katie's mom.

This is what he'd feared—an interrogation from a parent before he could talk to Katie. "Jared."

"Katie's not feeling well."

"I figured. She hardly ever misses school."

There was a pause. "We took her to the hospital last night. She has a high fever, and other issues." Her voice caught a bit as she said it.

"The hospital." Jared repeated. "Can I go see her?"

"I'm sure she'd like that, but I don't think it's a good idea."

"Why not?"

"It's a family time."

"She's my friend. I care about her, too."

"I'll tell her you asked after her." She seemed ready to hang up.

"You said she would like me to come—" Jared let it hang in the air hoping she'd feel too guilty to deny her sick daughter something she'd like.

"You can't stay long," she said eventually.

"I won't. Thank you."

"She might not know...well, it's a very strange illness, Jared. Sometimes she talks to us and we know she understands and other times she's delirious, talking nonsense. I don't want to scare you; I just want to prepare you."

"Thanks, Mrs. Smith." The hospital was on the other side of town. It would take more than half an hour to walk it and the roads were too slick from the recent snow to make riding his bike an option. He'd dress warm.

The phone rang as soon as Jared hung up, startling him. "Hello."

"Hi Jared." It was Dad.

"Hi."

"Dinner tonight? What do you say?"

Would he ever give up? "How about a ride to the hospital, instead?"

"Jared, what's wrong!"

"Not me. My friend, Katie." Jared explained, and in five minutes Dad pulled into the driveway. Instead of leaving him at the front door of the hospital, however, Dad parked and came in with him. He didn't want to admit it but Jared was glad. He hadn't been to the hospital since he was little.

"I don't know what room she's in," said Jared.

"They'll tell us at the front desk."

They got in the elevator and pushed the button for the third floor, where the woman at 'admitting' directed them. "You don't have to stick around. I might stay for quite a while and I can walk home."

"Okay. But I want to see her, too."

Jared wondered if he meant it.

Jared knocked lightly on the door that was standing open at room 314. He could see Katie sitting in the bed with her head leaning against two big pillows. "Hi," she said, her pale face brightening.

"Hey," said Jared.

"Hi, Mr. Thompson."

They came forward and stopped, Jared at the side and Dad at the foot of the bed.

"How are you feeling?" asked Jared.

"Really warm."

"Um, yeah, you look hot."

"Jared!" said Dad in a fake shocked tone. "She's not feeling well; she doesn't need to fight off your...flattery."

Katie smiled.

Jared felt his face go red. "I meant you look like you have a fever."

"Hmmm," said Dad.

"'Kay Dad. Thanks for coming. Don't you have somewhere to go?"

"I'll be down in the cafeteria. I told you I'd take you for dinner and I've heard this place has the best eats in town. What do you think, Katie?"

She wrinkled her nose. "I think you've been misinformed." She tried to sit up higher in the bed, but struggled with the pillows.

"Let me do that," said Jared as he and his Dad moved to help.

"My head's burning up," admitted Katie as she settled back on the lower pillows. She looked so pale.

"Should I call the nurse?" asked Dad.

"No."

"Well then, I'll be downstairs," said Dad. "I hope you're feeling better soon," he added.

"Thanks," she said.

Jared sat in the chair next to Katie's bed. After an awkward silence, he said, "You're lucky you weren't in math today. It was so boring. But so hard, too. I hate trigonometry. It's so stupid! How will I ever need this in life? Why would I ever need to find an angle? Are they lost?"

Katie's eyes fluttered closed then opened again. Was he boring her?

"Oh! You'll be happy to know that I quit Lavascape," Jared continued. Katie nodded so he went on. "I have to tell you, it wasn't easy, but now it's like I'm free. At six o'clock I get a moment of panic and a feeling that I'm missing something but then I remember it's just the troll feast and I don't have to be there. I'm free to do whatever I want. I'm not a slave anymore."

Katie nodded again. "I know what you mean." Then after a pause she added, "I'm glad you're here." She closed her eyes.

Jared stared at her closed eyes for a minute. Then he said, "I'm going to grab a bite to eat, then I'll be back," he lightly touched her hand. She was on fire.

Her eyes fluttered halfway open and she nodded.

When Dad saw him approach in the cafeteria, he pointed toward the line up area. Then he got up and met him there. They both got the special, beef stroganoff. The soda sizzled as it hit the ice cubes making Jared think of venom hitting the lava sea.

"How's she doing?" Dad asked as they sat down.

"She's..." Jared smiled a little, "pretty hot."

"You have to admit, it made her smile."

"Yeah. I still wanted to kill you, though."

Dad laughed.

They dug their forks into the stroganoff. It was good. Dad cleared his throat and fidgeted in his chair. "This isn't how I wanted things to turn out, Jared." It was clear he wasn't talking about their dinner or Katie's illness. "I'm sorry about that. But it's going to be okay."

"I guess."

"I know things haven't been good lately." Jared rolled his eyes and Dad continued. "They haven't been good for quite a while, but I want to be a bigger part of your life, if you'll let me."

Was there a point in shutting him out? He didn't need to hold on to hate. Jared shrugged. "Okay." Was the word meaningless or would it really change their relationship? He slurped back the rest of his orange soda. "I'm going back up to see Katie."

"That's one sick young woman. Her eyes are so glassy."

Jared nodded. He got up.

"Do you have your cell phone?" asked Dad. When Jared nodded he said, "Call me when you're ready to leave and I'll pick you up."

"Thanks."

Jared was back in the chair beside Katie's hospital bed when she started to mumble in her sleep. She said, "Back off! I agree!" And then she said something too low to hear clearly about a volcano. Were these the unintelligible ramblings Katie's mom warned him about?

It was unnerving to hear bits and pieces of her nightmares, if that's what they were. Jared reached out to touch her hand, hopefully to bring her back to consciousness. He stopped. There was something in her face he recognized— it was like a phantom from another life. The set of her jaw, her determined mouth—the image echoed through his mind.

"No! You've got to be kidding," he said out loud. "It can't be; she can't be!" Katie hated Lavascape. She tried to get him to quit. A niggling voice in the back of his mind reminded him of the conversation he'd had with Sass. He'd done the same thing.

Katie's laptop was on the hospital nightstand. Jared slipped it open and did an Internet search for 'Lavascape sick'. There were pages of links including the PAL website. Words jumped off the screen: fever, deteriorate, death. Jared was sweating and the hairs of his arms were standing up.

Katie stirred. "You're back," she said.

Jared leaned over her. "Sparket!" he said.

Katie looked away. She didn't say a word. Not 'What about her?' Not 'What's going on with her?' Nothing.

"It's true isn't it," said Jared.

She nodded.

"What have the doctors done for you?"

"Different drugs. Nothing worked. Now they say the problem is with my blood. Leukemia. They're talking about a bone marrow transplant."

Jared felt like he'd been punched in the gut. "Katie, have you died in Lavascape before?"

Katie nodded.

"How many times?" Jared leaned closer to the steel frame bed.

She wouldn't meet his eyes as though afraid to admit it. Then in the strong Sparket way she looked at him. "I've lost count."

"Were you sick like this?"

"Never this bad. Flu-like stuff before." Suddenly Katie brought her hands to her temples and squeezed her eyes shut.

"What is it?" whispered Jared.

It was a couple of minutes before Katie lowered her hands and answered. "A shooting pain in my head. I've had a few of them."

The doctors weren't going to be able to do anything against the power of Lavascape. She was too invested. Sparket must be alive, but injured. They were crazy-outnumbered. Of course she was injured. The ache in his stomach radiated throughout his body. "I have to go back in. The only way to save you is to go to Lavascape and save Sparket."

Katie shook her head. "No, Jared! You escaped. That's what I really wanted—more than being rescued, more than stopping Antonio."

"But it has hold of you." Jared gulped and whispered, "It's trying to kill you."

"And it will do the same to you, if you return. I can't let you end up like me."

"Katie," Jared ran his hands through his hair, "I can't give up on you."

"If you go back, Lavascape will get you, Jared."

"It won't. I'll be careful."

"It's not that simple. You know what it's like. You *can't*."

"I *have* to."

They stared at each other for long moments, silent but intense.

Then Jared asked, "Why didn't you tell me you're Sparket?"

Katie shrugged. "You liked her better than me."

Jared chuckled uncomfortably. He bit his bottom lip. "No. I like you both the same."

She raised her eyes to him and a small smile graced her lips. "My troll friend."

About the Author

Susan Bohnet has an Associate Degree in Arts and Letters with a major in psychology from Ricks College and a Bachelor of Science degree with a major in Human Resource Development from Brigham Young University.

She lives in Alberta with her husband, five children, and a cute (but rather naughty) Yorkshire terrier. She has written a newspaper column called *Family Frenzi* for eighteen years and has had two short stories published. *My Life as a Troll* is her first novel.

Books by Five Rivers

NON-FICTION

Al Capone: Chicago's King of Crime, by Nate Hendley

Crystal Death: North America's Most Dangerous Drug, by Nate Hendley

Dutch Schultz: Brazen Beer Baron of New York, by Nate Hendley

Motivate to Create: a guide for writers, by Nate Hendley

Shakespeare for Slackers: Romeo and Juliet, by Aaron Kite, Audrey Evans, and Jade Brooke

The Organic Home Gardener, by Patrick Lima and John Scanlan

Elephant's Breath & London Smoke: historic colour names, definitions & uses, Deb Salisbury, editor

Stonehouse Cooks, by Lorina Stephens

John Lennon: a biography, by Nate Hendley

Shakespeare & Readers' Theatre: Hamlet, Romeo & Juliet, Midsummer Night's Dream, by John Poulson

Stephen Truscott, by Nate Hendley

FICTION

Black Wine, by Candas Jane Dorsey

88, by M.E. Fletcher

Immunity to Strange Tales, by Susan J. Forest

The Legend of Sarah, by Leslie Gadallah

Shadow Song, by Lorina Stephens

YA NON-FICTION COMING SOON

The Prime Ministers of Canada Series:

Sir John A. Macdonald

Alexander Mackenzie

Sir John Abbott

Sir John Thompson

Sir Mackenzie Bowell

Sir Charles Tupper

Sir Wilfred Laurier

Sir Robert Borden

Arthur Meighen

William Lyon Mackenzie King

R. B. Bennett

Louis St. Laurent

John Diefenbaker

Lester B. Pearson

Pierre Trudeau

Joe Clark

John Turner

Brian Mulroney

Kim Campbell

Jean Chretien

Paul Martin

WWW.FIVERIVERSPUBLISHING.COM

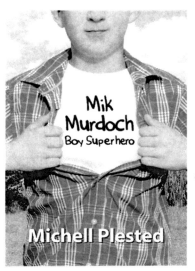

Mik Murdoch, Boy Superhero
by Michell Plested
ISBN 9781927400111 $23.99
eISBN 9781927400128 $4.99
Trade Paperback 6 x 9
226 pages
August 1, 2012

A delightful and truly Canadian tale of a 9 year old boy's quest to protect his prairie town of Cranberry Flats, and in his search to acquire super-powers finds the most awesome power of all lies within his own inherent integrity.

Out of Time
by D.G. Laderoute
ISBN 9781927400371 $23.99
eISBN 9781927400388 $4.99
Trade Paperback 6 x 9
294 pages
November 1, 2013

For Riley Corbeau, moving to a small town on Superior's north shore was an opportunity for his family to find a new beginning after the death of his mother. For Gathering Cloud, living on Kitche Gumi's shore now meant it was time seek a vision and become a man. There on a beach of this legendary lake, two boys meet across time and impossibilities, brought together to face an ancient evil from Anishnabe folklore, and in doing so forge a friendship that defies time.

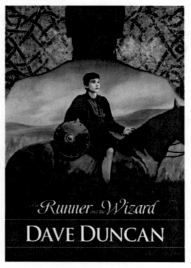

The Runner and the Wizard

by Dave Duncan

ISBN 9781927400395 $11.99

eISBN 9781927400401 $4.99

Trade Paperback 6 x 9

100 pages

October 1, 2013

Young Ivor dreams of being a swordsman like his nine older brothers, but until he can grow a beard he's limited to being a runner, carrying messages for their lord, Thane Carrak. That's usually boring, but this time Carrak has sent him on a long journey to summon the mysterious Rorie of Ytter. Rorie is reputed to be a wizard—or an outlaw, or maybe a saint—but the truth is far stranger, and Ivor suddenly finds himself caught up in a twisted magical intrigue that threatens Thane Carrak and could leave Ivor himself very dead.

The Runner and the Saint

by Dave Duncan

ISBN 9781927400531 $11.99

eISBN 9781927400548 $4.99

Trade Paperback 6 x 9

114 pages

March 1, 2014

Earl Malcolm has reason to fear the ferocious Northmen raiders of the Western Isles are going to attack the land of Alba, so he sends Ivor on a desperate mission with a chest of silver to buy them off. But the situation Ivor finds when he reaches the Wolf's Lair is even worse than he was led to expect. Only a miracle can save him now.

CPSIA information can be obtained at www.ICGtesting.com
Printed in the USA
LVOW10s1628040815

448798LV00002B/347/P